DEFY

Book One in the Rise of the Empress Series

C. S. Doraga

Dragon's Nest Books

Content Warning

This book contains physical violence, moments of peril, and some images that may be disturbing to some readers. Please, read with care.

To my family, without whose quiet support I might not have made it.
And to those of you who do not have the same.

Xandrin's Cave
Imperial Capital
The Mount
Tak's Village
Aigiae Mountains
ERIDIAN EMPIR

Degeraturi Mountains
Esuni Desert
Legend
Mountains
Dormant Volcano
Active Volcano
Plateau
Hills
Desert
Canyonlands
Lake
Water
Forest
Moderately Dense Forest
Thick Forest
Evergreen Forest
Plains
Marshland
River
Coral Reef/Keys

Pronunciation Guide

Redrinna:	REH-dree-nah
Brion:	BREE-awn
Eridia:	e-RI-dee-uh
Cel Tradat:	chehl TRAH-daht
Timothon:	ti-MU-thawn
Esunia:	eh-SOO-nee-uh
Xandrin:	ZAN-drin
Agicae:	A-ji-kay
Degeraturi:	deh-JAIR-ah-too-ri
Osiris:	oh-SY-ris
Korijin:	KOH-ree-jin
Landor:	LAN-dohr
Renoan:	reh-NOH-un
Amaris:	ah-MAH-ris
Matte:	MUH-tay

Tak:	tahk
Reyna:	RAY-nah
Kürtőskalács:	KUR-tish-KOH-lach

Chapter One

Redrinna sighed as the report she'd be giving to her parents in a few minutes ran through her head again. Fruit dropping from trees before they were even ripe. Plants withering before they were fully grown. An unusually dry winter in the east. Rampant flooding in the west. All of it inevitably harming the upcoming growing season, the harvest, and thousands of people's livelihoods.

She stared at her slim sheaf of papers bound together with a leather string, doing her best not to crease the pages bearing the report she'd slaved over for the last week, though she desperately wished she'd had more time. If she was honest, she had no idea how to even begin to fix one of those problems, but as heir to the Imperial Throne, she should have. With less than a year until she ascended the throne, she was supposed to have answers.

Half-heartedly, she glanced around at the dark, wood-paneled walls of the antechamber as if they had an answer for her, but they didn't. They were as silent as the smooth but frail paper in her hands.

Redrinna found her gaze wandering to the drape-framed window she stood next to, out at the world beyond. There was a sweep of sleepy, blue mountains pushing up against the palace on three sides, snow still hugging their crags, convincing them to stay asleep for just a little while longer. A thin, cobblestone path weaved its way through the narrow valley made by those mountains, vanishing behind the gray stone of the palace's outer wall, the wall that was supposed to protect the royal family—her family—and the small town nestled in the palace's shadow. The wall that should've protected them all from the assault last week.

Her gaze dropped from the gate to the town it'd failed, taking in the quarter of it that was stained black with the skeletal remains of charred buildings sagging in the dim light of the late winter sun. A shudder raced down her spine as she looked away.

"Are you feeling unwell, Your Highness?"

Redrinna's heart skipped a beat as she startled back to reality. Slowly, she managed to glance over at the person who'd plowed through her thoughts.

Captain Brion, her appointed knight, ever since she'd been six. With his height, broad shoulders, and a skill with weapons a league above any other soldier in the castle garrison, he'd seemed perfect for the job. When he'd been assigned to her, he'd seemed invincible in her child eyes. Now, with the grey gathering at his temples and the growing number of weathered lines on his sun-tanned face, she couldn't help but wonder if his age was bothering him more than he let on. If it was, how long would it be until...

Quickly Redrinna shook her head, a few wisps of her vibrant red hair getting caught in her eyelashes. "I'm fine," she said as she swept them away.

He could probably tell that was a lie. Between the assault on the Imperial City that'd happened on her seventeenth birthday a week ago and an attempt on her life at the trial of the leader of the group responsible, she was anything but fine. But it was better not to admit it. It was better to bury those feelings deep down and out of sight.

Almost against her will, her gaze returned to the burned scar in the Imperial City, the sick uneasiness in her stomach clenching a little tighter. After a moment, she managed to turn away again.

"It's still bothering you, isn't it?"

Immediately, Redrinna shot the captain a glare, matching his calm, green gaze with her red one, the closest she could ever come to reprimanding him.

At least, in their eleven years together, he'd never seemed bothered by her red eyes. Most people were and went out of their way to avoid her for it. That was probably the reason the antechamber was empty now. Not even the guards stayed in a room with her longer than they had to, duties or no.

"My apologies, Your Highness," he said, his expression softening, making him seem a little less worn out. "But you know, after all these years, I know you better than you like."

"Maybe so," Redrinna began, crossing her arms. "But I still wish you would have listened to me and let me stay in the library longer to investigate this more." She flicked the papers in irritation, making them rustle.

He folded his arms over his blue tunic—the color signifying his official rank as captain—matching her stance. "I do listen to what you say. But you and I both have to obey the Emperor's orders, Your Highness."

"His orders," she hissed, pressing her arms tighter to herself. "I'm seventeen, so I should be perfectly capable of taking care of myself and my assignments, which are best done in the library. After all, he's the one who keeps insisting ruling is in my blood, so I—"

Chomping down on the end of the statement, she huffed and looked away. If she was honest, she wanted to run away from this life, to leave everything behind. But that wasn't an option for her.

The captain stayed quiet.

Her gaze gradually shifted to the window, returning to the city. "I can do this...right?" she whispered.

After a minute, Redrinna risked a glance at the captain, who stared at the floor, an expression she knew well on his face. That was the one he always got when he didn't know what to say.

Looking away again, she caught hold of the pendant hanging around her neck, trying to find some comfort from the spiral pattern carved into the unyielding, dark stone. Her parents had given this to her when she'd been little, little enough she couldn't remember a time when it hadn't hung from her neck like a shackle. They'd told her—and frequently reminded her—to never go anywhere without it, as it was a sign of her birthright. If she lost it, she couldn't prove who she was if something happened.

She'd been tempted to lose it more than once.

At that moment, the dark, oak doors of the great hall opened, and someone who never failed to brighten Redrinna's day entered the dim antechamber.

"Lady Cel Tradat," she called.

The tall, bronze-skinned woman glanced over, a grin appearing on her features. Flipping her braided black hair over her shoulder, the woman came over. "There's my favorite princess! Have you grown again? I swear you'll be as tall as me soon." The woman's dark brown gaze turned to the captain. "Ah, Captain Brion. Practically an old man now but still convinced you're going strong, eh? It never ceases to amaze me how you manage to do our Princess' hair with such skill even with the arthritis setting in those fingers of yours. You're so...dedicated, aren't you?"

As usual, the captain didn't respond to Lady Cel Tradat's taunting, but Redrinna could feel the tension simmering in the air regardless. They were still always like this even after she'd asked them to be civil. So, to keep the peace, she took a small step forward, putting herself between them, just enough to return the woman's attention to her.

"What are you doing here today?" Redrinna asked. "Aren't you usually training the soldiers about now?"

The woman flipped the end of the deep purple sash around her waist that signified her rank as the general of the Imperial Army. Redrinna had always thought the sash went well with the woman's white tunic and dark trousers, but it went quite well with her skin tone too.

A flicker of jealousy flitted through Redrinna's chest as she glanced at her own hands. Her pale skin seemed even more ghostly than usual today, especially against the clean white of the paper.

"I'd love to be doing that," Lady Cel Tradat said, twirling her sash again, "but we're still buried under the mountain of work from last week's messes. I had to delegate the privilege of running drills to one of my commanders."

Nodding, Redrinna stayed quiet, more than happy to let the woman talk, keeping her unwanted thoughts at bay.

"On a happier note, I should finally have some free time in a couple days, and if you're up for it, I'll spend it with you. It feels like it's been ages since we've been able to have a nice chat."

Redrinna's spirits perked up a bit. It seemed like they'd barely had the opportunity to do more than wave at each other in passing lately.

The woman wrapped an arm around her shoulders, pulling her close and speaking in her ear. "Let's get to the point. Things like last week always get under your skin and stick around for a while like nasty, little burrs. So be honest: are you feeling okay?"

Redrinna nodded, though it was only so she wouldn't have to talk about it.

A small smile touched the woman's mouth. "You aren't a very good liar, you know that?"

She winced. Lady Cel Tradat could always tell when something was amiss.

Gently, the woman lifted Redrinna's chin with a finger. "Keep your head up, okay? Eventually, your heart will follow, and the pain of this will pass from your mind."

Swallowing, Redrinna dipped her head.

"It won't do any good to stay down forever. I'd hate not to be able to show this country the Empress I know is in there. You were born to rule, I can tell." Lady Cel Tradat beamed. "It's in your blood."

Annoyance pulsed through Redrinna's chest. Her parents always said that. Lady Cel Tradat always said that. They'd all said that so many times, she wanted to—

Laughing, the woman stepped back, letting her go. "You know, when you make that face, all I can see is your father. There's no doubt in my mind whether or not you've got his blood."

Redrinna tuned out what the woman said next as anger sparked in her chest. She hated when people compared her to her father. It wasn't that she disliked him; far from it. But sometimes, she was convinced that was all they saw. She was more than the blood in her veins, even if nobody else seemed to see it.

A part of her wished they'd let her prove it. Yet, the rest of her forced that down, just in case she wasn't up to the task. That way she couldn't let them down.

"I suppose you shouldn't keep your parents waiting." Lady Cel Tradat put a hand on her shoulder, propelling her forward, towards the doors leading to the great hall. "Besides, blood isn't evil, Your Highness. It decided you get to live in this palace, right?"

The woman did have a point, she supposed. However, it wasn't the palace Redrinna had a problem with.

"Besides that, it makes you who you are, and you are the Imperial Princess of the Eridian Empire. Would you change that?"

Redrinna stayed quiet, afraid of what would come out of her mouth if she spoke. She wanted to change it. She wanted to change it so badly, there was almost nothing she wouldn't do.

"Well?" Lady Cel Tradat continued, taking her hand off her shoulder as they reached the doorway.

"Of course not," she said, not because she meant it, but because the last time she'd confessed her doubts to Lady Cel Tradat, she'd received a well-intentioned lecture that had lasted for hours.

Nobody had ever asked if Redrinna wanted to inherit an empire for her eighteenth birthday, or explained why it had to be so soon. They never listened when she tried to tell them she didn't feel ready, that she'd rather leave the Empire to someone else and spend the rest of her days studying, whether in libraries or the world itself. Studying was the only thing she was good at, so what good would someone like her do for the Empire, especially since people the continent over despised her family? She'd seen a sample of that last week, and once she inherited the throne, she was positive she'd see a whole lot more. That thought alone made her knees go soft like jelly.

Someone put a hand on her back, startling her enough to feel embarrassed about it. Captain Brion gave her a gentle push, urging her forward, but before she could take a step, Lady Cel Tradat snagged her wrist.

"One more thing." The woman's dark brown gaze turned serious, catching Redrinna off guard. "I know I don't say this often, but, given everything that's happened lately, be careful in there."

"I'm just going to see my parents." Her parents had been giving her these lessons for years, after all.

"I know it sounds odd, especially coming from me," the woman said, her mouth pressing into a line. "Maybe it's the stress from the last week, but they seem a little...off. I know you love them, but they continued a legacy of war to build and maintain this Empire. Remember that, and be careful. Promise me."

Redrinna nodded, and the woman turned and left. Taking a deep breath, Redrinna stepped into the great hall with the Captain on her heels.

Polished, gray, stone floors shone in the light of the sun streaming through the high windows at the far end of the hall. Sunlight also caught the dark wooden beams of the arched ceiling, making them shine like they'd recently been polished. The long tables and benches were pushed to the sides of the room, making the space feel enormous. In the vacant space left behind, the crackling, orange fire hunkered in the open hearth in the center of the room seemed even bigger than usual as well.

Unfortunately, the shoved-aside tables partially obscured the carvings and tapestries adorning the stone walls. Redrinna's gaze was instantly drawn to her favorite designs, like the colorful tapestry depicting a prince receiving guidance from a spirit—powerful beings rumored to guard the land, remaining aloof from human affairs. Though, if that prince's legend was to be believed, occasionally, a spirit would intervene in special circumstances. However, excluding the legend, Redrinna hadn't heard any stories about that happening...ever. But the story itself gave her chills every time.

There was also the one, done in more muted coloring, about King Timothon, the king who'd had the shortest, but one of the most exceptional reigns in their nation's history. Though, during his time, Eridia had still been a small country, not the enormous empire it was today. She wasn't sure why that one always caught her eye, but it did. Something about the way he was depicted with a bright, fiery-red dragon never failed to catch her attention. Or maybe it was the dragon itself since it was the closest she would ever get to seeing a dragon at all due to the race having been wiped out nearly a century ago.

As Redrinna neared the dais at the end of the room where her parents stood over a long, paper-strewn table—their thrones pushed back against the wall—her gaze moved to the largest and oldest tapestry in the hall. It hung behind the table, facing the room proudly like it had nothing to fear. Its threads spun into a retelling of the priestess legend, Redrinna's favorite.

The priestess allegedly had been gifted great power and used it to slay a demon bent on crafting the world anew in fire before she'd founded the kingdom of Eridia. According to the legend, it had been over a thousand years ago, so Redrinna wasn't sure how much of it she believed. She didn't doubt whether or not the priestess had been a real person though; she was a direct descendant. But knowing that didn't make her job any easier. Yet, if she could find just a part of her ancestor's supposed strength, then maybe Redrinna would be able to...

Her thoughts trailed off as her parents turned to her, matching images of consternation. They both had her own pale skin, but unlike her, they had similar shades of brown hair and their eyes were similar hues of brown. Her mother's were much lighter, more of a honey brown.

Redrinna's throat clenched as a sudden hoard of butterflies swooped through her stomach. Giving reports to her parents didn't upset her nerves; it hadn't for a while. But sometimes, seeing their faces and not being able to see herself...

At the age of six, she'd been graced overnight with hair and eyes a shade of red similar to roses. A red the color of the sun wandering in a sky smeared with smoke. A red the color of blood, the one thing she couldn't ever seem to escape no matter how many books she read. No matter who her parents had brought to examine her, there'd been no explanation, and her original colors had never returned.

Her mother stepped forward. As Redrinna met her gaze, she forced the unease wriggling through her chest down deep.

"I'm here to give this week's report," she said, her voice seeming loud in the empty space.

As she did so, she couldn't help but notice Captain Brion had descended to one knee, his head bowed. However, his eyes were still open, his gaze boring into the stone floor. A little desperately, she wished he didn't have to assume that pose. If he'd been able to stand beside her, if she didn't have to stand alone, perhaps the constant, nagging fear she always carried wouldn't be so intent on plucking her heart into tiny pieces.

Her mother smiled, the skin crinkling around her eyes, making her seem older than she was. Redrinna's heart wilted at the reminder neither of her parents were young and either or both could die before she turned eighteen. Losing six children wasn't an easy burden for them to continue carrying around, and her mother in particular had never seemed happy since then. Not that Redrinna blamed her.

"I'm happy you made it," her mother said, taking a few steps forward, her circlet catching the light of the sun, making a shiver trickle over Redrinna's skin.

When Redrinna had been young, she'd learned there were two sides required of her parents. Without their crowns, they were simply her parents, the two people she loved most. With them, they were the Emperor and Empress, rulers of the entire Eridian continent. She liked it better when they spent their time with her without their crowns, but empire lessons always came with the cold glare of those metal bands.

Her father stepped forward then, allowing the sun to make the circlet on his head gleam as well. He stood stiff like he was turning to stone, a dark shadow touching his face. "You may begin when you're ready."

All at once, Lady Cel Tradat's warning rang through her mind again, making her clench her hands tighter. No matter how badly Redrinna wanted out of this life, when she stood here with her parents, the disappointment her wish would bring them settled like a mountain on her shoulders. They were depending on her—counting on her—not just as parents, but as rulers. She couldn't fail, no matter what.

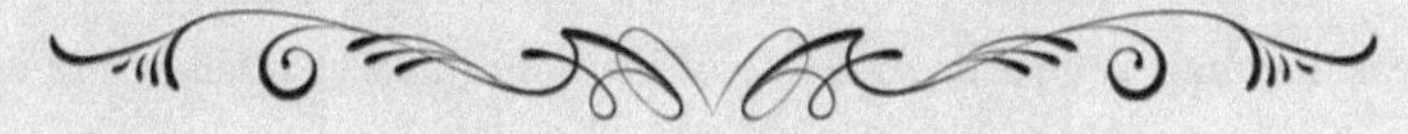

Chapter Two

The report went by in a flash, and before Redrinna knew it, she had nothing else to say. Her parents nodded a couple times after she finished before sharing a look she couldn't read.

"Please give us your written report," her mother said.

Her nerves almost got the better of her.

Even though meals were held in the great hall, Redrinna rarely ate them here. So many of their guests and members of the castle staff were put off by her hair and eyes, it was easier if she ate in her room. The last time she'd been in this room had been that day, during the trial, when that man had—

"You didn't forget to bring it, did you?" her mother asked, cutting into her thoughts.

"No. Sorry." Quickly, Redrinna shook her head, trying to shake those thoughts out of her mind. Steeling herself, she forced herself up the short staircase to the dais, only holding out the report when she was in front of her parents. Even still, she noticed the trembling of her hands, and she was certain her parents noticed it too. They didn't comment on it, but that didn't set her at ease at all.

Her mother pulled the string holding the papers together loose, and her parents proceeded to go over the report.

Redrinna tucked her hands behind her back again, trying to get them to settle while she waited. Almost of its own free will, her gaze began to drift to the side, towards the place where she'd stood during the trial.

Her parents' thrones had been at the center of the dais, so she'd been standing a bit behind them, just off to the side. About halfway through the trial was when— A shudder raced down her spine, shaking her so hard she had to take a teeny step forward to stay balanced.

She still remembered his face, his golden eyes burning with unspeakable rage as he'd broken free of his bonds and charged at her with a stolen knife clenched in his fist. He'd broken past the captain. Just when she'd thought she was going to die, a soldier she didn't know had stepped in and taken a stab in the arm—a blow meant for her—before he'd ended the man's life. She still remembered the man dying on the floor, the soldier standing over him with blood dripping from his fingers.

Redrinna's chest tightened painfully like she was drowning. Even now, she—

She forced those thoughts away as her parents lifted their gazes from her report.

"Well written, as usual," her father said as her mother turned and placed it on the table behind them. "Your insights will be of great value to us."

Would they? She hadn't found a solution—just a lot of potential ones. How helpful would she even be?

"Now then, we should talk about your next assignment."

Redrinna's nerves came alive like writhing snakes. Since they'd begun giving her assignments a year or so ago, she dreaded the day they'd give her one with more at stake than livestock and struggling crops.

Her mother turned to the table again and lifted a large report off it before turning back around. It appeared bigger than anything they'd given her before. Her nerves went taut as she tried to think of what it could be.

"The events from last week have kept us busy, and while your mother and I could handle it all by ourselves, we've been debating whether or not to drag you into this any further," her father said, his voice a shade deeper than before. "But, in less than one year, the Empire will be passed to you."

Redrinna's heart shivered. He only sounded like that when he was upset about something, and it was rare for anything to unsettle him that much.

"Since our time before you become Empress is growing short, we decided it's time to have you take on more responsibility." Her mother extended the giant report towards her.

Empress. More responsibility. A chill seeped through her veins. This was the thing Redrinna had been dreading.

For a long moment, she remained frozen, unable to will her hands to move, to unstick themselves from her sides. Hesitantly, she managed to take the papers. After spotting the words 'murder' and 'arson' about halfway down the front page, she held them close so she couldn't read them.

"What is this one about?" She could barely hear herself; she had no idea how her parents did.

Behind her, the fire popped, making her jump a little bit.

"It's a report on the remaining members of the group responsible for the assault on the Imperial City," her father explained. "To prepare you to take the throne, we are delegating this task to you. It's your responsibility to assess their crimes and determine the royal family's position for the upcoming trial. We would like you to study this information throughout the week and discuss it with us during next week's lesson. A written report will not be necessary this time."

Taking a quick step back, Redrinna dropped her gaze to the floor like it had caught fire. She didn't want to have anything to do with this.

"Redrinna," her father said, the stern note in his voice stopping her in her tracks. "Running away won't help anyone. Were you lying the other night when you said you wanted a chance to prove yourself?"

At that, she remembered mentioning something similar to Captain Brion while they'd been waiting to enter the hall. When she'd said it, she'd meant it. She always did. But then there came moments like this, reminders of what 'prove herself' actually entailed, and she trembled like she was about to receive a death sentence.

"How much do you know about the events that led up to last

week's trial?"

She glanced at her father, just for a second. "The man was part of a rebel group from the desert. He and some of his followers led an assault on the citizens of the Imperial City, during which he was apprehended and was later placed on trial. And there was where he..." Her gaze wandered back to where she'd been standing, where there was still a shadowy outline of where he'd died. A mere hint as to what had happened. She had to fight hard to keep her hands from trembling more than they already were.

"Yes," her mother said with a slight nod. Despite the topic, her mother seemed utterly serene, something Redrinna wished she could be. "Because of him, many people's lives were lost. Many more lost their homes and precious belongings to the fires and violence. It's unwise to believe something as simple as the threat of death will be enough to deter anyone else from attempting something like this, so you need to learn how to act when this happens under your leadership. That is why this task is being given to you."

A heavy silence fell over the room, heavy as a wet blanket, making even the crackling of the fire behind her seem distant and muted.

It was up to her to decide the fate of the rest of the rebels who'd besieged the city. The rest of the people who'd come to her home intent on killing anyone they could reach. Black gathered at the edges of her vision, the room spinning.

All at once, her mother cupped her cheeks with her hands, the warmth of her skin making Redrinna realize she'd gone as cold as ice. Slowly, she managed to meet her mother's calm, brown eyes. Unable to hold her gaze, she focused on the necklace her mother wore instead, the one Redrinna had never seen her without.

It was small considering some of the jewelry she'd seen before. The charm was only about as big as her two thumbnails side by side, but it was the most beautiful piece Redrinna had ever laid eyes on. It was two intertwining hearts, curling around each other in an endless loop.

Her mother's favorite necklace.

A thumb stroking her cheek dragged her away from those

thoughts. "My sweet Redrinna," her mother murmured, almost like she didn't want the rest of the room to hear. "We don't want to scare you even though I can tell we are. Nevertheless, there is something we, as your parents, have to tell you."

She couldn't bring herself to look up.

Her father approached, brushing her bangs from her eyes, coaxing her to meet his gaze. A deep sorrow rested there, one she'd seen in his gaze so often, it hurt a little. "Do you know how our people refer to you? They call you the heir to a throne of death, destined for nothing but ruin and destruction. There are certain people out there—not all, but some—who would do anything to hurt you, a fact demonstrated to us a few days ago. But they're wrong. When you take the throne, I know you'll be able to prove it. So prepare now, not when you're on the throne."

"I know," she managed despite the fear coiling around her heart like it always did. She hated this feeling, hated having it inside her all the time. It made her want to hide somewhere, a place no one would be able to drag her out of, and pretend the rest of the world didn't exist.

"Even when it's hard, you have to keep pressing forward," her mother said, dropping her hands so she could hug her instead. "That's how you'll succeed."

All at once, Lady Cel Tradat's warning rang through her mind again, but Redrinna couldn't bring herself to listen to it. She knew her friend meant well, but Lady Cel Tradat didn't know her parents like she did. And they didn't love the woman like they loved her.

"You know what you need to do," her mother said as she pulled back. "So you may go."

Turning, Redrinna struggled to find her balance. She wanted to shake her head to clear the anxieties crowding the space, but she was afraid she'd fall flat on her face.

"You should take the side door," her father whispered. "Since the counselors are probably in the antechamber, and you don't like bumping into them."

He was probably right about the counselors being out there. They usually were, impatiently waiting for her to leave. If she had to go out there and face them and their cold, calculating stares they reserved just for her...

Swiftly, she descended the stairs of the dais, Captain Brion rising as she did. They made it to the unadorned side door, the captain's hand just touching the doorknob that was hard to spot if you weren't looking for it.

"Wait! One last thing," her father called, making her jump a little. "We almost forgot something."

After being given this assignment, she wasn't sure she wanted whatever it was.

"Captain Brion?"

Redrinna's faithful escort turned immediately, bowing low. "Your Majesty?"

"Hold this for her?" her father said. "It's for next week's lesson. When she goes on a trip with the Empress and me."

"A trip?" Redrinna breathed, hope sputtering to life in her chest. She half-turned, not sure if she dared to believe her ears. "For real?"

"That's right," her mother said with a smile as the captain took a sack from her father. "For real. Just the three of us so there are no distractions. So study hard so we have plenty to discuss on our way, all right?"

The little fire in her chest flickered, threatening to go out. Right. Studying. Her heart dove under her toes, the feeling making her dizzy. An unbearable pressure wrapping around her head, she turned and seized the door handle, throwing the door open a lot harder than she'd meant to.

As she hurried through the opening, the bang of the door striking the stone wall made her trip over herself in her haste to escape. But, as the familiar click of the captain's heels against stone rang out behind her, the steady rhythm slowly coaxed her heart out from under her toes a little bit.

They ascended the stone stairs in silence, the narrow space lit intermittently by a flickering torch. At least here, in this staircase reserved for a select few, Redrinna wouldn't have to worry about bumping into anybody. Especially since just the other day, a young, nervous maid had tripped while holding a tray and spilled tea and jam all over her. The hot tea had stung a bit where it'd hit her skin, but it'd mostly been on her dress. She'd been fine, just a little embarrassed.

Even more humiliating than that though, the girl had begun sobbing, begging Redrinna on her knees, forehead to the ground, to spare her, to not harm her or her family, seemingly deaf to what she or her parents had said to try and calm her. In the end, the only solution had been for Redrinna to leave and let someone else try to smooth out the whole situation.

That alone didn't give her the confidence that she'd be able to handle her new assignment, but her parents had insisted she had to at least try. After a few more quiet hallways dimly lit by the weak sunlight, the door to her room came into sight, bearing a firm reminder of what she was about to do. Swallowing, she tried to muster a shred of courage, just an ounce of what the priestess must have had to fight her demon. The sooner she started, the sooner she'd be finished.

◦☜ ☞◦

Redrinna watched as the moonlight gradually trickled further into her room, deepening the shadows clinging to the corners like hulking spiders. The blue moonlight touched the white rug covering the stone floor, making it seem brighter than it was. However, unlike the rug, she hid in the shadows. She buried her face in her knees, hugging them tight to her chest as she tried to ignore the chill of the stone floor beneath her.

The report her parents had given her lay on her desk, closed now. She'd pushed through the heavily detailed report, but her stomach shriveled at the mere thought of it. She despised fighting with everything in her, but this...made it seem real. Fighting was real—she knew that—but this...this was different.

There came a knock at her door, distracting her from her thoughts for the first time that evening.

"Your Highness?" called Captain Brion. "May I come in?"

Her heart sighed with relief that it wasn't Lady Cel Tradat. The woman had spirit and knew how to motivate soldiers, but she wasn't great at helping Redrinna feel better at times like these. Then again, she wasn't pleased anyone was here right now.

"You may," she said, not moving from her place under the window.

The captain entered with something in his hands. He shut the door silently behind him before stepping over to her. "It's late. You should eat something," he said.

"I'm not hungry," Redrinna whispered, staring pointedly at a spot behind the captain's boots. She shifted her gaze further away, to the fireplace brimming with smoldering embers in the far wall, as he knelt on one knee, setting the tray of food between them.

"Did you read the report your parents gave you?"

She nodded.

"I see," he said before falling silent.

At length, she said, "I don't understand it."

"The attack?"

She shook her head once. "It's not that. I mean, it was terrible—a quarter of the city was burned. So many people were hurt. What I don't understand is why. All those people had families and lives and dreams, and now—Why would anyone—why would—" The words wouldn't come, so she stopped trying to speak.

The captain dipped his head. "I'm afraid the only answer I have is that there isn't a satisfactory answer I can give you, Your Highness. Angry people don't make sense."

Her heart clenched, making her squeeze her arms a little harder. "I can't do this. There's no way I can take over an entire empire." Her voice came out in a harsh whisper, not what she'd intended. "Captain, I—"

Cutting herself short, she closed her eyes. Her fears...weren't a burden she should share with the captain. She knew enough to make that choice. He was her guard, not her nanny.

"Captain," she said, her voice still hushed. "Your grandfather and father were soldiers, weren't they?"

Captain Brion nodded.

"And before my parents selected you to be my appointed knight, you became a soldier as well. In that sense, your path echoes your family's." She opened her eyes, briefly meeting his gaze before both of them looked down.

"In that sense, yes," the Captain replied.

"But," Redrinna continued in a hushed voice, "what if one day you realized you weren't meant to be a soldier? Yet, the only thing anyone ever said was your grandfather and father were soldiers, and because their blood runs in your veins, even if you felt otherwise, you had to become a soldier too. If that was the case, Captain, do you think you would have fought to do something different?"

Heavy silence suspended itself between them for a long moment before Captain Brion released a deep breath, not quite a sigh, but close. "That is an interesting question, Your Highness."

His tone was warm like a fire on a cold night, startling her a little. She risked a glance at him. He...was smiling? He almost never smiled. In fact, she hadn't seen him smile in such a long time, she'd forgotten what it looked like, like forgetting what the sun's warmth on her skin felt like after a long winter. A part of her wished she hadn't asked that question. At the very least, she hoped she hadn't hurt his feelings in any way. Yet, at the same time, it reminded her of all the times she'd tried to tell him this before, and how he always seemed to understand what she couldn't bring herself to say.

Releasing a short sigh, she hooked two fingers onto the edge of the tray he'd brought, pulling the food closer. "Thank you for bringing this. I...really do appreciate it."

He dipped his head, his smile melting like frost touched by the morning sun. "Of course. Knock on the door when you're finished, Your Highness." He rose and moved to the door. As he stepped out, he inclined his head with a final 'Your Highness' before leaving her to her thoughts again.

Her gaze flicked towards the report lying on her desk, but Redrinna didn't want to revisit it tonight. She'd thought and thought about the punishment for the criminals, but had only been able to conclude with the most obvious solution. And that made her insides shrivel up. Maybe she could think of another way in the week her parents had given her. She had to at least try.

Rising to her feet, she scooped up the tray her shadow had brought her and set it on the table, hiding the report beneath it. The dinner on the tray was simple, nothing more than bread and soup. Palace dinners were always more elaborate than this, which meant her thoughtful shadow had only brought her what he'd thought she'd be able to handle. Her gaze drifted towards her bookshelf. Sitting against the side of the bookshelf sat a pair of the most beautiful leather boots she'd ever seen, Captain Brion's birthday gift to her.

She had no idea how he'd managed to get them, but she'd been touched he'd been paying so much attention to her. It'd been several months since they'd perched on one end of the palace's terrace and commented on the soldiers' boots as they made their rounds. She hadn't expected him to buy her a pair of boots that had matched the one pair she'd taken a liking to.

The ones he'd gotten for her had a dull shine, nothing too flashy. He'd even managed to find the boot covers that had caught her eye. Several buckles ran up the sides and the top of the covers folded down, creating a short flap.

Perhaps she was simple, but she loved them.

It occurred to Redrinna right then she'd never even thanked him for them. He could've died trying to protect her from that man a few days ago—or any time since his job wasn't a leisurely stroll through the garden—and then she'd never get the chance to thank him for anything.

She rubbed her head before remembering her hair was still done up in its neat wreath, something else that was a byproduct of Captain Brion's care.

It'd been ages since she'd had ladies-in-waiting of any kind—since her transformation had happened, actually. After being chased around the castle by one with a pair of scissors and another who'd poured a foul-smelling liquid on her hair that had burned her scalp, all in the name of freeing her from her red hair—and neither one of them had stopped no matter how she'd screamed, not until the captain had been able to wrest her away from them—she didn't want ladies-in-waiting anymore anyway.

Redrinna knew they'd meant well, but with so many people afraid of being alone with her or being associated with her, she'd asked to be alone. The only task she still struggled with was her hair, and Captain Brion willingly did it for her every day.

She'd never thanked him for that either.

Shaking herself, she hurriedly ate the meal her devoted shadow had brought before scooping up the empty tray and knocking on the door with her foot. The door opened a second later.

The captain blinked once before taking the tray from her. He opened his mouth to say something, but Redrinna cut him off, her tongue getting the better of her.

"I forgot," she blurted out, knowing it didn't make sense the moment the words flew out of her mouth.

"Forgot what, Your Highness?" Captain Brion said, his eyes a bit wider than usual.

"Last week, to thank you." The words tumbled out like a rushing river. "I forgot. For the boots, I mean. They're exactly what I wanted, so thank you. I'm going to wear them on my trip next week." She paused, glancing away for a second. "A-and I wanted to ask if you were okay. After...you know."

The captain stared for a long time before the barest hint of a smile tugged on the corners of his mouth. Her mouth opened a little. Two smiles in one day? She'd seen more blue moons than her shadow's smiles, and now she'd seen not just one, but two.

"I'm glad they're to your liking, and I am perfectly fine," he said. "Thank you for the concern, Your Highness."

For the first time in hours, her heart lifted a few inches. "And the soldier who protected me that day, do you know if he's...okay?"

"I will ask."

She managed to give him a small smile, but it vanished almost immediately. "Thank you, Captain."

"Good night, Your Highness."

Redrinna nodded and closed the door. With a small shrug like she could shake off all the bad feelings inside her, she made her way to the bag from her parents—which she'd shoved under her bed—carefully tugging out its contents. Her eyes narrowed. Fingerless, leather gauntlets? A fur-lined traveling cloak? A shirt and an overtunic? And pants? She'd never worn a pair of pants a day in her life—not because she didn't want to, she'd just never thought about it. What kind of trip were her parents taking her on that she needed a pair of pants?

Chapter Three

With the report bogging down Redrinna's mind, she eagerly anticipated when Lady Cel Tradat would be able to fulfill their promise to spend time with each other. But a few days passed without any sign of her. Almost an entire week went by before the woman knocked on the door to Redrinna's chambers.

"You in, Princess?" the woman called.

Redrinna's heart rose an inch or two.

Eagerly, she set the report aside before glancing around the slightly disheveled space. Tomorrow was the day she and her parents would be heading out on their trip. It would take most of a day to get there and most of the next to come back, so she'd been trying to decide what to pack for a while. Things were still a bit of a mess. And the mess seemed to have carried into the sitting area with her a little bit.

She shrugged. It was fine. Lady Cel Tradat had seen her chambers in a worse state before.

Shaking those thoughts away, she went and opened the door.

"Hey!" Lady Cel Tradat didn't wait to be permitted before she entered, but Redrinna didn't mind. "Where's your faithful guard at?"

"My parents wanted to talk to him, so he's with them," Redrinna explained as the woman strode past the bear fur rug to the armchairs in front of the fire.

"That explains why your parents wanted more guards in the halls tonight. I really wish they'd explain why they want my soldiers somewhere instead of telling me to simply do it." As Lady Cel Tradat sat, she beckoned Redrinna over. "Come sit. It's been ages since we've been able to chat like this."

It certainly had. Quickly, Redrinna went, purposely not looking anywhere but the chair she intended to sit in so she wouldn't have to see the other doors in the room. Besides the doors that led in from the hall and the one to her room, there were two other doors. If things had been different, her siblings would've lived behind them. But they didn't, and the rooms beyond were empty. Shaking those thoughts away, she sat, trying to relax in the fur-covered leather chair.

For a while, they chatted about nothing in particular, but then Lady Cel Tradat said, "Are you ready for your trip tomorrow? I just wanted you to know this was my idea. I, for one, think it's impossible to rule a country you've never seen."

Redrinna smiled a little at the woman's enthusiasm. "But you're not coming?" She was sure there'd be some kind of escort. Regardless, that didn't mean the Imperial general herself would be among them.

"Nope," the woman said, playing with the end of her purple sash. "Your parents are adamant about having some family time, so I'll be holding down the fort while you're all out. Of course, I'm still sending a small but trusted group of soldiers along. Just to be safe."

The tension in Redrinna's chest eased a little. If it had ended up being only her, her parents, and Captain Brion (they'd never said he was coming, but she had no reason to think otherwise. They were rarely separated as it was), that would've made her plenty nervous.

"It's been a long time since I've left the palace," she said after a minute. "Not since before the Esunian War started."

Both of them went quiet. Esunia had been the last country on the continent that had refused to yield to the Empire, and the war to conquer them had erupted around the time she'd been eight. It'd officially lasted only a year; she scarcely remembered any of it. It'd been a vicious war, and the Esuni people—as demonstrated by the rebels—hadn't forgotten it. And that was why Redrinna had never been allowed to leave the palace since.

So doing so now... A chill raced over her skin.

"What assignment did your parents give you this week? I heard your last one was about crops or something?"

"That's right." Redrinna retrieved her report from the table she'd set it on, holding it out to the woman.

There were a couple minutes of silence as she flipped through the report before she thumped it back on the table with an irritated huff.

"I told them not to assign that to you," Lady Cel Tradat snarled, flipping the end of her black braid over her shoulder. "You shouldn't have to bother with something like that when you're only seventeen."

Redrinna didn't know how to respond to that.

The woman sighed. "Do you know what you're going to do?"

"Not yet."

"Things like that are difficult, no matter how simple the solution may seem. The best thing is probably to have all of them executed, however awful that feels to decide."

Redrinna didn't know what to say to that either, so she didn't say anything. The report curdled her stomach every time she sifted through it, so she also wished she didn't have to bother with it. But at the same time, giving her an assignment like this meant her parents trusted her, didn't it? If killing them was such a simple choice, why make her bother with it?

Settling back into her chair a little more, Lady Cel Tradat turned to her with a ghost of a smile. "What's done is done, I guess. At times like these, you could really use a Queen Reyna, huh?"

Queen Reyna... Redrinna supposed someone like her wouldn't have been a bad thing. According to her legend, after the ancient queen had had her kingdom stolen from her, she'd wandered from country to country helping its leaders until she vanished. She'd been fearless and devastating in battle, but also fiercely loyal and kind to those she considered friends. At least, that was how Lady Cel Tradat told the story.

There weren't any tapestries of the queen in the palace, but that was because she hadn't been from Eridia. She'd come from somewhere in the southeast. Either way, if someone like her ended up wandering into the palace one day, it would be a relief.

Though, also scary. The legend had imbued great respect in her for the woman but also fear. Redrinna wasn't sure she wanted to meet someone who'd supposedly taken on an entire squadron of soldiers alone and won.

"Actually, since we're on the subject," Lady Cel Tradat began, the cautious note in her voice making a chill settle in Redrinna's chest. "There's something I found out a little bit ago that you need to know. I've been debating whether or not I should tell you, but I think I should."

"What do you mean?" Redrinna asked, unsure if she wanted the answer.

"It's about," the woman paused, chewing on her lip, "this trip of yours. Isn't it odd your parents want to take you on a trip so soon after the capital was attacked?"

Well, now that she thought about it, she guessed it was odd. Even when it'd seemed like things were settling down after the war ended, they hadn't even let her visit the palace gardens. So going on a trip so soon after an assault on the city was a bit...

"Right?" The woman cast a glance her way, her expression mirroring the sudden doubt wheedling into Redrinna's mind. "To top it off, they've been acting odder than normal lately. I thought it was because of the attack, but the closer we get to this trip, the antsier they've become."

"Why?" She wasn't surprised though, in all honesty. Letting her leave the palace had made them nervous before war and rebels, forget after.

The woman stayed quiet for a minute. "Redrinna," she whispered, "I have no proof, so you don't have to believe me, but I think they're going to try to kill you."

Her heart all but stopped. "You think they want to kill me?" she breathed, barely able to speak through her clenched throat.

Lady Cel Tradat nodded, her expression solemn. "I do. While you're on your trip. They won't even tell anybody where they're taking you."

That couldn't be right. Her parents couldn't want to kill her; they were getting ready to hand the throne over to her. How were they supposed to do that if Redrinna, their only heir, was dead?

"B-but why? It doesn't make any sense."

"I think it's because of your hair and eyes."

"What?" Ever since her appearance had changed, her parents had been some of the only people who'd continued to be kind to her. To treat her like a human. They'd seemed sad about it for a while, but they'd never, not once, treated her like most the palace staff did.

"You remember those legends about the Dragon Kin your mom told you before, don't you?"

"That group of humans and dragons from a long time ago, right?" If she remembered right, they'd turned the tides in a war and ended another one or something. The legends weren't very detailed.

"Exactly," Lady Cel Tradat said, her gaze turning to the fire, the light of the orange flames reflecting in her eyes. "A long time ago, they appeared to save the land from a great evil, remember? And your father is an emperor who's brought the entire continent to heel through bloody conquest. What if the Dragon Kin is going to come back? This empire is a vicious creation, and with the unrest in the east, I think things are going to get worse. A legendary group of defenders would rise to put a stop to that, wouldn't they?"

"What would that have to do with me though?"

Lady Cel Tradat turned to her, her serious expression chilling Redrinna to the bone. "A lesser-known fact about the Dragon Kin is the human members all had strangely colored hair and eyes, just like you do. Whether the Dragon Kin is going to come back or not, your father won't stand for any threat to his empire. If he even thinks you're a threat, that would be enough for him to want to kill you."

Redrinna's hand curled around the pendant dangling from her throat. Her heart hammered against her ribs so hard, it almost hurt. Her parents had never mentioned that part of the Dragon Kin legend whenever they'd told her the stories. Had they not known? Or maybe...they hadn't wanted her to know? Was the change in her appearance really supposed to mean she was fated to join some group to overthrow her parents? How was she supposed to know if the Dragon Kin had even been real?

Swiftly rising from her chair, Lady Cel Tradat hit the ground on her knees in front of Redrinna, grasping both her hands. The most desperate look she'd ever seen shone from the woman's eyes, catching her off guard. "Remember, this is just my thinking. I can't prove any of it."

Even still, Redrinna knew Lady Cel Tradat's hunches were seldom wrong. She was renowned for it.

"Because of that, we can't say a word to anyone. Not even if you think you can trust them."

"Not even the Captain?" Redrinna could barely speak her chest was so tight.

"No. He is your appointed knight, but at the end of the day, he works for your father. Just because he does his job and your hair nicely doesn't mean he loves you."

Lady Cel Tradat reached into a pouch at her waist and pulled out a knife, pressing it into Redrinna's hands.

Redrinna almost stopped breathing. A weapon. She hated weapons and what they brought with them.

"I wanted to give this to you on your birthday, but things didn't work out, so I'm giving it to you now. In my country, when children reach the age of seventeen, they're given a knife to symbolize their strength to carve their own destinies. But right now, your life might very well be in danger. If something happens, protect yourself and do everything you can to make it back to me. I may be the general of your father's armies, but as your friend, I'm loyal to you first. I'll protect you as best I can, no matter what. So, if something happens, find me. Promise?"

Her hands shook. Was this some kind of nightmare? "O-okay."

All at once, a knock resounded through the room, making both of them jump. "Your Highness?" came Captain Brion's voice. "May I come in?"

Frantically, Redrinna looked at Lady Cel Tradat.

"Hide it," the woman hissed as she rushed back to her chair.

Redrinna hid the knife under her skirts before calling out, "All right." Her hands were shaking badly enough she partially hid them too.

The captain entered, pausing for the briefest of moments when he seemed to spot Lady Cel Tradat. "Ah, you have company. I don't wish to overstep, but it's growing late and you have an early morning ahead of you."

"He's right about that, Princess," Lady Cel Tradat said, sounding like her normal self. Rising, she stretched before turning towards the door. "I'll see you when you return."

There was a knowing look in the woman's eyes. Redrinna nodded, not trusting her voice enough to speak. A minute later, the woman was gone, leaving her alone with her appointed knight.

For the first time in Redrinna's life, a shiver of fear trickled down her spine at the idea of being alone with him. Could she trust him?

Doing her best to hide the knife among the folds of her skirt, she rose from the chair. "I guess I'll go to bed then," she said, doing her utmost to keep her voice steady.

"Of course," Captain Brion said, dipping his head.

Without even a sideways glance at him, she marched as calmly as she could to her room. Once inside, she hesitated for a long minute before she turned and silently locked the door.

To try calming herself a little, Redrinna studied the knife she'd been given. Dark leather with curling engravings covered the unadorned hilt. The scabbard was done in matching black leather, and when she withdrew the knife a fraction, its slender blade shone bright as a star.

Slipping it back into its sheath, she gazed around the room, towards everything she'd packed. She'd been thrilled about this trip; at least, a part of her had been. Now, she wished she could back out or pretend she was sick or something. Except, if she did, wouldn't her parents know something was up? That she'd somehow figured them out?

Lady Cel Tradat hadn't been sure either. Could she be one hundred percent certain her parents were going to try and kill her after all the effort they'd put into teaching her how to rule? Who would take over if she died? The rest of her siblings were dead, and she had no cousins or relatives to speak of.

A shudder shook her, and she tightened her grip on the knife. Very, very desperately, she hoped Lady Cel Tradat ended up being wrong.

๑๑ ๑๑

The next morning dawned bright and clear, a fact Redrinna only knew because Captain Brion roused her way too early. Once she was awake, though, an awful feeling of dread slithered through every organ inside her, making it impossible for her to go back to sleep. She debated feigning illness, but the allure of going outside the palace walls combined with the fear of what would happen if she didn't go was enough to coax her from the warmth of her bed.

Deathly quiet, she dressed in the clothes her parents had given her and the boots from the captain. She spied the knife from Lady Cel Tradat on her bedside table. After a long minute of staring at it, debating whether or not she could bring herself to use it if something happened, she strapped it to her belt (which took more tries than she expected).

Her agitation gnawed on her nerves so hard, Redrinna couldn't even handle standing still. Until the captain finally arrived with a light breakfast and to do her hair, she paced the length of her room like a wildcat in a cage.

At her request, he fashioned it into a braid almost identical to the one Lady Cel Tradat often featured. Perhaps looking more like the woman would help her find some confidence.

As she sat, nibbling through the fruit and milk he'd brought, her heart began to doubt her friend's warning. How could she not trust Captain Brion when he would brush her hair so gently, she rarely felt him work a snarl free? When he'd undo his work if he didn't think it was up to standard and start over, intent on making her hair look nothing short of amazing every day? He always listened to her complaints, even the stupid ones she regretted later, and offered advice whenever he could.

More doubts needled into her heart as they left her chambers and made their way through a few, quiet hallways and down the palace's long, curving staircases to the entrance hall. Lady Cel Tradat had never lied to her either. Not even once. So why would she do so now?

To distract herself and disguise her nerves, Redrinna studied the morning light streaming diagonally through the colored windows, painting rainbows across the gray, stone floor. If her parents were going to try to kill her today, then how could there be something this beautiful right in front of her? After a moment, she realized the captain was watching her, making her stiffen.

"What?" She folded her arms, trying to appear much calmer than she felt.

"Are you feeling all right?"

Of course, he'd be able to tell if something was bugging her. Thinking quickly, she said, "I'm just nervous. I haven't left the palace in so long and..."

The corners of his mouth lifted slightly, but not into an actual smile. It would seem his smiles were gone again. "That's understandable. But there's no need to fear. The world is dangerous, but it is just as beautiful. You deserve to be able to see it again."

His words touched her heart, making her nerves fade for a moment before they returned full force, adding to the doubts festering inside her. If he was merely doing his job and never cared about her, then why was he always so kind?

The soldier who'd protected her at the trial had just been doing his job and hadn't given her a second glance afterwards, even with blood dripping from his fingers.

At that moment, a soft clacking echoed through the room, distracting her from her thoughts. Her heart stuttered like a flame in the wind as her parents entered the room, both of them dressed in similar fashion to her. Neither of them were wearing their circlets. Crown-free time. Her favorite.

Despite all her doubts whirlpooling inside her, as her mother stopped in front of her, her brown hair in a neat, high ponytail, Redrinna couldn't help smiling a little.

"Ready to go?" her mother asked.

Redrinna nodded, a small part of her hoping they'd notice she wore the clothes they'd given her the other day. The clothes were more comfortable than she'd expected, though she had a pressing need to keep readjusting them. Tunics and pants functioned differently than dresses, it seemed.

"Let's get going," her father said.

Where were the soldiers Lady Cel Tradat had said she was sending with them? As they turned towards the door, Redrinna couldn't help noting how stiff her parents stood and that their smiles seemed a bit forced, like they always did when they were nervous. Was it because they were really going to try to kill her? That didn't make sense though. If her parents wanted her dead because of her potential link to this mysterious Dragon Kin she hardly knew anything about, why would they be nervous about it?

They left the palace and headed to the bottom of the steep hill it stood on, past the vast gardens whose trees swayed gently in the chill breeze like they were dancing to the burbling of the nearby stream. Redrinna pulled her fur cloak a little tighter to her as they walked. Her parents led her to the royal stables, where their horses were kept.

It'd been a long time since Redrinna had been in here, but the musty smell of hay and the faint, sweaty smell of the horses were instantly familiar. Despite how early it was, with the sun just starting to light the sky and illuminate the doorways of the stables, the young stable hands were already busy preparing three horses for them.

Wait. Only three?

Tentatively, she glanced at the captain, who caught her gaze and whispered, "Your father is allowing me to escort you to the end of the grounds before he takes over your care for the next couple of days. It may feel a bit strange, but he's more than capable of protecting you."

Or killing her, she couldn't help thinking, but she adamantly kept that to herself.

Desperate for distraction, Redrinna turned her attention to the horses. Her heart ached at the sight of them. It'd been so long since she'd been this close to the animals, ever since she'd been hidden away in the palace. The three horses were all similar shades of a dark brown, almost black color. They had short-ish, almost compact faces, with stout necks and broad chests. Their legs were kind of short, and she was pretty sure their shoulders were a little below her own, but they seemed fit and muscular, through and through. Mountain horses.

Just where were they going?

Once the stable hands were finished, one of them—a young boy—bravely approached her. He didn't speak, but a ghost of a smile appeared on his face as he ushered her towards the horse farthest to the right and helped her mount it.

"They're not very big," he said softly once she was settled. "But our mountain horses are stronger than most any other horse you'll ever meet. He'll keep you safe." He patted the horse's neck before turning and disappearing into one of the stalls.

Redrinna blinked after him, still trying to process what had just happened. He'd...spoken to her. Because he could. Maybe she was going to die today.

She shook that thought away and focused on adjusting to being on horseback again.

No wonder her parents had given her pants to wear. A long trip on horseback in a dress would have been quite uncomfortable. Plus, it'd been a long time since she'd ridden a horse, so pants meant one less thing on her mind.

At her parents' urging, she coaxed her horse to follow after them. Instead of heading towards the front gate and guard post that led into the town like she'd thought they would, they went towards the back entrance, the one that let out very close to the bases of the wild mountains that sheltered them.

Her heart thrummed in her throat, her grip tightening on the leather reins as they got closer. When they reached the gate, they stopped so her father could talk with the guards there.

Captain Brion stepped close, tenderly patting her horse's neck. "This is as far as I go," he murmured, and Redrinna could've sworn she heard a tremor in his voice. "Have a safe journey, Your Highness."

Her voice caught in her throat. "Of course," she managed.

"I'll be waiting for your return," he said.

If she returned.

Her father urged his horse forward, followed closely by her mother, leaving her little choice but to follow. She barely had time to glance back at the captain because balancing on her horse took a lot of her concentration. They passed under the deep shadow of the gate, and she just managed to look back at him once more before the gate grated shut.

There wasn't an escort waiting for them out here.

"Mom?" Redrinna called timidly, feeling very, very exposed outside the palace gates.

Her mother glanced back, one eyebrow raised. "Yes, dear?"

"Lady Cel Tradat was going to send soldiers with us, wasn't she?"

Her father glanced back. "That was what she said, but that's why we're leaving so early, beyond this being quite a long trip. If we want some alone time, we have to go before she catches us."

There was a hint of a twinkle in his eye as he spoke, the mischievous look painstakingly reminding her of when she'd been little. She and her father had always played games of hide-and-seek with Lady Cel Tradat, though the woman had been clueless about their game most of the time. Even still, Lady Cel Tradat's warning from last night rang in her ears so loudly, she almost thought the woman had leapt out from behind a nearby tree.

It was just her, her parents, and nobody else. Maybe they were going to kill her.

Chapter Four

Even though Redrinna's nerves were alive like a nest of wriggling spiders, that didn't stop her from taking in the mountain forests towering around her. A mixture of pines, aspens, and beeches spread as far as she could see, patches of white snow clinging to their bare branches and hiding in their deep shadows. There wasn't much color, especially with the morning mists limiting how far she could see, but if she hunted for them, she spied myriads of little buds on the trees and bushes, and the bright green heads of snowdrops and crocuses pushing their way through the rich brown soil. Despite the chill breeze, there was an undercurrent of warmth that promised spring wasn't long-off. And to top it off, like jewels in a crown, beautiful but quiet birdsong drifted through the air.

A definite sign of the arrival of spring.

As the mountains rapidly closed in around them, Redrinna managed to throw one last look over her shoulder at the palace, its turrets just catching the sun's first rays. The gray stone seemed a bit lifeless on its own, but she knew in the moonlight, it shone silver. At twilight, it blushed pink or sometimes glowed purple. In the early morning light, right before her eyes, it shimmered gold.

When she saw it like that, she could understand why people believed it was the Priestess' palace. Was she ever going to see it again?

Their horses plodded along the narrow mountain trail, and too soon, her home was out of sight, lost behind mountain and trees. The nerves tightening around her stomach became her foremost thought.

The palace was behind her, getting farther with each hoofbeat. Because of the narrowness of the path, they fell into a single file line, with her father ahead of her and her mother behind. Perfectly stuck between them. If something were to happen, would Redrinna be able to do anything? At that instant, she became acutely aware of the knife at her waist like it'd jabbed her leg. Would she even be able to bring herself to use it?

As the day trailed on, Redrinna's tension started to lessen as nothing happened, allowing her mind to find different things to focus on. The horse she rode was well trained. Once, a snake darted across their path, startling her at its suddenness, but her horse had been unfazed. As they continued, she rarely had to direct him. Instead, Redrinna scanned the forest more as the mists began to lift, burned away by the sun. She spied clusters of red and white mushrooms peeking out from the bases of the trees, thick patches of moss, and every once in a while, thin, trickling streams. The sun filtering through the snowy branches illuminated the ground, making everything it touched glow a little.

Once again, Redrinna found herself thinking if her parents were planning to kill her, how could the world be so beautiful?

They stopped around midday to rest and water their horses, and to rest themselves too. Already, Redrinna found her legs to be quite sore, with still a ways to go ahead of them.

When they set off again, her parents began chatting, and every once in a while, asked for her to chime in. They had yet to ask her about the assignment, and she didn't remind them.

While Lady Cel Tradat's warnings from last night beat like a drum in her ear with every hoofbeat, the relaxed way her parents talked about boring and mundane things set her at ease. Maybe Lady Cel Tradat's hunch was wrong this time. There was no question whether or not her parents were on edge after the attack, but it occurred to Redrinna as they traveled that perhaps her friend was on edge too. Maybe they'd all show up at the palace tomorrow evening and everything would be fine.

Well, as fine as things could be.

Even still, a tiny, incessant voice kept whispering otherwise, preventing her from relaxing. Every once in a while, she asked her parents where they were going, but they had yet to answer. If Lady Cel Tradat had sent soldiers after them—and knowing her she would've—they had yet to arrive. She couldn't hear a thing except for themselves and the burbles of the forest. If she thought about it though, the three of them would be able to move a lot faster than a squad of soldiers.

It was nearly dusk when they finally stopped. Redrinna's legs were so stiff, she couldn't move for a minute or two after dismounting. To her amusement, her parents were just as stiff, all three of them enjoying a laugh as they hobbled around for a few minutes.

As their laughter faded, Redrinna's father wrapped an arm around her shoulders and said, "Do you want to know where we're going now?"

Her curiosity ignited as easily as a spark striking dry leaves. More than a little eager, she nodded.

He pointed to something just ahead and to the side of the path. It took her a minute to spot what he pointed at, but once she had, her heart skipped a beat. A cave. A natural, real-live cave.

The forest raced right to the edges of the huge, shadowy opening, and with the way their branches hung over the top, she would've missed it if her father hadn't pointed it out.

"You've never been able to see one before, have you?" her mother said as she came up on her other side. "The closest you've come is the ice room back at the palace, but that was man-made, so I don't think it counts."

Redrinna shook her head. Man-made didn't count.

"It's a little late, but we have time to poke around a bit if you want to," her mother continued. "Or we could rest for the night."

Redrinna didn't even need a second to decide. She knew what she wanted to do. "Can we take a quick peek before we settle down?"

Her father smiled a little. "Always the curious one, aren't you? All right. If you insist, let's take a peek."

She didn't wait for them, hurrying forward and stopping once she reached the entrance of the cave. Lightly, she touched her hand to the rough, dark stone. She'd read a lot about caves before, but seeing one in person was much different than she'd expected. It was extremely dark. And cold.

A breeze tugged at her ankles like it was urging her in. Her parents caught up with her before she could take a step. They all stood there for a brief moment before her father strode inside. Her mother tugged playfully on her red braid before they did the same.

For some reason, Redrinna had expected it to be a long tunnel, but after a couple of steps, the space abruptly opened, the stone walls and stalagmites vanishing into the expansive darkness. A part of her was afraid if she moved, she wouldn't be able to find her way back out. But after a minute, her eyes adjusted enough for her to see a bit further ahead.

Her heart stilled. A short ways ahead, the stalagmites gave way to a giant chasm yawning open in the floor. It was a lot harder to breathe.

Caves were dangerous places. She'd heard of murder victims being found in them more than once. People just vanished in them sometimes, like the earth had swallowed them, without a trace. And she'd walked inside one like a brainless dim-wit. If she died here, there was a good chance no one would ever find her body. Her parents could make murder seem like an accident.

All at once, the stalagmites seemed alive, knitting themselves tighter together, fencing themselves around her. The darkness above crouched lower, the very mountain itself ready to swallow her whole. Folding her arms like she was cold, she gripped the hilt of her knife as discreetly as possible.

"Redrinna, come see this," her father called from near the edge of the chasm.

Since she couldn't think of a good excuse not to without potentially alerting them, she shuffled over, gripping the knife so hard it hurt a little, the leather digging into her skin.

When Redrinna neared her father, he held up a pebble before dropping it into the hole. She took a couple of steps closer, peering down into the unending darkness, her curiosity outweighing her fear. How far down did it go?

It took a minute or so before a tiny splash echoed out from the dark abyss. There was water down there? She leaned a little closer. Unexpectedly, her father grabbed her elbow, dragging her back a bit.

She straightened, biting her lip as she avoided his gaze.

He let go.

Should she say something? How could she? What could she say?

No part of her wanted to believe what Lady Cel Tradat had told her. Some of her couldn't. How could they want to kill her? They'd already had plenty of opportunities, yet they hadn't taken a single one. Was she panicking for nothing?

"Is this not very interesting for you?"

"No, i-it is," she said, her fingers aching from her tight grip on the knife. "It's interesting."

"Maybe not from up here though," her mother mused from the other side of her father as she peered into the darkness.

Was that a clue?

Her father leaned forward, pointing down into the darkness, his eyes sparkling just a bit. "You know what they say about this place? People say a dragon lives here."

She almost smiled, but her cheeks didn't cooperate. "A dragon? Everybody knows all of them were wiped out in the Dragon War almost one hundred years ago."

A sigh escaped her mother. "Yes, that is a war we should never forget. It changed this country's history forever."

Silence fell between the three of them at that. Redrinna caught herself relaxing, her grip on the knife loosening. Hastily, she tightened her grip.

"So," her mother continued, taking a step back from the ledge. "We haven't discussed your assignment yet, have we?"

"No," Redrinna said, her voice quieter than normal in the emptiness of the cavern. "We haven't."

"What's your decision?" her father asked, his normally loud voice also seeming quieter.

It occurred to her this would be the first time she reported on an assignment without her parents wearing their crowns. It would be the first time she reported to them as just her parents. Her grip on the knife loosened a bit.

Despite that though, her tongue grabbed onto the roof of her mouth. It took a few minutes to convince it to come back down. "According to Eridian law, murder alone is a crime punishable by death, and that wasn't their only crime. But I..." Her tongue clambered back up to the roof of her mouth, fear and frustration warring inside her.

"Speak your mind," her father said, folding his arms. "I want to hear every thought you put into this."

A sigh fought to escape while she pried her tongue down again so she could speak. Her heart shivered at the thought of saying what was on her mind, but it would be worse if she didn't say it. "The Esunian people hate us because of the war in the Esuni Desert and what they've suffered since. We claimed their lands as our own and destroyed their livelihoods, so I can imagine how angry they are bowing their heads to us and trying to adapt to a foreign way of life, thus why the rebels there feel justified in attacking us."

She remembered the Esunian man's trial, how he'd shouted about justice and taking back what rightfully belonged to his people. "Despite that, I...I can't see how adding to the bloodshed is going to change the situation. It'll make it worse. But I also don't know...how to..." She huffed, wishing she could just get all the words out. "Is it wrong to let them live? But, I also know if we do, there's nothing to stop them from coming after us again, or from hurting more innocent people. They already have, so what would deter them?"

Her parents remained silent.

"Even still...many of them claimed they'd had no knowledge of what their leader had planned until they'd arrived at the city, and the reports from the knights confirm many of them surrendered themselves willingly. So, executing them doesn't seem..."

Neither of her parents spoke for a while.

Her mother laid a thin hand on her shoulder. "Violence always begets more violence," she said. "You are correct. And there's nothing wrong with not knowing how to do something, Redrinna, no matter how old you are."

"Remember that, and I appreciate your honesty. Don't worry," her father said, flashing a smile, "your mother and I will take your thoughts into consideration and decide our stance. You did well."

Her heart lifted an inch or two. Redrinna...wasn't going to have to officially decide their stance after all? Her grip on the knife slackened even further.

Dipping her head, she recalled last night and the way Lady Cel Tradat had begged her on her knees to be careful and wary. But she couldn't do it, not how the woman wanted her to. She couldn't believe her parents would kill her after all this.

Swallowing her doubts, she let the knife go.

"Redrinna, I need you to do something for me." Her father turned to face her, the way his square jaw was set making him appear much younger. "I want you to promise your mother and me here and now that you will do everything in your power to be the greatest Empress you can be. Always remember your people must come first. You have to protect them, no matter what. Understand? Promise me."

Redrinna's gaze flicked to the gaping chasm of darkness at her side. She didn't want to, but they would insist until she did. "Okay."

"That's not good enough." Her father grabbed her shoulders, giving her a gentle shake.

Startled, she turned back to him, her mouth going dry at how serious his dark eyes were.

"I mean it, Redrinna. Don't just be 'okay' with this. Swear it."

Her stomach churned at the thought. However... "Okay, okay. I swear it. Do you want me to swear it on a sword or something?"

Her mother laughed a little, but for some reason, it sounded like her heart was shattering. "No, your word will do."

That familiar, sinking feeling settled in Redrinna's chest. Did they believe in her that much? "Even if I can't do anything right?"

Even though her parents had been nice about it, she knew the right choice for the assignment had been life imprisonment or execution, but she couldn't bring herself to make that call. It felt wrong.

Her father sighed, smiling a little. Gently, he took hold of her hands, meeting her gaze. "Redrinna, nobody can do everything right, not even an Empress. It's about doing what you believe and not letting your mistakes hold you back. Don't make difficult decisions lightly. Make sure the benefits outweigh the costs, and most of all, remember to act. Don't stand idly by or you will spend the rest of your days drowning in regret."

Her mother stepped up as her father released her hands, smoothing Redrinna's hair before kissing her forehead. "You are so brave, my love," she murmured before drawing back. "Don't ever forget that."

As she did, Redrinna noticed tears in her mother's beautiful brown eyes. She glanced back and forth between the two of them. Had she said something wrong? Why were they so sad?

Without warning, her father shoved her.

Wait.

Redrinna didn't have time to blink. One moment she stood beside him and her mother. The next she was falling over the edge of the chasm.

This wasn't supposed to—

Her eyes widened as her stomach dropped to her toes. She nearly choked as her heart lurched into her throat. Her eyes locked with her mother's and father's for a brief second that stretched into an eternity. They both mouthed three words she refused to believe. Then they were gone.

Darkness swallowed her. Wind tore at her face; she couldn't make sense of what was up or down.

Suddenly, a roar struck her ears and pain erupted across the right side of her body. Water filled her mouth and nose as her body went numb from cold and shock. Her heavy fur cloak tightened around her throat, pulling her down. She frantically looked up, the world she'd just been severed from nothing but a small glimmer of watery light far above her, shrinking until it faded to nothing.

≈≈ ≈≈

Something kept poking her ribs. It wasn't painful, but it wasn't pleasant either. For some reason, though, no matter how hard Redrinna tried to move her arms, they wouldn't listen. They weighed too much, like they'd turned to stone. Her mouth didn't seem to be working either.

Her head was all fog, making it impossible to discern anything.

A noise touched her ears, but she couldn't understand it. It was like she was straining to hear something through a wall. It was almost as grating as the incessant prodding in her ribs.

"Hey," said a voice, sounding a lot like the noise she'd just heard, except a little bit louder this time. "Hey. Hey!" The voice steadily got louder. She tried to wave her assailant off but she was only dimly aware of her arm moving. Without warning, her body lurched, air rushing into her lungs with dizzying speed. The world spun, careening wildly. Then, she sank back into darkness.

Chapter Five

Redrinna jerked awake, staying still for a minute before wave after wave of aches from all across her body battered her brain. She had no idea how long she lay there, alternating between having her eyes closed and open before a vivid memory flashed through her mind.

Falling.

Her body snapped into a sitting position, jerking upright as though her brain was trying to find the rest of her and make sure it was okay too. Pure agony surged from every muscle. As the pain intensified, arcing up her back and down her limbs, she squeezed her eyes shut, doing her best to hold back the cry in her throat. It took a while for the stabbing pain to recede to a bearable level, but once it had she was afraid to move at all, just in case doing so would ignite the pain again. She didn't like pain, and she'd never experienced anything like that before.

After a long moment, she risked opening her eyes, just enough to see. Worry pulsed in her chest. All she could see was a dark gray shifting in and out of inky blackness.

There had to be something wrong with her after that fall. She'd studied enough about injuries to know that. Steeling herself, she lifted her hands. Her arms screamed as she moved them, but she forced herself to push through the pain. This was important. She glanced down. She could see her hands, though they were dark and shadowy. So maybe her vision was okay and it was just dark.

Redrinna's chest constricted. Where was she? A dark, windowless, lightless place like this would only be the dungeons if she were in the palace. However, this place, something about it, was different. It was damp and cold, but it didn't smell like the dungeons. Here, it smelt vaguely of wood smoke with a faint but nose-curling smell that stung a bit lurking underneath. It reminded her of that one time some of the kitchen staff had accidentally smashed some rotten eggs and the smell had wafted through the palace for hours.

Was it possible she wasn't in the palace? Her heart shuddered, catching hold of her throat and refusing to let go.

Trying to stay calm but knowing it wasn't working, Redrinna took in as much of this place as she could without moving her head. Gray. Gray. Gray. Was...it possible she was still in the cave with her parents?

Closing her eyes, she took several deep breaths, convincing her heart to ease its grip on her throat though it refused to calm entirely. Panicking wasn't going to do her any good. It would make a situation seem scarier than it was, thus making it harder to react in a way that would keep her safe. Lady Cel Tradat had told her that once.

She studied her surroundings more. Biting her lip to stay quiet, she turned. The pain clawed at her for a few minutes before quieting down. Redrinna didn't know if she could handle much more of that.

A shaky exhale escaped her. Her heart squeezed a bit harder on her throat. It was a bit brighter over here with thin sunbeams poking through a hole in the ceiling, just light enough to make the surrounding space seem exceptionally dark. Blacks and grays were still the dominant features here, even with the little bit of light trickling in. After a minute though, she found another color too: dark blue, a blue so dark she almost mistook it for black. After staring at it for a while, it dawned on her it was water. Very still and quiet water. Her gaze returned to the opening high above, which was situated right above the water, so small and high above her she could have hidden it from sight with one hand.

As everything began clicking into place, a chill crept through her lungs. Lady Cel Tradat had been right. Her parents had tried to kill her by shoving her into the chasm. Thankfully, she'd landed in water, presumably the water lurking a short way from her, and lived. Somehow. How long she'd been unconscious, she didn't know. However, she was still in the cave and, mysteriously, no longer in the water.

All at once, it occurred to Redrinna there was something between her and the cavern floor. Something soft. Keeping her head as still as possible, she looked down. Her fur cloak lay beneath her and was partially wrapped over her legs. It was dry. So was she.

A foggy memory swam through her mind, a moment that must've happened sometime between falling and now. Someone had saved her from drowning. More than likely, whoever it had been was still here.

A noise struck her ears like they'd decided it was okay to work again. Heavy breathing echoed off the stones around her, and it wasn't coming from her.

The breathing was slow and loud, like a draft horse stood right behind her, breathing down her neck. How had she missed it before? After another minute of listening to it, she realized the breathing came from the other side of the water. It took considerable effort, but she forced herself to study the darkness beyond the pool.

At first, Redrinna couldn't see anything, but after a minute more, she spotted a faint gleam. Her heart sputtered like a candle in the breeze. The longer she stared, the more things she noticed. There was no way this was a person like she'd initially thought. It appeared to be something much larger, bigger than any living thing she'd seen before. She wasn't sure where its face was either, a fact that made it difficult for her to swallow. What exactly was she staring at?

All at once, something red flicked through the dim light as the thing in the cave shifted, becoming even bigger. A harsh scraping echoed through the cavern, reminding her vaguely of stone rubbing against stone, except it didn't sound quite right.

As a wicked set of four claws slid into view, rasping against the rocks, her throat constricted. Each of those black claws had to be at least half her height, all of them gleaming in the faint light. Another set promptly followed the first.

Her eyes widened, all coherent thinking dwindling to nothing.

A tall, lithe, muscular body followed after those claws, light reflecting off a smooth sheen of red scales. Long, black horns arched back over a gracefully curved neck. A smoky black frill ran down its neck, out of sight, and reappeared on its tail, the tip of which flicked in and out of the shadows like a lizard's tongue.

What grabbed her attention most, however, was its face. Small horns protruded from the underside of its jaw, accentuating its curved snout. There were also small spikes in place of its eyebrows, shadowing its gleaming, dark eyes. Its eyes were narrowed, almost in a glare, except the corners of its large mouth were turned upwards. To her horror, Redrinna realized the beast was doing something akin to smiling. Why was it staring at her like that?

"You're awake," it said, its voice deeper than thunder rumbling through the heavens. "I'm so glad. After I fished you out of the water, I wasn't sure you'd wake up." It took a few catlike steps towards her before stopping, close enough now to grab her in its claws if it leapt. How had it covered the distance between them so quickly?!

"You...you're a...a...dragon," she managed, her voice tiny in the enormous space. This couldn't be possible. There was no way. It couldn't—

The beast tilted its head slightly to one side. "And you're not."

Her mouth opened, but her heart squeezed her throat so tight no sound came out. Dragons were supposed to be extinct. They were gone.

The dragon took a few more steps towards her, its long tail sweeping across the pool's surface, disturbing the water. Every muscle in Redrinna's body wanted to move, but they all ached too much to even twitch. However, those thoughts were chased far from her mind as the dragon took a step forward, leaning down, head getting nearer, ear frills on either side of its head lifting. She leaned away, pain battering her bones, back hitting the wall—

"Don't!" she cried.

The dragon froze, eyes wide. Its eyebrow spikes twitched slightly as it assumed what appeared to be some sort of concerned expression. "What's wrong?"

Her breath came in spastic gasps, each one sharpening the ache in her sides. "Don't...don't..."

It withdrew its head, taking a step back. "Don't what?"

She squeezed her eyes shut against the pain churning her stomach and making her nauseous. When her breathing calmed enough that she felt a little less sick, she met the gaze of the large beast watching her with those big, black eyes that glittered like beetles.

"You're a dragon," she said. "A dragon." Why was it messing with her like this? Is this what a mouse felt when it saw its reflection in a cat's eye?

Everyone knew before the Dragon War, dragons were some of the most ruthless and vile creatures known anywhere in the world. Which meant she was in some serious trouble now. As Lady Cel Tradat often said: off the stovetop and into the oven.

"Yes." One of the dragon's ear frills twitched, drawing her back to the present. "I know that. I also know you're a human." It attempted what she guessed was meant to be another smile, but all those sharp, gleaming teeth did little to make her feel better. "What's the problem?"

Was it really going to make her do this? "Dragons, they, you know, kill people."

It recoiled, shaking its head so hard, its ear frills slapped against its cheeks. "W-what?! That's so gross! I would never do something like that. Why would you think that?"

Redrinna's throat constricted so fast, she couldn't breathe for a couple of seconds. She wished the captain were here. Or Lady Cel Tradat.

"I've never killed any of your kind," the dragon continued, one clawed foot touching its chest as it lowered its head closer to her level. The spikes on its chin grated against the ground, making Redrinna wince as the ache in her skull intensified. "At least, not that I know of. Wait! I-I mean—" it stammered as her eyes went wide, "your kind is very small. I could've accidentally squashed someone, I admit. But in my defense, it's not as easy for me to keep track of all my body parts around small things as it is for you!"

Its wings flared open for emphasis, the tips brushing the cave walls on either side, the loud snap making her jump. The dragon's eyebrows twitched up into that concerned expression again before it hurriedly folded its wings tight to its sides and crouched like it was trying to appear smaller. Even still, it was as big as the stables back at the castle. No, a bit bigger.

"I'm so sorry. I didn't mean to frighten you, honest."

"I-it's okay," Redrinna managed to say once her heart stopped racing. "I guess it's only..." she tried to think of something inoffensive, "your predisposition."

The dragon seemed to accept that as it sat back on its haunches. "I guess I should introduce myself because then we can be friends." It cocked its head to one side. "That is how your kind does it, right?"

Not exactly, but she wasn't going to argue. She nodded once, a motion that made everything from her shoulders up sting.

"Right. So my name's Xandrin." It stared at her, ear frills perked up. Xandrin sounded like a boy's name maybe? Was this dragon a male? Was that even a good way to tell?

After a minute, she realized he was still staring at her. It took her another second to figure out what he waited for.

What should she say? Should she tell him she was an heir to an empire and people would be searching for her? Would he even know what that meant? Better yet...perhaps, with this dragon, she could pretend she wasn't the heir to anything? That was what she'd always wanted, right?

"My name," she began slowly, not sure if she should be entertaining thoughts like these, "it's Redrinna. Just Redrinna."

"It's nice to meet you. Officially," Xandrin said, once again adopting that toothy expression she could only equate with smiling. Unexpectedly, his ear frills lowered at the same time as his eyebrows. Eyespikes? "Why are you in my cave? Don't humans prefer to stay together?"

Her heart skipped a beat before it shuddered, a sick feeling sweeping through her. Her parents had really...after everything...they'd actually— Her gaze fell as she fought back the urge to start bawling. "Someone tried to kill me."

The dragon half-snorted, moving his head a little closer. "Kill you? You seem like a very nice person to me. Why would anybody want to kill you?"

"I wouldn't know," she said, her voice becoming so quiet she almost didn't hear it. She couldn't comprehend why her parents had done it. She couldn't even begin to think of an answer to the relentless question pounding against her skull: why? She was their only child still living. She was the only heir to the throne. So why?

If she hadn't been there, if it hadn't happened to her, she wouldn't believe it. She didn't want to believe it, but that moment, being shoved, falling—all of it had been real. It'd been very real.

The dragon remained silent for a while before he shifted, causing her to look up. He stared over his shoulder, towards the pool of water that lay behind him. "If it hadn't been for the water, whoever it was would have succeeded. It's an honest miracle they didn't." He turned back to her, his head cocking to the side again. "After all, you seem rather...frail."

"Frail?" she snapped before immediately biting her lip. Do not anger the dragon. Even though he seemed trustworthy, she wasn't in a position to tempt fate.

"Compared to me, I mean," he said with a hint of a smile. "It's pretty amazing that you're still alive, right?" He shrugged, making his wings flap a little. "There's not much we can do about it, I guess."

She found herself nodding—an action she immediately stopped—while trying to ignore the fact that despite waking up in a strange place with a creature she'd been convinced no longer existed, she was relaxing in this dragon's company.

"I suppose you'll want to go back to...wherever you came from when you're feeling up to it?"

Go back? Fear dug its icy claws into Redrinna's chest. If she went back, would her parents try to kill her again? Would anybody believe what had happened? Most of the castle staff could scarcely stand her, forget the people of the Empire at large. Would anybody even want her to come back?

"It's okay if you want to," Xandrin continued. "We barely know each other, after all."

Redrinna wanted to shout no, she'd never go back, but all at once, she thought of the promises she'd made to her parents and Lady Cel Tradat. Never in all her life had she broken a promise, even if she didn't always like it. There was no way she could keep either one by staying here. A shiver slithered down the length of her spine. She couldn't travel in her condition; she could hardly sit up. Even if she tried to get back, would she make it?

"No," she said, meeting the dragon's gaze. "That's not a place I can go back to right now." She'd worry about it later. When she was better.

Xandrin blinked as he slowly lifted his shoulders in a shrug, making his wings flap again. "I guess—if you want to—you could always stay here. If you don't have anywhere else to go, that is."

"Stay here?" she stammered, unable to tell whether or not the dragon was messing with her.

"Well, if someone is trying to kill you and you've got nothing important you need to get back to, you could always just let them think..."

"They'd succeeded," she finished quietly, hardly able to believe how desperately she wanted that.

"I understand if you don't want to," Xandrin said, tripping over his words in his haste to get them out of his mouth. "A human living with a dragon is something I've never actually heard of. I mean, you'd be stuck hiding in this big, empty hole in the ground for the rest of your life. Nothing will ever happen to you...probably." He stopped, grimacing a little. "Maybe it's not such a good idea for you to stay with me after all."

She realized she was chewing her lip. Redrinna hadn't done that in years, not since she'd been little. Xandrin wasn't at all how she'd imagined a dragon. Sure, he was large, covered in scales, and kind of odd, but at the same time, he was surprisingly...kind. Despite the aches resonating from every muscle in her body, there was a flicker of warmth in her chest.

"You'd really let me stay with you?" she asked. Her promises nagged at her again, but she forced them away. Later. She'd think about them later.

"Sure I'd let you stay with me," Xandrin said, his ear frills lifting. "I've never been one to turn away someone who needs help. Besides, I never have company anyway. At least, not any company that can talk."

Despite his odd comment, Redrinna found herself smiling a little. "Then I'll stay."

The dragon's ear frills flared out as he lunged a little closer, the movement jerky since he pulled himself up short before he got too close. "You will?"

Once again, she found it difficult not to like this giant creature. "Of course. I don't have anywhere else I need to be, and I doubt anyone would mind." The lie rolled off her tongue so easily a chill trickled along her spine.

"Excellent," Xandrin said, leaping onto his feet with a loud clack. His claws hitting the ground, she realized. "Wait right there. I'll be back in a little bit."

Without another word, he turned and launched himself upwards, right through the opening above and out of sight.

For a few minutes, Redrinna sat in the semi-darkness, wondering where Xandrin had gone. Then ice flooded her veins. What was she thinking? Had she actually agreed to live in a cave with a dragon—a creature that, according to history, was one of the most vile and ruthless? Had her fall injured her brain?!

Gingerly, she touched a hand to her forehead, making her more aware of the dull pounding in the back of her skull. She had no idea how to tell how hurt she was. The darkness started to weigh on her, bringing with it a very powerful desire to sleep. At the same time, the chill radiating through the cavern made her aches even worse, almost to the point they were becoming unbearable.

An overwhelming urge to cry rushed in like the tide, threatening to drown her in all the pain and confusion flooding her mind. She wished the captain were here. Or Lady Cel Tradat. Or— No. For all she knew, the captain had been in on this. He'd let her go without a moment's hesitation. As for Lady Cel Tradat...

No. Redrinna wasn't a coward, and she didn't need someone to coddle her. She'd been insisting for longer than she cared to remember that she could take care of herself, and this was the opportunity she'd always wanted. Imperial Princess Redrinna of the Eridian Empire cried at times like these. Redrinna who lived in a cave with a dragon did not. Would not.

Shaking herself, she tried to stay focused on the present and her injuries. After taking a deep breath, she attempted to bend one of her legs. It was horribly stiff and tight, an arc of intense pain racing through her body when she tried to move. Maybe she ought to wait a bit longer before trying that again. On the bright side, it didn't seem like any of her bones were broken. That was better than nothing, she supposed.

Bit by bit, her gaze climbed to the opening in the ceiling. That really had to be where she fell, didn't it? It was a lot farther down than she'd thought. It dawned on her she was lucky to be as okay as she seemed.

To ease the tension in her stomach, Redrinna flexed her fingers and curled her toes. A small sigh of relief rushed out of her lungs. She'd loved reading ever since she'd been little, and she remembered reading about how injuries like hers could, and frequently did, result in paralysis. Fortunately, it appeared she'd dodged that too.

Casting a disproving glance towards the pool, she studied its still, dark blue waters. It stayed absolutely motionless like it was trying to feign innocence. The color was almost the same as her mother's favorite color, the one that comprised all of her favorite dresses. Blues like that had always been favorites of her mother's.

Redrinna growled to get those thoughts out of her head. She'd nearly died in that stupid pool, and her mother was partially to blame. It would be easier if she could just forget about her old life, even if she had no idea how.

The hum of wingbeats interrupted her thoughts and within minutes, Xandrin descended through the hole in the ceiling with more grace than she'd expected a creature of his size to be capable of. She half-expected him to glide across the water like a swan, honestly. He landed at the pool's edge, however, tucking his wings to his sides and cautiously ambling over to her with something in his mouth. The next moment, he set a dead deer at her feet.

Instantly, she observed two things: blood pooling onto the cavern floor and a harsh iron smell permeating the air. It made what little appetite she'd had shrivel to nothing. Her nose wrinkled as she gathered her cloak a little closer to herself.

Xandrin seemed to be watching her intently. "You slept for a long time and need to eat. Is this not what you want?" He lowered his head as though ready to whisk it away at a moment's notice.

Grimacing, Redrinna tried to swallow the urge to gag so she could speak. He looked so concerned with the wrinkle between his eyespikes, the last thing she wanted to do was upset him. "Well, I...it's raw."

"Raw?" His brow crinkled.

Of course, there'd be no way he knew what that meant. "You know, still bleeding."

"But it's good that way," he said, his brow wrinkling even more.

"I-I'm sure it is, but..." She fought to repress a sigh. She was too tired to explain this. "I can't eat it like that. I'll get sick."

His eyes became as wide as the pool behind him. "You can't get sick. You're so weak you'd die."

Wow. Such a stellar observation on his part. A few rude comebacks raced through her mind, but she squashed them. "Probably."

"How are you supposed to eat then? You can't stay in my cave with me if you're dead," he said, his claws tapping a rapid staccato on the ground.

"Can you breathe fire?" Hopefully, that wasn't an exaggeration from the history books.

His claws stopped mid-tap. "Technically, no. Breathing fire actually really, really hurts—don't try it. However, I can exhale fire." His ear frills rose, becoming almost vertical. "Are you saying that if I set the deer on fire, you can eat that? I didn't know humans could eat fire!"

Her eyes slid closed almost of their own accord. "I can't eat fire, but if the deer is on fire for a while and then you put it out, I can eat what's left."

Xandrin's eyes narrowed, his ear frills lowering. "That sounds gross."

She wanted to sleep.

The claw tapping resumed for a minute. He cocked his head to the side again. "Are all humans as fragile as you?"

If she wasn't injured and he wasn't a dragon... "I guess so."

"Oh," he said with a blink, wearing a thoughtful frown. "I'll try to remember that then." He inhaled sharply, his chest glowing with a red, fiery light. Without warning, a fireball engulfed the deer. She jumped, the heat of the flames washing over her, hot and soothing at the same time.

Momentarily, she was torn between leaning towards it and leaning away, but froze as Xandrin lowered his head closer to the deer. The light of the fire danced in his eyes and off his scales, a sight that briefly distracted her from the fact she was only a few feet from the dragon's face. He watched the flames with such intensity, she would've believed him if he'd told her it was the most fascinating thing he'd ever seen.

After a few minutes, he blew on the flames, quickly reducing them to embers. Another breath and the embers vanished like the stars at dawn. Gingerly, like he was afraid to break it, he cut out a small piece of meat with his claw and extended it towards her.

Redrinna readily took it, wincing at the heat radiating from it. She passed it back and forth between her hands, the heat almost feeling good compared to the chill of the cave, but hurting just as much.

"Thank you," she remembered to say. She didn't feel very hungry, but maybe she would if she started eating. After all, she hadn't eaten since—that thought stopped abruptly and so did she. "Xandrin?"

The dragon's eyes widened, giving him a peculiar expression that hovered somewhere between expectancy and surprise.

"How long was I unconscious?"

He frowned. "Unconscious?"

"Asleep," she amended, wondering how many words this dragon actually knew.

His face contorted like she'd asked him a difficult question. "I didn't keep track. I was too worried about you to leave, you know? It was only a day or two I think?"

Scowling, she paused before taking a small bite of her meat. The outside was burnt and it became less cooked deeper in, but the flavor reminded her of being back in the palace. They didn't have deer much during the winter, but in late summer and fall, it was often a welcome sight on the table. The thought made her pause, made the meat on her tongue a little harder to chew. She'd been gone for nearly two whole days, but no one had found her yet. Were they even searching? Did they think she was even alive?

"Is it bad?" Xandrin asked, barreling into her thoughts.

Redrinna shook her head, immediately regretting doing so as her muscles sent fire up and down her back. "No, it's good. I was just thinking." To prove it, she took another bite of the meat.

He nodded then lowered his gaze to the deer. After several minutes, he glanced at her before his gaze returned to it. All at once, it dawned on her what he wanted.

"Do you want the rest of it?" There was no way she was going to get down more than this; she'd never been a big meat eater, and as hungry as she'd been, she was already starting to feel full.

"Oh, I couldn't," he said, lifting his head off the ground so fast he had to scramble to keep his balance. "You need to eat as much as you can so you won't die."

As annoying as that last bit was, she smiled a little. "I don't need to eat as much as you, and this," she lifted the meat still in her hands, "is plenty for me."

The dragon's eyes narrowed. "No wonder you're so small," he muttered before stepping closer and picking the deer up in his jaws. He stared at her for a long moment before slinking to the other side of the cavern and into the shadows.

A little more alert with some food in her, Redrinna found herself studying the cave a little more as she ate. Because of the darkness, she couldn't be sure of the size, but it seemed huge. In fact, she thought the great hall back in the palace would've been able to fit in here twice with no trouble. Xandrin seemed to be the perfect size for it.

It took a lot out of her, but Redrinna managed to eat all of the meat Xandrin had given her. Her body was ready to collapse by then, something that annoyed her even though she was powerless against it.

All at once, the slender beams of sunlight slanting into the cavern seemed to brighten, lighting a portion of the water, making it glisten like a bunch of tiny gems.

Xandrin slinked back over from the other side of the cavern, settling next to her. He laid close enough to startle her, but it didn't last long because she was too tired to be afraid.

"The sun's setting," he said. "You should rest."

Despite the exhaustion tugging on her senses, she frowned. He didn't need to tell her what to do; this wasn't the palace. As she folded her arms, she mentally began berating herself. What was she doing?! If she made Xandrin mad, who knew what he'd do? He was probably a hundred times her size! Why couldn't she be smart and do what the dragon said?!

The dragon's brow wrinkled. "What...are you doing?"

She shouldn't argue with a beast a hundred times her size! "I-I don't want to go to bed," she said, not sure whether to commend her bravery or condemn her stupidity.

His head slowly tilted to the side. "Bed?"

"Er, I mean sleep. I don't want to go to sleep."

"Oh," he said, scratching at his cheek. "Then you don't have to? I only suggested it because you look really, really tired. I'm sorry."

"Oh," she said, her annoyance dissipating in seconds. "W-well, I mean, if you think it's best then—" She bit her sentence short when she spotted Xandrin smiling. "What's with that face?"

"You're funny, you know that?"

"I am not," she snapped, irritation coiling in her stomach. This dragon was nothing short of exhausting. Ignoring him, Redrinna began working up the courage to lie down. Sitting up had hurt. Lying down would most likely be about the same. Sucking in a slow, deep breath, she barely moved an inch before Xandrin's claw forced its way between her and the ground.

"Hang on," he began.

"What?" she demanded. She sounded a lot like a three-year-old but was too tired to care.

The dragon dipped his head, the way he peeked at her making him look a little sheepish. "I just thought you wouldn't want to sleep next to that." He motioned to the ground beside her, drawing her attention to it. Of course, he was right. She didn't want to sleep next to a giant smear of drying deer blood.

Feeling like she was sitting with her foot in her mouth for the second time in the last five minutes, she asked, "Where do you suggest?"

Glancing behind himself, he said, "Perhaps you would be better off on my back? I doubt it's very comfortable, but it isn't covered in blood. It's also warmer than the ground."

She hesitated again, but after a minute or two, Redrinna relented. After all, if he truly wished her harm, he could have let her drown. Or eaten her instead of the deer. Hopefully, he wouldn't roll over and squish her or something.

It required a great deal of assistance from him (Redrinna refused to admit it, but he pretty much did everything), but she managed to climb onto his back. It was much warmer than the ground. The warmth from his hard scales seeping through her cloak and into her bones left her sleepier than she'd been before.

Once she was settled, he strode across the cave, his movements much smoother and soothing than she'd expected. He walked a lot like a cat. By the time he made it to wherever he was going, she couldn't keep her eyes open. Sleep was coaxing her, so tempting, especially once Xandrin rearranged her cloak so it covered her a little better.

Somewhere in her mind, Redrinna reasoned she shouldn't feel safe, but the rest of her couldn't deny she did.

Chapter Six

The next time Redrinna remembered waking, she found herself lying in the sun. She could still feel Xandrin's hard but warm scales underneath her. A disoriented feeling clung to her mind as she tentatively sat up, rubbed her eyes, and tugged a few rogue strands of hair out of her face. Her muscles stiffened more than they had been before when she saw they were at the edge of the pool. The dragon beneath her basked in the small amounts of sunlight angling through the opening above, the tip of his tail swirling the water of the pond. His head turned without lifting off the ground so he could watch her.

A couple of butterflies trailed through her stomach at his unblinking stare, making it difficult to hold his gaze. "How long was I asleep this time?"

Xandrin blinked, frowning for a long, long moment before he said, "Almost all day."

She scowled and directed her focus away from him, trying to chase the butterflies out of her stomach. As she did though, her stomach growled. Loudly. She snuck a glance at the dragon. If Xandrin heard it, he made no sign.

In an attempt to distract herself from the fact there was nothing to eat, Redrinna studied Xandrin's cave again, not ready to be all buddy-buddy with this dragon yet. Unfortunately, it didn't appear there was much to study as the cave hadn't undergone a metamorphosis during the night. After a few glances around the space though, she spotted something she hadn't noticed yesterday.

From where she sat—it was kind of difficult to make out—she spied what appeared to be a precarious stack of large rocks. After a minute of staring long and hard at it, she couldn't figure out its purpose, though she was fairly certain it wasn't natural, whatever it was. Did Xandrin have a rock collecting/stacking hobby?

"Hey, Xandrin?"

"Mmm?" The dragon was still staring at her intently when she glanced at him.

Swallowing her nerves—because the last thing she wanted to do was offend him but at the same time she was dying to know—she pointed out the haphazard stack of rocks. "What's that?"

He turned his head in the direction she pointed, his head lifting a little off the ground as he did so. "Oh, that? It's just in case."

"In case what?" Redrinna asked, her curiosity piqued.

The dragon shrugged. "In the event I need to leave this place and keep anyone from finding it. All you have to do is hit the rocks so they strike the wall and bam," his ear frills flared open, "the cave will fall in."

Those butterflies zipped through her stomach again. "Are you sure?" Hopefully, he wouldn't bump into one on accident.

"Of course," the dragon said with a hint of a smile. His smiles never made her feel very good. "The rock in this cave isn't indestructible after all. Actually, it's a bit brittle." His smile broadened.

She supposed he thought the information was supposed to make her feel better. He seemed so pleased with himself she didn't have the heart to tell him it was doing the opposite of what he'd intended.

Xandrin's scales scraped against the stone floor as he turned away from her. She wobbled dangerously—and a bit painfully—as he shifted. When he was finished, his snout angled towards the hole in the ceiling.

"What are you staring at?" she asked.

"Nothing," he replied. "I'm just soaking in the last of the sunlight before it leaves. So little of it makes it down here when it's not summer."

She stared at the opening in the ceiling above them for a minute before shaking her head. Trying to be as gentle as she could, she laid on Xandrin's back again, stifling a groan, and started turning her face towards the waning light in the cave. As she made to do so, something jabbed her in the side, more startling than painful. Glancing down, she found it was the knife from Lady Cel Tradat poking her, reminding her it was there. Her mind started picking at her new wounds, but she shut it out. Not now.

Redrinna forced her attention back to the light in the cave. Late afternoon sun trickled into the cave, the little that managed to reach the bottom making the pool's surface sparkle a little. She cocked her head to one side; she hadn't known the cave opened to the west. That would mean the palace lay behind them. She already knew they were somewhere in the Aglcae Mountains, the massive range that sheltered the palace and its citizens from severe storms, among other things.

They were also the mountains that were said to be full of spirits and all sorts of odd creatures, a rumor she'd never believed. Though, now that she'd met Xandrin, she wasn't so sure. Maybe if she stayed in these mountains with him long enough, she'd be able to see some of the creatures herself and learn about everything the history books had never told her. After all, Xandrin wasn't anything like they'd said, so it was logical they could be wrong about other creatures too, right?

However, thinking of the palace made her heart skip a beat, despite her best efforts to ignore that and the memories accompanying it. Remembering that place brought Captain Brion and Lady Cel Tradat to mind, and they, in turn, made her think of her parents. Thinking of them made a hot rush of anger coil in her stomach, heat pricking her cheeks. She didn't want to think about them because doing so would also make her worry about them. Why should she worry about the two people who'd thrown her away?

Xandrin stood, drawing her back to the present. He stretched and left the pool's edge. Redrinna sighed. Well, the sun had abandoned them with astonishing speed.

"Finished with your sunbath?"

The dragon stopped, staring at her like she'd grown a second head. "Sunbath? W-what is—I don't do that."

A small laugh escaped her, hurting more than she liked. "I'm kidding," she choked out.

"Oh," he said, his head cocked as he resumed walking. "Kidding. Is that like bed?"

"What?"

He glanced back at her, grinning from ear frill to ear frill. "Kidding!"

She raised an eyebrow, her ribs protesting from held-in laughter. "You don't get out much, do you?"

He climbed back up to his sleeping spot, turning in circles before lying down. Then he said, "What makes you say that?"

She raised one shoulder. "Oh, no reason." Why else would the word 'kidding' be fascinating?

A long sigh escaped the dragon, but he didn't make another sound. He simply shut his eyes, sliding his head away from her. Redrinna carefully shifted so she could watch him for a little while before turning her attention towards the rest of the cave.

Without the light of the sun, the space seemed darker than it had been before. From here, in the dark, she couldn't see that funny rock pile anymore, which explained why she hadn't yesterday. She allowed her gaze to travel upwards, spotting the opening far above yet again. There was some light up there still, making the opening appear like the moon hanging in a sky devoid of stars.

The light, comfortable feeling she'd had melted away as all-too-familiar worry wormed its way in. Despite her earlier thoughts, she couldn't help wondering if anybody missed her yet. If Captain Brion had been in on the whole affair, he probably didn't. However, she had a hard time believing he would've done that even after what Lady Cel Tradat had said about him. The woman must miss her, though. Of that she had no doubt. Were either of them searching for her? Would they try to find her? Or did they think she was dead?

A thrill of fear raced up her spine. What would happen if they did find her? Did she even want to be found? Did she truly want them to come and take her back to a life that had made her miserable for so long? Would things go back to normal? How would she explain to

Lady Cel Tradat that while she had promised to find her if something went awry, she hadn't even tried? How long would it be before her parents would try to kill her again?

Her throat tightened a little. Being found would mean going back to the Empire, and it also meant going back to her parents, to the people she'd thought loved her, but didn't. And yet, if they had tried to kill her so some magic Dragon Kin wouldn't stop them, what would happen if she hid in this hole forever? Would more people keep getting hurt?

Pain in her fingers made Redrinna realize they had tightly curled themselves around her necklace, the one that marked her as the Imperial Princess of Eridia. If she kept this, it would give her away to anyone who knew what it meant. At the same time, if she got rid of it, there was no way she could prove her identity if she needed to stop her parents by seizing the throne.

Reality settled itself on her shoulders, the weight alone nearly stopping her heart. There was no way she could keep one foot in both worlds. She either had to be Redrinna, the Imperial Princess, or Redrinna, a girl who lived in a cave with a dragon. A cold weight settled in her chest despite the fact her necklace burned, like it was trying to sear her skin, to forever imprint its image on her flesh. She wanted to hold off this decision for as long as she could, but it crept in on her like the darkness of night. Desperately, she wanted to stay in this cave. But what if people died because of that choice?

As she lay there in the dark, the promise she'd made to her parents echoed from every rock and stone. Tracing the hilt of her knife, Redrinna hesitated.

⁂

A loud splash startled Redrinna awake sometime later, causing her to panic for a moment. She didn't remember falling asleep, nor did she have any idea how she'd ended up leaning back against the rough stone wall.

Splashing echoed through the cavern again, calling her attention to the pool. To her surprise—and amusement—it appeared Xandrin bathed like a bird did. With his wings partially extended, he shook violently in the water that nearly came up to his shoulders. Water splashed everywhere, causing reflected light to bounce all over the cavern. If the absurd, glistening red dragon hadn't been in the middle of it all, it would've been stunning.

Her limbs were stiff, but only her right side radiated soreness. She stretched, wincing at the sting. Gingerly, she got to her feet and limped just out of range of Xandrin's splashing.

"Enjoying yourself?" she asked, causing him to jump and look her way.

His eyes widened a little as he blinked a few times. He smiled that toothy grin.

Redrinna hesitated to admit it, but his smile was growing on her.

"You're standing all by yourself," the dragon said, splashing water all over as he crawled out of the pool. "You humans aren't as fragile as I thought."

She smiled at him, not sure what to say. He nudged her with his nose, making all the muscles in her shoulder and back smart, causing her to wince. She hissed at the sting.

Hastily, the dragon took a step back, gaze dropping to the floor.

Redrinna didn't understand what he was doing for a second, but, all at once, it dawned on her: he thought he'd hurt her.

Stuttering in her haste to get the words out, she managed to say, "You didn't hurt me. It's just a little sore, is all. And it's gotten better much sooner than I thought it would. Don't you think?"

He peeked at her. She smiled, encouraging a small smile out of him.

"How long was I asleep this time?" she asked, glancing up towards the opening above. There was some light up in the cavern, but not a lot. She was pretty sure she'd never been awake at this time of day since she'd dropped into the dragon's life.

Xandrin drummed his claws against the ground. "Not as long as usual. I think it's only early afternoon this time."

A warm feeling snuggled in her chest. That had to mean something good, right? "At this rate, I'll get better in no time," she said, making Xandrin's smile broaden a little more. A comfortable silence fell between them before the dragon rose to his full height and stretched his wings. She was so small compared to him. She barely reached his elbow, and she'd always faired on the tall side.

"I'm sure you'd get better even faster if you had something to eat," the dragon said as he flicked water off the tip of his tail. "The last time you ate was a day or two ago, you know."

That would explain why her stomach felt like an old, hollow log.

"I'll be back soon," the dragon said, turning towards the exit above them.

As he did so, the warmth she'd been basking in extinguished, making her feel like she was falling again. He'd left her alone in the cave before, so why did her heart want to burst at the thought of him going now? He spread his wings again, crouching low, preparing to take off. To leave her alone, like she'd so often been before.

Her breath caught in her throat before she managed to cry out, "Wait!"

Xandrin's head whipped around, his eyes wide. The two of them both froze, but Redrinna couldn't meet his gaze. The dragon remained quiet and still.

Words failed her. Redrinna swallowed, rubbing the side of her head with one hand. She didn't know if she could get the words out. Sharing her feelings had never been easy for her. Even though she was with a dragon she hardly knew, she...she didn't want...

"I just...don't...want to be alone."

The words seemed to echo in the silence of the cave, making the next moment stretch for an eternity. If Lady Cel Tradat had heard her say that, she would have been annoyed. The woman was stubbornly independent in every possible way. Redrinna had rarely told anyone how she'd felt before. At least, no one except the captain, but he hadn't been able to do anything to help nor had she wanted him to. At the very least she expected Xandrin to laugh.

Yet, to her surprise, he approached her with a hint of a smile. "Then maybe you'd like to come with me?"

She hesitantly met his gaze, not sure if he was teasing her or not.

He'd never done so before, but there was a first time for everything.

"Some fresh air ought to be good for you too, right? See the sky and all that?" He crouched next to her, his large head close enough to touch. "Climb up, right behind my head."

Tentatively, she approached. His eyes flicked in her direction but his head remained still. Redrinna had no idea where to put her feet, so she reached up and grabbed hold of his spiny frill. She tried to pull herself up, but her arms shook with the effort.

Redrinna refused to give up on this chance for freedom. Her foot found something to step on, and she tried to use it to push herself up. Xandrin made a funny noise when she did so, and she immediately stepped off. Then, she didn't have a good enough hold with her arms. She squeaked as she slid back towards the ground with no way to stop herself. Which was going to hurt.

Before she could hit the ground, Xandrin caught her in his claws. "Sorry. Let's try again," he said before lifting her a little higher so she could reach. Cheeks flushing, she scrambled onto his neck, grabbing hold of the crown of spikes behind his horns for balance.

"Hold on," he said as he lifted his head, his wings rising.

Redrinna's grip on his spikes was so tight, her knuckles went white. He turned to face the opening above, the muscles in his legs bunching. In one ear-popping, stomach-dropping, heart-stopping moment, they launched into the air. The force nearly sent her flying back, but she held on. Somehow. The opening rushed towards them. How did Xandrin fit through there?

As they neared the opening, he pulled his wings close to his sides. They cleared the hole, the light stinging her eyes. Her stomach lurched as they started sliding back.

Xandrin's wings unfurled with a powerful snap.

They launched out of the cave, the outside world so bright Redrinna squeezed her eyes shut and kept her head down. Wind ripped at her heavy cloak, tearing at her hair (which she realized was still mostly in the captain's braid), clawing at her hands like it wanted to pull them loose. All at once, it calmed.

Hesitantly, Redrinna lifted her head, blinking at the dazzling brightness she'd forgotten defined the outside world. When she could see again, the wind and the view both stole Redrinna's breath in a heartbeat.

A bright blue, cloud-flecked sky stretched out endlessly around her, cool despite the high sun overhead. Trying to ignore the wind pulling at her face—making it even harder to breathe—she looked down, watching the dark, sleepy forests and the mountain crags flash by. Sparkling blue flashes of ponds, lakes, and rivers burst from between the trees, accenting the range like a string of jewels.

Xandrin glanced back and grinned before angling towards a low cloud. Unable to help herself, she stretched a hand towards it, her fingers sliding through it like it was water. When they were past it, she grinned at her wet fingers. Clouds were wet! No book had ever told her that!

Unexpectedly, she wobbled, frantically grabbing onto Xandrin's spikes with both hands again. The panic was immediately swallowed by a rush in her veins, by a feeling she couldn't name. Drinking in the feeling, she closed her eyes. She wanted to lean into the wind, or lean back and let it carry her somewhere. As a flapping noise reached her ears—a lot quieter than Xandrin's—Redrinna opened her eyes. Off to their right flew a flock of birds. She frowned. It'd been a while since she'd studied birds, but they were crows? Maybe ravens? What was the difference between the two again? Redrinna shook her head. Did it matter? She was flying!

Her attention shot back to the ground. The mountains beneath and around her were unfamiliar, so she tried to find landmarks she knew. To the north, far in the distance, lay an ocean, and she knew if they went further west, over the Agicae Mountain range entirely, they'd run into another stretch of ocean. What were the names of those seas again? She was too distracted to remember.

Her gaze moved on, leaving her thoughts to scramble after. A very short way east, the Agicae Mountains curved a bit like a fish hook before melting into the rest of Eridia, stretching out as far as she could see.

Redrinna took a deep breath, her heart burning in her chest. It was like she'd been born to fly. She'd never had this fiery sensation in her chest before, and it took her a moment to identify it: freedom.

"So, how does it feel to fly?" Xandrin asked, interrupting her thoughts.

"Xandrin, this is amazing! I...I've never experienced anything like this," she said, not sure if he could hear her. "Does it always feel like this?"

The dragon flashed a grin at her, which she took to mean yes. He dipped lower, following the path of a small river as it wound its way through the forested mountains. She glanced at the never-ending blue sky one more time, drinking in the fresh air. A small smile crept across her lips. So this is what it was like to be alive. All her wildest dreams had never even come close to reality.

She settled back, Xandrin's hard frill pressing against her spine as he flew higher in the sky again. Noticing that he seemed to be surveying the ground below them, she turned her head so that she could watch him better.

"What are you looking for?" she asked.

"I came out to find you something to eat, don't you remember?"

Right. Flying had put that far from Redrinna's mind; she didn't even feel hungry. Well, she did now that that thought pranced through her brain. She was not enjoying being hungry all the time, something she'd never had to worry about back at the palace.

The light in her heart went out as the thought crossed her mind, her gaze starting to wander towards the palace she knew lay behind her somewhere, nestled in the crook of the Agicae Mountains. She stopped herself, forcing her gaze straight ahead instead. Putting the life she used to be living behind her was proving very, very difficult.

Without warning, Xandrin dipped into a graceful, terrifying dive, making Redrinna's stomach leap into her throat. Her grip tightened on his spikes as the wind tore through her hair like it would love nothing more than to rip out every last strand. She couldn't open her eyes because of the how hard it pressed against her face, but after a long minute, Xandrin launched back upwards. When he evened out, she opened her eyes again.

She wouldn't say it out loud, but she loved this, and a large part of her wanted to be able to do this and feel this way all the time.

The flight back to the cave was unbelievably short in Redrinna's mind, and after the light from outside, the space seemed abysmally dark. It took her eyes several minutes to adjust before they were dazzled once again by flames as Xandrin cooked whatever he'd caught for her (a boar, as it turned out). There was plenty of meat to go around, and for some reason when she compared this to palace life, this was heaven.

After she'd eaten her fill, Xandrin finished the rest of the boar and cleared his throat, seeming loud in the silence around them.

"Are you feeling better today?" he asked after a long pause.

"Yes," Redrinna replied, her heart hovering somewhere between the sky and the earth. All at once, it felt like it was sinking in a pool. Being back in the cave dredged up the memories she was trying to forget. Flying had been better than sitting in the dark because those memories towed guilt around with them. It was easier to avoid them when she was surrounded by miles and miles of blue.

"You've been awfully quiet since we got back," he said. "Did...it scare you?"

She glanced at him. He was half-looking at her, not quite turned completely towards her, almost like he was afraid of what she was about to say.

"No it didn't," she said, noting the visible relief that washed over him, making his wings sag a bit. "It just made me think."

"About what?"

"Before I ended up here," Redrinna began, hesitating for half a second before plowing on with her thoughts, "I'd never even dreamed of doing a lot of the things I've done with you, but having done them, I feel really happy. Yet at the same time, I can't help but feel like I shouldn't be as happy as I am."

The dragon turned completely to face her. "Are all humans as strange as you?"

For two seconds, Redrinna couldn't decide whether the dragon was serious or not. Then she spotted the corner of his mouth tugging up, and both of them burst out laughing. They talked aimlessly for a while longer before she was too drained to keep up their conversation, and they dwindled into a comfortable silence. Within a few minutes, Xandrin's breathing relaxed into the slow and steady rhythms of sleep, leaving her alone to watch the moonlight trickle into the cave like a strand of pearls slowly twirling through water.

The silence allowed the thoughts she'd been trying to avoid emerge from the depths of her mind, each one increasing the unease in her gut. She'd turned her back on an entire empire only a few days ago, abandoning them, but already, she'd been extremely happy. For reasons she couldn't understand, she couldn't shake the feeling that after all that had happened, the consequence shouldn't be happiness. At the same time, if it was the wrong choice, how could she already feel so at ease?

All at once, Redrinna became acutely aware of the necklace dangling from her throat and the knife hanging from her belt. Her heart thumped against her ribcage as she wilted under their combined weight. She'd almost forgotten about them, but now that she couldn't, sleep escaped her, leaving her alone with her thoughts.

Chapter Seven

Redrinna's eyes opened seconds before her stomach lurched with a sharp jerk. She bolted upright, scanning the cave in an attempt to figure out what had woken her up.

Where had Xandrin gone?

Worry coiled around her chest before a sudden memory swooped in, snuffing it out. Dimly, she remembered Xandrin trying to wake her before giving up and saying he'd be back. As her heart settled back down, a yawn escaped her. The sudden rush of relief made it difficult for her to shake herself awake. How long had she slept after the dragon had left?

Eventually, Redrinna worked up the ambition to stretch and make her way off the ledge to the main floor of the cavern. It must not be too late in the day since it was still pretty dark, even in the cave above.

After a minute or two of aimless walking, she found herself face to face with one of those funky rock stacks. When Xandrin had explained them to her before, she'd had serious doubts about whether or not smashing these pillar-like structures would do any good. However, now that she was close enough to touch one, she took his words a bit more seriously. The pillars were massive, at least five times her height and width. Perhaps if they were all hit hard enough, the cave would collapse. She doubted they'd fall over even if Xandrin accidentally bumped into one.

Shaking those thoughts from her mind, she turned, finding herself only a few feet from the edge of the pool, a faint glimmer clinging to the edges of the water. Out of a morbid sense of curiosity, she approached and crouched next to it, trying to spot her reflection. She didn't want to see herself (especially since she'd taken out the braid and tried to comb her fingers through her hair the other day and found some serious snarls. Then she remembered she didn't know how to braid her hair, so it now hung limply down her back) but wanted to try anyway. The only thing to see was a dark shadow surrounded by more shadow. Nothing set her apart from the pebbles beneath her feet here. It was kind of refreshing.

She leaned a little closer to the water, making the dark shadow a bit bigger and causing her necklace to swing under her nose. Catching it, she held on to it while she straightened, her gaze remaining fixed on the pool.

For a long moment, Redrinna fingered the chill stone, returning to her thoughts from the last few nights again. Her free hand settled on the knife at her waist, Lady Cel Tradat's words hissing through the quiet: *in my country, when children reach the age of seventeen, they're given a knife to symbolize their strength to carve out their destinies.*

The strength to carve out her destiny. With that kind of strength, even if someone found her, they wouldn't be able to force her to go back. She would've been able to protect herself from her parents and the man at the trial. She would've been more like the priestess.

All her life, Redrinna had always let someone or something else dictate her path, and even though it'd hurt, she'd walked it. But if she had the strength to carve out the path *she* wanted, one she wouldn't regret walking...

A chill raced across her skin. Vividly, Redrinna recalled promising her parents she'd be the best Empress she could. Despite the pain that lanced through her heart at the thought of them, unbidden memories of happy times flooded her mind. Their lessons together, the rare moments when they'd been able to eat meals together, and when they'd made it to the cave, the way they'd joked and laughed about being stiff from riding the horses. How could she let that go? How could that suddenly mean nothing?

Maybe they hadn't pushed her, and she was just confused. Had she slipped and her memory was distorted from the shock?

Yet, Lady Cel Tradat had been so convinced they were going to kill her, she'd given her a weapon and told her to trust no one. If the woman had sensed a reason for that, her parents couldn't be as perfect as her memories made them out to be, right? There wasn't smoke without fire, as the saying went. So if her parents had truly loved her and had no intentions to kill her, why had Lady Cel Tradat been so convinced of the contrary?

Redrinna's heart stilled as a new thought entered her mind. Not once in that entire thought process had she asked herself what she wanted.

"I want that strength," she whispered. The strength to choose her own path rather than have it decided by anyone or anything else.

This was a decision only she could make. Even though it hurt, in her mind, her father's voice said: *It's about doing what you believe.* Even if it wasn't what he'd meant, she knew what she was going to do.

Tightening her grip on the knife, she tugged it free of its sheath. It hissed as it slid out, and she couldn't tell if it was thrilled or if it was letting out a warning. Gritting her teeth, Redrinna tightened her grip on the pendant, pulling it until the string binding it to her was taut. She pressed the knife against one of the thick strings. The threads released a quiet squeal beneath the bite of the metal like they were screaming, trying to convince her to stop. Jerking the knife sharply upwards, she severed the string, the steel blade eagerly ripping through the thread. The ends of the thread wilted, hanging motionless and limp as she pulled the necklace away.

Tears clouded her vision, but Redrinna forced them back so she could take one last look at this necklace that had chained her to a throne she'd never wanted or asked for. Blood would not paint a picture of what her life should be; that's what she needed to do for herself.

Releasing a deep breath, she drew her arm back, ready to hurl it into the dark depths before her, but froze. Again. Still.

Hundreds of memories cascaded through her mind, the faces of

Lady Cel Tradat and Captain Brion appearing over and over again. Hours of her life seemed to flash by in seconds. She hated how much she missed it all, how much she still couldn't bring herself to part with it.

The longer Redrinna hesitated, the lower her hand dropped until it was level with her waist. She found herself gazing at the necklace again. For a long time, she stared at it.

She didn't want to let it go, but she also refused to go back and risk being killed again. Refused to live a life oozing with the blood of her ancestors' burdens and mistakes. Refused to attempt living a life where she'd possibly been chosen to overthrow an empire and been relentlessly punished for it. She wouldn't go back. Not even for Lady Cel Tradat or the captain. Not for anyone.

Closing her eyes, she flicked her wrist, flinging the necklace into the water, where it struck the surface with a soft plop. Redrinna opened her eyes in time to see the circular stone on the water's surface, clinging there like it was terrified of drowning, ripples rushing away from the stone, making the water lap at the rock beneath Redrinna's feet. The necklace hovered for a long, agonizing moment before it succumbed, slipping under the water's surface and being swallowed by darkness.

Habitually, she reached for her throat, the emptiness there making her heart wriggle like a worm just ripped from the earth and tossed on hot stone. The deed was done. The Empire was no longer hers. No one could prove she belonged to that world any longer. Her shoulders lifted like they'd been relieved of a heavy burden, yet her heart sagged, sinking with the necklace.

Turning away from the water, Redrinna returned her knife to its sheath, trying to shrug off the unsettled feeling clinging to her. But even Xandrin's wingbeats singing in the distance couldn't drive it away.

⁂

Three days later, Redrinna stared at the cavern ceiling, hard stone digging into her spine, the heavy breathing of a sleeping dragon filling the space around her. Butterflies danced in her stomach before her gaze flicked towards the pool. With an irritated huff, she rolled over so her back was to it. If she ignored the desire to charge into those waters and retrieve her necklace, it would pass. The urge to fetch her necklace was fading the more she ignored the pressing need to find it. She only felt it in quiet moments like these when she was awake and Xandrin wasn't. Flying was a good cure for the urge, but she couldn't go flying at the drop of a hat. She was learning even dragons ran out of breath.

Despite that, her mind drifted back to the world above, back to the world she'd left behind. Did people miss her? Was anyone still searching for her or holding out hope she was alive? It'd been at least a week since she'd met Xandrin if her math was right, so had Lady Cel Tradat given up hope of her returning yet? What was Captain Brion doing now that she was no longer his responsibility?

It seemed like it had been ages since she'd been trapped in that stifling palace surrounded by stuffy, demanding people even though she knew it hadn't. She wanted to believe she didn't miss it at all, that she didn't miss a thing about it, but she couldn't do it. Whenever she thought about her home, she couldn't stop her heart from sinking a few inches.

A muffled boom shook those thoughts from her mind. Redrinna blinked, trying to decide if she was hearing things or if she'd actually heard something. What could possibly make a noise like that? Straining her ears for the slightest sound, she waited.

Another boom reached her, still muffled and quiet. She couldn't be hallucinating if she'd heard it twice, right? She glanced at Xandrin. He hadn't moved an inch, so maybe she was just hearing things. Squeezing her eyes shut, she listened hard, waiting for the sound to return, but the harder she tried to listen for it, the less she seemed to hear it.

Her stomach abruptly growled so loud it echoed. She wrapped her arms around her waist, intensely aware of the fact she was starving. Yesterday's meal seemed to be forever ago too. Why did everything in her past seem so distant? Could significant life changes do that to a person?

Shaking herself, Redrinna turned towards Xandrin and found him on his back, legs sticking up in the air. He vaguely reminded her of a sleeping cat she'd seen once.

Smothering a laugh, she got to her feet and ambled towards him. Mustering up a bit of courage, she poked him in the side. Hard.

With a loud snort, the dragon's head shot off the ground. His tail lashed wildly, wings flapped awkwardly, claws rent the air as his eyes frantically spun in their sockets. Abruptly, he froze. His head snapped towards her.

She couldn't suppress her grin, and her ribs ached from holding back her laughter. And from having to hurriedly dodge one of his wings. "Good morning," she managed to say.

His eyes narrowed. "That's the last time I wake up after you."

Her laughter broke loose, and even though he looked a bit annoyed, Xandrin eventually managed a smile.

The dragon rose and stretched. "So, what do you think we should do today?" His gaze shifted to the pool she knew crouched behind her. "Want to go swimming?"

She shuddered. "No." Almost drowning in that sly, sneaky, and suspicious pool had been one time too many in her opinion. She was quite content to never attempt swimming. Ever.

"Okay then," he said as he walked past her. "You figure out what we should do while I go and hunt down some breakfast."

Without giving her a chance to reply, he took off, leaving her alone in the cave. With a small sigh, Redrinna stomped over to the pool, picking up all the flat stones she could find. How should she know what they should do? As tempting as it was to ask if they could go flying again, she'd gotten sunburned across her cheeks and nose last time, and they still ached. Truth be told, there was hardly anything to do in Xandrin's cave, but she didn't dare say so for fear of hurting the feelings of the only friend she had.

Redrinna paused, thinking on that last thought. Since when had she begun thinking of the dragon as her friend?

Shaking the thought away, she gathered a few more flat rocks before attempting to skip them across the water. It took her several tries to figure out how to throw them right before one of her rocks would jump, but Redrinna smiled once she'd gotten the hang of it. Couldn't take care of herself? Please, she'd just figured out how to bounce rocks across water. Not that it was too impressive, but it was a start, right? Redrinna, the girl who lived in a cave with a dragon, had taught herself how to skip rocks.

She drew back her arm to skip the next rock, but another muffled boom made her freeze. That one was louder than the ones before. It wasn't really just her imagination, was it?

Feeling ready to jump out of her skin at a moment's notice, Redrinna warily eyed the cavern, waiting for the sound to return. It didn't. For some reason though, that didn't make her feel better. Dropping her rocks, Redrinna scurried back onto the ledge, hugging her knees to her chest until Xandrin returned. The sight of him dispelled the fear gripping her heart.

The mysterious noise she'd been hearing remained in the back of her mind while they ate, keeping her from relaxing. After they finished eating, Redrinna worked up the courage to ask Xandrin about it.

He paused, tilting his head to the side. "What sound?"

She strained to hear it, but it was gone. Just like before. "I can't hear it now, but there was a sound," she insisted. "I promise."

The dragon smiled a little. "I believe you. Honest. It was probably just the earth. It makes the weirdest noises sometimes."

She smiled, the worry gripping her heart dissipating in an instant at Xandrin's reassurance. That was also strange. No one had ever been able to put her at ease that quickly before. Perhaps though, if a dragon decided something wasn't worth worrying about, it wouldn't be so bad to believe them.

The rest of the day passed with Redrinna barely aware of it doing so. Before she knew it, she was curled up on Xandrin's back once again, the world above them settling into the night's darkness. There had to be a full moon tonight though since Redrinna could make out the pool's water a little better than usual. Dozens of thoughts clambered for her attention, but she shoved them all away, forcing herself to close her eyes and get some sleep.

The next time Redrinna opened her eyes, the cave was a bit brighter. She must've fallen asleep, at least for a while. For a bit, she listened to Xandrin's slow breathing before rolling onto her side and closing her eyes again.

A thunder-like boom shook the air. A jolt raced up Redrinna's spine, instantly waking her. What in the world had that been? That...couldn't just be the earth making weird noises again, could it? Another boom rent the quiet, making Redrinna sit up, her breath locked in her throat.

Glancing down, she noted Xandrin still slept like a rock. Was this noise really normal or could the dragon sleep through anything? Redrinna honestly couldn't say, and her thumping heart made it difficult for her to keep her thoughts straight.

Another enormous boom shook the air, so loud and deep it resonated in her chest. Pebbles skittered, rattling against the stony ground. Xandrin jerked awake beneath her with a muffled 'whazzat?'

An awful sensation she hadn't felt for almost her entire time in Xandrin's cave seeped into her veins, sending shivers down her spine and tying knots in her chest. She'd forgotten how much she hated feeling this way.

The dragon's head lifted off the ground, his face within an arm's reach of her in an instant. "Redrinna, what's wrong?"

There wasn't enough air in her lungs to speak. She tried to say something but she could only shake her head.

Another boom rang out, causing Redrinna to jump and Xandrin's head to whirl towards the rest of his cave. After a pause, the dragon scooped her off his back—an action she disagreed with—and glared at her so fiercely she was immensely glad he was her friend and not her enemy.

"Stay here," he hissed before slinking into the darkness of the cave. As he vanished from sight, Redrinna pressed herself against the wall, trying to make herself as small as possible. Xandrin would take care of it, she just needed to stay put and stay—

Another boom rang out, this time accompanied by the bang of larger rocks striking the ground and bursting into lots of little pieces. She jumped, her heart leaping into her throat.

She didn't know what was happening, but she desperately wanted to be at Xandrin's side. Her heart beat so fast it almost hurt. It was like she'd fallen back into the pool, water swarming over her face—she couldn't take a deep enough breath.

A final, cracking boom rang out, shortly followed by an enormous thud and more splintering and skittering. A thick silence fell like she'd shoved wool in her ears or suddenly gone deaf.

For two seconds, Redrinna wondered where Xandrin was. Then, as the silence grew heavier, she heard something different, something she hadn't noticed over the pounding: the heavy panting of something large. Immediately, she knew it wasn't Xandrin.

A low, gravelly voice spoke, so low Redrinna could've sworn she could hear the air reverberating. "Is this the...place?" The cave stayed silent for a moment. Sniffing rang out, slow and deep. "Where is...the girl? Is...she the one?"

Chapter Eight

Redrinna smothered her mouth with her hands to try to keep her frantic breathing quiet. It didn't mean her, right? Heavy footsteps echoed all around, making her want to run or hide where she was all at the same time. A crackling hiss cut through suffocating silence. Xandrin.

"I don't...want you," came the voice of their intruder seconds before a high whine and a thud. Silence prevailed again.

Redrinna could barely feel her own heartbeat. Xandrin? Had something happened to him? Was he all right?

She leaned forward slightly like she was going to move, but stopped. Xandrin had told her to stay here. Staying here...would keep him safe right? He wouldn't have to risk getting hurt to protect her if she stayed out of the way, right? But what if he was already hurt? All she could hear was the slow, heavy pant of the intruder.

Where was Xandrin?

Once again, the pant changed to sniffing. Then, the gravelly voice said, "She is here...somewhere. I can smell...her but...I don't see...her."

Ice crackled in Redrinna's veins.

All at once, it dawned on her that if she stayed put, the creature would undoubtedly find her and trap her on this ledge. Mustering up all the courage she could find, she rose, pulled her cloak tight around her, and took a quiet step. Then another. Warily, she made her way off the ledge and to the main floor, the heavy breathing ringing in her ears with every move she made.

Once she reached the cavern floor, Redrinna paused again. Desperately, she wanted to call out to Xandrin but didn't dare. However...if she could find him, she'd be safe. Yes. This nightmare would be over. Yes.

Taking a deep breath, she risked another step. She closed her eyes in relief when nothing happened. The tension in her chest eased a little so she took another step forward. And ran into something painfully solid. Stumbling back, she crashed into the wall, pain lancing up her spine. What in the world—

Shaking her head, she glanced up. Redrinna's heart stuttered. She couldn't make out many details in the dark, but whatever she'd run into bore some human-like resemblance, except it had to be at least half the height of Xandrin. Enormous muscles rippled across its shoulders with each long, slow breath it took. It was as wide as a boat—at least—and it seemed to be built of solid muscle. Despite the darkness clinging to it, she could see its eyes peering out from beneath dark, unkempt strings of hair. They glowed in the dark, shining like blades in the moonlight. As soon as she saw them, her body went stiff and rigid. She couldn't move. She couldn't breathe.

She'd found whatever had broken into their cave.

"Found her. I found...you," the thing said, its gaze boring into her. "You're...the one Father...wants. Won't hurt...you. Be good...little girl."

Her chest burned with the desire to breathe.

A chill, meaty finger tapped her jaw. That hurt a lot. "Want you...want you," the creature chanted like a spoiled child who'd gotten their favorite candy. "Special...girl. Daddy's girl."

Her heart banged against her ribs, desperate to escape this body of hers that couldn't move. She had to move. She was going to get abducted. She needed to move. Now.

Her fingers didn't even twitch. She couldn't feel her legs. Redrinna couldn't move.

Without warning, Xandrin pounced on the beast, yanking it backwards, breaking the glare from those weird, gleaming eyes.

Air rushed into Redrinna's lungs. Her knees threatened to buckle from the sudden dizziness, but somehow she stayed on her feet.

A loud crack shook the air, making her flinch. After a second, she risked a peek to her right. Air rushed out of her lungs again, but not because of their intruder. Xandrin and the beast still tussled, but they'd crashed through one of the pillars Xandrin had said could destroy the cave.

It turned out the dragon had been right about them. Cracks she heard more than saw raced up the wall like fire through dry grass, harsh grinding filling the air around her.

Redrinna had thought she'd been scared earlier. The panic that rushed into her chest made her earlier fear seem childish by comparison.

"Xandrin!" she cried, clinging to the wall behind her like it was the only thing that could keep her upright.

The dragon glanced her way the instant she called out. Whirling, he kicked the beast square in the chest with his hind legs. In one smooth motion, the creature sailed into another pillar, sending it crashing down, chunks of rock banging and bouncing all over.

He leapt across the space between them, his claws scraping against the hard stone. "On my back," the dragon said as he stopped by her side.

She tried. She did. Despite her best efforts to hop on, she slid back down his scales.

From the other side of the cave, the creature snapped, "Not take...my prey!"

Xandrin snarled as he glanced at the beast. He snatched Redrinna in his claws, his sharp scales biting her skin. She squeezed her eyes shut, trying to block out whatever was about to happen next.

He leapt, making her stomach drop. With a grunt, he smashed his tail through another pillar. The massive rocks pounded into the wall. A deafening rumble groaned underneath the high crack of the rock. With a powerful, sharp leap—making Redrinna more light-headed and nauseous than she'd been feeling before—Xandrin launched into the air.

It was now she learned Xandrin had been gentle the times they'd gone flying before. His turns were sharp, fast. If she hadn't been pinned between his claws she would've been chucked off. The rumbling intensified, becoming a booming roar. A chunk of rock struck Redrinna's cheek, making her flinch. Something hot trickled down her face.

Without warning, frigid air rushed in, needling her wherever she had skin showing. It snatched her breath away, just for a second. Xandrin's heavy wing beats were nothing compared to the rumbling below.

After a long minute, silence fell, alighting around them as Xandrin haltingly made his way back to the ground. A brisk wind blew over Redrinna's cheeks as he opened his claws, the chill making her injury ache more than it had before. She peeked an eye open, stepping onto the ground after he nodded. The grim expression on his face startled her. She'd never seen him so stern or serious. Casting a glance over her shoulder, she realized why.

The mountainside that had housed Xandrin's cave had collapsed, the land raked over and uprooted. Trees caught in the fray jutted out of the debris at odd, broken angles while chunks of earth and stone clawed at a sky they would never reach.

"Your cave," Redrinna whispered, taking a few steps towards the destruction.

Xandrin stopped her, touching one claw to her shoulder. "I know," he said.

She blinked, taking in the fractured outline of the mountainside again. It was gone. Just gone. Glancing up at the enormous dragon, she tried to find words to say but there weren't any. This was her fault. That creature had come after her, and as a result, Xandrin had lost his home.

"Whatever broke into the cave came for you, Redrinna," he said, nudging her with his snout. "You didn't expect me to let it have a second chance to get you, did you?"

"What even was that thing?" she whispered, grabbing at the hem of her shirt to try to quell the shaking of her hands. "Have you ever seen anything like it before?"

"Never."

Her grip on her hem tightened. "Who sent it after me?" She

struggled to form the words, barely able to get them out.

Xandrin crouched down next to her like he could shelter her. "It couldn't be the person who tried to kill you before, could it?"

"How? If they thought I was dead, why would they send something after me?"

He studied the fractured outline of the mountainside. "Maybe they know you're not dead. Or maybe it was somebody else."

Her hands trembled so hard she couldn't keep her fists curled. Even if her parents knew she wasn't dead, where in the world had that thing come from? She'd never seen anything like it back at the palace. If it wasn't them, there were myriads of disgruntled citizens to choose from, but she doubted many of them had a giant creature that could break through solid stone to send after her. Beyond that, how would anyone have known where she was?

"You're shaking so hard," Xandrin breathed, burying his snout in her side.

Her jaw chattered so hard, she couldn't speak. She buried her face against his snout instead.

"You don't have to be afraid. No matter who comes after you, I won't let them take you anywhere. I swear it."

Slowly, Redrinna met his gaze, his dark eyes brimming with warmth, framed by his red scales that seemed almost purple in the night. All the fear threatening to strangle her dissipated, leaving nothing except heavy guilt dragging her heart lower. She couldn't hold his gaze any longer.

"Xandrin, what are you going to do now? You lost everything because of...because of..." She couldn't bring herself to say 'me.' It hurt enough as it was, and saying it out loud would drive the pain even deeper.

"I still have you," he replied, giving her a gentle nudge. "And it was just a cave. This world is littered with thousands of holes in the ground, but there's only one of you on it."

Warmth blossomed in her chest. Did that mean they were truly friends? They weren't just a girl and a dragon in a cave, but actual, real friends? Words escaped her. Gradually, Redrinna managed to lift her head, meeting his gaze.

Xandrin cocked his head a little to the side, and she thought he might be smiling. "You really are a strange human, you know."

She almost smiled but was a bit too shaky. "Oh really? And just how many other humans have you met before?"

Xandrin tilted his head. After a moment, she realized he'd taken her question seriously. "One, actually," he said.

That gave her pause. "Really?"

He nodded. "It was a long time ago though, so I don't think he's still alive. But he was a lonely, miserable man. I pitied him."

"Oh," she breathed.

"His family had died, and he believed it was his fault. I think he wanted to die too." He shook his head a little. "Either way, I couldn't help him. There's nothing I can do about guilt. This time though, someone's hunting you. I can do something about that."

She blinked. He was right. This wasn't a terrible fear hounding her and threatening to crush her. This was a person, a living being. That was a problem that could be solved, like a math equation.

"So what do we do now?" he breathed, probably to himself. He glanced over at the unnervingly still mountainside.

That was a good question.

"We should probably find a place to sleep for the rest of the night first. And somewhere to hide, just in case whoever sent that thing isn't too far behind." He yawned, making her do the same. Exhaustion settled on her shoulders.

Since she couldn't think of something to say, Redrinna settled for a nod. Despite what had just happened, her heart was light, almost as though it would float away if it weren't trapped in her chest. That was new feeling.

"Shall we?" he asked with an inclination of his head.

She nodded again.

They began walking, heading away from the destruction behind them. The fact that Redrinna had no idea where they were going to go didn't bother her. It didn't even seem all that important. So long as Xandrin was with her, she'd be fine. It was an odd feeling, one that took her a while to figure out. Even then, she couldn't put a name on it.

For the first time, Redrinna didn't feel so afraid. Was there a word for that feeling?

Chapter Nine

Once they'd rested as much as they dared, Xandrin and Redrinna ate a quick breakfast before debating their next move. While the giant was most likely dead, whoever had sent it would figure out something had happened when their pet didn't return. They both agreed they needed to put a good deal of distance between themselves and the collapsed cave.

"We could head south," Xandrin suggested as they walked.

She folded her arms, a little surprised at how well she could stay balanced astride his neck while doing so now. "We could, but there are a lot more people living down there than up north. And the southern mountains are harsh. Entirely unlivable in some places."

At that, he shook his head. "That's not going to work."

She thought for a minute more before an idea struck her. "We could stay in the mountains."

"Stay here? But that's dangerous."

"A lot of people believe these mountains are haunted, so they avoid them as much as possible. Staying here would make it safer for you."

He nodded, a thoughtful frown on his face.

Even Lady Cel Tradat had always tried to avoid these mountains. Some people had been terrified of the spirits they claimed roamed through the woods, but her friend had been convinced that the Dragon

Kin's souls prowled these mountains as well. While it was true that the Dragon Kin, if the stories were to be believed, had protected the land and stopped a couple of wars, it was also true that they'd died during the Dragon War, the mass slaughtering of the dragon race. And Lady Cel Tradat had never tolerated ghosts, not even rumored ones.

Redrinna had never been bothered by ghosts. Having to take over an entire empire someday had been more terrifying than any ghost story she'd ever heard.

But if the Dragon Kin had been real and all killed? All the more reason she wanted nothing to do with it, regardless of whether or not Lady Cel Tradat thought she might've been chosen for it.

She shook those thoughts away. All she needed to focus on was one thing: escaping whoever had sent that giant after her.

After a while, Xandrin decided flying would be faster and wouldn't leave a trail, so they launched into the sky. The sky was a clear blue with high clouds drifting idly by like leaves in a slow stream. She sighed as she watched them. Flying had been better when she hadn't been so tired and her mind hadn't been packed with thoughts that made shivers run up and down her spine like they were holding a circus.

She'd been sure staying with Xandrin would convince her parents she'd died as they'd intended, but was there a chance they knew she'd survived? She'd never seen that giant back at the palace though, and it had been big enough it wouldn't have had a place to hide. Not without someone seeing it, at least. She was certain somebody would've seen it. Furthermore, unlike her parents, it hadn't wanted to kill her.

Rather, it'd come to drag her off. Her memory of the event was fear-frazzled, but she recalled it saying someone called 'Father' wanted her. Had it meant its father? Or was there someone who went by the moniker 'father'? The memory of the man at the trial flashed through her mind again. Could it have been connected to the rebels somehow? But how would they have known where she was? The rebels also avoided the mountains, more than the people who lived in their shadows did, despite the advantage it would give them.

Redrinna shook her head to clear it. Her thoughts were going in circles like dogs chasing their tails, giving her a headache.

Xandrin dipped into a descent, bringing her back to the present. From where the sun rested in the sky, she guessed the day was half over. The dragon landed lightly, touching down on the outskirts of the forest that draped over the mountains like a cloak.

"What are we doing now?" she asked as she hopped off his neck and stretched stiff muscles.

"I don't know about you, but I'm starving. Stay here and don't move," came the reply before he romped off into the woods, leaving her alone.

Redrinna cocked her head. Mentally, she noted to never doubt the appetite of a dragon. If he was hungry enough to leave her alone this soon after being attacked, who knew what else he would do in the future? Despite the worries still clinging to her, she couldn't help a small smile.

He returned a short while later with a few rabbits caught in his claws. While he—discreetly—prepared them, she remembered something that made her heart shiver.

"Xandrin?"

"Hmm?" he said as he handed her some meat.

"Did that thing in the cave hurt you?"

His eyes widened and he froze for a few seconds. Then he relaxed. "Oh right. Not really. I heard him and growled at him, and then he yanked on my tail and threw me into the wall. I was dazed for a second, but I'm fine. Why?"

"Oh, um..." A sudden rush of embarrassment made it hard for her to speak. Nameless people she never saw again had been protecting her for as long as she could remember. Only once had she thought to see if they were okay. And it bothered her. "I just—I-I didn't want you to be—" Rubbing her head, she huffed and did her best to force the words out. "I was worried about you, is all."

"Oh." He paused before flashing a grin. "Thanks."

She nodded, but her thoughts went back to the palace. Captain Brion hadn't been able to tell her about the soldier who'd protected her during the trial. Was he all right?

Sighing, she stared at the ground, swallowing past the shame creeping through her. She'd never even tried to learn his name.

๛

Redrinna and Xandrin traveled as far as they could before night settled in around them and exhaustion overtook them. They spent the night hidden amongst the dense forests of the mountains, and she wondered where they were. The Agicae Mountains were the second largest mountain range on the continent, only slightly smaller than the treacherous, ice-ridden Degeraturi Mountains that ran across the eastern half of the continent. She was profoundly grateful they weren't running across that mountain range.

Regardless of which mountain range they were on, it took Redrinna forever to fall asleep since she'd gotten used to the near complete darkness of the cave. Here, the stars were annoyingly bright, incessantly poking at her eyelids and keeping her awake. When she did manage to fall asleep, she had weird dreams about that giant chasing after them again.

Relief became her companion when morning came and they continued, alternating between walking and flying as they pushed deeper into the wooded mountains. They encountered no one, and nothing came after them.

In the afternoon, a cold, end of winter downpour struck, sending them scurrying for cover. When they found a rocky outcropping that looked big enough to mostly cover both her and Xandrin, they ducked underneath it.

Xandrin's warm scales dried fast, but Redrinna was another matter. She wrung water out of her hair, leaving it hanging in limp strands that stuck to everything they touched. Her clothes and cloak were too thick to dry quickly, making goosebumps race across her skin. Even when they laid out her cloak on Xandrin's back and she curled up on his neck, she and her belongings stayed wet for a long time.

However, as she lay there, listening to the rain fall, the towering trees around them creaking in the faint wind, it was so easy to forget they were on the run. The rain was so calming, it was tempting to forget all her troubles.

97

The rain slowed to a steady drizzle just in time for the last bit of the sun to set in a watery orange smear on the distant mountaintops. It had grown late enough they decided to stay the night where they were. Shivers still intermittently shook her, but she was a lot closer to being dry than she'd been before.

The rain died off as the moon climbed into the sky. It wasn't full anymore, so mercifully, it didn't overwhelm her with its brightness. The stars didn't seem as bright as they had the other night either, which helped ease the tension knotted in her heart even further. Crickets chorused all around her, their sound lulling her to sleep. It was almost like the world was trying to give her a sign that it was okay to relax.

She must've dozed off, because the next time she glanced at the sky, the moon shone from a different place. Redrinna stretched, her clothing stiff, but mostly dry. As the chill night air settled on her, she checked her cloak, but it was still damp, so she figured she'd be better without it. Too cold to relax, she decided to explore a little bit.

She'd never had the chance to investigate a forest. It was a mysterious place she'd only encountered in books and from windows. She was too nervous to wander far from Xandrin's side, but if she stayed where she could see him, she'd be okay. After all, who knew when she'd have the chance to explore again?

Carefully, she slid off Xandrin's neck, landing quietly on the damp grass. Redrinna couldn't resist running a hand through it, even though it made her hand wet. And the smell. She'd never smelt this scent this strong. Almost earthy, but also wet and clean. Is this what the forest always smelled like, or was it because it'd rained?

It didn't matter, she decided as she trotted to the nearest tree. She stared at it, trying to remember one of the books Lady Cel Tradat had brought her once. It'd talked a lot about trees, the different kinds, identifying features, potential resources, and the like. This tree...was an Eridian Pine.

Smiling, Redrinna touched a hand to the bark. Sticky. Just as she'd suspected. This tree grew in the high altitudes of the northern stretch of the Agicae Mountains and smelled nice when it burned.

When she removed her hand from the bark, thin tendrils of sap stretched between her and the tree. An Eridian Pine, no question. The trees were renowned for creating so much sap that they could trap anything and everything. They'd rightfully earned themselves the nickname: the Eridian Pin Cushion.

Which was all well and good, but now, her hand dripped with sticky sap, making her afraid to touch anything. It was a good thing there wasn't any fire nearby, as the sap ignited at the mere sight of a spark and it burned hot. They used the sap for the torches in the palace, or so she'd heard.

Rubbing her hand in the grass, she grimaced. It didn't work as well as she'd hoped. It took a lot of rubbing to get the sap off, and even then, small bits of grass stuck to her palm. That was annoying.

When she finally had her hand clean—well, cleaner, anyway—she rose, scanning the forest around her for something else to investigate. She spied snowdrops on the verge of blooming in the shadow of a clump of aspens, a signal that spring was well on its way.

As Redrinna stepped towards them, the hairs on the back of her neck rose. She stopped, unsure why her skin crawled like bugs were swarming her.

Then it struck her: a lot of animals would be sleeping, but the forest hadn't been this quiet a few minutes ago. Unease slithered up her spine, making her regret leaving Xandrin's side. As she began to take a step back towards him, the squelch of mud rang through the trees. She froze. That wasn't natural.

All at once, she heard muttering.

"There's no way," she breathed, not wanting to turn around to see what was coming. It couldn't have—it had to be impossible. Xandrin couldn't have destroyed his home for nothing!

"—smells close by..." came its voice, muttering in monotone. "Little girl...moves too much...so hard to...follow."

Slowly, she turned back. Something large pushed through the trees, coming towards her. Moonlight filtered through the leaves, making its pale skin glow with a ghost-like ethereality. Its eyes were hidden in shadow, giving them a sunken appearance. She managed to step backward, not sure if she was even breathing. She didn't think it'd seen her yet, but one wrong move and the spell would break.

Redrinna had covered half of the distance between her and Xandrin by the time the creature stepped out of the trees and into better light. She almost didn't believe her eyes.

The giant was back. Its dark, raggedy hair hung to its shoulders, its hauntingly sunken eyes shone out from behind the strands that looked so brittle, she would've been able to snap them in half. It was covered by an eclectic mix of furs—she spied cow and wolf, fox and sheep, rabbit and horse, and dozens of others—but the makeshift tunic failed to conceal all the sinewy muscle bulging in its neck, arms, and calves. It had a bad overbite, giving a very, very animalistic appearance.

That thing had been through a cave-in—she knew that. She'd seen it with her own eyes. Yet the creature stood in front of her. Alive. Unscathed. Not even a bruise standing out on its pale skin.

It should've been impossible.

The giant stopped, half the height of the pine trees towering around them. Its head turned towards her with painstaking slowness. "Found you. Now...stay put. Must take...with me. Daddy's...girl...daddy's girl."

The moment their gazes met, her muscles went rigid. Redrinna couldn't move. Just like before, in the cave. Its narrow eyes were like a snake's, holding her fast like she was bound in irons. Her chest tightened.

She couldn't breathe.

She couldn't call Xandrin.

She couldn't do anything.

Its enormous, meaty hand was coming towards her, its jagged nails catching the light of the moon and lighting up with a revolting yellowish color.

She had to do something. All her life, she'd been desperate to prove she could take of herself. Now she had a chance, but what in the world was she supposed to do?!

It was getting close. She needed something. Anything to fight with. She didn't know how to fight, but trying was better than getting dragged off.

The giant's massive hand came at her, blocking her vision when it was about a foot away. The second its eyes vanished from her sight, air rushed into her lungs. Life raced through her body again. Redrinna bolted, its nails raking across the back of her tunic.

She had to find a weapon. Something. Anything. The creature took a step forward. Redrinna dashed behind a tree seconds before the beast slammed into the one beside it, sending branches and leaves raining down. She eyed its shadow, heart racing.

A weapon. Anything.

All at once, she sensed something in the back of her mind, like someone had stood and raised their hand, calling all attention to themselves. 'Use me,' it seemed to say. Before she could, the creature swiped at her again, just missing, leaving thick gouge marks in the tree. The tree groaned from the wound.

Heat started building in her chest, like a bed of embers coming to life.

Redrinna forced her gaze to the ground, watching the giant's feet. She couldn't look into its eyes. If she froze, she'd be finished. Biting her lip, she raced out from behind the tree as the giant grabbed it, forcing a splintering protest out of its wood. The top half shattered against the ground seconds later, a branch or something striking the back of her knee, making her wince. If she went closer to Xandrin, there'd be more room to release the heat building inside her, so hot, it almost hurt. But her mind was faster than her feet. One minute, Redrinna was running. The next she fell flat onto the uneven ground.

The creature's heavy footfalls came closer. Her hands smarted, but she closed her eyes, focusing on the heat pounding through her. It reared in her chest, burning hot. It begged her to let it go, to set it free.

So she did.

Crackling hissed from behind her. There was a massive boom followed by a rush of heat. She buried her face in her arms, skin stinging.

The creature made a funny noise as the heat vanished. An acrid stench filled the air. Redrinna risked a glance back and immediately regretted it.

The feeling deep inside her must've been magic. Fire magic, to be precise. She'd roasted the giant. Its charred body smoked, not moving. Not even breathing.

A dozen different aches making themselves known, Redrinna climbed to her feet and stepped away from it. What had she done? She could use magic? Had she just killed someone—no, something with a power she'd never even known she had? Nausea creeping up her throat, she turned away.

Something she'd always hated, the power to kill, had been in her veins all her life. She couldn't decide which was worse: knowing it'd been slumbering inside her or now knowing it could've sprung out at any time.

Without warning, crackling ripped through the silence that had fallen. Redrinna nearly leapt out of her skin, frantically searching for the source of the sound before her gaze landed back on the creature. Its charred flesh had vanished, revealing the white of its bones. The moonlight glared off the reds and pinks of muscles and other things she knew belonged in a body but couldn't name off the top of her head. Its skin began reforming before her eyes. Pale flesh raced to cover the parts that had been exposed, stitching back together like cloth. Even the makeshift tunic reformed, its repair just as flawless. Within moments, it was as though she'd never even touched it.

The creature blinked. "That...hurt," it said, its voice raspier than it'd been before.

What...had just happened? She'd thought...hadn't she just...? Her muscles seized as its eyes glittered in the moonlight, focusing on her, turning her to stone. Her heart plummeted, hot tears pricking her eyes. She'd done everything she could to protect herself. She'd tried so hard and yet, she'd failed once again to prove herself. Like always.

Without warning, Xandrin's tail slammed into the creature with a loud snap. The giant flew back into a tree, a nasty crack trembling through the air as the creature crumpled at a grotesque angle.

"Are you all right?" the dragon asked, flicking the end of his tail as though trying to get dirt off it. "It didn't hurt you, did it?"

For some reason, all the nasty comments nobles and servants alike had hissed when they'd thought she hadn't been around flashed through her mind, all the snide remarks about how she'd been born weak, or that she'd been lucky to be born. That of all her mother's children who'd died, she should've been the first to go.

Almost as if to validate what they'd always said, she'd used magic and had promptly failed to protect herself with it. Xandrin had had to come to her rescue again.

"I'm fine." Redrinna rubbed her palms together, trying to get them to stop hurting. Maybe it was the aftermath of the fight, but, all at once, it was cold like her window had burst open on a winter night.

"Why did you take that thing on by yourself?" he asked, casting a wary glance towards the creature.

Unexpectedly, it sat up with a strained groan. Didn't that thing stay dead?!

Without a moment's pause, Xandrin snatched her, put her on his back, and launched into the sky. "You're fragile, remember?" he called over the wind.

What had he just said? She didn't need another reminder of her shortcomings, not from him. A hot sensation swept over her, awakening a beast slumbering inside her that wanted to roar. And it wanted to roar loud.

Even if she was weak, she did not need to be coddled like a child.

"I am not fragile," she snarled. "Don't treat me like I'm made of glass!"

"Hmph," he said with a snort.

That stung like he'd slapped her across the face. Despite the fact she was trying to suppress shivers, her cheeks burned. Hot tears pricked her eyes, but she refused to let them fall.

"I'm not a child, Xandrin. Don't treat me like one."

"I wouldn't have to if you didn't act like one."

Her cheeks flushed hotter. She did not feel right, and not because the dragon was making her unspeakably angry. Sweat trickled down her back, which made her shiver so hard she couldn't speak. Then her skin raged with blistering heat. She tugged her hair off her neck, which helped a little but not enough. It was like she stood in the direct sun on the hottest day of the year. Just as quickly, it was like she'd fallen face first into ice-cold water. To make things worse, her head spun. Her stomach lurched like she was falling. She managed to grab onto Xandrin's spikes, but her grip lacked strength.

"Hey," the dragon said, his voice seeming to come from far away. "I'm sorry if I hurt your feelings. You scared me, okay?"

She touched a hand to his scales, which were so warm they hurt her skin. Why did she feel like this? Had using that power done this to her? Maybe it was good they'd ended up skipping dinner; she would've lost it.

Without warning, a strong, cold wind rushed over them. Xandrin wobbled a little. What little warmth she'd acquired vanished. She collapsed against Xandrin's neck, unable to stop shivering.

"H-hey," she heard the dragon say, his voice even more distant than before. His scales were warm, but not enough.

The world slipped into a hazy state, like she hovered on the verge of falling asleep. It was too cold. Much too cold. Maybe if she brought her arms closer...but they wouldn't respond. They just clung stupidly onto Xandrin's spikes, stiff and unresponsive.

Redrinna had no idea how much time passed before they were back in the frigid shadow of the forest. Hard ground dug into her side. When had she left Xandrin's neck? He prodded her with his nose, but she couldn't stop shivering. She couldn't even speak. It was a struggle just to breathe. Was she dying?

All at once, a warm hand touched her cheek. A human hand. She tried to look, but the world was blurred, like it filtered through warped glass.

"Hurry," an unfamiliar voice said. "If we're fast, she'll be fine."

Chapter Ten

Redrinna's mind stayed in a murky state for hours. She was neither asleep nor awake, but somewhere in-between, like she was trapped in some place devoid of anything except a strange fog. No dreams wrapped her in their tender arms, but she did keep thinking she saw her father. It was the same face, but also not. The eyebrows were more expressive, more dynamic. The nose a bit more pointed.

When she did come around, darkness blanketed everything. She blinked several times—just in case—noting little difference when her eyes were closed compared to when they were open. It was brighter than Xandrin's cave, but darker than the forest. Where was she? Where was Xandrin?

A sigh slipped out of her. Exhaustion dragged on every muscle and joint in her body. Trying to remember the events that had led her here made her head pound like little dragons were using it as a stomping ground. Everything after fighting the giant in the forest was a fuzzy blur she couldn't pick apart.

Her body cried for sleep the way a child woken from a nightmare cried for comfort, but her mind refused to relax in such a strange place. After a long, indecisive moment, she tossed the covers back—wait. She'd been in a bed? She glanced around, waiting for something to jump out at her, but nothing did. Where in the world was she? A surge of panic raced up her spine, making her shudder.

Shaking herself, Redrinna left the bed, the cool ground beneath her feet making her shiver, but it had the roughness of...stone? She'd been wondering if she'd somehow ended up back at the palace since she was in a bed, but a bare stone floor meant no. Not that the palace didn't have stone floors, but per Eridian custom, there would've been a rug.

As Redrinna walked through the dark, she held her hands out in front of her, hoping she'd run into things with them before she found them with her face. In less than a minute, she ran into something (with her hands, thankfully). After a moment of investigating, she realized she'd found a door. Pulling it open, she was startled by what she saw.

She stood at the edge of a wide hallway that had a long row of doors on one side and a wall of large openings strung down the other, each spaced quite a distance from each other. It was unclear how many openings and doors there were, as the hall curved out of sight. The ceiling was so high, there would've been plenty of space for Xandrin to walk through. The walls and floor were a smooth, dark gray stone, all gleaming with soft orange light. She wasn't one hundred percent certain where the light came from, but at least she knew her eyes were still working.

The temptation to explore blossomed in Redrinna's chest, strong enough she started to step forward, but a rush of worry flooded her veins, making her hesitate. The last thing she wanted was to get lost in an unfamiliar place.

While she stood there thinking, she heard familiar, heavy breathing coming from the nearest opening in the other wall. She peeked inside, unable to see much in the dark. The space seemed large, but she couldn't tell how big.

Something lay in the cave, something enormous. After she studied it for a moment, her heart leapt and did a little jig at the sight of Xandrin's sleeping form. At least he was still here with her, wherever here was.

Trotting to his side, Redrinna paused, trying to decide if he was asleep or not. She didn't have to wonder too long. The dragon's large head lifted off the ground, coming to a rest near her. "You're awake."

A small smile touched her mouth for a second. "Where are we?"

she whispered. "What happened?"

"I don't know where we are exactly," Xandrin said, half-closing his eyes. "We're still in the mountains somewhere though. You collapsed for some reason and this person found us. He saved you and brought us here. As far as I know, he's still here somewhere."

Someone had saved her? Who could it have been? Was it the person who'd sent the giant after them? Or somebody else?

At that moment, it occurred to her she wasn't dressed the way she remembered being. She now wore a simple tunic and pants which were lighter and softer than the clothes her parents had given her. Xandrin was right. There had to be a third party. Fear wrapped its fingers around her heart until Xandrin nudged her with his nose.

"If you want, you could always stay in here," he suggested, blinking his dark eyes.

"Stay here?" Her gaze sank to the floor, their last conversation resurfacing in her mind. Guilt crawled into her throat, making it hard to speak. What she'd said to him... Xandrin hadn't deserved it. Regret burned like bile in her chest. "But I yelled at you."

The dragon laughed, albeit quietly. "You'd also just finished fighting for your life. I'm guessing you've never had to do that before, right? And on top of that, you were sick almost right after."

It pained her to admit it, but he was right. Her life had been turned upside down since meeting him, in more ways than one.

"So, given the circumstances, why should I be mad at you?" he continued, no longer laughing but still smiling. That smile was unquestionably growing on her.

Redrinna didn't deserve a friend like him.

"You might have a point," she said with a sniff, fighting back the urge to cry.

With a minor, itty bitty bit of assistance from the dragon, she managed to climb onto his warm shoulders. Even though Redrinna had just woken up after who knew how much sleep, the second she laid down, fatigue tucked itself in around her like a blanket, coaxing her into sleep's waiting arms.

Maybe hours, maybe minutes later, Redrinna gradually became

aware of a hand touching her head. Her eyes shot open.

Red. For a second, that was all her bleary, sleep-filled eyes could see. Blinking to clear her vision, she tried to figure out what she was looking at. Leaning over her stood a man with skin maybe a shade paler than hers and vivid red hair and eyes. She rubbed her eyes. That couldn't be right.

The man remained unchanged when Redrinna looked a second time. The man's hair and eyes really were red, giving him a striking appearance.

He...was like her.

"Good afternoon!" the man said, withdrawing his hand as a grin erupted across his face. "I hope you aren't regularly in the habit of sleeping in for half the day."

Her mind still reeled from the fact his eyes were as red as hers, so it didn't occur to her to speak.

"Hmm," the man glanced at Xandrin. "She's not a great conversation partner, is she?"

A growl reverberating low in his throat, Xandrin whipped his head off the ground, ear frills flared, stopping maybe a foot away from the man.

The man laughed, the sound almost infectious. "Yes, yes, I'm already quite aware of how you feel about me. Don't worry, your friend is doing fine and I'm finished examining her."

As the man stepped back, Xandrin growled again—giving Redrinna chills. Without even flinching, the man flicked him on the nose. Xandrin recoiled, shaking his head.

"You're very cute, but I told you I was done, and I will not tolerate the attitude," the man said, turning back to face them. Even still, Redrinna couldn't help staring at his vivid, red eyes that reminded her of leaves in autumn. He seemed close to her age, but there was a maturity to his face that made her think he was older than he seemed.

The man's gaze was focused somewhere else for a long moment, but then he glanced back, meeting her gaze. He raised an eyebrow as the corner of his mouth turned upwards.

"You're not very shy, are you?"

Heat rushed to her cheeks as she hurriedly looked somewhere else.

"Anyway, your fever broke, so in a day or two you should be back to whatever your normal self is." The man flicked his hair out of his eyes though it came right back, a half-smile on his face. "Was it your first time using magic?"

Panic shot through Redrinna's veins. How did he know that? Had he been watching her in the woods? Or was he the one who'd sent the giant after them? Was this a trick? If he—

"Woah, easy there," he said, eyes widening a fraction. "I don't know what your thought process just was, but relax. I've seen this a few times, that's why I asked. I could have been wrong though. You also could've had vermillion fever, but given the fact you're so much better after only one night's rest, I'm going to say that's not the case."

Something about this fellow seemed trustworthy, but she couldn't quite decide why. Maybe becoming friends with a dragon made everyone feel more trustworthy.

"I feel the need to say you can trust me, but since that line usually belongs to either a villain of some kind or the hot village boy who's going to sweep you off your feet within the next five minutes, I don't think I will." His smile broadened, though she couldn't help noting it didn't quite reach his eyes.

Despite that, she couldn't hide the tiniest smile of her own.

"I suppose I ought to tell you my name," the man said. "It's Timothon, but feel free to call me any nickname you like. Well, except for Moth. Not fond of that one." He swiped at his bangs again, to no avail. "So, who are you?"

Timothon? He had the same name as the king in one of her favorite tapestries.

Her mind warned her not to trust him, but at the same time, her heart wasn't cowering in fear. That had to count for something, right? "I'm...Redrinna," she offered, earning a warning glance from the dragon. "The dragon's name is Xandrin. How...did you know...?"

"About the magic?" Timothon finished, shifting his weight from one foot to the other. "Do you want me to tell you how I knew it was magic or how I knew it was your first time?"

"The second one."

"Let me put it this way: using magic is a way of manipulating the world around you to make certain things happen. So—and correct me if I'm wrong—you used your powers for the first time, and it ended up being fire magic. What does a fire need to burn?"

"Air," Redrinna began, "and heat...and something to burn, right?"

"Right," Timothon said, "so I'm going to assume there was plenty of air, yes?"

She nodded, sitting up as her curiosity flared to life.

"And something to burn?"

The giant had been what she'd burnt, which, while gross, still counted she supposed.

"That leaves us with what you used to start the fire: the heat. You most likely did this in one of two ways," Timothon said, scooping a rock off the ground. "Either you used some kind of force to make sparks," he chucked the stone at the wall hard enough a few sparks flew through the air, "or you made the air so hot whatever you wanted to burn spontaneously combusted. Is it safe to say you did something along the lines of the latter?"

She thought back to the fight with the giant. The details were still fuzzy like she was staring at the memory through murky water. As far as she could remember, there hadn't been any sparks. It'd just been her and the beast in a forest soaked from hours of rain. Meeting his gaze again, Redrinna nodded.

"Which means you had no idea what you were doing and you took the heat from your own body to give your fire life," Timothon said, his eyes glittering like steel in the dim light. "I'll be honest with you: you were lucky. Very lucky. Most people die for making a mistake like that. Unless you learn how to use your power safely, don't use it all."

Her heart dropped an inch or two, but she tried to shake it off. What he said made sense, even if she didn't like it.

"Anyway," he continued, a smile once again gracing his cheeks, "anybody hungry? You've both been a bit out of it, so I argue that we should all grab a bite before we go any further."

As thoughts of food waltzed through Redrinna's mind, her stomach growled. Xandrin's stomach answered seconds later, making them grin at each other.

Timothon turned towards the exit. "I thought this would be a good idea. Let's go."

Once she was on the ground, Redrinna took measured steps behind him, feeling more confident once she heard Xandrin's heavy steps behind her. She couldn't help admiring the architecture of...wherever she was. It was light and undemanding. No fancy decorations or sculptures. Just smooth, polished stone, beautiful in its simplicity.

"Where are we?" she said to Timothon's back since she didn't trust him enough to walk beside him.

"This place?" he said, pausing and casting an appraising glance around the hall before allowing his gaze to rest on her. "Nothing fancy. Just the Mount."

Oh? So they weren't just in the mountains, but inside one of them? Remarkable, though it was kind of an odd place for someone to live.

Timothon resumed walking. "It was also the home of the Dragon Kin about a century ago."

She stopped. The Dragon Kin. Not again.

"The Dragon Kin?" Xandrin asked from behind them. "I've heard about them. Weren't they that group of dragons and humans that fought alongside each other a long time ago?"

"Yes," Timothon replied, his voice somewhat hushed.

"You mean they were real?" Redrinna whispered. First Lady Cel Tradat and now this guy had mentioned them. She wanted nothing to do with them, so why did it seem like they were following her everywhere she went?

Timothon didn't meet her gaze. "Of course. Has it really been so long people are forgetting?" He shook himself, his easy smile returning. "Set that aside for a minute or you'll get so worked up you'll have to go back to bed. You two need to eat."

The hallway with the myriad of doors abruptly opened into an enormous room. It seemed a bit brighter than the hall, more yellow than orange. A large set of double, stone doors gleamed in the far wall to her left. To her right branched two more passageways, one angling down somewhat while the other climbed upwards. Timothon led them into the hallway that sloped down. They walked the entire way in silence, passing a room that looked invitingly like a library and another she couldn't name what it would be. There were a lot of stuffed dummies in it though.

The third room they encountered was the one Timothon led them inside. This one Redrinna likened to a great hall, though it was far too empty. One, long table rested in the center of the enormous room, ten chairs standing around it.

The dimensions made no sense until Xandrin slid through the door. There was enough room in here they could've fit more dragons, no question.

At their host's request, she sat in one of the chairs, Xandrin settling behind her. "I didn't know what food you two liked, so you'll have to wait until I make you something. What do you want?"

Redrinna stared. What did she like? She'd never been given the option of liking something or not before. She'd always just eaten whatever had been put in front of her.

"Well?"

"I like fish," the dragon behind her offered.

"Fish?" Redrinna asked before she could help herself. She knew a lot of people ate fish, but she couldn't even remember what it tasted like.

"Have you never had fish before?" Timothon asked, his eyebrows vanishing behind his bangs.

"Well I..." she began. The last time she'd had fish, she'd been little and had eaten too fast, choking on a bone. Since then, her parents had never requested fish to be brought to the palace, at least not unless they'd been hosting some kind of celebration or something. Not...that...she should mention anything about her home here, at least, not until she figured this Timothon fellow out. "Not exactly."

He and Xandrin gave her such startled expressions, she thought she might've said something wrong.

The dragon leaned down, putting their heads level with each other.

"But Redrinna, fish is divine."

"I just—"

"Fish it is!" Timothon said before turning and exiting the room, leaving them alone.

Xandrin's head moved forward, a little closer than before. "He's not the person who tried to kill you before, is he?"

She shook her head before resting her chin in her hand. "I've never seen him before."

The dragon nodded before retreating a bit.

That said, Redrinna couldn't deny that the man's hair and eyes were so like hers, it was kind of uncanny. He knew about the Dragon Kin too. Did that mean he was a part of it or joining it or whatever? If that was the case, maybe she didn't need to worry about it. Unless all the members of the Dragon Kin's hair and eyes changed to red?

Either way, she wasn't going to be a part of it.

Her thoughts continued to meander until Timothon re-entered the room. A lone fish was set in front of Redrinna, while a small mound was given to Xandrin. Where had he gotten so much fish? And how?

"Try it," the red-haired man said to her, directing her attention to the fish in front of her.

It smelled...odd. Redrinna cocked her head at it, her stomach churning to remind her it hadn't received any food for a while. She took a bit of the flaky, pink flesh, placed it on her tongue...and winced. This...this wasn't what...what she'd...

"What do you think?" Xandrin asked, peeking over her shoulder.

She shoved it toward him. "You can have mine."

Chapter Eleven

When Redrinna startled awake the next morning, it took her half a second to remember where she was. Sighing, she rubbed a hand against her forehead; she should be getting used to waking up in foreign places by now.

After dinner last night, she'd returned to the room she'd woken up in yesterday. Timothon had said it was hers to use while they stayed in the Mount. Which, if she was honest with herself, shouldn't be for long. If the giant came after her again, she'd rather not ruin someone else's home.

Redrinna shook those thoughts away as best as she could before getting up. She walked out of her room a few minutes later, glad to have her old clothes back on, before stopping, unsure where to go. Glancing up and down the hall, Redrinna debated barging into Xandrin's room. All at once, she spotted their red-haired host heading into the main room with the two other passages.

"Timothon," she called, biting her lip when he didn't turn around or stop. Should she try again? Maybe she should chase after him to get his attention? Or maybe she should follow him and see what he was up to? After all, if she wanted a better idea of what he was like, what better way than watching him when he thought he was alone?

A shiver of fear raced up her spine, but to be honest, both the giant and her parents attempting to kill her were scarier than he was.

She'd be more frightened if he attacked her without warning than if she suspected it might happen. Well, maybe that would be the case. At least, that was what Lady Cel Tradat had always said. Her mother had mentioned it a time or two as well.

She scowled. Even here, away from her old life, she still couldn't stop thinking about them. Like she hadn't been abandoned by the one and abandoned the other. She wished the pain inside her would go away, that she'd stop thinking about the people she'd thought had loved her. She wished she could forget her life before meeting Xandrin. Forget all of it.

Shaking herself, Redrinna hurried after Timothon with all the stealth she could muster. He'd taken the tunnel they'd gone down last night. Due to it being rigidly straight, she had to go much slower than him to keep him unaware of her presence. As they passed the room Redrinna suspected was a library, she peeked in. All she managed to see were a few large windows, but the fragrant smell of old paper wafted out of the stone walls. A library, without a doubt.

She continued on, following him past the dining room and to the last room in the hallway. Tiptoeing as she got closer, she peeked around the doorframe, trying to keep her breathing as quiet as possible. It took her a minute to put a name on the warm, well-lit room.

From where she was, Redrinna could see a long table in the center of the room, an assortment of pans and dishes stacked on a shelf underneath the table. A fire danced in a stove pushed against the wall opposite her. An enormous pile of wood stood tall in the only corner she could see, creating a natural barrier between the stove and the oven three-quarters of the way up the wall.

The word for the place came to her: kitchen.

It'd been ages, it seemed, since she'd seen one, let alone been in one. The cooks at the palace had often welcomed her when she'd been young, letting her eat snacks to her heart's content. Then, like everyone else, when her appearance had changed, they'd treated her like a wild animal. After that, she'd never gone back.

What was Timothon doing in a kitchen though? Immediately, she kicked that thought out of her head. Fully cooked meals didn't leap out of tabletops, so someone had to be doing the cooking around here, and it wasn't odd Timothon was capable of doing so. After all, one of Captain Brion's secret talents was making the most amazing pastries she'd ever tasted.

As that thought waltzed through her mind, she pressed her forehead against the doorway. Redrinna wished he would get out of her head too.

As she refocused on Timothon, he approached the oven, the gleaming silver handle releasing a high, grinding squeal as he turned it, jerking the door open. The crackling of a fire sang out of the oven's depths, an orange glow lighting Timothon's face, the rush of hot air tugging on his hair. He grabbed a long, wooden tool that reminded her of a shovel—aside from the fact the actual 'shovel' part was flat on this thing—and he stirred the fire with it. The fire crackled mutely a few more times before falling silent. He pulled his tool out, flicking embers off the end with one smooth movement before resting a hand on his hip and gazing into the oven for a long time.

"So, how long do you plan on spying through the doorway, Redrinna?"

Heart leaping into her throat, she jerked straight, stiff as a board, smacking her fist on the doorframe as she did so. Wincing, she occupied herself with examining her reddening fingers so she wouldn't have to meet his gaze. Frustration at being caught so fast pounded through her. More proof she couldn't take care of herself.

"You can come in, you know," he continued. "The oven doesn't bite."

Heat rushing up her neck, she slinked in, stopping near the edge of the table. Glancing up beneath her bangs, she found Timothon watching her, brow lowered.

"Was there something you needed? Or am I just that fascinating?"

Rubbing her head, Redrinna scrambled to think of something to say. "I...wanted to thank you." That wasn't untrue, even if it wasn't what she'd actually come here for, so she didn't mind saying it. "For saving Xandrin and me."

"Oh. You're welcome," he said depositing his weird shovel in its place and approaching the table. He unwrapped four rather small, cloth-bound mounds she hadn't noticed, releasing a smell similar to bread but with a hint of sourness. Bread dough, she realized. Using his weird shovel again, he placed all the mounds inside the oven's belly, leaving the door wide open.

"Isn't it too hot in there for bread?" she asked, forgetting her embarrassment.

"Not really. The fire sounds bigger than it is. It's mostly just embers." He set aside his weird shovel and dragged two stools over from the other side of the table. She sat on one when he motioned towards it, but she sat on the edge, ready to bolt in a split second.

"How about I ask you a question now? Tell me, Redrinna," he began as he rested his elbows on the counter and studied his flour-coated hands. "Why are you out in the mountains with a dragon?"

Her stomach squirmed like a fish out of water. She should've expected this to come up sooner or later. "I...want to study...the plants and things," she whispered.

"Really?" Timothon glanced sidelong at her.

She hurriedly fixed her gaze on the table.

"Where's your weapon? I mean, knives are great, but not against bears or wolves or even a lynx. And it's mating season for the chamois, so there's always a chance of getting attacked by an overprotective male. Unless, of course, you were planning on having the dragon do that?"

"Huh?"

"To protect you in case you got attacked by a wild animal while you were out doing your research or something. Plus, why were you using fire magic if you were studying non-fire-proof plants? Also, you've never eaten fish? That's pretty much all there is to reliably eat out here right now, beyond the plants, of course."

Each question hit her like a slap across the face. Was she that transparent? What was she supposed to tell him while avoiding the truth if he was so good at seeing through her?

"Don't expect me to believe you were trying to make a campfire," Timothon continued, tapping his fingers together, making little puffs of flour fan out. "If you had, you wouldn't have almost died. And what kind of life were you living that you've never figured out you could use magic? I would imagine a scholar would have pursued finding something like that out?"

Redrinna had never had the luxury. It'd always been about the throne, getting ready to take the crown. Lowering her head a bit more, she grimaced. Lying or keeping secrets had never been her strong suit, especially when she was under direct pressure like this.

"The truth is," she began softly, hating the way the memories made her chest constrict and her heart dig little, invisible fingers into her throat. "Someone...I trusted a lot tried to kill me. Xandrin was the one who saved and hid me. But there's this giant that keeps coming after me no matter what we do or where we go. I don't know if it's connected to the people who tried to kill me or not. I don't think it is, but I don't even know what that thing is." Her vision blurred a bit but she forced the tears back. "It's because of the giant I found out about the magic."

She hadn't thought about her futile fight against the giant since it'd happened, but as she talked about it, a remnant of the fear and frustration she'd tasted echoed inside her.

Frowning, Timothon said, "So, you're hiding from whoever tried to kill you, and whoever is trying to get a hold of you now. You and Xandrin tried hiding in the mountains and out running it, but none of it worked?"

Nodding made shame burn in her belly. How long ago had it been since she'd said she could take care of herself if she only had the chance? Being able to escape that thing would've proven she could—

"Then...have you ever considered learning how to fight back?" Timothon's voice was quiet, almost like he was suggesting something they both knew could be dangerous.

"Fight back?" Those words left a strange taste in her mouth. It wasn't a bad taste, but it was peculiar all the same.

"Right. From the sound of it, that thing is going to keep coming after you until it gets you. While you're safe in here, it'll only be a matter of time before it catches up and drags you off if you leave."

Even though Redrinna didn't want to acknowledge it, she knew he was right. It'd almost succeeded twice already. At this rate, how would she stop it the next time they met?

"You could resign yourself to that," he continued, slowly meeting her gaze. "Or you could get stronger. Become strong enough to fight back and survive. It wouldn't be easy, but it's better than hiding in a hole and waiting to die. Or worse."

The way Timothon said that reminded her of how Lady Cel Tradat had often tried to convince Redrinna to learn how to fight. All at once, a sharp ache reverberated in Redrinna's chest for the days when she used to watch the woman train or the quiet evenings when they'd sat and talked.

As Redrinna thought about Lady Cel Tradat, her hand went to the knife on her belt. Fingering the cool leather grip slowed her thoughts, made them easier to examine. She'd been too fixated on what the woman had told her about her parents when she'd given her the weapon, but now maybe taking her words to heart was worth trying.

"Who would teach me?" she asked, a small fire timidly dancing in her chest. "Are there books I can read or something?"

Timothon laughed, throwing his head back. "What do you take me for? A bump on a log?"

"You?" The question slipped out before she could catch it. Stumbling in her haste, she added, "I-I mean, you're already doing so much for me. I shouldn't ask for more." She grimaced when he laughed a bit harder.

"Let's just say it wouldn't sit well with me if I turned an inexperienced kid like you out on your own. So, this is more so you won't sit on my conscience if something happens to you. I wouldn't mind teaching you a thing or two. Honest."

He grinned at her for a second before leaping to his feet, sending the stool to the floor with an enormous bang and bolted towards the oven, hissing something along the lines of: "Oh! My bread!" Skidding to a stop in front of the oven, he squinted into its glowing depths before extracting the loaves and shutting the door.

Just the look of the crusty, golden brown loaves was enough to make Redrinna's mouth water, forget the fragrant smell of hot bread wafting through the kitchen, soaking into everything it could touch. Her stomach rumbled, making Timothon smirk.

"Anyway," he said as he returned to her side of the table, calmly righting his stool like he hadn't just run across the room like a maniac. "I was going to say I know more than I look like I should. So if you want, I can teach you how to stand on your own two feet. What do you say?"

"You're different than I expected," she said, hoping he'd take that as the compliment she'd intended since it'd kind of just popped out.

"Well, I've been around long enough to acquire a secret or two," he said, lifting his eyes to meet her gaze while his head stayed lowered, something about the way he did so putting her on edge. "Like the one about your empire, Princess."

Ice coiled around Redrinna's spine, her heart almost stopping. What had he just said? How did he...?

The silence pressing its heavy weight on them intensified as Timothon stared at her, his expression not changing no matter how long she stared back.

"How do you know about that?" she asked, her voice barely audible.

Smiling a little, he shrugged. "I don't think you're ready for that secret, so for now, I'm going to hold on to it. When you've proven yourself a bit, I'll tell you. Anyhow, where's that dragon friend of yours?" Turning, he left the room.

Closing her eyes, a shudder shook her body. He knew. Would he force her to go back? It didn't seem like he cared whether she did or not, so maybe he wouldn't. Especially since his last smile reminded her of the first one of his she'd ever seen: it didn't quite manage to reach his eyes though it seemed like it was really trying.

⁂

A few hours later, Timothon took Redrinna to the one room in the hallway she hadn't been able to identify at first glance: a training room. The musky scent of straw filled her lungs, reminding her of the few times she'd been able to get away from soon-to-be-ruler life and watch

Lady Cel Tradat spar up close.

Unlike back at the palace though, this room was nearly as large as the great hall—twice the size of the training grounds at the palace—and a rack holding all sorts of wooden weapons stood proudly against the far wall. Dummies stuffed with straw lined the wall perpendicular to that, each with a different weapon shoved in their straw fists, from swords to maces to things she couldn't name.

Timothon's gaze flicked towards her. "I'm going to take a wild guess and say you've never done this before. But maybe you've read a bit about it?"

"Kind of," she said, wishing she could go hide with Xandrin in his cave. Despite Lady Cel Tradat's efforts, she hadn't ever been interested in books about weapons and fighting. She preferred ornamental weapons over the ones designed for killing. Those weapons were pretty, not practical. But if Redrinna wanted to protect herself from that relentless giant, perhaps this was the best way to do it.

Timothon chuckled a bit. "I hope you studied well because we're going to put theory to practice."

"What?" Redrinna's heart fluttered uncomfortably. She hadn't read any of those parts with the intent to use it! How was she supposed to put theory to practice when the only theory she had was from watching Lady Cel Tradat—one of the most renowned swordswoman in the Empire—who moved so fast she couldn't tell the moves apart?

He tossed a wooden sword to her, which she fumbled since it was much heavier than she'd expected. It clattered against the ground. "All right, we're going to start your training with close-range weapons first before we move on. In order for this to work, you need to imagine your opponent is the thing that's chasing you."

Retrieving her wooden sword, Redrinna straightened just in time to see one of the dummies coming towards her, brandishing a wooden sword of its own. She was supposed to pretend this dinky dummy was the giant?

"It's too small," she said, shooting a panicky glance at Timothon.

He tilted his head to the side, brow furrowing. "Too small? How big are we talking here?"

She pointed up with her sword. "Its head is up there."

Timothon nodded, a thoughtful frown on his face. "I get it, but there's no way I'm stacking the dummies that high. That's asking for trouble. Besides, it doesn't matter how big your opponent is. Size can give people an advantage or a disadvantage depending on the situation, but it's not absolute. In this case, we don't need an accurately sized opponent. Your body just needs to believe you're fighting that thing. Fight that dummy like it's going to kill you."

How was she supposed to think of this puppet as the giant?

She turned back just as the dummy swung its sword at her head. Redrinna barely brought her sword up in time. The impact jarred her wrists and she narrowly avoided dropping the sword for a second time.

Wait. That hurt just like when she'd tripped and fallen while running from the giant.

The dummy brandished its sword. She could almost imagine the giant's beady eyes glaring down at her. Her pulse sped up.

It swung again, and she managed to pull off a block that hurt a little less. Or maybe her arms were still numb from the first hit. Either way, she took a step back. Don't let it get close. That's how she'd evaded the giant before. Keep it at a distance.

Redrinna managed to parry the dummy's sword five consecutive times before it smacked her on the shoulder. It stung. A lot. Crap. It was like the giant's eyes had her frozen, like its giant hand was stretched out to grab her again. Crap. All at once, its sword clocked her in the ribs, hard enough it knocked her down. Its blade touched her neck, sending a chill down her spine.

"And the stalker wins," Timothon said.

She winced, her fist tightening on her sword. She hadn't even lasted five minutes against this stupid dummy that was less than half the giant's height. There was no way she'd be able to stand up to the stupid giant like this. Not as weak and helpless as she was.

"Don't get angry," Timothon said, standing over her, his expression stern. "That was only your first try. This is why you practice. If you keep at it, when it counts, you won't fall so easily. So, if you want to get stronger, get up."

Glancing down, she forced herself to take a deep breath. If Lady Cel Tradat had been here, she would've said the same thing. So would the Captain. So would her parents.

Setting her jaw, Redrinna stood, trying to ignore the lingering sting in her hands.

The dummy approached, but it didn't attack.

One hand on his hip, Timothon stood off to the side. "All right. This is going to be sword fighting for beginners, first lesson, so listen well. First thing to remember: the sword is an extension of yourself, not just a stick in your hand."

"Well, it kind of is," she whispered.

Timothon scowled, his expression reminding her a lot of the face her father had always made when she'd showed him a new bug she'd found and he'd been anything but impressed. The next second, she had to hurriedly block another wrist-jarring smack from the dummy.

"As I was saying, when you're sword fighting, the best option is to rely on brute strength. You, however, don't have that advantage."

It was Redrinna's turn to scowl. She came up to Timothon's shoulder, and he was a pretty tall guy. Considering that, she wasn't so disadvantaged. Was she? Though, against the giant, she only made it up to its thigh, giving it an enormous advantage.

"Because of that, you have to be fast and hit where it counts. Our dummy friend is better at that than you." He motioned towards the stuffed figure, who still looked ready to attack at any second. She shot a glare at Timothon. Then she had to duck another swing from the dummy. "When you're being attacked, the best thing for you to do right now is to avoid it and do something they won't expect before they can strike again."

Something the giant wouldn't expect? What would that be?

"So, you said that thing is huge, right? I know the dummy doesn't compare but remember: big things need more room and time to move around. It has a wider reach and can cover more ground than you, but you are smaller and faster. You can dodge most of its attacks, don't you think?"

He was right. The giant did tend to move pretty slow. Even before, in her panicky states, Redrinna had been able to evade its assault. What always stopped her were its eyes and the weird power it had over her.

"But, in order for you to do that, you'll need to learn the basics so well you won't even have to think about them." Timothon glanced at the dummy before fixing her with a smug look she didn't like.

The dummy lifted its sword, holding it perpendicular to the ground.

"Horizontal swing," the man called.

Redrinna swung, lightly clacking against the dummy's wooden blade.

"Again, from the other side."

She did, though Timothon had to guide her through doing that one with the correct posture.

"Upper hand, swing down." Then, "Under hand, swing up. Thrust."

The dummy moved its sword to counteract each of Timothon's instructions.

As the man continued to call out instructions, Redrinna had to scramble to keep up. Her hand stung more with every strike. The instructions came faster. Her arms burned so badly she was sure they were going to fall off. By the time the man stopped, Redrinna was gasping for breath.

"Not bad for your first time," he said with a slight shrug. He shot her a grin. "At this rate, you should be ready to take that thing on in a year. Maybe two."

She was pretty sure that was an insult of some kind, but she was too tired to care.

"I think we can call it a day there. You're going to need a lot of practice, but don't worry too much. You're not half bad. And we don't want to wear you out completely, since the dummy did manage to get in a couple good hits."

He touched two fingers to her shoulder. She flinched away. A strange look passed through his eyes, one that almost made her feel guilty, but neither of them said anything.

Chapter Twelve

After three days of relentless training and studying, Redrinna could barely keep her eyes open. The few books she'd read had made fighting seem much simpler, but she supposed it would be if she had the brute strength or the technique to make it that way. She was ready to give up on that already. She'd had no idea so many muscles could ache so much or all at the same time. There had to be a better way to fight off the giant than dashing around and poking it with a sharp stick.

Though, despite the fact she could hardly think straight, she didn't want to go to sleep. The library had so many books, so many things she'd never been able to read before. The Mount itself was so fascinating; she wanted to spend hours exploring every inch.

Fortunately, on her first day of training, when she'd been stiff from sore muscles, Timothon had introduced her to the second room hidden inside hers, a small one she hadn't paid attention to. Inside rested a hot spring, which worked wonders for taking the aches away for a time.

Since she was feeling better after using it today, she wanted to go check out the third passageway they'd never been in. Everything they needed seemed to be in the two she knew, so what was the point of the third? She'd never even seen Timothon go up that one.

Peeking out into the hallway, she made sure the coast was clear before leaving her room. She peered into Xandrin's cave as she passed.

She didn't see him, but his heavy breathing rang out from inside. A melancholy feeling settled in her chest. She hadn't gotten the chance to spend time with him much since they'd arrived here. Odd how she'd already come to enjoy his company.

Glad there was always a soft, orange light in the halls of the Mount, Redrinna paused at the entrance to the third tunnel. Biting her lip, she cast a glance over her shoulder for reasons she didn't know before entering the tunnel. The floor slanted up at a bit of a sharp angle, and she was sure it curved as well. In the silence hanging in the air, her breathing seemed far too loud. The higher she climbed, the colder the air became, but she didn't quite feel it since the hike was taking its toll.

The passageway opened to a vast room filled with silvery streams of moonlight. Her eyes stung a little from the intensity, but once they were used to it, she gasped at the sight.

Before her was a short staircase leading up to a large circular platform. Nine gigantic statues painted and sculpted with incredible detail stood around the circle, each one depicting a different person with different colored hair and eyes. None of them bore the color red, though. Behind each statue was a stained glass window—depicting a different dragon—muted, multi-colored light streaming through each, bathing the room in quiet rainbows.

Redrinna padded up the stairs, her soft leather boots silent, leaving the still hush over the room intact. She turned in circles, trying to see everything at once. All the statues stood on a pedestal, keeping them out of the moat of water ringing the platform. However, directly across from the door stood a bare pedestal. Why was that one empty? Had this room's creator been unable to finish? Or maybe it was still being worked on somewhere?

"What are you doing here?"

Timothon's voice shattered the fragile silence of the room, almost making Redrinna leap out of her skin. Whirling, she spotted him standing at the base of the stairs, his expression not entirely friendly, but also not one that made her think she was in danger.

"What is this place?" she asked, forgetting about his question in her excitement. "I've never seen anything like it."

"It doesn't have a name," he replied, glancing away. "But I've always thought of it as the Hall of the Dragon Kin."

The Dragon Kin again? All her excitement dissipated. The last thing she wanted was to hear about them.

"Do you not like the Dragon Kin?" he asked, ascending the stairs. "Every time I mention it, you get this grumpy look on your face."

"I do not," she said, shooting a weak glare at him.

He raised an eyebrow.

She looked away.

"Why do you dislike them so much? You've heard stories about them, haven't you? About how they protected this continent and that kind of thing?"

"I have. But—" She barely managed to stop herself. Just thinking about when Lady Cel Tradat had said that she, Redrinna, had possibly been chosen as a new member filled her with unspeakable dread. If she hadn't been chosen, then her parents never would've...

"But what?" Timothon tilted his head, his expression expectant, though still gentle.

Well, maybe it wouldn't be so bad to tell him. After all, she suspected he'd been chosen too, so he'd probably understand, wouldn't he?

"Well," she began slowly, the words sticking in her throat like they were afraid of coming out. "I don't know for sure, but a friend told me that they believe my hair and eyes...that they turned this color because I was chosen to join the Dragon Kin. And it's because of that...that someone tried to kill me."

Timothon took that in without a word, not moving for a long minute. "So, because of that, you've acquired some animosity towards them?"

She guessed that was the case.

"Do you even know who they were or what they did?"

That made her pause. She shook her head.

"Fear of the unknown breeds hatred. So then, how about I tell you a story?" he said with a sigh. He walked to the center of the platform and sat cross-legged on the ground. Patting the ground beside him, he said, "Come on. We haven't got all night."

She sat, glancing at him before staring at the ground instead. "Are you going to tell me about the Dragon Kin?"

"That's right. Then you can decide whether or not they're something worth being bothered by." He lifted his head, staring at the windows above. "The legend I know goes something like this: it's said that deep within the earth of this continent slumbers a fearsome power, one that awakens whenever the inhabitants of the land are threatened by something that could destroy them all.

"The Dragon Kin was a group of ten humans, all gathered from the different tribes and countries, upon whom this legendary power chose to bestow itself. Because of the power's nature, this group petitioned the help of the dragon race, asking for help to guard the power with which they were entrusted. This help came in the form of ten, powerful dragon warriors. The group grew in strength, able to put to rest any threat to the continent they all loved.

"However, the history of this continent and its Dragon Kin is also the history of Osiris, a man who sold his soul for power. It's unknown how he obtained this power or where it came from, but almost overnight, he upended the peace the Dragon Kin had worked so hard to build. In his grab for a power beyond most people's reckoning, he turned this continent upside down, rewriting its history in blood. The Dragon Kin were the only force with the potential to stop him. But for some reason, the people turned on them. Despite that, they managed to subdue Osiris, putting him to rest, but at great cost. A few of its members were found dead. The rest disappeared. The power they were entrusted with also vanished, leaving the continent vulnerable to any threat wishing to claim it." He closed his mouth, turning away like he was finished.

Redrinna wasn't sure she was breathing. The legends she'd heard before hadn't been anything like this one. Osiris had never been mentioned in any of them before. Neither had the power.

"What's the power you're talking about?" she asked, hoping that would convince him to keep going. "I've never heard of it before."

"I'm not surprised," he said, softly, like her question had made him sad. "Back then, the power was known as the Dragon Gems. Maybe you've heard of them?"

She shook her head, her gaze fixed on his face.

He smiled, but this one seemed like it was having a harder time reaching his eyes than any of his earlier ones. "I thought that might be the case. I don't think you're quite ready to learn about them, but I can tell you this: your friend was right. The gems, when they sense their power is needed, will hunt for individuals they think could be worthy of their power and mark them. Their mark expresses itself in the altering of the color of your hair and eyes. So the fact your hair and eyes are red means one of them, at some point, marked you."

She frowned. Some ancient power had marked her? Then why hadn't it been...she didn't know...more special?

"Don't believe me?"

"I never said that."

"It's all over your face," he said, almost smiling again. "All right, try this on for size: did something happen right before the change? It doesn't have to be big, per se, but important enough that you remember it."

Something from around the time when her appearance had changed? She'd still been a kid at the time, so most of her memories were patchy and worn out like an old quilt. But, her sixth birthday had been the time when she'd first tried (and choked) on fish. Her hair and eyes had changed sometime after that, she was pretty sure...

There was that one day. She didn't think about it often, and a chill raced over her skin as the memory played through her mind.

⚘ ⚘

Redrinna glanced at the little boy—son of the visiting noble—doing her best to keep a scowl off her cheeks since her mother had told her it wasn't a nice thing to do. Even still, she could feel the muscles in her face twisting of their own accord.

She'd seen the nobleman when he'd arrived and had been unable to keep herself from wondering how such a tiny, imp of a boy was related to such a large, heavyset man. The two were like a horse and an annoying horsefly. Even she was taller than the midget of a boy next to

132

her, though she supposed it wasn't much in the way of bragging rights; she was taller than every kid her age.

The boy (she couldn't remember his name anymore. It'd been Davi or Doru or something that sounded similar...maybe?) caught her staring at him and grinned, a wide, obnoxious grin that made the hairs on her neck stand on end.

"I bet I'm braver than you," he quipped, and she gave in to the scowl that had been threatening to take over since she'd laid eyes on him.

"I doubt that," she said. "If you were brave, maybe you'd be tall."

His cheeks flushed. "Height has nothing to do with being brave! Don't blame me for things beyond my control. But I am braver than you. Any day of the week."

She knew what game he was trying to play and refused to take the bait. Just because she was supposed to keep him entertained didn't mean she had to act like a love-struck puppy.

"I'll even prove it," he said, leaping to his feet and setting off down the hall. Rolling her eyes, she trailed after him, more because she'd get in trouble if he got lost than because she wanted to go with him.

He left the palace, hunkering behind some bushes on the grounds. He didn't say anything. They waited until a wagon passed by, heading towards the guard's gate. Ducking beneath the wagon, they used it to sneak out.

Once in the town, she itched to explore, but the boy she was keeping tabs on dove into the nearest alley. "Did you see that? I was pretty brave to sneak out here. If my dad had seen that, I would've been grounded."

Pursing her lips, she scowled at him.

It was his turn to scowl. "Fine. Let's keep going."

"Where are we going?" she asked, tucking her hands behind her back as they walked down the alley. That made her feel a bit like her dad.

"Does it matter? You're just going to follow me anyway."

She scowled again, but he was right. She'd be in trouble if he went missing, and he knew it.

They rounded a final corner, entering a dirty alley that made her skin crawl. Very human-like shadows hunkered in the doorways and corners, seeming to grow larger as the two of them stepped onto the street.

"We shouldn't be here," she hissed at him, falling a step behind.

"You scared?" he asked, flashing that obnoxious grin again.

"No," she said quickly. "But—"

"But nothing. Do you know what this place is?" he asked, stopping in the middle of the street. "This is the shadiest alley in the entire city. I heard my dad's knights talking about it. See, there's a rite of passage in my town where if you can walk the entire way down the scariest alley, then you become a man."

"Like magic? You're full-grown by the time you make it to the other end?"

"I don't know, that's just what they say."

"So what would that do to me? I'm not a boy and I don't want to suddenly turn into a man."

He stared at her for a long time—she could almost see the gears in his head grinding before he shrugged. "That's not important. Are you going to walk down the alley with me? Or are you too chicken?"

"You can't walk down the alley by yourself?" she asked, crossing her arms.

His cheeks flushed. "Fine! I'll do it first, then you can follow me." Spinning on his heel, he crashed right into a filthy, stocky man.

Redrinna's eyes went wide. Pale, almost translucent skin, snow-white hair, icy blue eyes—Korijin. The Korijin hated her family. It was written in the man's glare.

"What's a noble brat like you doing out here?" he said, his voice like ice scraping against itself. "Are you lost?"

"No, we're fine," the boy said hurriedly, taking a large step back, bumping into Redrinna. She shot him a glare, but then spied lots of other Korijin men slipping out of the shadows. Grabbing the boy's arm, she took a step back.

The man took a giant step forward, towering over them despite how stocky he was. "Are you now? Do you know where you happen to be right now? No?"

Reaching out, he fingered a lock of Redrinna's then-brown hair, the smell of his hands making her flinch. Her tiny heart raced, frantic to escape back to the palace where her parents were. To safety.

"Do you know how much the pair of you would sell for, little blue bloods?"

Alarm bells clamored in her skull. Leaving the palace had been stupid, but since she'd gone along with it, it was up to her to get them back. Leaping forward, she kicked the man in the knee with all the strength she could muster. When he staggered back, she grabbed the little boy's hand and raced back up the alley. A couple of hands swiped at them, but being little and fast had its advantages.

Rocketing down the streets, she sensed the man and his friends hot on their heels, so she refused to stop. She didn't know the way back to the palace since she'd never been allowed to come here and she hadn't been paying attention before. But if they could find a busy street, maybe their pursuers would be intimated by all the people.

The sound of people struck her ears, and she shot towards it. Seconds later, they burst into the middle of a bustling street, a wagon flashing by with a loud rumble as people shouted all kinds of things. Pausing, she glanced over her shoulder. The Korijin man came straight for them. Without a thought, she leapt into the street. A monster of a horse reared, hooves flashing. The little boy tripped, crashing into her backside, sending them both to the ground.

Panicked shouts rang out as the horse reared again. Shoving the boy off, Redrinna grabbed him and dragged him away from the horse. A shadow fell over her, making her turn. The street went silent.

"Anyone moves, the brats get it," the Korijin man shouted, a knife flashing in his hand. Several Korijin encircled them, backs to them, but she kept her gaze focused on the one threatening them with a knife.

Dropping the boy, she grabbed a handful of crushed cobblestone and chucked it at the man's face. He flinched and swiped his knife at her, missing by only inches. Stumbling, she hit the ground. Scrambling to her feet, she stood over the tiny boy, arms out.

"Not one of you will touch him," she snarled.

"Bold words for a little blue," the man said, pressing his palm against one of his eyes. "I'd like to see you try and stop me from taking you and that boy." He shoved his knife away and reached for her, making her lean back, but she refused to stand down. Her heart thrashed against the confines of her chest like a bird trapped in a cage.

A roar echoed through the street. The Korijin man looked up.

Sun gleaming off his blade, her father leapt right at the man. Her eyes went wide. Her father was here?! Fighting? Chaos erupted around them, soldiers and Korijin alike leaping all over. She crouched next to the boy, her heart thrumming in terror at the blood splattering the cobblestones and her dad snarling like a wolf as he fought.

It ended in a matter of seconds, leaving her trembling like a leaf being tussled in the wind. Soldiers were leading away some of the men, carting away the rest. Then her father was there, wrapping her and the little boy in his arms.

"Are you two okay? None of them hurt you, did they?"

They both shook their heads, not speaking a word as they were taken back to the palace.

⚜ ⚜

Redrinna shivered, the silence between her and Timothon heavier than it had before. It'd been so long since she'd thought about that day. Regardless, she was sure the next morning had been the one where she'd woken with altered hair and eyes, the morning when her parents had stared at her with wide eyes before they'd never looked at her in quite the same way again. Less than a week later, Captain Brion had been assigned to her.

Moreover, remembering how her father had dived into the midst of the mob, just to protect her, made the turmoil inside her worse. He'd risked his life to save hers. He could've died. So did that mean if she hadn't been chosen, none of this would've happened in the first place? That her parents would still—

"Did you think of something?" Timothon asked, breaking her out of that downward spiral of thoughts.

"I tried to protect a little boy when I was a kid. People were trying to kidnap us," was all she said. She didn't want to think about it any more than that.

"That would be a valid reason to be marked." That sad expression of his melted away.

"What else can you tell me?" she asked.

To her surprise, he rose, shaking his head. "I think that's enough for tonight. I don't think you're ready to hear the rest of what I know yet."

She frowned, but a different thought popped into her head as he started walking away. Hurrying after him, she said, "Wait! Why did you get marked?"

Pulling up short, he turned back, eyes wide. "Me?"

She nodded. Before, she hadn't been sure, but now she was. Red probably wasn't his natural shade either.

He closed his eyes for a minute before shaking his head, a rueful smile twisting his mouth. "I wouldn't worry about that."

"Huh?"

"I know you won't get it, but I don't...I don't count." He turned away so she couldn't see his face. "Anyway, I wouldn't stay up too much longer if I were you. If you want to know the rest of my story, then you need to show results in your training. You won't be able to do so without any sleep." Without another word, he left.

Frowning a bit more, she dipped her head. Why didn't Timothon think he counted?

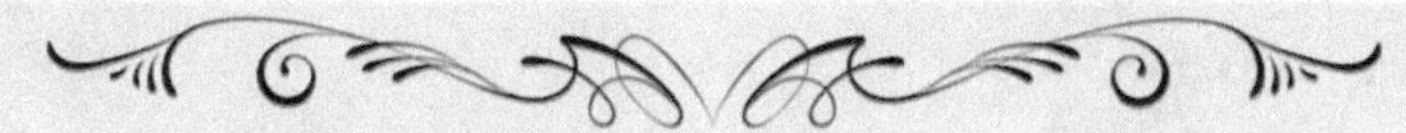

Chapter Thirteen

Redrinna went back to bed as Timothon had insisted, but her mind refused to relax. Timothon's story about the Dragon Kin hadn't made her any less freaked out, but what he'd said about the Dragon Gems... That had caught her attention.

According to him, one of those gems had seen her, seen the moment when she'd tried to protect somebody, and thought she might be strong enough to wield its power. That she wasn't some kind of failure or mistake. If she could get a little stronger, if she could claim a gem and it's power, she wouldn't keep needing someone to protect her.

Joining the Dragon Kin might be worth it if she could just do that.

So, the next morning after nowhere near enough sleep, Redrinna went and found Timothon first thing. A bit to her surprise—though she probably shouldn't have been—he was baking bread in the kitchen yet again.

"You're up early," he said as he spotted her. "Or did you not go to sleep?"

"I did sleep. A little. Anyway, I wanted to ask you something."

"Give me a second." Turning, he messed with something inside the oven. When he finished, he came and sat on one of the stools. "What's up?"

After a moment's hesitation, she sat on the next stool over. "It's about the Dragon Gems you mentioned. What do they do exactly? You said they choose people who could join the Dragon Kin, but what about after, when someone is chosen?"

He tilted his head to the side. "It's kind of difficult to explain since it depends on you, but from what I know, with a gem, a person could enhance their magic or increase their strength. A gem will protect you as much as it can, whether by warning you or releasing some power of its own."

She nodded. "If I could find one, would that prove I'm strong?"

Timothon hesitated, brow furrowing. "I guess that depends on what you think strong means. But, you're on the right track. Being able to claim a Dragon Gem would definitely prove you're strong."

"Then I just need to train harder, right? If I do—"

"Hold on," he said, lifting a hand. "The strength we're talking about here isn't necessarily physical. This strength is more the strength you've already got inside you."

The strength inside her? Doubt wheedled into her mind. She didn't know if she had anything like that. But one of those gems had marked her, so there had to be something inside her somewhere, right?

"How would I find one?" Redrinna wanted to prove her strength. If she could find a gem, she'd be able to take on the giant. She wouldn't have to keep running.

Shaking his head, Timothon spun on his stool to face her. "Woah there! You don't slow down at all, do you? That's a massive step. You're skipping a few—"

"I can do it," she said, shoving her doubts aside. She had to do this, regardless of what he thought about it. Joining the Dragon Kin wasn't something she wanted, but the gem was. "Just tell me how."

"You're not going to listen to me, are you?"

"I can do this," she repeated, staring him dead in the eye. "I have to, or else I'll—the past is going to haunt me forever." If she couldn't overcome the giant, if she couldn't leave the memories of the palace behind, how would she keep going forward?

"Redrinna," he whispered, something about the way he did making her pause. "Do you remember that secret I mentioned?"

"You mean the one about the Dragon Gems?"

"No. The one about your empire."

Her heart shuddered. She'd done her best to forget he'd said that.

"I'd rather keep it to myself. But I think you need to hear it. There's something you need to understand because this isn't a game. This is serious."

"I know that," she said, trying to keep her unease at bay. Of course she knew this was serious. "I'm not playing around. I know getting a gem means joining the Dragon Kin. It means fighting." It would mean fighting her father. She understood that.

"It's not that simple." Timothon closed his eyes. "You remember what I told you last night?"

Hesitant now, she nodded.

"Do I need to remind you that the last Dragon Kin died? They didn't even finish their mission."

"What?" He hadn't said that last night. His story...it'd seemed like they'd won, but at the cost of their lives.

Rubbing the side of his head, he sighed. "I didn't want to do this yet, but, I think it's time for me to tell you your Empire's history." He opened his eyes, lifting his gaze to meet hers. A bit of fire flickered in his red eyes, making her insides shrivel up. "The look on your face tells me this isn't what you wanted to hear, but I think you need to."

Nausea flexed its claws in her stomach.

"At the time in question, the Empire didn't exist and your home was still a little mountain country. The ruler was King Landore."

That was vaguely familiar.

"He was loved by all his subjects and his children. But an illness swept through the country, and he was one of its many victims. He left three children behind: a daughter and two sons.

"His daughter ascended to the throne, since she was the oldest. The next oldest, the first prince, was called to be a member of the Dragon Kin, leaving the third child, the second prince, in both of their ever-growing shadows. For a long time, a war had been threatening the borders of Eridia, and that was accelerated by the Queen's ascension to the throne. With the Dragon Kin's help, that war was subdued, and the people thought it was an era of peace.

"But, Osiris, the new ruler of the nation that had lost the war with Eridia—and that man who sold his soul for power—corrupted the heart of the second prince, taking his soul and twisting him into a monster. With his help and the help of another queen, Osiris launched an assault on the dragon race. That was the catalyst for the Dragon War. The second prince declared war on his own kingdom and every dragon on the continent.

"By some foul trick, he managed to turn the people of that kingdom—almost overnight—on their queen, the Dragon Kin, and the dragons. After that, the queen," Timothon squeezed his eyes shut, his face twisting like someone had stabbed him through the heart, "was executed by her youngest brother."

Redrinna's heart shuddered. That was similar to what had happened with her and her parents. Betrayed by family.

"The first prince and the Dragon Kin fought to their last breaths to end the bloodshed and the mass slaughtering of the dragon race. In the end, all they could do was shatter Osiris' power, make him so weak he had to retreat, but he survived. For that Dragon Kin, all was lost. They failed. People searched everywhere for them once Osiris retreated, but all they ever found were a few broken bodies."

Timothon glanced at her, a fire smoldering in his eyes again. "Since then, with the help of the second prince, Osiris's power still seeps through the ground, writing the history of this continent in blood, waging war after war in order to create the Empire you know. The one you were born to rule."

Redrinna's breath caught in her throat, her stomach clenching like it was getting ready to hurl. None of this was the history she was familiar with. But at the same time, given her recent experiences, this history made a frightening amount of sense.

"Eventually, the second prince had a change of heart. Rumors say it's because his sister lectured him with her last words, her strength piercing his twisted soul with the light he'd been starved of. Regardless of the reason, it's because of him there are still a few dragons alive and scattered across the continent in hiding, like Xandrin. And as far as I know, the second prince is the only soul on this continent who knows where they are to this day."

Would that...explain why the history books had painted dragons as demons? Was that a remnant of the Dragon War? Wouldn't that explain why Xandrin wasn't anything like Redrinna had expected him to be? If most dragons had been good and kind like Xandrin before being turned on, that would explain why history had—

"Wait," she said, turning fully towards him, her heart fluttering weakly, trying to stop her from asking the question on her tongue. "You said the second prince *knows* where the rest of the dragons are, implying he's still alive. How is that even possible? He'd have to be over one hundred years old—"

Timothon's gaze slowly turned towards her, the fire there making her throat clam up. "He would be, wouldn't he? Remember when I told you Osiris traded his soul for a power we can't even begin to comprehend? One of the effects of such power taking root in your body is longevity, the kind that makes you stay young and ageless for a very, very long time. So, yes, the second prince *knows* where all the dragons are hiding. Renoan still *knows* what he did with all the dragons."

Redrinna knew that name. She knew it very, painfully well. A terrible, excruciating thought pierced her mind. She shook her head from side to side, Timothon's unblinking gaze making her want to vanish into the ground and never come back out.

Without her meaning it to, the word 'Dad' slipped out of her mouth. The fear trickling inside her roared like a flood that had just broke through its dam. Timothon's red gaze didn't move from her face, the look there confirming her fear with the decisiveness of a judge's gavel being slammed down.

"Renoan...is my father's name," she whispered, fear digging its icy claws into her throat. "And he's the Emperor of Eridia. He...he can't be the same one who did... It can't be."

But Lady Cel Tradat had said her father wanted to stop the Dragon Kin's return. Was that because he was afraid of what would happen if they came back, if he had to fight them again? Yet, if that had been his goal all along, why hadn't he killed her as a child? If he'd hidden the last of the dragons, why would he start trying to undo it all?

On the other hand, he had tried to kill her. Or had he? The more time that passed, the more she doubted it. After all, if her parents had wanted her dead, why had they seemed so sad? Why had they made her make that promise first? Why bother making her vow to protect their people at all costs if she was just going to die a minute later? Had it been an act?

To top it off, her father had taken an active part in raising her, something she knew many royals and nobles alike didn't do. He'd taught her how to read, write, do math, science—all of it—by himself. There'd never been any tutors brought in to teach her. How could someone like that be the same person Timothon painted for her? How could he have killed his own siblings?

"Redrinna, I know it's hard, but think. Do you know when your father came into power? Do you know anyone who can remember a time when he wasn't ruling?"

Her heart shuddered at the thought. She'd never met her grandparents. She had no aunts, uncles, or cousins, not even on her mother's side. Never heard about any of them, ever, not once in her childhood. Her mind stopped, not wanting to comprehend the look in those scorching red eyes.

Timothon mercifully looked away. "I'm sorry to be the one to tell you this, Redrinna, but you can see the truth, can't you? The man who you call father...Renoan? He is the second prince, the one who wanted power and attention so badly he destroyed his own family and slaughtered thousands of innocent people."

Her heart stopped beating. At the very least, she couldn't feel it beating. Her father shoving her in the hole made perfect sense from how Timothon described him.

But it didn't add up. It never had and this made it worse. He'd been strict, but never cruel. Stern, but compassionate. Not the best advice giver, but he'd always listened to her. And he loved her mother. Redrinna had seen enough evidence of that, enough of the moments they carved from their busy and dangerous lives to be together, that she had no doubt how they felt about each other.

The person Timothon described though, he was a tyrant. In that light, she could see the murderer. A part of her could imagine he'd even killed his own children. But the man she knew wasn't the same. Even though he'd tried to hide it, she knew every time one of her siblings had died, for each one of his other children, he'd grieved. It'd been quieter, harder to see than her mother's, but she'd known, even as a child, he'd been devastated every single time.

And again, if he'd truly thrown her in a cave to die, why had he seemed so upset? Why had he told her he loved her? Better yet, of all the caves he could've chosen, why one with a dragon, something only he would have known?

"And I," Timothon continued, more crestfallen than he'd been any moment prior, "I am the one who couldn't save his older sister from being murdered. I couldn't save any of my friends or my people, not even my own little brother."

Lightning rocketed down Redrinna's spine as she understood. It was so obvious. His name was Timothon. One of the tapestries back at the palace had featured King Timothon—with a dragon. It'd never occurred to her he could've been part of the Dragon Kin, but it made perfect sense. It explained why last night he'd said he didn't count.

"You're the first prince, aren't you?"

"I am." He bowed his head like she'd given him a death sentence. "I am the prince and king who failed to save a kingdom I swore to protect. Because of my failure, it no longer even exists. Because of me, the Dragon Gems couldn't protect the continent and are lost."

"Wait," she said, realizing something that made her feel like she'd eaten something rancid. "You...you're dead? But if you're dead, how can you be...?"

"This is why I need you to understand how serious this is and not chase after it on a whim. When a gem accepts you, it binds itself to your soul until its mission is over. The gems didn't complete their mission, so even though I died, I'm still trapped here, powerless to do anything but watch."

So if Redrinna got the gem, and then failed or died, she wouldn't just be letting down thousands of people, but she'd been trapped here, an aimless spirit until a third Dragon Kin was found. Or the world ultimately ended. A very, very real feeling of panic settled in her chest.

However, at the same time, something else occurred to her. "So, this means you're my uncle, doesn't it?"

The startled expression on Timothon's face made her feel bad for asking. "Do you really want to think of someone like me as your uncle?"

When he put it like that, she didn't know what to say that wouldn't make the situation worse. Not to mention she didn't feel capable of giving any sort of encouragement.

"So, you're telling me this because me chasing after a gem is foolish?"

"No. A gem marked you as one who can potentially inherit its power. It's fine if you want to go after it, but make sure you're completely ready before you do," Timothon said, shaking his head before turning to face her so abruptly she nearly fell off her stool. "As a king who failed his own kingdom, I have no right to ask this of you, Redrinna, but please. Please, claim the Dragon Gem's power and save this land. I want you to be sure before you commit, but please. With you alive, there is still a chance to stop Osiris and your father and save your empire."

Her Empire? No, no, no. Joining the Dragon Kin was one thing, but this was another. Shaking her head so hard she actually fell off her stool, red hair partially obscuring her vision, she barely managed to keep from falling to the ground. "I-I can't promise that, Timothon. I'm so sorry, but I can't."

Everything Redrinna touched turned to ruin, even though she always wanted to convince herself of the contrary. She'd never been able to do something right or protect herself. That's why she'd had a bodyguard, and a knight had gotten hurt saving her life. It's why without Xandrin, she'd already be dead or captured.

"You can't?" he asked, eyes narrowing. "If you couldn't, the gem never would've marked you, Redrinna. Besides, even without the gem, you have an obligation to the people who bow their heads to you—"

"They're not my people!" she said, hands bunching into fists, her heart racing a hundred miles an hour in an attempt to escape her chest. "I'm not going back to the Empire because they hate me. Nobody wants me anyway!" Unbidden, the panic from servants at the mere sight of her sprang to mind, swiftly followed by the fire burning in the rebel's eyes as he'd flashed his blade, seconds from taking her life.

Timothon stared at her like she'd smacked him across the face. Then he sighed. "Listen to me. You are overreacting, and I need you to think for a minute. Until a few minutes ago, I was the only person, besides your father, who knew about what is happening, but I'm stuck here in these mountains, and even then, I'm a spirit. A ghost. However, you can do something now that you know. If you decide to do nothing about it, do you think you could convince anyone to do anything in your place?"

Backing away from him, Redrinna shook her head, darkness gathering on the edges of her vision. The entire rooming tilted like she was in some sick dream world. She couldn't breathe, she couldn't think, forget coherent thoughts. She wasn't going to go back to being a princess or the palace, to any part of her past, no matter what he said! Not even for a Dragon Gem!

Timothon grabbed her wrist, saying something she couldn't hear over the fear roaring in her skull. Jerking back, she banged her head against the door frame before turning to run. Xandrin was there, his scales closer to the dry pink of a dying rose than their normal smoky red, and she almost crashed into him. Panic flared through her chest at the thought of being trapped in here. She couldn't do this again. She couldn't.

Desperate now, she pushed past him, bolting to her room like a mouse racing for its hole with a cat on its heels.

Once there, Redrinna frantically searched for somewhere to hide, somewhere Timothon wouldn't be able to find her. After a second, she scrambled beneath her bed, pressing herself as far back as she could.

Tears blurred her vision, soaking her cheeks in a cry for relief that wouldn't come. Her red hair fell into her sight, a vivid reminder of everything Timothon had just said. She didn't want it. She didn't want the gem anymore. She didn't want to be here. Timothon, her uncle, had died because of this.

All at once, an even worse fear constricted her chest. Timothon had said she'd be safe from the giant as long as she stayed here. If she refused to join, would he turn them out? How long would she last out there without a Dragon Gem?

Grabbing fistfuls of her hair, she was tempted to rip it out. But that was stupid. It wouldn't change anything.

Even still...Redrinna had been chosen. A gem had thought she was strong, and she still wanted to prove she was. But if she got it, if she joined the Dragon Kin, she'd be on the front lines in a war. She'd have to fight her father.

Despite what he'd done and what Timothon had told her, she still loved him. A lot. Enough that her heart ached and she wanted to be little again and crawl in between her parents while they slept. When they'd woken up, they'd always stayed until she had too, even though she knew they must've had important things to do. She'd stared up into their brown eyes, and for a while, hers had matched.

Until they hadn't.

Redrinna wanted things to go back to the way they were. She wanted her parents back. She wanted to forget all of this and pretend it'd never happened.

Chapter Fourteen

Redrinna woke because of a violent sneeze, startling herself enough she nearly started crying again. What was she? Six? The next moment, she spied Xandrin's snout resting on the ground about a foot from her bed. What was he doing there?

"Are you awake yet, Redrinna?" he asked softly, making her heart jolt like it had been the one to wake itself up by sneezing.

"What are you doing?" she asked, her nose plugged from falling asleep amid several layers of dust she hadn't noticed when she'd crawled under her bed.

"Waiting for you." He shifted, scales rubbing against the floor. "You missed breakfast and lunch. I was really worried about you."

She curled into a tight ball, not wanting to think about that morning at all. Not a single part of it. "You don't have to do that."

"Why not? Isn't that what friends do? Did I mess that part up?"

Oh, Xandrin. Sighing, she dragged herself half out from under the bed. "No...that wasn't what I meant. You got that part right, I think."

Blinking his big, dark eyes, he lifted his head a little. He still had a bit of that ashy tinge clinging to his scales. "You look so sad. But you're training, right? You're getting stronger so we can fight that giant? Isn't this what you wanted?"

Her heart slipped out of her chest and buried itself beneath her toes when she thought about how much she'd have to explain for him to understand. "Xandrin, the thing is, I wasn't honest when we first met. I'm so sorry. But, I'm not just Redrinna. I...I'm supposed to be the one who leads all my people. That someone I told you about? The ones who tried to kill me? They were my parents. My parents tried to kill me, and I decided hiding with you was better than going back to a life I didn't want anyway."

"Oh," he breathed, blinking those eyes, those two endless pools that had never, not even now, made her feel like he didn't care about her. Haltingly, she summarized what Timothon had told her, trying to explain everything in as few words as possible.

"You know what this means?" Redrinna whispered, tears on the verge of falling again. "If I join the Dragon Kin, I have to go back. I'll have to fight my father. I know what he did was wrong, but I just—he wasn't like that in all the time I've known him. Not until he tried to kill me. If I go back, I won't just have to fight him, but people will expect me to take over that awful Empire. I can't. I can't handle it anymore."

He frowned at the floor for a long time before he said, "If you join the Dragon Kin, I will too. If you don't, I won't. I'll never force you to do something like this, not ever. I promise I'll be right with you, no matter where you go, Dragon Kin or no. If your father wants to hurt you again, I won't let him touch you. I won't let anyone hurt you. I swear it."

Her tears fell without her permission. Why couldn't he ever just be mad at her? She'd feel a lot better if he would. "Xandrin, I..."

"Besides, all he said was that you had to save the Empire. You don't have to rule it. You don't have to ever go back to it if you don't want to. If people try and make you, I'll fly you somewhere far away where they won't ever find you."

A glimmer of life beat in her chest. She knew Xandrin was no liar. "You'd do that for me? Even though I lied to you?"

"Yeah," he said, stretching forward and touching her forehead with his snout, his hot breath ruffling her hair, stirring up the dust she'd accumulated. "To me, you were doing the best you could do. You're confused and hurt. I'm not going to abandon you because of something like that."

Her heart nearly melted, but instead, it decided to crawl back to its place in her chest. There was no way she could rule the Empire, but maybe Xandrin was right. Ruling it and saving it didn't mean the same thing. If Xandrin was with her, then maybe it wouldn't be so scary.

Swiping at her eyes, she dragged herself the rest of the way out from under her bed. "I guess...I can try. As long as you're with me, right?"

That won her a grin from him.

◈◈◈

Timothon seemed more tired than he had earlier when Redrinna and Xandrin found him again. He was still in the kitchen, sitting on the same stool, staring at the same wood table like it could give him an answer. He jumped when they entered, looking as guilty as a kid caught with the ball that had shattered the window.

His brow wrinkled as he rose and approached her. Gently, he tugged a cobweb out of her hair, watching it drift to the ground before speaking. "Were you hiding under your bed or something?" His voice was so soft Redrinna almost couldn't hear him.

"Timothon," she began, not sure if her voice was any louder than his had been, "I'm sorry. For how I reacted. I'm sure it wasn't easy for you to tell me. And I pushed you, so it's my fault."

A sigh started to escape him, but he cut it off. "I told you too soon. And with the intent of making you unsettled and slow down, but instead, I made you distressed. So, I'm sorry too."

Shaking her head, Redrinna said, "I know it's difficult and things could go wrong, but I still...I want to try and find a gem. The giant isn't going to stop chasing me because I hide."

"Are you sure?" He stepped back, his gaze flicking to Xandrin for a second. "If you do manage to convince the gem you're worthy, there'll be no going back. You will be stuck in this mess as much as I am."

Her thoughts turned back to the moment she'd thrown her necklace into the pool in Xandrin's cave, and by extension, the promise she'd made. Retrieving the necklace was impossible, but maybe the promise she'd abandoned was not. All she had to do was protect the Empire—protect its people, not lead it. That would mean keeping her promise while keeping her out of a life she didn't want.

"I am sure," she said after a minute. Xandrin touched her hand with his snout. "I thought before that attempting to do this would mean I'd have to be a princess again, but I jumped to conclusions. I won't promise to rule this country or put myself in a position to do so, but I will promise to try my hardest to keep it from being destroyed more than it is. I-I think I can handle that."

Timothon's mouth opened like he was going to say something else, but it slowly closed as he stared at the floor. "All right. For now, you should eat and keep up on your training. Focus on getting stronger."

⁕ ⁕ ⁕

Xandrin shifted beneath Redrinna, waking her. She remained still, her eyes cracked open, before spotting a slim ray of sunshine peeking through the entrance of the dragon's room. It must have been coming from the window she'd discovered in her room. It'd been a while since she'd been outside the Mount and in the sun.

All at once, her conversation with Timothon bubbled to the surface of her mind, chasing out any trace of sleep. Everything about it still scared her and she didn't want to think about it, although she couldn't help it. Even still, Redrinna wanted to prove she was strong enough to claim one of the gems. Even if Lady Cel Tradat never saw it, just proving it to herself would be enough. Maybe Xandrin would even let her help him a bit more instead of treating her like she'd fall apart if the wind blew too hard.

Timothon's story made her think of something that had never occurred to her before. For the first time, she wondered just how involved her mother had been in plotting her attempted murder. Did her mother even know what her father had done in the past? Or was she another victim?

After a while of trying to sort through the thoughts crowding in on her, Redrinna gave up and got up. She considered leaving Xandrin behind, but they'd barely spent time together yesterday and she wanted to make up for it. Facing him, she gave him a quick jab in the side. He snorted and twisted onto his side, legs flailing, his eyes snapping open. After a moment, he spotted her.

"Wha-what—"

She bit the inside of her cheek to keep from laughing. "Are you hungry?"

His eyes closed as his head drooped back to the floor, but Xandrin pushed himself up anyway. "Okay," he said before opening his jaws in a massive yawn. He staggered forward a few steps, his eyes seeming desperate to stay closed.

It dawned on her she'd never seen him awake this early. "You're not much of a morning dragon, are you?"

He yawned in response.

She left the room, Xandrin trailing behind her as she headed towards the dining room. It seemed early, earlier than usual. Just how early in the morning was it anyway?

Nobody was in the dining room so, after leaving Xandrin there, Redrinna headed to the kitchen. To her surprise, and a bit to her relief, Timothon was there, already baking his bread. Wait, he wasn't just Timothon anymore. He was her uncle. She'd never had an uncle before. Was there something special she should do or say?

He turned, jumping when he saw her. "Hey," he began, almost unsure of himself. "How are you feeling today? Any better?"

After a minute of second-guessing, she nodded. "I am. Also, I have another question for you."

"Another one?"

"Yesterday, you mentioned a queen who sided with Osiris. I got so caught up in the other details I forgot to ask about her. Is there...anything else you can tell me about her?" Redrinna wasn't sure why she wanted to know, but she was curious regardless. After all, the history books had hardly mentioned any of the things Timothon had told her, especially this queen, and she'd rather know as much as she could if she was going to go through with this.

"Her?" His mouth hung open for a moment before he shut it and looked away. He stayed quiet for several minutes.

Had she brought up something painful? She should've thought before she'd said anything. Hurriedly, she said, "I'm sorry if you don't want to talk about it."

"No, it's not that." Timothon waved a hand. A big sigh rushed out of him. "It's a fair question, so I'll give you a fair answer. Her name was Reyna."

"Reyna?" Redrinna repeated. That queen Lady Cel Tradat had often told her stories of had had the same name. Was that just a coincidence?

"Yeah. She was a queen from a southern land that fell in with Osiris after her kingdom was taken from her. Honestly, she was nothing short of terrifying. The damage she could do on her own—even if she was very disadvantaged—was unreal. It was a nightmare." A shudder shook him, tugging on her heartstrings.

His Reyna sounded an awful lot like Lady Cel Tradat's. They couldn't be the same person, could they?

"She isn't the one who...who...you know." Redrinna made nonsensical gestures with her hands, not wanting to say it out loud.

Shaking his head, Timothon said, "No. Osiris did that with his own hands, not her. But...she was the one who killed my dragon, Amaris. I just—" Another shudder cut him off, and he turned back to the oven.

Oh. Now she felt horrible for asking about it at all. If something like that happened to Xandrin, she'd— A shudder shook her. She didn't know if she could take that. All the more reason she needed to get stronger.

"Sorry," she said. He didn't respond, and she hoped that was because he hadn't heard her.

They didn't speak again until after the bread finished baking and they were in the dining room with Xandrin, who was fast asleep once more. After Redrinna had begun eating their usual breakfast of bread and fruit, Timothon plopped in the chair to her right and leaned forward, watching her with an unblinking stare. She stopped chewing.

"I've been thinking of something you could do to make sure you're ready for your gem," he said.

She finished chewing the food in her mouth and swallowed. "What do you mean?"

"Well, I've been trying to think up a task for you to do, something that'll help you prove to the gem that marked you that you're strong enough to claim it like you want. So I'm thinking you should take a test."

"A test? Are you serious?" Redrinna went still like that would make her invisible so he wouldn't be able to see her anymore. How was taking some test supposed to help her out? She wouldn't have agreed to this if she'd known he was going to be giving her a mystery test. Well, maybe.

He nodded. "That's right. I think that's the perfect way to make sure you're really ready for this."

"What kind of test will it be?"

"I haven't worked it all out yet, so I'm not telling." He flashed her a grin she did not appreciate. "We'll get you started on it tomorrow, but in the meantime, all you have to do is keep up on all those sword moves I've been teaching you. If you don't, I won't ever let you take my test."

❧ ❧

"Wait, you want me to take the test today? Like, right now?"

Timothon nodded, an annoying grin fixed to his face. "I did say we'd get started today, didn't I? That's what we talked about yesterday, isn't it?"

"Well, it is," Redrinna began, glancing around the entrance hall for a second while she tried to think of how to explain herself. "But I didn't think you were serious about doing it so soon."

"I didn't want to stress you out, and I came up with the test much faster than I thought I would anyway," he said. He shot a glance towards the hall where her and Xandrin's rooms were. "As soon as that dragon friend of yours is ready, we can go get started. Aren't you excited?"

It was a little harder to swallow. Her parents had never given her tests, so she had no idea what she should expect from this. "How long will it take, do you think?"

"A month."

"A month?!"

"Yep, but don't worry. I promise to take good care of Xandrin while you're busy."

What kind of test was she taking?

Xandrin dragged himself into the room, looking like he was either half-asleep or miserably ill. That did very little to boost her confidence. She and Timothon climbed onto his back (Timothon did so with much more grace than she'd expected) and they left the Mount, launching into the sky. Instantly, Redrinna fell in love with flying all over again.

They flew over a few mountain peaks and an enormous carpet of forest before they descended into a small meadow. When they landed, Redrinna spotted a massive, lone tree in the center of the clearing. Its trunk was gnarled and twisted in a way that made her picture a dragon rearing on its hind legs. It had no leaves she could see, and its bark shone a pale, bone white.

"This is where you will take your test," Timothon said, motioning for her to disembark.

"Here?" Redrinna asked, her heart getting smaller by the second once her feet hit the ground. "W-what am I supposed to do?"

He smiled. "Don't worry; it'll be simple. All you have to do is survive out here in the wild for one month."

She blinked in surprise. "That's it?"

"That's it. Think you can handle it? You've got that knife of yours and everything?"

She turned slightly so he could see it hanging from her belt. "I've got it."

"All right," he said, glancing upwards before his head jerked towards her. "Oh, a word of caution. You mentioned before someone was chasing after you, which is why I brought you here specifically. I'm not going to bother explaining, but stay near the tree and this meadow. Also practice your basic sword stances while you're here. If you don't improve, you're going to be doing drills until you wish your arms would fall off."

Her insides twisted. Timothon nudged Xandrin, but the dragon's gaze was fixed on her. He let out a tiny whine, his claws digging into the earth. Trying to smile encouragingly, Redrinna rubbed a hand over his snout. Words clogged her throat, so she didn't try to speak. After another minute, Timothon coaxed him back into the sky, though he kept glancing back. She made sure to wave until she couldn't see his brilliant redness anymore.

"Don't worry about me," she breathed. "I will take care of myself this time." Doubt coiled in her stomach but she tried to convince herself she believed those words. She couldn't quite do it, but she kept trying.

Turning, Redrinna studied the clearing, taking in her new surroundings. Morning sunlight gilded half of the clearing, making the greens brighter and more vivid while the shadows were deep but inviting. The trees towering over her looked so similar to all the pines, aspens, and beeches that had decorated the mountains around Xandrin's cave that, for a moment, she almost thought she'd gone back. Tiny flowers of all colors swayed in the faint breeze, almost like they were dancing. It looked like spring had finally arrived in the mountains.

One month would be a long time. But, she didn't need to be too worried. She'd read plenty of books on nature and survival. All she had to do was apply that knowledge to the real world. Then she'd be able to earn the gem and get rid of the giant dogging her steps.

It couldn't be all that hard, could it?

For the rest of the morning and part of the afternoon, Redrinna fought to make a little lean-to for herself, just like all those books had shown her. She'd fantasized about running from the palace and living in the wild enough she had them memorized. It took several tries, but she eventually got it right. By then, the sun beat on her with all its strength, like it was trying to boil her to death. She'd worn her old clothes and cloak, which had been ideal for drafty caves, but not sunny forests. Redrinna shed her cloak and hid in the shade.

As she began cooling off, her throat itched with thirst. She listened for the sound of water, which she found to be incredibly difficult with all the birds twittering and the wind rustling the leaves. After several minutes, she managed to detect what she hoped was the sound of running water and moved towards it.

As she walked, Redrinna took note of landmarks—like the massive moss-covered stone and the tight cluster of aspens that almost looked like one enormous, ropey tree—so she could find her way back to the clearing. The last thing she wanted to do was get lost since Timothon and Xandrin might think she'd gotten herself killed or something. Or get far enough away from the clearing that the giant managed to find her again.

The river was farther away than Redrinna had expected, but relief rushed through her when she spotted it. The water rushed over the rocks, lapping at the shore, throwing spray high into the air. Lady Cel Tradat had always told her she was more likely to get sick from drinking standing water than from flowing water. The river moved so fast it was almost rushing, tumbling over itself in its haste. She took that as a good sign.

Kneeling at the water's edge, she cupped her hands and drank a few handfuls of the clear, bitingly cold water. She'd forgotten mountain water could be so cold.

For some time, she remained there, listening to the powerful rush of the water. It struck her that she should figure out how to carry water back to her shelter so she wouldn't have to walk so far every time she needed a drink. Timothon had warned her to stay near that funky-looking tree, and she didn't want to think about what would happen if the giant found her out here.

After a few minutes of thought, Redrinna gathered the largest leaves she could find and did her best to fold them together like her parents had shown her once.

As her fingers trailed over the leaves' smooth surfaces, she got lost in the memory of sitting in the garden and folding leaf bowls with her parents, both of them acquiring enormous grins when she held up the first successful one she'd made. She couldn't remember if that was before or after Captain Brion had been assigned as her personal knight, but either way, it'd been a long time ago. If she remembered right, it hadn't been too long after her mother's third child—her newborn baby brother, not even two days old yet—had been found lifeless one morning for no reason, or, at least, no reason anyone could explain.

Even now, all these years later, she hated thinking about what had happened to her siblings. Not a single one of them had even lived to be more than five days old.

After everything that had happened between her and her parents, she couldn't prevent the thought that maybe her parents had been involved somehow from creeping into her mind.

Just as swiftly as it had entered, Redrinna forced it back out. That didn't even make sense. If her parents had tried to murder her because of her potential link to the Dragon Kin, then why kill all her siblings too? Why keep having children just to kill them right away?

Closing her eyes, she shook those thoughts out of her head too.

After several tries, Redrinna managed to fold the leaves into a lop-sided bowl. Hoping it would hold, she dunked it in the river, filling it with as much water as it could carry.

Moving slower than she had before, she carried her water back to her shelter. The bowl's weight constantly shifted as she walked, requiring a lot of her focus to not splash it all over herself. The sun dipped closer to the horizon, reminding Redrinna that she hadn't eaten anything since the bread Timothon had given her that morning. Her stomach curled into a tight ball like an ant that had just been stepped on, making her wince.

Trying to be as careful as she could, Redrinna set the water under the shelter of her lean-to. If spring had arrived in the mountains, then she firmly believed there'd be some kind of berry or something for her to find.

If she didn't find something, she wondered how long she could survive without eating. That sounded miserable though, so she'd do her best to avoid it as much as she could.

The final task Redrinna gave herself for the day was to find a branch similar to the training sword she'd been using. If Timothon expected her to have the basics mastered, she'd have to work on it every single day, even if the thought alone drained her.

She practiced a little, but the further the sun crawled behind the mountains, the harder it became for her to see what she was doing. Not that she was sure she was doing any of it right to begin with.

As the sun vanished, Redrinna retreated beneath her shelter, watching the sun's dying rays cling to the sky like they didn't want to leave, leaving a trail of fiery orange in their wake. Too bad Xandrin wasn't here. He'd catch something for her to eat without a second thought. Maybe tomorrow she could try and figure out some of those traps the books had talked about? After all, she'd survived today with little incident. How hard could this be?

Chapter Fifteen

Redrinna jerked awake sometime during the night, her eyes taking a bit to adjust to the faint moonlight. For a moment, she couldn't figure out what had woken her up.

A shiver raced across her skin. Once it started, she couldn't get it to stop. When had it gotten so cold? She snuggled deeper into her cloak and lean-to, tired enough she didn't want to move and hoping that would be enough to keep her warm.

It quickly became apparent it would not. The books had never mentioned a lean-to would not keep one very warm. They also hadn't said what to do about staying warm in the middle of the night. Or that the nights in a mountain forest during early spring could be so frigid. She supposed she could build a fire, but she wasn't sure she wanted to risk using her magic to try that yet. She still had yet to learn a thing about magic, and the last thing she wanted was to repeat her mistake from before with the giant.

Timothon probably wouldn't be able to save her this time.

With a slight sigh, she rolled onto her back, forgetting her bowl of water lay under the lean-to with her until it was too late. Her elbow dipped into the frigid water, causing her to jerk her arm back, which dumped the rest of the water onto her side. Gasping, she bolted upright, smacking her forehead against the lean-to with a loud thunk. It didn't fall, but her eyes watered as she furiously rubbed her aching head.

With a resigned sigh, Redrinna scrubbed the sleep from her eyes, shivering harder now. She probably wasn't going to get back to sleep so long as she remained cold and wet. Maybe she should try building a trap? It might help her warm up a little.

She was hungrier than she'd been earlier. Enough so that nausea made her head swim a little as she got to her feet. Or maybe that was the exhaustion speaking.

She paused long enough to stretch, feeling stiffer than a fallen log. Trying to keep the drenched part of her clothes off her skin as much as possible, she turned to begin her search for materials, but her gaze was drawn to the star-speckled, inky darkness above. She'd read lots of poetry that had made the night sky out to be enchanting and romantic. However, as she stared at it, it left her feeling tiny and helpless. The stars twinkled, as they often did, but instead of something enchanting, it reminded her of ladies at court hiding their contempt behind their fluttering, silk fans. Frowning, she turned and stalked through the shadows of the trees so the stars wouldn't be able to see her.

By the time Redrinna had finished stumbling around gathering everything she'd thought she'd need, the sun was beginning to rise, a pale yellow smear on the horizon. Fighting a wave of irritation, she made a few, half-hearted attempts to craft a working trap. None of them worked.

The sun was halfway across the sky by the time she gave up. Shaking with fury and hunger, Redrinna tried to take a nap to make up for staying awake for half the night. However, it was far too hot now, no matter where she went. Abandoning the attempt at sleep, she tried to build another trap.

The sun beat a steady trail across the sky, heading for the western horizon. By the time the sun rested on the tops of the mountain peaks, Redrinna had managed to construct one working trap. A rush of pride shot through her, making her feel a little giddy. All she had left to do was find somewhere to set it.

She picked a spot a little far from her camp since she figured that was where more animals would be. It took her a few minutes to set it up, but once she had, she sat back, staring at it. A huge grin spread across her face. Couldn't take care of herself? She'd just set a trap.

As she rose to head back to her lean-to, her stomach churned, and her pulse pounded in her skull for a second. A painful reminder she hadn't eaten all day. After the feeling subsided, she dismissed the thought. Now that she had a trap, she'd be eating tomorrow. So no need to worry. In the meantime though, she hunted for some berries to munch on.

After a bit of searching, she found some ivy-like plants that still had some purple berries clinging to them. Most of the berries were shriveled, but there were a few good ones once she looked hard enough. Once she had a small handful, she considered setting some aside for later, but her stomach churned again, making her light-headed for almost a full minute. She ate them all at once.

The second the juice exploded on her tongue, she regretted putting these berries in her mouth. They were so terribly bitter, like eating dirt. Or rocks. Or something so gross your tongue kind of goes numb. But she was famished, so she swallowed them all before racing to the river to drink the taste away.

⚜

Redrinna had been expecting to wake up the second night, but she hadn't been prepared for her stomach to ache like a draft horse had stomped on it. She also hadn't expected to find her mouth as dry as burnt wood and pulsing with a sharp ache. Rolling onto her side, she intended to go back to sleep. However, the instant she shifted, a stabbing sensation shot through her stomach, the strong urge to vomit following close on its heels.

Scrambling onto her hands and knees, she just managed get out from under the lean-to before she threw up. It hurt a lot. More than she thought it had ever hurt before. Afterwards, the pain in her stomach didn't go away. If anything, it got worse.

Crawling away from her lean-to, she made it to the edge of the clearing before she vomited again.

The berries she'd eaten, they must've been poisonous. That was the only explanation she could think of. She'd been so hungry she hadn't even bothered to check. Berating herself, she hunched into a ball, trying to will the pain away.

The vomiting turned to dry-heaving as the night wore on. Neither it nor the terrible pain in her stomach and face receded until morning. Her stomach was an empty void that pulsed with a dull ache.

The only other time Redrinna had gone this long without food, she'd been unconscious for most of it. She'd eaten shortly after waking, so she hadn't had to feel this. Even then, she hadn't eaten poisonous berries and become horribly ill.

Redrinna struggled to get to her feet; she'd never felt so weak. Her body had never been so heavy, so taxing. Slowly, she shook her head, finding it difficult to focus on anything but what was right in front of her without starting to teeter.

Once she had her balance, she headed back towards the river. Maybe some water would help? Her mouth was still bone-dry like it was stuffed with wool.

By the time Redrinna managed to find the water, her legs were so spent they dumped her at the water's edge, the spray striking her face eventually coaxing her back up. Her hands trembled as she dipped them into the water. Somehow, she managed to drink it, making her dry mouth pasty. Her stomach was okay for a second. Then it clenched so hard she doubled over.

It hurt so much a small whine managed to escape her. Redrinna didn't know how much time passed with her hunched over—oblivious to anything but the hot-iron pain twisting in her gut—before she managed to get back onto her feet. She needed to go check on the trap. Now.

Desperation gave her the strength to move. With any luck, she'd managed to catch something that could end this nightmare.

Once she'd stumbled across the trap, Redrinna almost burst with pride and cried in relief at the same time. She'd caught something! It was a little, brown rabbit. Its paws were tied together, just like they should have been. She'd done it right! Taking a deep breath, she extracted the rabbit from its cage, leaving its legs tied. It took both of her hands to hold on to it; it squirmed more than Xandrin did when she woke him up.

After a few minutes of fighting it, she managed to pull out the knife Lady Cel Tradat had given her. The rabbit stilled as the metal blade flashed in the light of the rising sun. Redrinna readied her knife. She'd never done this before nor had she ever wanted to, but desperation made her willing to try. Her gaze met the rabbit's. Its big, brown eyes glistened, making it look ready to cry. Its nose quivered.

Immediately, she knew she'd made a mistake. She froze.

The rabbit trembled beneath her hand, making it hard to swallow. She needed to eat, but her arm refused to move.

What was she thinking? She couldn't do this. This was why she hated fighting and violence. She had to let it go.

As she moved to put the knife away, she froze again. All at once, it became a terrifying reality that if she didn't eat she would die. She needed food. If not now then soon. She hadn't eaten for nearly two whole days and she'd accidentally poisoned herself. Her books had drilled into her people could starve to death within a week in dire circumstances. Or be so weak, they'd die from something else.

Tears of absolute frustration pricked her eyes while she sat frozen. Why had she agreed to this stupid test in the first place?! She should've figured something like this would happen and she'd mess everything up like always.

All of the sudden, a red fox darted out of the woods and nicked the rabbit from her, passing so close its fur brushed her face. That spurred her into action.

"Hey!" Redrinna snarled, jumping to her feet and racing into the woods after it. It was fast, but she was hungry. Branches whapped her face, but the sting in her cheeks paled in comparison to the pain twisting in her stomach like a knife.

She skidded to a stop as she found the fox. It had already killed the rabbit and was busy feeding it to an energetic bunch of baby foxes. Kits, she was pretty sure they were called. She couldn't take their meal. Even if she'd been brave enough to try, she wouldn't have anyway.

She released a long sigh as her sharp hunger nestled deeper into her stomach. Turning on her heel, she spent most of the morning in a blur, trying to find her way back to her camp. She somehow ended up where she wanted to be, but she didn't remember walking there.

Once she'd made it, it took her the rest of the day to build a second trap. Before she could finish, she found herself lying on her side. After a minute, she tried pushing herself up, but her arms lacked any strength. Her stomach had gone numb; she could no longer feel any pain. It was replaced with a haze, a fog shrouding her brain.

Somewhere, she'd heard there was a difference between living and surviving. It struck her as she lay helplessly on her side that by surviving, it meant just staying alive. Doing whatever it took to not die. Maybe being reckless, but not acting like a fool.

It would be an awful time for the giant to find her.

She'd been so stupid.

Redrinna's throat burned with the desire to cry, but tears refused to form. Hunger and poison had not only taken her strength, but they'd stolen her only release from the anger and frustration pent up inside her. She wished Xandrin were here. Captain Brion. Lady Cel Tradat. Timothon. Even her parents.

Or to just go home, even though she didn't know where that was anymore.

Black gathered on the edges of her vision. Time began to skip, and she couldn't figure out whether she was awake or not. Had her siblings felt something like this before they'd died? This nothingness? Would they have understood what they were feeling was wrong and they were in trouble? At the rate things were going, she'd be able to ask them herself.

Eventually, her thoughts shut off, her eyes closed, and the darkness swallowed her.

◈ ◈

The next time she was aware her eyes were open, night had fallen. Redrinna drifted in and out of sleep, sometimes because she was cold—but couldn't do anything about it—other times, because her body had become stiff and needed to move, a problem that sapped her of her strength whenever she figured out what to do about it.

Later, when the sun was shining through the trees, Redrinna woke in a hazy state. Everything seemed distant, almost unreal. She was no longer aware of the passing of time. All she knew was, for now, she lived. When that would end, she didn't know.

Gradually, Redrinna became aware of a presence nearby. Someone was watching her. Gathering what little energy she had left, she opened her eyes and looked. A pair of large, creamy white paws sat not too far away. Slowly, she managed to look up, meeting a pair of glowing, golden eyes.

For what could've been a long time or a short time or no time at all, she stared at those eyes, unable to do anything else.

"You have much to learn, human child," said a voice that seemed far away, like someone whispered from across a large room. Then, Redrinna knew nothing else.

⚬⚬⚬ ⚬⚬⚬

Her mind was nothing but fog. Redrinna knew someone hovered nearby, though she lacked the energy or desire to find them. Whoever it was, they kept trying to feed her something. She couldn't taste whatever it was; in fact, she could hardly eat it. Her mouth refused to work properly. That someone kept making cooing noises, which struck her as strange. One bite at a time, she managed to eat whatever it was. By the time she'd finished, she was utterly exhausted. Something soft and velvety nudged the side of her head, somehow coaxing her back to sleep.

⚬⚬⚬ ⚬⚬⚬

Redrinna had several, vague memories of someone feeding and caring for her, but they all spun and swirled in her mind, creating a kaleidoscope of broken images. Her body lay heavy and lifeless, like she'd stayed in one place for too long and had rusted over. However, she managed to force her eyes open. Sunlight filtered down through the trees, shimmering like it passed through water. A pleasant breeze stirred the leaves above her, the sound reminding her of the river. Or at least, that's what she thought it sounded like.

There was a different noise to her right. She only had the strength to turn her head to investigate. Sitting a short distance away was an elegant lynx, the dappled sunlight making its creamy white and golden fur radiate a hushed glow. Its golden eyes were trained on her, unmoving. Somewhere in her mind, she thought she should probably be scared, or at the very least a little wary. She was too tired to care.

One of the lynx's tufted ears twitched. "How do you feel?"

Redrinna slowly blinked, her eyes trying to close. "Tired," she managed.

The lynx nodded once, making it look like a wise sage from a fairy tale. "Human child, you nearly perished. You are very weak. It is fortunate you are still alive."

Timothon had said something similar once. So had Xandrin.

"You need to eat again," the lynx said. "Your body needs energy to recover."

The creature stepped forward, placing some plant she didn't recognize in her hands. It took a lot of willpower to eat whatever it was. She was so exhausted she couldn't even taste it. When she finished, sleep tugged at her senses the way a sleepy child pulled on their parent's sleeve.

The lynx stepped over, nudging the side of her head with its velvety nose. "Rest now."

Something about that called to mind a time when she'd been young and very sick. Another one of her siblings (the fourth or fifth one, she couldn't remember which, though both had been girls) had just been found dead for no apparent reason, yet her mother had spent the night at Redrinna's side anyway. Her mother had coaxed her back to sleep every time she'd woken from feverish dreams, stroking her head, saying things she couldn't remember.

For some reason, this lynx reminded her of that night. Something small and wet made its way down one cheek. Redrinna wished her mother was here. She wished she could stop thinking about what had happened that day, that all of it had been a lie, a bad dream that would go away if she could just wake up. She wished things could be different.

If her mother had appeared before her then, she would've believed it had all been a nightmare.

⁓⊙⊘⊙⁓

The next time Redrinna woke, the sun shone through the trees again. A slight breeze ruffled the bright green grass around her and the green leaves above, throwing dappled shadows over her face. Where was she? What day was it?

Her mind was clearer, and though she was shaky, she managed to sit up. This wasn't the first time she'd woken up like this. If she wasn't more careful, she'd make a habit of it. A shiver ran up her spine as she became aware of a presence nearby. Turning, she spotted the lynx sitting a few feet away, its gaze never moving from her.

"It seems you are recovering well," the creature said.

It struck Redrinna that she should probably be freaked out an animal was talking to her. All of the sudden, a jolt of alarm shot through her. "How long was I...?"

"In your time? Almost a week."

She sighed in relief. Timothon wouldn't have come to find her yet. Eyeing the lynx, she asked, "Who are you?"

The large cat raised its equivalent of an eyebrow. "I am the guardian spirit of these mountains. You may call me Matte."

Wait. A spirit? A spirit had saved her life like the one in the old legend? She couldn't even begin to process that, let alone comprehend it. "You saved me?"

The spirit nodded. "That is correct."

"But...spirits don't interact with humans, right?"

"Usually no. Protecting the race of men isn't my charge. But, in your case, the land I protect will need spirits like yours to survive the darkness I feel drawing near."

The darkness. The spirit had to mean Osiris. Did that mean he was coming back like Timothon had said?

Turning to the spirit, Redrinna tried to stay calm despite the fog of her brain. "A spirit like mine?"

"A strong spirit," Matte continued, seeming unfazed by Redrinna's confusion. "A powerful spirit, just untempered." The spirit rose to its

171

feet, glancing off at something before returning its gaze to her. "One hundred years ago, this land was shaken to its core. Now, I sense something even worse is lying in wait. If this land is to survive, spirits like yours are vital. As a guardian spirit, it's my duty to ensure you survive."

Redrinna had no idea what it meant, but she kept her mouth shut.

The spirit blinked once, its golden eyes piercing her in a way that made her uncomfortable but also unable to look away. "However, in your current state, your homeland's future is quite bleak. Therefore, I will start you on the correct path. Do you have the strength to stand?"

Trying to shake off the spirit's insult, Redrinna pushed her way to her feet. She was a bit shaky, but she managed it. Matte nodded, and, with a flick of its ears, moved off through the trees at a leisurely pace. Redrinna hurried to follow. The spirit led her back to the river, the roar of the water making her mouth dry up like earth longing for rain. The spirit sat on the river's damp shore, one of its large, black-tipped ears flicking while it waited for her.

"Let's begin."

Chapter Sixteen

Within a few days of the spirit, Matte, taking her under its wing, Redrinna felt better than ever. The spirit had been teaching her things none of her books ever had, like *where* to find those unique plants that healed certain wounds and other ailments, and how to tell them apart from similar plants that were harmful. Being here in the forest was different than she'd expected, but in a good way.

Today, however, the spirit had said it would show Redrinna how to hunt, a prospect that made her more than a little nervous. Just the night before, she'd made a trap under the spirit's watchful gaze. Somehow, it had turned out much better than her earlier attempts, though they appeared as though they should have been the same.

They arrived back at the place where they'd set the trap. Redrinna was a little pleased to see they'd caught a rabbit. However, the feeling fizzled out like a candle in the blusters of a storm when the last time she'd been in this situation came to mind.

"Remove it from the trap," Matte instructed.

Taking a deep breath, she obeyed, trying to ignore how hard her hands shook. Once again, it required two hands to get the squirming rabbit out of the trap.

"Make sure it is male," the spirit said, catching Redrinna off-guard. "If you are going to take a life to ensure the continuation of yours, then you must do your part to ensure the safety of its kind."

Taking a steadying breath, Redrinna did as the spirit had instructed. "It's male," she said, her voice already trembling like a leaf being buffeted by the wind.

"Take its life."

Trying to steel her nerves, she drew her knife. The rabbit stilled beneath her hand. She'd spent most of the morning hoping the second time wouldn't be as hard, but if anything, it was worse. Her muscles stiffened again, like they'd turned to ice.

If this rabbit had been the giant, if she'd had no choice but to kill him with her own two hands like this, it already would've snatched her. She was painfully aware of that.

A long minute passed before Matte's claws flashed, swiftly ending the rabbit's life. Redrinna shuddered as the heartbeat brushing her fingertips stopped. She didn't like that.

The spirit said nothing, which was worse than being yelled at. She wanted the spirit to say something, to be mad, to scold her. Otherwise, she would suffocate under the weight of this silence.

Face burning with shame, she slid the knife back into its sheath. "I'm sorry," she said.

"As you should be," the spirit said as they rose, the rabbit heavy in Redrinna's hand like it was chaining her to the spot. Matte took off, leaving her to follow. Anger churned inside her, but she stomped it out. Matte had saved her life. She would not get angry at the spirit, no matter how much she wanted to. Xandrin may have forgiven her when she'd made that mistake, and maybe the spirit would too, but she'd rather not repeat it.

She'd been the one who'd messed up, not the spirit.

The spirit waited for Redrinna at camp, already having fetched wood for a fire so they could cook the rabbit. As she arrived, Matte took the animal from her.

The spirit set the rabbit on the ground, its tongue flicking over its lips once it had done so. "Have you ever used magic, human child?"

"Once," she said, fighting hard to keep a snarl out of her voice. "It didn't end very well."

"Would you like to learn then? Or would you rather sit and

watch?" Matte held its claws close to the rabbit.

Blood drained from Redrinna's face. She wasn't quite ready for that yet. "I-I'd rather learn."

Matte nodded towards the wood. Redrinna knelt in front of it, putting her back to the spirit while she arranged the wood like her books had shown her.

"The ability to use magic is not a talent that every human possesses. Being able to master the ability will take a considerable amount of practice as mastering any skill requires patience and diligence. It will require much from you, but your efforts will bear fruit in time."

Butterflies waltzed through her stomach. "Last time I used it, I hurt myself. What if something bad happens again?"

"The first thing you should know," Matte continued calmly, "is magic is not yours. It is something you have to ability to use. The power you pull on flows all around us. To use magic, you simply need to tap into that flow. You act as a conduit of sorts, understand?"

She nodded. If this had been Lady Cel Tradat, she had a feeling the woman would not have been so patient. The woman had never been one for walking her through things one step at a time. Her mother and Captain Brion had always been the patient ones. A small pang went through her at the thought, and she immediately brushed it aside.

"Give it a try," the spirit said.

For a long minute, Redrinna stared at the pile of wood, wondering how she was supposed to tap into this flow Matte had mentioned. Would she be able to feel it when she did? Or would things just happen?

"Focus, human child."

Releasing a short huff of irritation, she tried harder. All at once, she sensed something, but she wasn't sure how to describe it. Closing her eyes, she searched for it, unsure if she was pulling it to her or if it was the other way around. She put a hand to the ground, which seemed to make whatever she was feeling a bit stronger. All at once, it became clear. There was movement beneath the earth, somewhere deep. It was almost like...a heartbeat.

"You feel it, don't you?"

Redrinna's eyes popped open.

"That is the flow I told you about. It's the earth's flow, its spirit, you could say."

Redrinna took a deep, calming breath. The second she became aware of the power flowing beneath her, she couldn't seem to un-notice it. It was in everything around her—the trees, the grass, even the wind. Concentrating on what she wanted, she tried to nudge some of the power beneath her to accomplish it.

There was a hiss and a pop, making her jump. The wood crackled as a tiny flame bit into its bark. The flames grew stronger the longer she stared at them, pushing more life into the fire. A grin burst across her face. She'd done that. Her.

"Not bad for your first attempt," the spirit said. That wasn't very encouraging, but all things considered, Matte didn't hand out praise lightly. Redrinna supposed she ought to take it for what it was worth.

Under the spirit's instruction, she cooked the rabbit. Once it had cooled enough for her to hold, she took a bite of the crispy flesh. It occurred to her she'd never seen Matte eat, making her wonder whether or not the spirit needed to eat. She knew as much about spirits as she did about dragons: next to nothing.

Matte gathered what was left of the meat, doing something she didn't pay attention to.

The two of them remained by the fire as the sun set behind the trees, and the stars began to light the sky. With a small sigh, Redrinna leaned back so she could study the dark expanse above her. They didn't look like laughing ladies tonight. Right now, they were just little lights far away. That got her thinking.

When she'd been back at the palace, she'd heard some of the soldiers talk about the animals they'd tracked and hunted. They'd never seemed to hesitate like she did. Even Lady Cel Tradat had told a tale of her own exploits a time or two with such enthusiasm, it'd never occurred to her that hunting could be difficult. At least not in this way.

"Matte?" she said, earning the spirit's attention. "Why do I have such a difficult time with the...you know."

The spirit stretched and laid in the grass, watching her with those eyes that held all the brilliance of the setting sun. "There are merely things you don't yet understand. It is only natural for one as young as you. It's nothing to be ashamed of."

"What things?" She found herself cocking her head to the side, the action reminding her of Xandrin. Her heart ached at the thought of him too.

"Allow me to put it this way," Matte said. "Everything in this world lives in harmony with the flow of the earth. It is always moving forward, never turning back. What you don't yet understand is how death fits into that flow. Here, the death of one provides the means for another. Taking life to save your own is a very solemn responsibility that should be treated with the utmost respect."

"Respect?" she asked. The soldiers had never talked about their hunts with respect. To be honest, she wasn't sure what the spirit meant at all.

Finding such a significant lack of understanding in herself was...oddly frustrating. It wasn't like Redrinna had assumed she'd known everything. She'd just never considered there could be things that difficult to understand.

"You hesitate when life is placed in your hands. This does not mean you are weak, only that you are human. Killing is not an easy task for those who still retain their humanity. It should never be easy. Never take a life unless it is absolutely necessary and there is no alternative. I ask that you show nothing but respect for the life you take when the need arises."

She frowned, taking that in.

The spirit nodded towards the rabbit's bones Redrinna had put to the side and added a few more to the pile. "Begin with this one."

She stared at the bones for a while before understanding dawned on her.

Grabbing a nearby rock, she dug a hole in the earth. Then, she carefully laid the bones inside, arranging them close to how they'd been when the rabbit had been alive. When she finished, she placed the dirt back in the hole, finishing the grave.

"Well done."

Redrinna sat back, her gaze returning to the sky. For a few minutes, she mulled over everything Matte had told her. It sounded a lot like...the responsibility of being an Empress. Her parents had spent hours during their lessons drilling into her that taking charge of a nation meant taking responsibility for her actions and doing her utmost to do right by the people in her care. A chill raced across her skin. She'd rather not think about that.

Her thoughts turned anyway, taking a path she didn't like. She hated the idea, but if she joined the Dragon Kin, then she was sure there'd come a time when she'd have to kill someone. She'd didn't want to. Yet, if something came for Xandrin, wanted to drag him off or worse—how far would she go to protect him? Would she be willing to kill if she had to then?

A shudder swept through her.

"Matte?" she said after a minute, once again earning the spirit's gaze. "How long have you been a guardian spirit?"

"A very, very long time."

In a hushed voice, she asked, "So...were you around when Osiris first tried to...?"

Slowly, not saying a word, the spirit dipped its head.

"So he is real," she breathed, hating the awful feeling curling inside her. If Osiris was real, then her father really must've been trying to kill her. If Osiris was actually out there, then it couldn't have been possible for her father to love her once she'd been marked, right?

"Those were dark days," the spirit said. "The magic that man employs is against nature. It throws the world off-balance."

That gave her pause. "What do you mean?"

"You recall your magic, yes? That is natural magic. It flows in harmony with the world around you. However, the magic of that man does not. I do not know if the human race has records, but as his powers grow stronger, the seasons lose their order. It would snow one hour then the sun scorched the earth with blistering heat the next. The elements were out of hand, with natural disasters striking almost constantly; earthquakes, floods, volcanic eruptions. It seemed as though the earth itself was dying."

All at once, Redrinna thought back to her second to last assignment, where she'd poured over reports from farmers all across the Empire. Droughts in places normally abundant with water, floods coming earlier and with more force, crops dying with little explanation. Osiris had to be coming, getting stronger. She'd seen the evidence with her own eyes, and it was already bad. As he got even stronger, would it get worse? How much worse?

"It's starting again," Redrinna whispered. "The world is already starting to teeter."

"Yes," Matte said, making her heart clench. "That is why it was necessary for me to intervene on your behalf. There is only so much time remaining in our favor."

They remained quiet after that, and for a while, fear squeezed on Redrinna's chest, making it hard to breathe.

At the same time, a new feeling budded in her chest. She'd grown a lot since she'd left the palace. There was a way to stop Osiris and her father, so things couldn't be so bleak, could they? On the other hand, the first Dragon Kin had failed and been killed. Maybe things were quite bleak after all.

Unexpectedly, something touched her hand, making her glance down in alarm. To her relief, it was just a little, black ant. Curiosity giving her a bit of courage, Redrinna lifted her hand, watching the small insect as it crawled across her fingers.

Despite how much bigger she was in comparison, the ant had tried to climb over her. Regardless of how daunting a task that would be, it believed it would succeed.

Smiling, she lifted the ant a little higher, framing the insect against the starry night sky. The bug seemed tiny, diminutive against such a massive expanse. It probably had no idea how little it was. It was purely determined to survive.

"You're not frightened by what's out there at all, are you?" she breathed before letting the ant scurry on its way. She instantly lost track of it in the dark.

Was that what Timothon had meant by the strength already inside of her? If she could be more like this ant, would that make her stronger? If she could do that...then what else would she be able to do?

As the fire faded to embers, Redrinna laid near it. She listened as the forest settled in around her—the wind making the trees sigh like a mother comforting a child, the quiet rush of the river in the distance, the faint hum of a few brave crickets—all things that had startled her a short while ago, but were soothing now. As she closed her eyes, she couldn't help but smile.

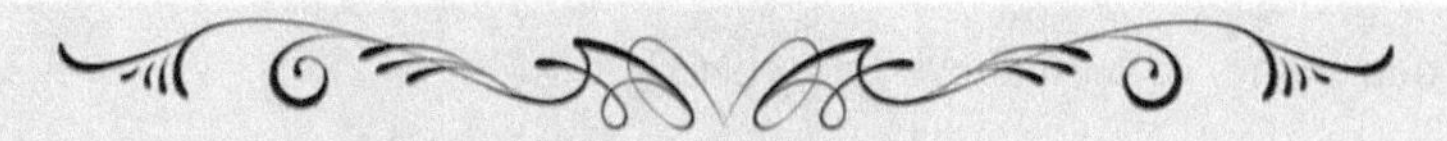

Chapter Seventeen

The remainder of the week flashed past, and before Redrinna knew it, the month of time Timothon had given her was already half gone. To be fair, she'd been unconscious for nearly half of it.

As the sun crested the mountain peaks, she watched the early morning sky, listening to the first birdsongs of the day. Matte approached, instantly catching Redrinna's attention. The spirit carried a certain air about it that always grabbed her attention.

"Human child, I have business elsewhere I can no longer ignore, so I must leave you."

Her heart stuttered a little. That meant she would be on her own. Again. She'd been alone so much in her life, but after meeting Xandrin, she'd forgotten how much it hurt. Even if she still couldn't decide what to make of her parent's actions, her chest ached when she thought about them, like someone was repeatedly stabbing little holes in it.

Though perhaps that pain came from the fact she missed who she thought they'd been, not them specifically. Regardless, knowing they were no longer going to be a part of her life was painful, like losing her siblings all over again.

"Do not fear, human child. I have taught you many of the skills you will need to survive. You will be all right." The spirit's paws barely ruffled the dewy grass as it turned to leave. "If you ever need me, focus on the power of the earth and call my name. Farewell."

Before she could say a word, the spirit vanished, and complete emptiness filled her again, seeping into her bones. For a long moment, she remained where she was. Then, she decided she'd better gather the things she'd need to make more traps. Without Matte to help her out, she would have to find food all by herself.

A short time before noon, Redrinna returned to camp and set what she gathered under the lean-to. Smiling a little, she tapped on the wood frame. At least she'd done that right.

She set to work making the traps. Once she'd finished with them, she hid them in various places throughout the forest. As she worked, she refused to hesitate or let herself question what she was doing. It wouldn't help her, nor would it change what she had to do.

A few hours later, after gathering some of the plants Matte had told her were okay for eating, Redrinna went and checked the traps. One had been successful, holding a young squirrel. Gently, she extracted it from the trap. It remained eerily still.

Then she discovered it was a female. Matte had never allowed her to take the females. So, despite her stomach's complaints, she let it go. It hesitated for only a second before shooting back into the forest, its bushy tail bobbing like a banner in the wind. She reset the trap and hid it in a different spot before heading back to her lean-to.

She made a small fire to keep herself warm—a thrill running through her chest when she used magic to do so—and ate some of the plants she'd gathered. They didn't taste very good, but at least she wasn't poisoned or hungry. After being poisoned and nearly starving to death, what food she had, regardless of what it was, sent a rush of gratitude through her. Food would never be the same after this.

As the fire began to dim, Redrinna laid on her back, partially under the lean-to so she could stare at the stars. An emotion she didn't understand settled in her chest as she watched all those little lights twinkling as they poked their heads through the blanket of darkness overhead. She got why so many people called them beautiful now.

⁂

It was mid-morning when Redrinna set out to check her traps. She'd woken up underneath the lean-to, finding the forest soaked from a midnight rain, filling the air with that fresh, wet earth smell she was starting to love. A part of her hoped the traps were empty and no animal had been trapped in the storm. But she still hoped she'd find something.

While the first trap lay empty, the second did not. As Redrinna got close, she frowned. Whatever was inside was squished. From where she stood, she couldn't tell what kind of animal it was, but it seemed bigger than anything she'd caught before. Her heart twinged in sympathy as it shivered, its fur soaked.

Moving carefully, she worked the creature out of the trap, its small body limp. A bit startled, she studied it. It wasn't like any animal she'd ever seen or heard of before. Its face was fox-like but it had enormous ears. It had a long, fluffy body—or it would have if it hadn't been soaked—with a great floof of a tail. It was coated in muddy splotches, giving it a brown patches, but she was sure its fur was actually white. There were swirling blue markings around its eyes that were strangely calming and serene if she stared at them, which she caught herself doing. She forced her attention away.

She had no idea what it was, but regardless, the poor animal was sick. Momentarily unsure what to do, she decided to carry it in her arms as she checked the rest of the traps. It wasn't like she would nor should eat a sick animal. One of the other traps held a rabbit, though this one appeared dry, fortunately. After setting the unusual creature down in a dry place, she pulled the rabbit out of the trap.

This one was male.

For a brief instant, Redrinna considered letting it go. However, she needed something for the sick animal to eat. If she failed, it would die. She had to do this. She had to stop relying on other people to do the hard things for her.

Drawing a deep, calming breath, she drew her knife from its sheath.

Meeting the rabbit's gaze, she said, "I'm sorry."

A flash of metal, and she'd taken the rabbit's life.

Swallowing the tears, she took both of her finds back to camp and set to work cooking the rabbit. While she waited, she did her best to make sure the strange creature would be comfortable beneath the lean-to. Promptly, she ran out of things to do while waiting for the rabbit to finish, and her mind wandered back to when she'd looked into the rabbit's eyes. Unlike the first rabbit she'd tried to kill, which had been terrified, this one had had a strange expression. Almost like acceptance.

Maybe she'd imagined it.

Shaking herself from her thoughts, Redrinna checked the rabbit. It was done. She took it away from the heat of the flames, and while it cooled, put the fire out. The heat from the sun was more than sufficient.

Turning towards the strange animal, she debated for several minutes how she should feed it. She nibbled a bit on the rabbit while she thought.

She'd just have to see what worked and hope for the best. Ripping off a small piece of meat, she pried open the creature's mouth. She hesitated. It had a lot of little, sharp teeth that weren't very inviting, but she'd have to brave those teeth if she wanted to keep this creature alive.

As gently as possible, she placed the meat as far back in the creature's mouth as she could. Its eyelids fluttered, and it attempted to swallow. It choked instead.

Panic flooded her senses as she struggled to dislodge the meat. Once she'd succeeded, she had to take several deep breaths to calm herself back down. It'd be easier if it could chew on its own.

All at once, Redrinna remembered something she'd read about wolf mothers and their young, giving her a weird, but promising idea. She put the first piece of meat to the side and got another one. After she'd chewed on it for a bit, she put that in the creature's mouth. It swallowed without any problems.

A little disgusted at her ingenuity, she continued feeding the creature that way until her jaw ached. The animal had been somewhat conscious towards the end but had fallen into slumber. She hoped it would rest a little easier now.

Redrinna watched the creature while she finished a bit more of the rabbit. When she was full, she left the rest a ways away from camp, close to where she'd seen the fox with her babies. As she turned to leave, she spotted little black noses poking out of their den, which almost made her smile. This way, it wouldn't go to waste, and the foxes would take care of the bones.

For the next couple days, Redrinna kept a careful eye on the unusual animal she'd found. She even cleaned most of the dirt out of its fur, though that had taken more work than she'd expected. At first, it stayed pretty much the same. Then, it began to get better.

When it woke up for the first time, it stared at her for a full minute before tucking its tail between its legs and flattening its ears against its head. It pressed itself as far back as it could under the lean-to, its lips curling back to display all those tiny, gleaming teeth. It poofed up, becoming fluffier (it was hard to believe it could've), as a low— almost unbearably adorable—growl shook its little frame.

Redrinna knelt in front of it, holding out her hands, palms up. "Hey," she breathed, trying to imitate Matte's calm voice. "How are you feeling? You're looking a lot better than you did before, which is good."

The creature watched her hands intently before doing something she should have expected. It lunged and bit her finger, hard enough to make it bleed. And refused to let go.

It took a lot of her willpower not to cry out. Wincing, she grit her teeth. "It's okay. You don't need to be afraid of me. I promise I won't hurt you." She picked up some of the meat beside her. "See? I brought you something to eat, to help you feel better."

Its dark, brown eyes flicked between her and the food as it hesitated. Mercifully, it released her finger. Its nose quivered as it licked her finger with its rough, warm tongue. To her surprise, the wound immediately closed over and healed. An unusual creature indeed.

Trying to shake off her surprise, she gave the meat to the creature, who meekly took it from her. It ate quickly, finishing with a small hiccup.

It nudged her hand with its head. Its fur was soft, like a blanket her mother had given her for one of her birthdays after her parents had returned from a diplomatic trip on the east coast. A blanket she knew had been intended for one of her siblings who had died hours after being born a few weeks after her parents' return. Redrinna had never let on that she'd known.

"It's okay," she said, giving the creature a small smile. "No harm done. I'm going to sleep now, so be careful."

Turning, she laid down with her back to it, trying to give it some space. After a few minutes, to her astonishment, it curled up against the small of her back, it's breathing settling into the easy rhythms of sleep. She remained there for a while until the sun began to sink beneath the horizon, not wanting to move until she had to.

Extracting herself from its presence, Redrinna checked the traps one last time. She lit a small fire upon returning to the lean-to and almost settled down again when she spied the wooden stick she'd used on the first day to train.

Training had completely slipped her mind while she'd been with Matte. Now, she'd have to practice twice as hard to accomplish anything. Scowling, she spent a long minute debating going to sleep and worrying about it tomorrow before deciding against it. Maybe a few swings would be good for her.

It wore her out fast, faster than it had before. A dim image of the giant loomed in front of her eyes. If it showed up now, it would win. But a fire burned inside her that hadn't before. She'd saved that weird creature. It wasn't much, but it was a step in the right direction. And she would keep walking.

As Redrinna laid back down, intense exhaustion swept over her. She must not be completely better yet. Or maybe two weeks off were enough to make her weak. With a small sigh, she snuggled as close to the creature as she dared and fell asleep.

Chapter Eighteen

When Redrinna woke the next morning, the creature had moved, stretching out and pressing against the length of her back. It was remarkably warm because of that, which explained why she hadn't woken during the night. As she sat up, it did the same, stretching its surprisingly long body with a squeaky grunt that was way too cute.

Still feeling a bit sleepy, she rubbed its head, earning herself a lick. "Are you feeling better?"

It nuzzled her palm in response, making her smile.

She rose, pausing to stretch before heading in the direction of the river. After a moment, she heard the padding of soft footsteps from behind. To her surprise, the creature trotted after her. For half a second, she thought about discouraging it, but she didn't mind the company.

It stayed with her for a few more days, making her time in the woods easier to bear when she wasn't distracting herself with her sword training or testing out her magic a bit. Then, it too took its leave. While she wandered the woods, she kept trying to piece together what kind of creature it'd been, but she drew a blank every time. It was a complete mystery to her.

Redrinna saw it many more times and became fond of seeing it. Sometimes, it even stopped by to share a meal with her, usually bringing something to contribute, which never failed to lift her spirits. However, when it brought her a bat, she respectfully declined. It didn't seem to mind too much.

Before she could believe it, Redrinna was settling down beside her fire on the eve of her last night in the woods. As she watched the flames dance, she reflected on her life before she'd met Xandrin. She'd thought she'd been pretty grown-up before, but it was easy to see she hadn't been. Especially compared to now. Though in her defense, that had been as grown as she could've been at the time.

Her gaze moved to the stars, another sight she'd grown fond of seeing. Maybe when she returned to the mount, Timothon would let her make a hole in the ceiling? The thought made her grin. He probably wouldn't be pleased with her suggesting they drill holes in the roof of the Mount.

With the sounds of the forest sighing in her ears, her body relaxed, coaxing her eyes shut. Before she knew it, she drifted to sleep, feeling at peace for the first time in quite a while.

⋅◦◖◗ ◖◗◦⋅

The next day dawned bright and clear, and Redrinna woke with the sun. She settled in the shade of the strange, pale, dragon-like tree, munching on a few non-poisonous berries while watching the forest as it woke. Birds flitted through the trees while squirrels and chubby-cheeked chipmunks scurried through the underbrush—some even brave enough to venture in her direction to see if she would share her breakfast. They scattered when she rolled a couple berries their way, but they returned seconds later, stuffing the fruits in their cheeks before scampering off. Sunlight streamed through the tree branches, the leaves shimmering gold and bright green.

Her heart longed to stay here, something that startled her a bit. It was odd to think that after a short month, she was already attached to this place. Despite the fact there was a chance of the giant showing up, an ache blossomed in her chest at the thought of leaving and hiding in a cave again.

All the more reason she needed to be stronger.

Around mid-morning, Redrinna heard flapping, causing her to look up. A shadow rushed over her face and moments later, Xandrin and Timothon descended into the clearing. They were a sight for sore eyes. She rose before nearly being knocked back down by the dragon barreling into her like he'd thought he'd never see her again. He didn't say anything, just buried his nose in her hair, the red and smoky black of his scales more brilliant than she remembered.

Rubbing his chin, Redrinna smiled a little. "It's nice to see you too."

Timothon grinned from Xandrin's back, his eyes and hair seeming brighter and more fiery in the light of the sun. "You made it! I told you it'd be easy, didn't I?"

A laugh almost bubbled out of her chest, but she kept it in check.

"So," he continued, the smile on his face seeming to be one of the few genuine ones she'd seen. "Unless you really want to stay here, you ready to go?"

Redrinna started forward, pausing when she thought of all the traps still out in the woods."Wait a second."

Xandrin's brows furrowed, ear frills pressing flat against his head. She didn't pause to explain before turning and dashing into the woods. She should have taken care of the traps last night, but at least she'd remembered to take care of them at all.

Quickly, she found all her traps, letting any animals ensnared in them go before breaking them so nothing else would get caught. After splitting the final one, she turned to head back. Her unusual friend blinked at her from a nearby tree branch, pulling her up short.

It chittered at her, and she stretched up on her tiptoes to rub its head. "It's nice to see you too, but I have to go. So try not to get stuck in any more traps, okay?"

It huffed and licked her palm before rocketing off through the trees. Her gaze drifted over the surrounding forest before she turned and left. Timothon and Xandrin were waiting in the same spot. As she climbed onto the dragon's neck, settling behind Timothon, her heart let out a tiny sigh.

If she was honest, she didn't want to go. However, staying here wouldn't make her father or Osiris go away.

As Xandrin lifted into the sky, a shiver raced up Redrinna's spine, making her turn back. She knew that feeling. Standing just out of the trees was Matte, those unblinking eyes focused on her.

All at once, she could've sworn she could hear the spirit's voice again, saying, "Your spirit is strong enough for the journey ahead. All you have to do is walk it." It was so faint, she couldn't be sure.

She lifted a hand in farewell. The spirit inclined its head before vanishing. For a moment, she wondered if she'd ever see Matte or the strange fox creature ever again. Then, she turned back to the front, keeping her gaze trained ahead.

If Matte believed Redrinna could do this, perhaps she truly could.

In the distance, a short way beyond the mountain peaks, she could just make out the tips of the Eridian Palace's four towers. It seemed like it'd been years since she'd last been there, even though she knew it hadn't been that long. Funny how that kept happening.

It wasn't long at all before they landed on the ledge of the Mount a few feet from the massive stone doors Redrinna couldn't recall if she'd ever seen from this side. To be honest, they were far less impressive out here. She could only just tell they were even there, but perhaps that was the point.

Xandrin strode inside before she had a chance to dismount, but once her feet were back on the ground, Timothon glanced at her with a hint of a grin.

"Ready to go get the gem yet?"

She couldn't tell if he was being serious or not. "H-how about in a day or two?"

That made him laugh. "I'm teasing, honest. We'll worry about it later. In the meantime, why don't you go take a bath while Xandrin and I make something to eat?"

A bath didn't sound like a bad idea. If her clothes were anything to go by, then she had to be downright filthy. As Redrinna turned towards her room—already aching at the thought of sleeping on a bed instead of the ground—she glanced back at the other two, who were chatting quietly as they headed down the middle passage towards the kitchen.

It struck her then that Xandrin seemed a bit different. A bit bigger maybe? No, he wasn't bigger, but he seemed more sure of himself? Frowning, she resumed walking towards her room. She couldn't quite name it, but the dragon was different. It hadn't occurred to her until right then, but now she couldn't stop wondering what Xandrin had been up to while she'd been taking her test. At the very least, he and Timothon appeared to be getting along now.

⁕

Two days later, Redrinna stood on the outside ledge of the Mount, the cool morning air sending chills down her back. Xandrin stood beside her, his head dipping towards the ground before jerking up. He really wasn't a morning dragon.

A quiet thrill of excitement rushed over her skin while she waited for Timothon to arrive. Today was the day she was going to find one of the Dragon Gems, something that would prove she wasn't weak, that she was strong enough to join the Dragon Kin. Today was the day she made a choice for herself, the day she did something because it was what she wanted. Part of her still hesitated, but the rest of her was itching to go, wishing Timothon would hurry with whatever he was doing.

Doubt flickered in her chest like a candle in a light breeze, but she shoved it aside. She shouldn't doubt whether or not the gem was waiting for her. After all, she'd been marked by it. A long time ago, it'd chosen her as someone that could claim its power. Besides that, her parents had tried to kill her because of it. Not trying to get the gem after that seemed kind of pointless.

A chill wind brought Redrinna back to the present, and she scooted closer to Xandrin to avoid the breeze. He stirred when she bumped against him, blinking for a moment before his eyes decided to stay closed.

"I need bed," he whined, his voice thick with sleep.

"Normally, you'd say 'I need to go to bed,' not that you 'need bed,'" Redrinna said, trying not to smile. It was difficult to keep a straight face. She'd missed him.

"Whatever," he mumbled, ear frills drooping as his head started to drift towards the ground again. "I just want to sleep."

That smile finally managed to snag her mouth right before Timothon waltzed out of the Mount with a small sack in his arms.

"Good morning!" he said for what had to be the fifth time that day. For reasons unbeknownst to her, he was in a curiously good mood. "Since we don't know how long it's going to take to find the gem, I figured you should take something to eat. There should be enough for both of you provided Xandrin doesn't hog it all."

Xandrin's head jerked up at the sound of his name, but it only hovered there for a second before drifting towards the ground again. Redrinna and Timothon shared a smile.

"Where are we supposed to go?" she asked, taking the sack from him and slinging it over her shoulders. It was heavier than she'd expected, but it wasn't a burden. Maybe her sword practicing was starting to pay off. Timothon had deemed her skills passable yesterday, after all.

"That I wouldn't know. One of the other members took the gems and hid them when things took a turn for the worse. We never saw her again," Timothon said, his smiling fading for a second. "But you'll be able to feel it. Since it left its mark, you already have some form of a connection, so you just have to draw on it and you should head right to it."

Helpful. Very helpful. Turning, Redrinna nudged Xandrin awake before climbing up behind his head. The dragon ambled around, turning to face the pale morning sky framed by the dark outlines of forest-blanketed mountains. She glanced back at Timothon one last time, half-hoping he'd offer some kind of advice, but he just waved.

She'd tried.

With a surprisingly powerful leap despite his sleepiness, Xandrin launched into the sky. As the wind tugged through Redrinna's hair, she closed her eyes. She hoped this feeling never got old. They flew silently until they were high above the sweeping, dark green of the forests.

"So, where do we go?" Xandrin asked, drawing her out of her thoughts.

A sigh slid out of her as Redrinna opened her eyes. "I don't know. It'd be easier to figure that out if we land, but I'm afraid that giant might find us again."

He nodded. "Agreed."

A part of her wanted to fly in a direction until they found something—and she couldn't help thinking that before her test, she would've chosen to do something along those lines—but that wouldn't help them. What she needed to do was stay calm and think.

All at once, there was a tug in the back of her mind, almost like a few strands of hair had gotten stuck on her clothes. "Xandrin, wait," she said, trying to decide if the sensation meant something or if she was so desperate to prove herself she was imagining things.

The dragon slowed his flight though he didn't stop.

The feeling persisted, vaguely reminding her of when she'd discovered her magic. Turning, she scanned the dark mountaintops to the west. In the distance, she spied a faint blue streak of water. The ocean.

The sensation in the back of her mind seemed to be stronger that way. Doubt wriggled through her stomach, making her hesitate. What if she couldn't find it or guessed wrong? Timothon had seemed pretty confident she wouldn't have a problem, but a lot of people had also thought she'd make a good Empress. And look where she was now.

"Redrinna?" Xandrin asked, freeing her from the downward spiral of those thoughts.

The feeling was something, a start. She should at least give it a try. "Head that way. I think there might be something there."

He nodded, soaring in the direction she'd indicated. As they flew, the faint smear of ocean expanded, growing bigger and wider just beyond the Agicae Mountain range.

Within an hour or so, the landscape beneath them shifted from towering, green mountains to a sloping, vibrant green coastline that ran past them a ways longer until it dove into the soft blues of the ocean. The sturdy pines and aspens of the mountains gave way to towering oaks, elms, and hazels as the forests raced down the slopes. The tree line dwindled a short distance from the base of the mountains. Despite that, the land remained a startling shade of green. Redrinna had thought the mountains had been green, but this was in a whole other league. She'd never seen a green quite this shade.

Her heart skipped a beat as her gaze stumbled onto something she hadn't expected to see squatting near the coast: a village. She'd never been in an actual village or town beyond the Imperial City before, though she'd read a lot about them. Lady Cel Tradat had always advocated for her to be able to see the real world for what it was, though her parents had never given in.

Gripping Xandrin's sleek, black horns, she said, "Go down."

He didn't hesitate to do what she asked, though he did stare at her like she was a two-headed sheep once they'd landed. "Is something wrong?"

"No," Redrinna said as she slid to the ground. "But since we don't know where that giant is, flying over a village in broad daylight isn't a good idea."

"A village?" Xandrin's eye spikes twitched upwards. "Is that like bed?"

She was smiling before she knew it. "Not quite. A village is a place where lots of humans all live. Didn't you see it?"

"I saw a weird open cave thingy with humans so tiny they looked like ants."

"Well, it is a village, and since we don't know what kind of people live there, we shouldn't risk you getting spotted."

His head cocked to the side, eyes narrowing. "We shouldn't risk you getting caught either."

She almost jumped when he guessed her plan. He hadn't been able to do that before her test. What had he been doing with Timothon?

"You're right," she said with a nod. "But I also really want to see what a village looks like. I've never seen one either. I promise to tell you all about it."

He frowned. "But what if something happens to you?"

"You can stay close by in case something happens. Just don't get too close or they'll spot you, okay?"

Sighing, he nodded. "If you get in trouble, I'll sit on you when we get back to the Mount."

Not wanting to commit to a deal like that, Redrinna turned and took off through the shade of the trees, heading in the direction of the village. Distantly, she could hear the dragon's heavy footfalls, but they grew quieter the closer she got to the village. She knew she needed to be careful, since there was a chance someone could recognize her, even out here. A shudder shook her at the thought of what would happen if her parents caught word.

The trees parted to reveal a tall, stone wall, stretching as far as she could see in either direction. After a moment of debate, Redrinna climbed the side, just until she was high enough she could peek over. A short distance from the wall stood the village she'd seen from above.

Her nose wrinkled at the smell coming from it. Her mind said it couldn't be a good sign, but since she didn't know what villages were supposed to smell like, she didn't know if it was all that bad. It was pretty noisy too. People milled about as kids raced between the simple, wooden houses. Their dress was a bit different than what she'd grown up seeing. There wasn't any embroidery edging their hems, which in the town around the palace, almost everyone had. Even Redrinna had some on her overtunic.

Redrinna rested her chin on the wall. So this was a village. Were the people happy? Did they get enough to eat? Were their crops being affected by Osiris' powers too? There was no way she could tell from here.

All of a sudden, a prickle raced up her spine, like someone was watching her. No one hung around the wall in the village, so that had to mean... She looked over her shoulder. Her heart stuttered, nearly leaping out of her chest.

A young man stood a short way behind her, just outside of the trees ringing the town, staring at her with wide eyes.

Chapter Nineteen

The young man appeared to be somewhere around Redrinna's age and wore a dull brown jacket, a baggy tunic, and long trousers that made his already stark white skin even paler. However, what caught her attention the most were his eyes. They were a startling shade of green, greener than even the hills sweeping into the ocean. His hair was a similar, alarming shade of green. Granted, they were very dark shades of green—it'd probably appear black in the right light—but undeniably green.

He didn't say a word, just stared at her like she was some kind of ghost.

"Hello," she said.

He stared for a while longer before giving her a tiny nod. "H-hi." His gaze flicked between her and the town beyond the wall. "You shouldn't stand on that."

Redrinna noted his voice was quiet and had a breathy quality to it, which she didn't know if she'd ever heard before. Most of the people she knew had loud voices, but she supposed Captain Brion's voice was kind of similar.

"Why?"

The part of the wall she currently used for a footrest let out a harsh, grinding before abruptly shifting, snatching her balance away. She fell back, somehow managing to stay upright when she hit the ground. Sharp bolts of pain lanced through her feet, but she did her best to ignore them.

"That's why," he said, the way his eyebrows were scrunched up making him look extremely concerned. "A-are you okay?"

"I'm fine," she said. She couldn't help noting his gaze dropped so he stared at her feet. After glancing at them just in case, she asked, "Are *you* okay?"

"O-of course," he said.

"Then why won't you look at me?"

He turned a shade paler. "Well, because...y-you know."

"I do?"

"Well, you're, you know," he shrugged a little, but his shoulders stayed up like he was a turtle trying to retreat into its shell. "The Imperial Princess."

Her stomach dropped. She'd already been found out? That fast?

"But I won't tell anyone," he added hurriedly.

"I'd appreciate that," she said, just as fast. If people would recognize her on sight, then there was no way she could go into the town like she'd wanted. Maybe it served her right for abandoning Xandrin so she could satisfy her curiosity.

"W-why are you here?" he asked, interrupting her thoughts. "It's not very safe."

Could she trust him? He had said he wouldn't tell anyone about her, and while she did have an odd feeling he would keep his word, the paranoia her parents had always had about her safety made her hesitate. What would they have had Redrinna—

Perhaps it was more important to decide what she wanted to do.

"Actually, I'm looking for something. Maybe you've heard of it?"

"Heard of what?" The young man cocked his head to one side, his entire demeanor changing almost instantly. He reminded her of Xandrin when he stood like that.

"It's something really powerful, known as a Dragon Gem. I think there might be one around here somewhere," she said.

Redrinna mentally kicked herself. How had he gotten so much out of her? If she didn't try to be a little bit more suspicious of strangers, she was going to get herself into a lot of trouble. Maybe frequently running into strange creatures was giving her a bad habit.

His forehead scrunched up again, this time making him look thoughtful. "I've never heard of a Dragon Gem, but maybe I can still point you in the right direction." He nodded towards the ocean, which she knew lay behind her. "A few years ago, lights came out of the ocean from that area pretty erratically, but it hasn't happened for a while. Plus, there's a water drake guarding that part of the ocean; some people say it's a spirit. Either way, it's been out there for as long as anyone here can remember. Whenever anyone gets too close, it attacks. Otherwise, it doesn't seem to do anything."

That had to be it. Though if there was a water drake guarding them, this could be harder than she'd anticipated. If it didn't let them get close enough to investigate, would they have to fight it?

After a minute, Redrinna remembered the young man was there. She supposed she ought to thank him at least. "What's your name?"

For a split second, he looked like she'd just asked him to solve the universe's greatest mystery. Gaze moving to the side, he said, "It's...Tak."

That made her pause. His name sounded an awful lot like the word 'talk,' but she didn't want to say anything about it. She doubted he'd chosen his own name, and she did not want to hurt his feelings.

All of the sudden, a man shouted something vile, a word that instantly put her on edge. Tak leapt a foot in the air, the color draining from his face (not that it had all that much to lose). Redrinna didn't quite understand what the word meant, but she knew it wasn't kind. As she turned to see what was going on, Tak shoved her behind the nearest tree.

After the surprise wore off, she peeked out from around the trunk of the young oak. A man dressed in similar fashion to Tak approached, wearing a nasty sneer while cracking his knuckles.

"What do you think you're doing out here?" The man spat that insult again, making anger churn in Redrinna's stomach.

Tak didn't respond. Instead, he kept his gaze fixed off to the side.

"You should stay inside and spare everyone the pain of seeing your horrible face. We've had to suffer you long enough as is."

That was more than enough. Redrinna stepped out from behind the tree, stopping in front of Tak. She knew firsthand what it was like to have someone say something things like that to you, and she wasn't about to sit idly by while it happened to somebody else.

"Who do you think you are?" she demanded, clenching her fists to keep them steady, her heart racing like it would leave her behind if it could escape her chest.

"What?" the man said, recoiling back a step as he stared at her. "There's another one?"

The way he said that made her grimace. "I asked who you are, but now I don't care. Get lost. Now." It didn't sound impressive, but it was the best she had.

Tak made a small noise behind her, but she wasn't sure why. The man took a step forward, but she refused to back down. Compared to the creature that kept coming after her, this guy wasn't scary at all. If she accidentally roasted him, she was pretty sure he'd stay dead. Not that she wanted to cook him but—

Without warning, someone yanked on her hand, throwing her off balance. Redrinna scrambled to stay balanced as Tak ran, dragging her with him. The man behind them shouted and thundered after them.

"What are you—" she began.

Tak cast one, frantic look back at her, and she understood. Kind of. But if they wanted to get away, they needed to go faster. She took the lead, but she didn't have to pull Tak along.

"Where's the shore?" she asked, doing her best to keep her breathing even. One way or another, she'd prove she could protect herself, even if it had to be the simple stuff.

The young man pointed a little to the right. Redrinna went in that direction. As they burst out of the trees, she glanced back. The man was gaining on them. He sure was determined.

The grassy hill beneath them switched to sandy beach, making her feet seem heavier and harder to lift. A surge of desperation gave Redrinna the energy to keep going, but Tak lagged behind. All at once, he tripped. She skidded to a stop so fast, she ended up on her knees. Spitting sand, she fought for breath as her heart lost all its courage and leapt into her throat as the man rushed closer, still shouting vulgar insults.

She glanced at Tak, who gasped for air. She clapped a hand to the sand. Power rushed beneath her hand, and she seized it. First crackling. Then fire. It flashed between them and the man, the bang shaking the air. The man skidded to a stop, eyes wide.

"You take another step," she said, panting a little, "and I will hurt you." Secretly though, she was glad he was still kind of far away since a fireball hadn't been what she'd had in mind. If she wasn't careful, she'd accidentally hurt someone.

The man glared at her, but he didn't step forward. Before any of them could move, a shadow rushed over them. She didn't have to look to know: Xandrin.

Redrinna jumped to her feet, pointing at Tak. "Take him too!"

The enormous dragon nodded once as he dove for them. In a matter of seconds, he scooped them up and they left the beach behind. He held her in one claw, and a quick glance confirmed he'd grabbed a visibly shaken Tak in the other.

"I'm glad to see you!" Redrinna called to the dragon.

He grimaced. "How come every time I take my eyes off you, you get in some kind of trouble? I'm sitting on you when we get back home!"

Her heart was still pounding, making the world around her seem sharper than usual. It was just like when she'd fought the giant, except this time was better. She'd definitely done better.

As her pulse began to calm, she noted the town coming to life, people running everywhere. Her heart dropped a little, that good feeling melting away. That was her fault, and not in a good way.

As they flew out over the ocean's water, a shock shot up Redrinna's spine. She straightened. "Tak," she called, quickly catching his attention. "Which part of the ocean does the drake guard?"

He pointed. Xandrin glanced down before flying in the direction he'd indicated. After a few minutes, that feeling rushed up her back again, stronger than before.

"Here," she said, not sure how Xandrin heard.

The dragon slowed, floating from side to side, as close as he could get to hovering, Redrinna decided. The claw he held her in tilted a bit. She scrambled to hold on.

"Would you like me to drop you here?"

"Don't you dare!" she snarled, pulse racing.

His eye spikes rose before he smiled. "You don't know how to swim?"

Redrinna suddenly spotted a small island and pointed it out. "Land."

Xandrin did so, and she hopped out of his grip as fast as she could. Tak stumbled out, but he didn't fall. The dragon tilted his head at him, but Redrinna didn't hear whatever he said.

"Wait here," she said. It felt like someone tugged on her fingers, pulling her towards the waves splashing against the sand, leaving wet splotches everywhere they touched. Her stomach clenched at the sight of water, but that incessant tugging pulled harder. Removing the sack from her shoulders, she set it at Xandrin's feet before stepping just out of the water's reach.

Not entirely sure why, Redrinna stepped into the waters, hesitating before walking in deeper.

Chapter Twenty

The water tugged at her knees, making Redrinna pause. She'd only been in the water for a few minutes, but already something swam towards her. Something massive. Despite the fact it wasn't very close to the surface, the water rippled, agitated. The closest thing she'd ever seen size-wise to this were the mountains behind her. Not even Xandrin came close.

All at once, saltwater sprayed high in the air. A large, reptilian head emerged from the ocean, the blue of its scales blending perfectly with the water around them like it was formed from the ocean itself. Water streamed off it, cascading around them, splashing Redrinna. The shape of its face was similar to Xandrin's, but it was longer and more narrow. It seemed to have ropes and ropes of a long, snake-like body and giant, sail-like fins that jutted out of the water like rocks.

Tak had called it a drake, but the feeling she had—it was exactly like being with Matte. She should've been scared, but the calm warmth inside her made that impossible. If this was a spirit like she thought, then she'd met not just one, but two. This definitely was starting to feel like some sort of legend, and she kind of didn't like it.

"Are you a spirit?" she heard herself say, though she hadn't meant to.

"I am." The drake leaned closer, tilting its head one way, then the other. "You are the one it chose? I wonder... No, clearly you have been marked." Its eyes narrowed as it studied her.

It became very difficult to swallow the longer it stared at her with its bright, sea-green eyes.

"Let us see," the drake said, extending a claw beaded with moisture towards her. "Come."

Xandrin hissed behind her.

She cast a reassuring glance back towards him. "It's okay." Spirits were powerful guardians by nature, according to Matte. So, if the drake wished her harm, it wouldn't need to lure her away from a dragon to do so, she was pretty sure. Still, as she took the drake's outstretched claw, her hands were trembling.

The drake pulled her forward, and the next moment they were beneath the waves. It took her deep under the surface in mere seconds. She held her breath for as long as she could as the surface got farther and farther away. Her chest tightened the deeper they went. Panic at having water on her face with no escape was not helping.

In less than a minute, her lungs were burning; she couldn't hold it anymore. The air burst out of her lungs, and she coughed, expecting salty water to rush into her mouth. To her surprise, she didn't choke on water.

Redrinna breathed.

This had to be the spirit's magic or something. This had never happened before, and when she'd been little, she'd tried.

She didn't get long to marvel at it. The drake slowed as they neared a jagged, barnacle-clad rocky shelf with a small cave opening sitting right in front of them. Tiny, colorful fish and all sorts of other sea creatures she couldn't name swam to and fro. She wished for a minute—just a minute—to stare at it all. There was nothing quite like this on land.

"They await you in the cave," the drake said, dragging her forward and depositing her at the entrance.

Nodding, she half-swam half-walked through the short entrance before leaping into a small chamber, startled to find it filled with air, not water. She dropped like a rock the last few feet, but she landed okay. Watery sunlight danced on the dark stone walls, and when she looked up, she spied a dome of water above her, in the upper half of the chamber, almost like a glass ceiling. This had to be some kind of magic.

More importantly, resting on little rocks—almost like pedestals—all around her were ten gems, their colors ranging from blue to white, black to amber honey. They were large too, each one almost the size of her palm.

So these were the Dragon Gems. One of them held the answer she'd been yearning for: the strength to stand on her own, regardless of who or what came after her. Which one was it? Was she supposed to choose or wait for something?

"Which one calls to you?" the drake said from above, making her jump. She glanced up, surprised to see its head protruding through the cave's entrance.

Turning back to the gems, Redrinna glanced around, her gaze coming to a stop on a blood-red ruby. That one. How she knew, she didn't know, but it was the one. It would make sense too. After all, her hair and eyes had turned a similar shade of red to the one it sported.

After a moment's hesitation, she approached and knelt in front of it. Was she supposed to take it? Or was there something else she should do?

"The gem is willing to accept you," the drake said, startling her again. "Touch it. If it truly accepts you, you may leave."

"What if it doesn't?" She couldn't keep herself from asking that.

"You will be made to forget everything you know about this place."

Something about the way the spirit said that made chills skitter across her back. She didn't want to find out what it meant. Taking a deep breath, she began to reach for it but stopped. What if it didn't accept her? What if it remained silent, confirming what so many people had said about her for her entire life? Could she handle that?

If she didn't try, she'd never know.

Reaching forward, her fingertips brushed against the gem's smooth surface. Nothing happened. Then there was a rush in her chest and a weight hung from Redrinna's neck, causing her to look down.

The gem hung from a chain around her neck. Did that mean...?

Not sure, she glanced at the drake.

It stared at her with its head cocked to the side again, brow furrowed. It made a noise like it was thinking before it spoke, something about it making her very nervous. "Very well. The gem wishes to be with you for the time being. Allow me to return you to the surface." It reached down to her with a claw. Readily, she accepted it and let it pull her back into the water.

৶৫ ৯৹

Redrinna's head broke the surface of the water a short distance from the gleaming, white shore. Her heart rattled in her chest until her feet found the sandy bottom, but it didn't relax until she got her face and chest fully out of the water. Xandrin scrambled to his feet, meeting her before she'd reached the shore.

He nuzzled her wet hair and then snorted. "You're all wet."

She laughed a little. "What did you expect?" A chill raced up her arms as a breeze blew through her wet clothes. "Where's Tak?"

The young man shuffled into view, eyeing Xandrin warily and keeping some distance between the two of them. "I-I'm here."

The dragon glanced at him before turning to her. "Why is he here? You know it's hard enough keeping track of you, forget two, small, fragile humans for me to make sure I don't squish?"

Tak's already pale skin went whiter than a sheet so fast, she thought he might pass out.

"Don't scare him!" she said, pointing a finger at the dragon. "He helped me get out of trouble." Glancing at the young man, she hesitated for a second before stepping over to him. "Though, I guess I got you into some trouble."

His gaze hit the ground. "Oh...n-no, it wasn't your fault."

Even still, the idea of sending him back to that village, to that man, made her chest ache. Maybe...she wasn't the Imperial Princess anymore, but that didn't mean she couldn't help people when they were in trouble.

"Can I tell you something?" Redrinna waited until he nodded before she continued. "I know you said you wouldn't tell anyone about me, and I believe you, but I need you to understand that someone is trying very, very hard to find and kill me. If they figure out I came here, then they might target you, and I don't know what they might do."

Whether or not this troubled him was difficult for her to say. He just stared at the ground, looking decidedly concerned.

"What are you going to do?" His voice was very quiet, like she was about to deliver a death sentence.

Pausing, she glanced at Xandrin, who was wearing a concerned expression similar to Tak's. Well, it was nice to know he had so much confidence in her. Turning back to Tak, she couldn't help the small smile that touched her mouth. He still looked ready to shrivel into a ball.

"Do you want to come with us?"

Both he and Xandrin exhaled at the same time. Slowly, he met her gaze, his head still lowered. "Are you serious?"

She nodded. Why else would she have asked?

He closed those striking green eyes of his before nodding. "Okay. I'll go with you."

"We should get going," Xandrin said. "Before that thing can find us again."

Without hesitation, she climbed onto his neck and held out a hand to Tak. He hesitated before accepting it.

Once he was settled, Xandrin launched into the sky. They soared over the ocean, past the village, and back to the shelter of the mountains. They flew high to avoid being seen, but she didn't mind.

Glancing back, Redrinna almost laughed at the shock written on their passenger's face. Tak stared at her with eyes round as the moon.

Smiling, she said, "It takes a bit to get used to it."

"The world is so small," he breathed, swallowing as he eyed the ground flashing by beneath them. For a few minutes, he seemed lost in thought before his gaze began to shift back towards the village. He stopped before he actually looked, a strange expression crossing his face, one she didn't understand.

He met her gaze instead. "Where...are we going?"

She pointed towards one of the distant peaks of the Agicae Mountains on the horizon. "That's where we're going. A...friend of ours lives there."

The young man accepted this without complaint. Hopefully, Timothon would do the same. They shared the food Timothon had packed them (which were mostly rolls), Tak whispering a subdued 'thank you' every time she handed him something. It was a bit of an odd habit, but it wasn't a bad one either, so she kept quiet.

The sun sat low in the sky by the time Xandrin's claws touched down on the ledge that led into the Mount. Timothon was waiting for them inside, one eyebrow lifting when he spotted Tak.

"Who's this?" he asked, sounding startled but still polite, like he was questioning a child who'd tracked mud through the house to find a towel to clean said mud off their shoes.

Redrinna made the introductions. "Since the thing that chased after me is still out there, Xandrin and I decided it was best to bring him with us to keep him safe." She glanced at Xandrin and Tak in time to catch them sharing a worried glance. Scowling, she ignored them.

"I see," Timothon said, shifting his weight from one foot to the other. "I also see you managed to find the gem." A shadow flickered across his face as he looked at it, but he didn't say anything .

"What?" she asked, worry taking root in her chest.

"There's...something I need to talk to you about, but how about we get your friend settled first? He doesn't even have any shoes."

He didn't? Redrinna glanced at the young man's dirty, bare feet, a bit startled. Tak went bright red and shuffled back a half step. Now she felt really stupid for not noticing.

Timothon smiled a little, but it didn't even come close to reaching his eyes. "I'll get him settled. Wait for me in the kitchen, okay? And Xandrin, you look like you could use a nap. How 'bout it?"

The dragon didn't even hesitate before romping towards his room. At least he was settling in, she decided. Turning towards the kitchens, she tried to convince herself everything was fine. However, the worry growing in her chest left her feeling otherwise.

Chapter Twenty-One

As Redrinna stepped into the kitchen, the familiar scent of warm bread washed over her. She was starting to associate the smell with the feeling of being home, something she hadn't expected to do. It was nice that after everything, there was a place that felt like home.

It was a short while later before Timothon arrived, dropping onto one of the stools like he was an old man worn to the bone by the weight of the world. A trace of fear curled around her spine. He hadn't been like that this morning, right? So what had brought it on?

"What did you want to talk about?" she asked, not sure she wanted the answer, whatever it was.

"Redrinna," he said, the seriousness of his tone making her tense. "We have a bit of a problem."

A sensation she knew all too well clenched her heart. She should've known this had been going far too well. What had she done this time?

"You see...the gem," he paused, glancing at it with a pained expression, "it didn't wake up."

The temperature in the room seemed to drop several degrees like ice was creeping up the walls.

"What do you mean? The spirit said it wanted to come with me. You said it marked me. It chose me."

"That may all be true, but it didn't bond to you. Being marked and being bonded are two different things. Several people will be marked. Only one can be bonded." Shaking his head, he continued, "When the gem accepts someone they've marked, there's a bright flash of light and the gem will glow like an ember all the time afterwards. It'll even speak to you sometimes. It literally binds itself to your soul."

Redrinna's heart plummeted faster than a stone tumbling down a mountainside. So she'd failed again. Like always. After all this, the hours of training and the test in the forest, she hadn't proved anything? Why couldn't she just do one thing right?!

"We're not going to give up," Timothon said, turning towards her. "I'm sure you'll be able to wake it given the right amount of time. We just need to find things that'll prove you are the one it's been waiting for."

That was easier said than done, and she wasn't in the mood to try to figure this out. "Okay," she said, more to the table than to him.

He didn't speak for a minute. "Don't be so down on yourself, Redrinna. I believe you can do this."

Matte had too, and the ocean spirit had let her take it, so maybe it wasn't completely hopeless. Maybe.

"Also, there's another thing, something I hadn't expected. It's Tak."

"What about him?" she asked, trying to put her emotions away for a minute.

"There was someone in the last Dragon Kin whose hair and eyes turned a shade similar to his. I think he's been marked too."

Really? It would make sense, she supposed. Though, if that were the case, why hadn't the spirit taken him to find a gem? Was the gem not ready for him yet or had it already decided on someone else?

"If he's up for it, I'll train him right alongside you. Who knows? Maybe having another member around will help you too."

She knew he meant well, but it didn't make her feel better. It did the opposite. "Okay."

He seemed out of things to say after that, so without waiting for permission, she headed to Xandrin's room.

"What are you doing here?" he asked, scrambling a little.

Redrinna didn't care what he was doing; her gaze was on the ground anyway so she didn't see it. She didn't speak as she approached and hid her face against his shoulder.

"What's wrong?" he asked, tenderly nudging her with his snout. "You got the gem. Aren't you happy?"

"No. It didn't wake up," she said. "I didn't get it." She'd done something wrong, but she didn't know what. They were going to have to try to convince the gem that whatever mistake she'd made wasn't serious enough for it to give up on her.

"Oh," Xandrin said. "What do we do now?"

"Timothon said we'd have to find other ways to convince it to wake up."

"So there's a chance we can still join the Dragon Kin, right?"

Biting back a fresh wave of tears, she nodded. There was still a chance, but she couldn't shake the feeling it was getting smaller and smaller. If she wasn't careful, it was going to slip out of her grasp altogether.

⚬⚬⚬ ⚬⚬⚬

Redrinna stood in the middle of the training room, wooden sword in hand, straw dummy before her when Timothon found her the next morning. Turning, she was a bit surprised to see Tak padding after him, quiet but staring at everything, his gaze zipping from one corner of the room to the next until he noticed her staring. Then he seemed to be trying to make himself as small as possible.

"Well, someone's diligent," the man said, the usual, cheerful fire back in his eyes. Not even his broad grin had limitations today. "I'm going to test you on that later. Anyway, your new friend seems hungry, so why don't you pause so we can eat breakfast? Even Xandrin is already waiting."

Still a bit down from yesterday, she merely nodded, put the sword away, and followed him to the dining hall. Xandrin was there, but he was sprawled against the back wall, fast asleep. At least some things never changed.

Shaking her head, Redrinna turned her attention to the table.

Their usual breakfast of bread and fruit waited for them. Today's fruit was a few apricots. Her mouth was watering before she'd even sat.

Timothon took the chair to her left while Tak took the one to her right. The green-haired young man glanced at her, waiting until she took a roll and an apricot before he did the same. Before she could even take a bite, Timothon spoke.

"So, Redrinna, I've been thinking about the first thing we should try. I remembered there's this old legend from thousands of years ago about a priestess who prayed while standing in these springs to unlock some grand power—I forget the details."

Redrinna let out a quiet sigh almost the same time Tak did. It wasn't a priestess, but *the* priestess, the one who'd slain the demon and founded Eridia, according to legend. Everyone who knew the story—except for Timothon, apparently—knew she'd been pleading for the power she later used to seal the demon away. She'd stood in springs that had been bathed in a spirit's power, and through them had found her power.

"The important thing to note is that it worked. For her, she had to prove her devotion and commitment to earn her power. If it worked for her, maybe something similar would work for you. What do you think?"

"That legend's ancient, you know, and I doubt standing in any puddle of water is going to cut it. Do you even know where we'd have to go?" She asked more because she'd rather not stand in a cold spring for hours to prove her resolve than out of curiosity.

He grinned, pleased as a dog with a bone. "As a matter of fact, there's one on this mountain we could use. Of course, we wouldn't go right away since we'd have to prepare a bit, but if that doesn't show how serious you are about this, then I don't know what will."

"It sounds dangerous," Tak said, his voice so soft Redrinna had to think for a minute before she understood him.

"You're not supposed to stand in the spring for a long time," she said, trying to recall the finer details of the legend. "In the legend, she wore special clothes and would stand in the spring for as long as it took to complete whatever it was she was supposed to say. It was more about that than the spring itself."

Tak's nose wrinkled. He and Xandrin both wore worried expressions she kind of agreed with.

Timothon rose from his seat. "I'll go start preparing. You," he pointed straight at Redrinna, "don't neglect those new sword stances I showed you. I'm going to test you on those eventually. Also, you should start teaching the basic stances to Tak too. That'll help both of you out." Walking with a definite swagger in his step, he waltzed out of the room.

The bread in Redrinna's hand steadily disappeared while she stared after him. Agreeing to try and win over the gem must have been what he'd been hoping for. His spirits were soaring so high, she was partially worried he'd float away.

"Re—Your Highness?" Tak asked quietly.

It'd been long enough since someone called her that, she froze, not sure what to do.

"Wait, is that what I'm supposed to call you since I know who you are?" Xandrin butted in—literally—his eye spikes lifting higher than she'd thought they could. "Is it bad that I called you by your name...a lot?"

No, no, no," she said hastily. "When I met both of you, it wasn't as a princess, and since I'm technically not a princess anymore, both of you should call me by my name."

Xandrin exhaled. "I don't have to learn a new name," he said, mostly to himself, as he withdrew his head.

Tak's gaze dropped a fraction of an inch. "Re...Redrinna? What should I do while I'm here?"

'No idea' was the first thing that popped into her head, but she thought it might hurt his feelings if she said it out loud. He seemed more sensitive than the people she'd had been around at the palace, so, for the time being, it would probably be best if she approached every conversation like she was walking across broken glass barefoot.

"Has Timothon said anything to you?"

"He mentioned the Dragon Kin a little bit, but I don't know what that is."

With a sigh, she stared at the table, gathering her thoughts. She guessed this was going to fall to her. As quickly as possible, she told Tak most of what Timothon had told her. When she finished, he stared at her with wide eyes.

"Wait, so Timothon was part of the original Dragon Kin?"

She nodded. "Yes, but his spirit is still trapped here. So if you want to do this, you have to be serious." There were enormous consequences. "There's no going back."

He stared at the table for a long time, a sad expression creeping onto his face. "That's fine. I have nothing to go back to, so I might as well make the most of what's here."

She understood that. "Then when we're finished eating, we'll go and do sword training."

He nodded, not speaking.

Once Redrinna finished, she rose—Tak following suit—noting that he'd only eaten half of his roll and a quarter of his apricot. "Tak, do you not like apricots?"

His cheeks flamed bright red. "I do, but I-I'm not very hungry."

Without meaning to, she gave him a once over, noting how he was barely taller than her and his clothes seemed to hang off his painfully thin frame. Coupling that with the guy from the village who'd definitely had not been painfully thin, she wondered just how much he'd been able to eat before.

"Bring it with us," she said, hoping it wasn't too obvious she was trying not to stare. "Weapon training always makes me a bit hungry, so maybe you'll work up an appetite."

Nodding, he gathered his food and followed her to the training room, Xandrin's claws clacking against the ground after them. There, she found a sword for Tak and they went over the basics together. He had to hold the sword with both hands, but despite that, he seemed to catch on to the movements much faster than she had. An hour into their practicing, he ate the rest of his breakfast while Xandrin's quiet snores echoed through the room. Turning her back to him, she couldn't help smiling a little.

Making sure Tak got enough food here was a simple way of paying him back for uprooting him from his life, however frail those roots had been before she'd arrived.

When it was nearing noon, they were too tired to practice any longer. Tak mentioned being hungry again, so they rooted through the kitchen with Timothon's permission—since he happened to be in there—and had a quick snack. Afterwards, Tak followed Redrinna to the library, where she tried to locate any book she could find on magic or anything that could help her find the key to waking the gem up.

After a while, she glanced up, finding Tak nearby, staring at the shelves like they were a mystical creature he'd never seen before. Which he might not have.

She froze as something occurred to her. "Tak?"

He jumped. "Y-yes?"

"Do you...know how to read?"

For the second time that day, his cheeks flamed as red as the sun at sunset. "No."

Hesitating for a heartbeat, she said, "Did you want to learn that too?"

The fire coloring his cheeks was immediately snuffed out. "You want to teach me how to read? W-why?"

Her search for a good answer left her resorting to Xandrin's tactics. "Well, because we're friends, aren't we? And since I like reading, I thought maybe you would too."

Tugging at the ends of his sleeves a bit, he stared at the ground for a long time. Little by little, he lifted his head. "If you want to..." There was a hint of a smile in his voice, though he didn't outwardly show it.

With a nod, she led him to a table tucked away in a corner. They started with the alphabet since it seemed to be the most logical place to start. By the time Timothon found them and raged they weren't at dinner yet, they'd made a good deal of progress. Better than Redrinna had been expecting, in fact.

After they'd eaten, Timothon took her aside and asked how Tak had been. She told him about how she figured he'd rarely been able to eat before—which, to her surprise, the man had also picked up on—

and that he'd caught on to the sword techniques with remarkable ease.

"Interesting," Timothon mused. "I was busy planning a bunch of things today, but tomorrow, I want to watch him. I have a hunch he might have a gift for sword fighting, which means he'll need a special kind of training."

When Redrinna went to bed, her energy felt well spent, but an unsettled feeling hovered in her chest. Could Tak have an inherent gift that she didn't? He'd seemed more receptive to the idea of joining the Dragon Kin than she had too. Even though she'd only known him for two days, why did it already seem like he was a better fit for the Dragon Kin than she was?

Chapter Twenty-Two

A chill raced over Redrinna's skin and straight into her bones as she stood at the edge of the spring Timothon's map had led her and Xandrin to. Why couldn't he have sent them during the daytime? Her gaze flicked towards the mounds of snow hunkered beneath the trees still, a vivid reminder it was still spring in the mountains.

The quiet trickling of water in the dim moonlight cast a gentle hush over the entire place, making her want to either stay quiet or speak no louder than a whisper. A myriad of stars reflected in the surface of the dark water, their thin lights illuminating the pebbly bottom below. It wasn't large, but it seemed deep. A faint power radiated from the spring, reminding her of both Matte and the water drake.

So this was one of the supposed springs the priestess—her ancestor—had proved herself in? Honestly, Redrinna didn't know if she believed that. Yet, she wasn't sure she disbelieved it either.

Though, for some reason, staring at it reminded her a lot of when she and her parents had stared down into Xandrin's cave together. Her chest surged with a painful, confusing ache.

She couldn't help wondering again if her mother had been a willing participant or if she'd been a victim too. Her mother could almost always keep a tight lid on her emotions, but she hadn't been able to then. Redrinna had seen the sorrow in her eyes.

She shook those thoughts out of her head.

"Even I'm a little cold," Xandrin said, his breath sending wispy cloud-like puffs into the night sky. "And Timothon said you could only wear your normal clothes."

It took a lot of effort to repress a shiver as she left Xandrin's warm neck."It'll only be for a little bit, so I'll probably be fine. But, you're going to pull me out if I'm not, right?" She hated that the fear making itself at home in her chest convinced her to glance back at the dragon.

He nodded, a faint smile on his scaly face.

It bothered her how much that made her feel better. She wanted to be brave enough to do this on her own. How else would she win the gem over?

Swallowing her nerves and taking a deep breath, she removed her boots and stepped into the frigid water. For the first few steps, it was fine. After the fourth step, her feet were already aching from the cold. A wince twisted her face the further in she went, and by the time the water was waist-deep, her feet were going numb.

Through her chattering teeth, she said, "I, Redrinna, swear to pledge my life for the good of the land and all who are in it, to keep myself strong in mind and body, and to strengthen and uphold my fellow Dragon Kin members in their times of need." She paused to breathe since the cold was diving into her lungs and kicking all her air out. A violent shiver ran through her, making Xandrin whine. Almost finished. So close. "I will rise above any threat to this land and vow to protect the life of every creature who graces it. This is my word, and I vow my blood will be spilt before I break it."

Hopefully, it wouldn't resort to that, but she should probably expect it to. That thought made her heart shiver as much as she was.

After another violent shiver shook her, she raced out of the water as fast as her numb feet could carry her. For two solid seconds, the night air was so much warmer than the spring. Then it got colder.

Xandrin held out a towel for her legs and a blanket for her shoulders. Hopping onto his back, she wrapped herself up, shivering for a long while before she started feeling warm again. She checked her toes multiple times to make sure they were getting feeling back.

"Do you think it worked?" Xandrin asked, though his tone said he knew it hadn't.

The gem around Redrinna's neck was ice cold. "Maybe it'll take more than once," she said, trying to stay optimistic. "Timothon is basing this off an old legend, and the legend says the priestess had to do this in several springs before her powers awoke."

Xandrin frowned, glancing towards the spring, but he remained silent. Her voice hadn't betrayed her, but her insides recoiled at the thought of stepping into the spring again.

Once she had warmed enough, she entered the spring again, just managing to make it through the speech before she raced out of the water. All at once, as she curled against the warmth of Xandrin's scales, she remembered asking Captain Brion that if someone had tried to force him to be a soldier, would he have fought for something else rather than tread the path that had been rolled out for him.

The towel and blanket became a bit too heavy, like they were also trapping her on this path she didn't want. If Redrinna let herself be honest, just for a second, she had to admit she didn't want to do this. Any of it. All she wanted was to be strong enough to keep the giant at bay. But if this was how she would find her strength, then she was willing to put up with almost anything.

Even still, why did it always seem like someone was trying to shape her instead of letting her be what she wanted?

⚜

Timothon made her return to the spring a week later, despite the fact it was pouring. Redrinna hadn't slept much the night before, dreaming of the water freezing over with her still in it, and Xandrin not being there to pull her out.

It didn't help Timothon had drilled her on her new sword skills, deeming her passable and moving her on to trickier skills, ones that required more of her. They had also begun branching out to other weapons that were more difficult to use. She lived in a constant, unending state of exhaustion. To top it off, Tak was progressing faster than her. Even though he'd had much less time, he was already in the second set of sword stances and well on his way to the third with her.

Whenever she found a free moment, she scoured any book she thought might help. At night, when Timothon finally let her be, she practiced her magic, often waking in the morning with her face stuck to the page of her book. Fortunately, she'd always put out whatever little fires she made before falling asleep.

So far, Redrinna had been sticking to mastering simple little fires instead of anything flashy. Most of the books stressed having a mastery of control before anything else. Luckily, unlike with the weapons and physical stuff, magic came easy to her.

On the plus side, Tak was steadily learning more of the alphabet. It wouldn't be long before he could start trying to read.

However, that was the furthest thing from her mind as she stepped into the cold spring again. It was colder than she'd remembered. She made it three-quarters of the way through her recitation before she bailed, scrambling for the heat of Xandrin's scales. Shame like she'd never experienced before crept up her cheeks. The rest of the night, she refused to answer any of the dragon's questions or get back in the spring.

When Timothon heard Redrinna had left the spring early because she had been too cold, his gaze had narrowed before he'd clucked his tongue once and said nothing. In that moment, she'd felt like she was standing in front of her parents again while they dictated a task that made all her insides shrivel up, or reprimanded her for falling short of their expectations.

She was trying. Why couldn't that be enough?

That night in her dreams, Timothon appeared there, urging her to follow him. She was chained to the book in her hand and her legs were stuck fast in a frozen pond.

"I can't, I can't!" She tried to yell but she couldn't make a sound. Eventually, the man shook his head and left, leaving her alone and trapped. She woke from that dream drenched in a cold sweat, dreading returning to the spring even though her next trip was a week away.

After her third, fruitless trip to the spring, she escaped to the library as often as she could, searching through every book she could reach for answers that would keep her out of the spring. Knowledge had always put her on the right track, even if it felt like she was trying to scale a steep mountainside. That was abruptly cut short when Timothon barred her from the library, cutting her down with those burning red eyes of his.

On the third day after being denied entry to the library, Redrinna woke early and went there first thing. The door was still locked.

Slumping against the wood, she closed her eyes, soaking in the coolness of it against her forehead, fighting the burning urge to start bawling. For the first time since she'd left the palace, she found herself longing for a quiet life on some secluded mountain where there was no one to bother her. At least, when she'd been in the palace, her parents had let her have the books. Without them, everything was too bright and colorful, making her head pound like a dancer had used it for a stage.

"Here again, Redrinna?" Timothon's voice made a shiver race down her spine.

Keeping her head against the door, she half-heartedly glanced at him. It'd only been a few weeks ago when he'd been so excited she was pursuing the gem. Now, the look in his eyes dragged old memories out of where she'd buried them, memories of how people had shifted from being kind to cruel like she'd sprouted a second head instead of her hair and eyes changing to unnatural colors. That look had made her stomach curdle then, and seeing it in Timothon's eyes made it curdle now too.

"You're not going to find answers in there. If there were answers in there, I would have found them for you. As far as I know, this hasn't ever happened before, so why would there be some kind of record?"

There was more than one way to find an answer to a problem, she thought, but the crackling fire behind his eyes made her too afraid to say it.

"Books make me happy," Redrinna whispered, not caring if he heard or not. "Everything makes more sense when I see it in black ink."

"You don't listen to what I tell you, do you?" Timothon said, one hand resting on his hip. "Just do what I say, and you'll find a way to convince the gem you're the one it needs."

Huffing, she pushed off the door and strode back up the hall. Maybe if he was the one standing in a freezing cold spring every week, he'd realize how much he was asking of her. She nearly ran headlong into Tak on her way back to her room, momentarily surprising her.

With Timothon's last words ringing in her ears, she went back to bed, ignoring Tak's puppy dog eyes on her way. After all, as of yesterday, he'd already caught up to her in their weapon's training. It seemed he had a natural gift after all.

Even though she knew she shouldn't, Redrinna couldn't help the envy that burned inside her every time he mastered something with so much ease when it had taken her so long to just be passable.

Burying herself beneath her thick blankets, she welcomed sleep's warm embrace and found herself dreaming about everyone leaving her behind again, her parents, her siblings, and even Xandrin.

⚬୧ଓ ଓ୧⚬

When Redrinna emerged from her room the morning after another failed attempt in the spring, she leapt out of her skin when she found Tak waiting there, sitting across from her door. He went pink when he saw her, but he climbed to his feet, a meager sheaf of papers in his hands.

"Good morning," she stuttered, her heart beating a spastic rhythm against her ribcage.

He dipped his head. "I-if you're wondering what I'm doing, I was waiting for when you woke up so I could ask you a question. Since Timothon keeps us super busy, I haven't been able to ask you yet." He peeked at her from beneath his dark bangs.

Well, Redrinna wasn't sure she'd called them bangs. They were more like thick strands of hair a bit too long and unruly to fall in line with the rest of his hair. None of his hair seemed to stay in line. It seemed to stick up all over like it was intent on giving him some kind of mane.

"I-is that okay?"

She squared her shoulders. She could handle a question, couldn't she? "What's your question?"

His cheeks went a bit pinker as he sucked in a deep breath. "D-do you want to see the letters I've been practicing?"

"Of course," she said, a bit surprised. She wasn't sure what she'd been expecting him to say, but it hadn't been that.

Hesitantly, he held his papers out to her. She took them, shivering at the feel of paper against her fingers again. The letters started out shaky but became more sure as they went on. He'd become proficient very quickly, though she couldn't quite remember how long ago it'd been since she'd shown him these letters.

Handing them back, a tiny smile tugged on Redrinna's mouth for the first time in weeks. "These are really good. The next step is for you to start reading." That thought brought the library to her mind, which made the smile on her face scurry out of sight.

"You can't go in the library, though," Tak said. "A-and Timothon would be mad if he even saw you with a book." Frowning, he took his papers back, staring at them for a minute before that concerned expression he often wore graced his features. "But...I might be able to help you get into the library. If you want."

It was Redrinna's turn for concern to contort her face. "You'd do that?"

He nodded. "You saved me from my village, so I'll help you however I can in return. If you want to get in there, I'll help you do it. W-we'd have to be careful though."

Frantic butterflies swooped through her stomach at the thought of going into the library without permission, but she kind of liked the feeling.

Chapter Twenty-Three

A couple hours later, Redrinna stood outside the doors of the library, sucking in a quick breath before she knocked. Xandrin had been hiding in his cave a lot lately, but he'd come out long enough to spy on the red-haired man for her. He'd said Timothon was making bread in the kitchen, meaning the man would be distracted for a while. And, since Tak was allowed in the library, the young man just had to open the door and she'd be inside.

Moments later, the door grated open just enough for her to slip through. Tak twitched the ends of his sleeves as she pulled the door shut, the butterflies from earlier doing a few victory laps in her stomach. She was back in the library! Her gaze drifted around the room, taking in the rows of bookshelves while she drank in the smell of leather and paper. The library was a bit dreary today, but that was more because of the rain pounding against the large windows set in the far wall than anything else.

"He didn't see you?" Tak asked, jumping at the sound of his boots—a recent gift from Timothon, though Redrinna had no idea where he'd gotten them from—scraping against the ground.

"Nope," she said, all but skipping over to the shelves. "But let's focus and find a book. Anything in particular you want?"

He trailed a little ways behind her, his gaze on the books' spines. "Not really."

That wasn't very helpful. She poked around a few minutes longer before finding a book that appeared interesting. She opened it and, after a few moments, put it back.

"That one's a bit complicated," she said in response to Tak's inquiring look.

She searched for another minute before spotting a book that looked promising. Grabbing hold of it, she glanced at the young man. "Maybe this one," she said, starting to pull it down.

Without warning, he grabbed her wrist. Glancing at him, a bit alarmed, she was startled to see Tak's eyes so wide, she thought they might pop out of his head.

"What?"

"Redrinna," he said, catching her a little by surprise. That was the first time he'd ever said her name without tripping over it. "Don't move."

Frowning, she glanced at the book in her hand. Immediately she froze, all her limbs going rigid like ice. Clinging to the top of the book's spine was the largest spider she'd ever seen, its fat body and thick legs bristling with dark fuzz, eight beady eyes seeming to stare straight into her soul. It was so large, she could see its pincers flex in and out, as though it was trying to decide whether or not to pounce.

"H-hold still," Tak said, his voice shaking like a leaf in a thunderstorm. "I'll crush it."

"With what?" she hissed, staring at the spider like her life depended on her not blinking. The beast had to be at least the size of her palm. "If you hit the book too hard, you'll break it." Her voice came out in a high whisper like it feared incurring the spider's wrath.

"I'll figure som—it's moving!"

Thick silence curled around them as the spider crawled a little closer to Redrinna's hand. Then it leapt.

Without meaning to, she chucked the book in the air and hit the ground. Frantically she looked to see where the spider had gone. It hunkered on top of the shelf for a brief second before scuttling towards Tak. The young man rapidly backed up, smacking into a bookshelf.

"Redrinna help!"

Leaping to her feet, she drew her knife. Desperate times called for desperate measures. "Not on my watch, you creep." She leapt in between Tak and the spider, causing the beast to pause and wiggle its pincers again. A chill raced across her skin as they stared at each other.

It pounced. She flinched back. The next second, Tak was in front and swiped at it, knocking it to the ground. It scurried off, and she quickly lost track of it.

"Over there," Tak said, pointing towards the nearest wall where two bookshelves almost touched, forming a dark space between them.

Swallowing, Redrinna held her knife out to Tak. "You can do it."

"Me?" he cried, his face going paler. He stopped, taking a deep breath. Then he took the knife. "Okay."

Together, with him in front, they approached the gap between the bookshelves.

"All right, creepy. Come on out," Tak called.

Peering around him, Redrinna frowned. It was too dark for her to see anything in between the shelves, forget trying to find the spider. "Tak, I can't see it."

"I thought for sure I saw it scramble in here," he said. He stared at the dark space for a couple minutes before shaking his head and returning her knife. "I-I guess it's gone."

She forced out a sigh, trying to convince her heart to come out of wherever it had decided to hide this time despite the fact she was still trembling from head to toe. The spider could come back at any second and—oh seriously. It was a spider.

Cheeks flaming hot, she slipped her knife back into its sheath. "I think that got a little bit out of hand," she said.

"But it was huge—" Tak began before his cheeks flushed too. "I guess you're right. It's just a spider."

"Admittedly a huge spider," she said, turning towards the shelves to hide her embarrassment. "Anyway, let's get back to—"

"It's back!"

Redrinna jumped a foot in the air as she whirled around. The spider scrambled between them, running as fast as it could go. Not again! Thinking fast, she raised her hands. Forget the knife; she could use her magic.

Fire crackled on her hands. Tak grabbed her arm, making the flames go out. "Don't use your powers in here. You could set all the books on fire!"

"How else are we going to kill the spider?"

Without warning, a booted foot slammed down on the spider with a loud crunch that made both of them wince. Timothon lifted his foot off the ground, grimacing a bit before turning his gaze to the two of them.

"All that racket over a spider? Seriously you two?"

Redrinna's heart dived back into its hiding place, burrowing out of sight. She'd just been caught red-handed.

"S-sorry...Timothon," Tak said, his cheeks so hot she could've sworn she felt the heat. "It snuck up on us and it was really big and—we got carried away."

The man put his foot back down, crossing his arms. "A better question is how Redrinna got in here when I've told you multiple times you need to be out there looking for answers instead of locking yourself in here."

Tak's gaze dropped to his toes. Redrinna turned her head away, chest tightening.

"Well?"

"I," she began, her voice very close to a squeak. Clearing her throat, she tried again. "I'm trying to help Tak find a book so he can learn how to read. He's my friend, so I just want to—"

"Redrinna." Timothon's gaze quickly became fiery, threatening to burn her to ash. "You need to think about what's most important. Osiris could show up at any time, and obtaining the gem's power needs to be your top priority."

"It already is!" Her fists clenched. She was so tired of being lectured that she wasn't doing enough when she knew she was doing everything she could. "Can't you see that I'm trying? What else do you want me to do? I go to the spring every week and do exactly what you ask, every time."

"Are you trying to fail?" Timothon snarled with enough ferocity she flinched. "People are counting on you. If you don't give this your all, you're going to let them down. Or worse, they're going to die."

Throat and eyes burning, she lifted her chin, matching his fiery glare with one of her own. Words stuck in her throat, so she tried to pour what she wanted to say into her gaze.

Redrinna was trying. She was doing her best. Why wasn't that enough? He looked away. She did the same. Her heart shaking like a stranded baby bird, she left the library, fighting to hold in her tears, determined to head straight for her room.

Before the door was all the way shut, Timothon started talking again. For some reason, she stopped, hand on the doorknob.

"You distracting her isn't helping," the man said, his tone still stern. "She already has enough to do."

"I-I know. I'm sorry," Tak said quietly, so soft she almost couldn't hear him. "But she just seems upset, so I thought—"

"I know, I know. I get it. You're trying to help. But this isn't helping her, so don't do it again, okay?"

If Redrinna hadn't agreed to have Tak let her into the library, he wouldn't be getting in trouble.

"W-wait," Tak said, making her jump. "There's something I wanted to ask you."

"Oh yeah? What is it?"

"Well, i-it's...lately, I've been having a weird dream. I'm at the ocean, and there's a voice that keeps calling me and telling me to open my eyes. I-I keep having it, and I can't sleep afterwards. So...I was wondering if...maybe..."

"It was related to the Dragon Gems in some way?"

Tak didn't say anything, so she figured he must've nodded or something.

"As a matter of fact, it is."

Her heart stopped.

"That dream means the gem that marked you is ready to bond to you. It's calling you. The dream won't go away unless you refuse it or you go get it."

The worst feeling Redrinna had ever had dumped over her like she'd just stepped under a frigid waterfall. She'd never had a dream like that. No gem had called her. After a month of having this gem around her neck, it didn't seem to want her anymore.

"So if you want, you could go get it now. I'm sure Xandrin wouldn't mind taking you."

Redrinna didn't stay to hear the rest of the conversation. She went straight to her room, pausing at the door. Xandrin's claws clacked against the ground from inside his cave, but like he had been for the last little while, he remained distant. Somewhere she couldn't be. She slammed the door shut behind her.

As soon as she was alone, the awful anger inside her melted, leaving a horrible, empty feeling in its wake. In just over a month, Tak already had a gem asking for him. While in the nearly three months since she'd started hunting for one, she still had nothing.

What hurt even more was that she agreed. Tak, so far, was every bit the budding legendary figure a gem would want, seemingly perfect in every way. He was smart, nice, a much better fighter than her, and against the spider? He'd protected her when it'd pounced. He'd been willing to corner it with the knife. She should've been able to do that too instead of hiding behind him. But she hadn't. Like always, she'd hid behind someone else.

Glancing down, she stared at the cold, dark gem hanging from her neck for a minute before she took it off. Mutely, she set it on the bedside table before she laid across her blankets with her back to it. For the first time, she wished she hadn't come here. Maybe it would've been better if the giant had gotten her after all.

⊱⋅ ⋅⊰

The hostile blueness of the spring loomed in front of her, a violent shiver running down Redrinna's spine at the sight. Xandrin sat silent beside her. For the first time since they'd met, she found herself wishing he wasn't here. Whenever he and Timothon talked, Timothon seemed so excited...and she just...

Bracing herself, Redrinna stepped into the water. Tonight, she'd prove she was trying her hardest so Timothon couldn't scold her or lock Tak out of the library too. Her ancestor had stood in these waters once, bathed in the power of the spirits, and things had worked. A part of her wanted to believe if she kept trying, it would work. The rest of her no longer did.

Once she was deep enough in, she began her recitation. About halfway through, she stopped. She'd said those words so much, they'd lost their meaning, congealing into a muddled mess that didn't make sense no matter how she poked at it. After a month of coming here and saying them, they'd never stirred anything in her or the gem.

Tilting her head back, she studied the stars like they'd give her some kind of answer. Like everything else though, the stars in the sky remained as silent as their glittery reflections in the water around her. Wrapping her arms around herself, a violent shiver shook her. Hopping out of the water crossed her mind, but she fought it off. Maybe she'd never stayed in the spring long enough to prove herself. Maybe she never would no matter how long she stayed in the waters, but she was going to prove she was trying.

"Er...Redrinna?" Xandrin called, just the sound of his voice making her want to stay in the water longer, even though her head was starting to feel like it was going to float away. "Haven't you stayed in there long enough?"

"I'm going to prove I'm serious," she said. Talking took a lot more energy than it had a little bit ago. Breathing seemed harder than it had a little bit ago too.

The dragon scrambled behind her, but she ignored him and the pounding in her skull. She closed her eyes against the rush of heat that reminded her of the first time she'd used magic. Darkness crept into the fringes of her mind. Her ears were ringing, and her body was heavy, like she was turning to stone.

The next thing Redrinna knew, she was in Xandrin's claws, swaddled in towels and blankets. Stop it, she thought, or maybe she said it. How was she supposed to prove herself if she'd been dragged out of the spring?

As the world sharpened back into focus, she realized Xandrin had her pinned, trapped between his hot chest and the cool ground. He'd pulled her out. The stupid dragon had taken her out!

"Xandrin get off me!" she said, trying to whack him, but her arms didn't have any strength.

"No way. If trying to win the gem over means you nearly dying, then I'm going to personally throw that rock back into the ocean you pulled it out of!"

Hot anger pounded through her veins even though she was shivering so hard she couldn't see straight. Curling her fist, she hit him once. Again. No matter how many times she did though, he didn't move. Not even when she'd said she hated him.

Later, to make things worse, he told Timothon what she'd done. The man hadn't seemed mad but he'd scolded her, reminding her yet again people were counting on her and she couldn't help them if she was dead. Like that lecture had ever helped her before. She'd ignored him until he'd gone away.

A day later, with faint bits of moonlight streaming through the tiny window in her room, Redrinna studied the gem hanging from her neck again. It didn't appear any different, even after all this time. All at once, she remembered the night Timothon had told her about the Dragon Gems, in that room with the statues and windows that broke the moonlight into a myriad of colors as it streamed through. The thought of it made her shiver. There had been something special about that place.

What if she tried going there? She'd felt something when she'd been there the first time, so maybe she'd feel something again?

Crawling out from under the covers, Redrinna didn't even bother to put on her boots before leaving her room, heading towards the third passage. Claws clacked against the ground behind her, but she didn't look back.

"Hey," came Xandrin's voice, making her stop. "Where are you going? Are you feeling better?"

She already regretted getting mad at him for pulling her out of the spring when she'd passed out. If he hadn't, she would've drowned. She turned back towards him. His eye spikes were tugged upwards, as high as they could go. Even his ear frills were a bit droopy.

"I feel all right," she began, knowing that physically she was fine, but that was about where 'fine' ended. "I thought I'd try something different tonight."

"Something different?" The dragon cocked his head as he repeated her words.

Nodding, she said, "No matter how much I train or practice my magic, it hasn't woken anything in the gem, and neither has the spring. But there's a special room up there. Maybe going there for a while will change something."

Silence drifted between them like a snowdrift gently but surely piling up.

"Xandrin...can I...be honest with you?"

The dragon met her gaze, the dim light that always filled the halls of the Mount reflecting off his red scales, giving them a quiet shine.

"After everything I've tried, I don't think this will change anything, but," she managed to give him a small smile, "I'm going to at least try."

He nodded, and she resumed walking up the passage. Xandrin didn't follow.

A little bit later, Redrinna was embraced by quiet, blue light streaming through the windows, creating gentle halos around the heads of the nine statues. The place was still as beautiful as she remembered, bringing a brief, tiny smile to her face.

Stepping up the staircase, she paused in the center of the platform, glancing at the gem in the moonlight. It was the same as ever. Taking a deep breath, she recited the words Timothon kept having her say, half-hoping something new would happen.

A tiny shiver raced down her spine. Then nothing but silence.

"I don't get it," Redrinna hissed, her frustration threatening to boil over. "I'm doing everything I can, but no matter what, I don't hear or feel anything from you."

Sighing, she closed her eyes against the sting of tears. Couldn't she go a day without crying anymore? An ache to be able to spend just one night in the library again blossomed in her chest, but that brought to mind of all the times Timothon had told her she wasn't doing enough. Wasn't giving it her all. Wasn't even trying.

Someone had said that to her mother once. The memory leapt into her mind unbidden, and once there it wouldn't leave. It'd been after either her fifth or sixth sibling had died. That was the only time she'd ever seen her mother angry, livid at some noblewoman who'd dared to say her children were dying because she wasn't doing enough to keep them alive or protect them. That was the one time she'd seen her mother confront anyone, her glare so hot, Redrinna had thought the noblewoman's flesh would melt right off her sharp cheekbones. And that had been the one time she'd ever seen her mother strike anyone.

All of the sudden, Redrinna realized she no longer believed her mother had tried to kill her. She'd known, but after everything, all the memories they'd shared, there was no way her mother could kill her. That's what she believed. If anything, her mother was another victim of her father, though she still struggled to believe he could be a villain.

Dipping her head forward, Redrinna's fiery red hair slipped off her shoulders and into her vision. Despite all her recent shortcomings, she still bore the gem's mark, the sign that she had the potential to be its wielder. Or, at least, she'd had the potential once.

Scooping up the gem, she stared at it for a long time, a lot of thoughts crossing her mind.

At length, she said, "You chose me once, and Timothon believed in me at some point. I don't think he does anymore." Dropping the gem, she glared at the moonlight reflecting off the smooth stone of the platform. "Why can't you just tell me what it is? What is it? Why aren't I good enough now?"

Chapter Twenty-Four

Dawn came sooner than Redrinna was ready for, but since it was impossible to claw the sun back beneath the horizon, she guessed she'd have to accept it. Sometime during the night, she'd fallen asleep on the stone platform, making her ache all over. Sitting up, she rubbed her eyes, her heart hovering somewhere near her toes. The cold weight of the gem rested against her chest, just like it had all night.

She thought about staying there for a little longer, but the room and the statues weren't as magical in the morning sun. Sighing, she forced herself onto her cold feet and, after a moment more, left the room.

Was there nothing she could do to convince this gem she was worth its power? Was it time...to consider putting the gem back? If it wouldn't wake as long as she held it in her hands, did she need to consider letting it go?

A rock shifted beneath her foot, making her scramble to catch herself before she hit the ground. Her hand flew out, skidding against the wall to stop her fall. Her palm stung. She supposed that was what she got since she hadn't worn her gauntlets when she'd decided to spend the night here. Staring at it, she watched specks of fiery red blood bead out of the scrape.

It'd been a long time since Redrinna had thought about the blood running in her veins, the blood that had always dictated how her life would be laid out, how and where she'd take her next step. Was this stupid liquid twisting through her veins the reason she couldn't prove she could be a part of the Dragon Kin? She'd thought that by staying with Xandrin, escaping into the mountains where she'd longed to be for years, she'd repaved the road she'd been forced to walk for as long as she could remember.

Maybe there wasn't a way for her to ever escape the world she'd been born into, or the failures she'd left everywhere she went. Fighting to swallow the hot tears stinging her eyes, she ignored her irritated palm and kept walking down the tunnel.

At the bottom, Redrinna's heart dropped even further at the sight of Xandrin lying in the main hall, his snout pointed in her direction. She tried to tug the tears into submission but they refused to yield, so she kept her head bowed.

The instant the hiss of her feet against the stone echoed through the main hall, Xandrin's eyes opened. Purposely avoiding his gaze, she stopped, not wanting to talk, but also unable to drag herself away.

"Did...anything happen?" the dragon asked, his scales scraping against the floor as he lifted his head, the harsh sound almost a relief after the gem's silence the entire night. "You can tell me, right? Did you feel anything?"

Her throat went dry, and she was sure she wouldn't be able to make a peep even if she wanted to. Shaking her head would have to suffice.

"Oh," the dragon said, somehow managing to make her heart burrow even further down with that one word. After a moment's hesitation, he reached out, his claws scraping the floor again before lightly touching her foot.

A hand rested on her shoulder. She turned her head away, already certain she knew who it was.

"It's okay, Redrinna. It's not like that was your last chance." Timothon was one of the last people she wanted to see, and his words did nothing to make her feel any better. "You've been pushing yourself every day; don't think I haven't noticed. Why don't you just rest for today? Tak's been missing your company."

"Why are you being nice to me?" she asked before she could think about it. Even then, she wasn't sure she regretted saying it.

A moment of silence followed before his grip on her shoulder tightened. "How about we focus on getting food in you instead? Going without food isn't going to get you very far."

Redrinna knew that. She'd had that lesson drilled into her when she'd almost starved to death in the forest. Jerking out of his grasp, she stormed down the second passage that led to the dining room. Xandrin stuck to her side like he was a blade of grass glued to her hand. The dragon made a few attempts to talk, but when she didn't respond, he stopped trying.

Tak was at the table already when Redrinna walked in. Xandrin curled up behind her usual seat instead of retreating to the corner. She sat, fixing her gaze on the table, trying to keep her emotions in check. Tak pushed a small bowl of strawberries her way. After staring at them for a long while, she hooked a finger on the bowl's edge and pulled it the rest of the way over.

"I found a book," the young man said at length.

"Oh." Her voice fell flat and she didn't have the energy to change it.

"Yeah. Timothon let me go in the library again provided I was under his supervision the entire time, so he helped me find one. Want to see it?"

She nodded as she bit into a strawberry, letting the tangy sweetness of the juice sit in her mouth for a minute before swallowing it.

He pushed a book titled *Mysteries of Eridia's Oceans* towards her. It was bound in achingly beautiful azure blue leather, and she longed to thumb the pages, but didn't.

"Do you like the ocean?"

His gaze dropped to the book. "It was m–my favorite place to go when...well, before I came here."

Unable to think of anything to say, she nodded. They both stayed silent after that, turning their attention to their breakfasts.

While they ate, her gaze drifted over to the young man, eyeing that dark green hair of his. It'd seemed a bit darker when they'd been in the forest, but it was still pretty dark. He and Xandrin hadn't gone to fetch a gem for him, even though she knew he could. Why?

As Redrinna studied him, the Dragon Kin's story began weaving through her mind. Even though there was only the two of them for the time being, there were more people out there. More people like them. And there were—

Her thoughts halted. Wait. An important part of the Dragon Kin were the dragons, and they only had Xandrin. That meant they needed to find a dragon who'd be willing to help Tak protect the gem once he got it. She'd found Xandrin by chance. She didn't have a clue where to find a second dragon.

However, there was someone who did. Her father knew, or at least, that's what Timothon claimed.

Her lungs tried to freeze up and Redrinna had to fight to breathe through the shards of ice climbing her throat. She had to go back...didn't she? Even if she obtained that information but didn't earn a spot here, then at least whoever came after would have a head start. Something she hadn't gotten.

But maybe—there had to be a chance—that this would be the task that would prove to her gem she was worthy of its power. Better yet, if her mother really hadn't wanted to kill her and was a victim of her father and Osiris, maybe Redrinna could at least save her.

When they finished eating, Tak hovered near the table, so she told him to meet her back here in an hour. She'd be ready to help him then. Smiling a tiny, timid smile, he hugged his little book to his chest and left.

Once he was gone, Redrinna shot Xandrin a very pointed look—making his eyebrows wrinkle—before leaving too. He stayed hot on her heels, not saying anything until she stopped in the main hall. She'd thought about ducking into a room, but she'd be able to see anyone before they came in here. Hopefully.

"What's wrong?" the dragon asked.

Beckoning him closer, she laid a hand on his snout and whispered into his ear. "I have an idea for something else we can try to wake up the gem."

His eyes flicked in her direction, but he remained quiet.

"Tak is probably going to join the Dragon Kin," she began. "Even if he doesn't, other people will. Which means they need dragons too, right?"

"Right. Timothon said every member had their own dragon companion."

"Do you have any idea where to find another dragon?"

Xandrin's claws rapped against the ground for a minute before he shook his head. "Nope."

"Me neither," she continued, the hand on his snout tensing. "But Timothon said...he said my father does."

The dragon pulled his head back, staring at her like she'd told him the worst secret he'd ever heard. "But that's—he's the one who tried to kill you!"

"I know," she said, trying to get him to lower his head so she could speak into his ear again. "I don't want to, but those dragons are in trouble so long as he's the only person who knows where they are."

"So you think if we can steal the information, maybe the gem will wake up?"

"Maybe." Her throat clamped shut before she could explain her earlier thought process. This would be her last shot. If this didn't work, she was through. Redrinna was running out of options and tired of always coming up short. But even if she didn't make it into the Dragon Kin, she could still save her mother.

The dragon stared at her for a long minute, his eyes glittering like flint in the moonlight. "When should we go?"

Her heart fluttered from relief and chest-crushing terror at the same time. "We're supposed to head for the spring in a few days, right? If we go then, Timothon won't know we went somewhere else for a while." He wouldn't worry or try and stop her. Her chest tightened at the thought, but she was pretty sure the man would tie her down to keep her from going. If she was honest, she was tempted to tie herself down. However, she wanted to at least be able to say she tried.

All at once, Redrinna sensed someone's gaze on her back, making a chill rush across her skin. Whirling around, she found Tak standing a short distance behind them.

One of Xandrin's ear frills twitched as she glanced at him. Tak had caught her again?

Tak was paler than usual, and after a minute, he tipped his head forward so she couldn't see his eyes. How much of their conversation had he heard?

"Tak," she began, her heart thrumming as panic flooded her chest. "You can't tell Timothon."

The young man swallowed. "I-I wouldn't have anyway...but—" His voice was hushed, barely disturbing the silence that had settled over them like a heavy rain cloud. "You're doing this to help me, even though I..."

"I promise we'll come back, but this is something I have to do. Trust me."

"I don't want you to get hurt because of me," he whispered, his voice so quiet she almost didn't hear him.

"I won't." She knew she couldn't promise that, but she said it anyway.

Slowly, he nodded. Somehow, that did little to make Redrinna feel better.

⋅⊙⋅ ⊙⋅

Even though Redrinna spent most of her time either training or helping Tak read his book, time flew past too fast. Four days wasn't a long time.

When night finally arrived, she waited for Xandrin to knock on her door—their normal routine for when they went to the spring—her knees threatening to give out any second. She paced back and forth, her chest tight. There were so many ways this could go horribly wrong, and few ways it would go right.

The dragon finally tapped on her door, nearly launching her out of her skin. Throat too tight for speaking, she opened the door. Xandrin waited outside, and he didn't speak either. He merely nodded, and she managed to return the gesture. What they were about to do was such a momentous task, her heart lay frozen in her chest like she was going to butcher it at any second and it was trying to hide. Even still, this was something she had to do.

Taking a deep breath, Redrinna left her room, making sure to close the door. The longer it took Timothon to realize they were gone, the better. She didn't want the others to worry about them for too long.

Both of them staying silent, they headed to the entrance hall where Timothon and Tak were both waiting for them. The silence hanging in the room threatened to smother her, but Redrinna managed to nod in Timothon's direction. Tak held his book tight to his chest and stared at the floor like he could become one with it if he tried hard enough. She tried to swallow past the lump in her throat, but without success.

No. She needed to strengthen her resolve. The gem wouldn't find any speck of worth in her if she backed away from the ledge of the metaphorical cliff she was about to leap off of.

"Hey, just do your best," Timothon said, a weak smile on his face. "This will be the last time you go. If it doesn't work, then we'll figure something else out."

"Right," she managed to say, unable to hold his gaze.

"Be careful."

With a final nod to both Timothon and Tak—who still refused to look at anything other than the ground—she and Xandrin left.

The earth basked in the scent of fresh rain as they flew, and normally, Redrinna found the smell relaxing, but tonight, the smell seemed to heighten her fear, making the panic more alive than usual. It was like she had her own tempestuous thunderstorm rolling through her chest. She hugged her sack stuffed with food instead of the usual towels and blankets close. Bringing the sack had been Xandrin's idea. If they had it, it might keep Timothon from figuring out what they were doing sooner.

They stopped for the night at the base of the Agicae Mountains, resting for a few hours before the sun rose, quickly growing too hot and bright for them to relax.

Xandrin scanned the skies before he took off again. "It's going to rain again soon."

Redrinna nodded, her throat dry enough it hurt. The palace began looming larger on the horizon, its pale turrets gleaming weakly in the sun like polished bone. She kept her gaze away from it, not wanting to be there mentally until she was there physically.

It was almost noon by the time they drew near enough to the palace Redrinna could see its gates and the trees on the mountains behind it. The gray palace stood so bleak against the vibrant green and purple of the snow-capped mountains, she couldn't help wondering how she'd lived there for so long.

All at once, she spotted something that made her heart skip a beat.

"Xandrin, we need to land."

The dragon did so, descending on the outskirts of the Imperial City. He glanced around, his claws drumming against the earth in a rapid staccato. "It's very quiet."

Her heartbeat thrummed in her ears as she approached the town entrance. It stood empty, devoid of any life. There wasn't a single soldier at the gates or a person waiting to get in or out. Even if nobody needed in, there should've at least been guards on duty. The place couldn't shut down during the day. She'd heard there were places farther south that did to help cope with the heat, but that was there and this was here. In the cold north. Squaring her shoulders, she walked through the gates, the cobblestone crackling beneath her feet.

There wasn't a single movement from the town. No people shouting. No horse-drawn wagons rumbling. No stray cats yowling or spitting. The town was so barren, the stagnant air threatened to choke her.

"Is this normal for human cities?" Xandrin asked, his voice seeming small against the oppressive silence of the town.

Redrinna shook her head, her throat clenching so tight, she fingered it with one hand. Was this some kind of messed up joke or something?

Steeling herself, she took a few steps forward before something caught her eye, making her pause. Xandrin stopped beside her.

A house stood to her right, the door ajar and the windows still and gray. Tiny streams of dried blood encrusted the entrance step. Despite the fact her stomach began twisting itself in a maze of knots, she stepped towards it. Xandrin's claw touched her shoulder, making her pause.

"Redrinna," he said, even his voice sounding strained, "that blood is old. Whatever's inside might not be pleasant. Let me look first."

Reaching up, she laid a hand on his claw. "I appreciate that, but...I need to look."

Fear wriggled its way through the knots in her stomach as she stepped forward. If something had happened to her people while she'd been gone, then it was her problem, not Xandrin's. It registered dimly in the back of her mind that she still thought of these people as hers despite abandoning them, but that was the least of her concerns.

Taking a deep breath, Redrinna stepped up to the house, keeping her gaze focused on the ground until she was ready to look inside. The door squealed like an angry bird as she pushed it open a bit further. It took her eyes a minute to adjust to the darkness, but when they had, she could do nothing but stare. The blood drained from her face.

It'd been a long time since she'd seen a dead human body. Even then, waking up after sleeping in her newly born baby brother's room to try and protect him and finding him lifeless and cold had been finding one body, not an entire families'.

Seven people were sprawled across the floor, as still as stone. Dead. Motionless in pools of their own blood.

Chapter Twenty-Five

"What is it?" Xandrin asked, pulling Redrinna away from the house when she didn't respond. He asked again, but she couldn't speak, her mind not able to comprehend what she'd just seen. He looked, pulling back almost immediately, shaking his head like a wet dog.

When had this happened? What could've done this?

Once she could feel her legs again, they continued on through the city. The further in they went, the more an indescribable, sickly sweet stench clung to the air, soaking everything it touched in its smell. Every house or building they looked in had bodies, not a single soul still living anywhere. The closer they drew to the center of the city, the worse the smell and bodies became. Homeless people had died in doorways, their remains baked by the sun. Dogs and cats had died in alleyways, still as the cobblestone beneath her feet. Birds had fallen from the sky, lying in broken heaps in the shadows of buildings.

Xandrin rubbed at his nose and shook his head. Redrinna buried her face in her hands, but that didn't block the smell or keep her from gagging. By the time they neared the center of town—haunting compared to how she remembered it being—Redrinna was horribly light-headed and on the verge of vomiting.

However, they both froze when they arrived at the town's center. Redrinna had no idea what it was exactly, but a large circle with strange runes ringing the edge was smeared across the cobblestone. From each rune, there extended a line, each line meeting at the circle's center. What made her blood ice over, however, was that it looked like it was drawn with blood.

"This...is..." she began, her voice nothing more than a harsh whisper.

When she found the strength to look at Xandrin, she was startled to see his scales had taken on a faint, ashy red color.

Hesitantly, Redrinna stepped forward. Pain lanced through her chest like a stake had been driven through her heart, plunging deeper the longer she stared at the circle. While she'd been shirking her duties, hiding in Xandrin's cave and enjoying herself in the forest, something had butchered the citizens of the Imperial City like they were cattle.

Despite how much she'd hated the idea of being their leader, she was supposed to have been here. Keeping watch. Protecting them had been the reason she'd been born, the reason this blood flowed in her veins.

And she'd failed.

Her breath rushed out of her, making her shoulders sag once it was gone. A memory swam to the surface of her mind: her promise. She'd sworn to protect these people. When she'd broken it, it'd never occurred to her that something like this could...or ever would happen.

Before she knew it, she stood at the edge of the blood circle, transfixed by the bright red glaring up at her. For some reason, seeing that shade of red stare at her from the ground made her feel like she was staring at her reflection. She stopped. If this blood was red, did that mean it was still wet? All the other blood they'd come across had been dry and brown.

Redrinna nudged the circle with her toe and frowned. Dry. A loud crack split the silence as a bright flash of light pulsed against her eyes, so bright the pain pierced the back of her skull. Panic flooded her veins.

Xandrin roared, rattling her bones. When she could see, she glanced back. Her breath stopped in her throat.

Between her and Xandrin, as far as she could see, stood a shadowy, gray barrier that almost looked like it was made of glass. She raced towards the dragon, hitting the barrier with her fist. It rippled slightly where she struck it, but nothing else happened. What in the world was going on?

"Xandrin?!"

"Don't panic," the dragon said, spreading his wings. "I'll find a way to—"

Rumbling cut him off. Redrinna turned back towards the palace, her heart pounding like a war drum as dark mist began tumbling from behind the inner wall's distant gate. The rumbling grew louder, harsher in her ears. The ground shuddered beneath her feet.

Without warning, the gates exploded outwards. Chunks of stone struck the barrier behind her, shattering on impact. The rest of the gate was devoured by black mist, crumbling to dust. Her insides froze over.

Long, clawed feet appeared, hauling a long, dark body out of the mist. She didn't know what it was, but its skin twisted and shifted like it was made of black sand. It bore a strong resemblance to a dragon without wings, but it wasn't as big as Xandrin. It was bigger than the giant though. It had a long snout, curving into a wicked, sharp beak— almost like an eagle's. The creature paused in the archway before it opened its eyes. They were smoldering orange, like vats of churning, spitting fire, both fixed on her.

For a second that stretched into forever, they stared at each other. The beast's burning gaze bore into her skin, almost melting her into a puddle right there.

What was she supposed to do against this thing? The only other thing she'd seen like it was the giant, and compared to this, he seemed as harmless as a daisy. All this time, she'd been preparing to take on a giant. Not this. She was no match for this.

Ribbons of black, dusty shadow twirled off the beast while it stared at her. Its muscles bunched.

"Run!" Xandrin shouted.

It charged.

She bolted.

The creature rammed into the barrier with enough force it shivered. She risked a glance back. It was getting ready to come at her again.

Xandrin swooped by above her. No matter how fast she ran, there was no way she'd escape that thing or be able to keep pace with the dragon.

"Go left!" Xandrin roared from somewhere above.

She did. The creature skid past seconds later. A loud thud shook the air, immediately followed by splintering and a heavy shattering that reminded her of the night the giant had broken into Xandrin's cave.

"Go right," the dragon said. "Freeze!"

Gasping for breath, she crouched low behind the building, terrified of Xandrin's request, afraid if she stopped moving, her muscles would lock up and refuse to move again.

The next second, she heard sniffing, long and loud. Her heart leapt into her throat, but she stayed where she was.

Claws crunched against the ground, the sniffing ringing in her ears, getting closer by the minute.

"Get ready to run," Xandrin said, his voice softer than before. After what seemed like a mere heartbeat, the dragon roared, "Go right!"

She took off. Claws scrambled against the ground. The beast broke into a sprint, thundering after her.

Xandrin called out some direction, but she didn't hear it over another building shattering against the ground. Wildly, she turned, stumbling into an alley with a body strewn in her path. Skidding to a stop, she fell and slid across the ground. Her foot bumped against the unrecognizable corpse. Her body recoiled, pushing her backwards.

Hot breath washed over her skin, blasting her hair into her face.

Her heart stopped. Slowly turning back, she sat face to face with the creature, the black, swirling mist inches away. Those orange eyes threatened to sear the flesh off her cheeks the longer she stared at them, but she couldn't seem to look away.

Xandrin roared. Her power tugged on her fingers, but she couldn't remember how to use it.

Without warning, someone yanked on her hand, jerking her to her feet and off to the right. The world flashed by in a blur. She glanced back at the beast. The beast's roar pounded the sky, making her teeth rattle. Shaking herself, she tried to catch a glimpse of whoever was tugging her on before they could turn another corner.

Her heart almost leapt out of her chest. "Lady Cel Tradat?!" she gasped.

The dark-haired woman threw a wicked grin over her shoulder. "Long time no see, Princess!" Her gaze flicked behind them. Her grin vanished. She didn't say another word as they flew around a corner.

Redrinna glanced back too, spotting the beast's mists leaking out between the buildings and houses but not the actual creature. Above, Xandrin stuck as close to her as he could despite the barrier.

The beast seemed confused, but only for a second. It roared, hurting her ears, before taking off towards them again.

Lady Cel Tradat skidded to a stop as they raced back into the center of town, where Redrinna had gotten trapped in the barrier in the first place. The woman scowled over her shoulder at the beast.

"What now?" Redrinna asked.

Before the woman could answer, footsteps echoed behind them. They were way too light to be the beast's.

Glancing back, Redrinna didn't know what to think for a long minute. The world around her screeched to a halt.

"Dad," she breathed.

Somehow, he heard her and looked back. Her mind went numb. He was the same. Just how she remembered him. The same brown hair, the same eyes, the same tired look on his brow.

He didn't wear his crown. That meant—

No. It didn't mean that anymore. Her father had tried to kill her. He'd left her in a cave to die, and possibly killed her siblings too. Maybe even hurt her mother.

Even still, there was a part of her that wanted to bury herself in his arms and never leave. If he really wanted her dead, then how come instead of being shocked or angry, he just seemed so sad?

Had he...truly intended to kill her? Was he disappointed she was still alive? A crack spider webbed across her heart, threatening to shatter it. She wanted to be wrong. She wanted to be wrong so bad—

All at once, the beast burst into the square, hissing and spitting as it glared at the three of them. Her father stepped between them and the beast.

"Stop where you are," he demanded, the authority in his voice sending a chill down her spine. That she hadn't missed. To her surprise though, the beast halted, staring at them with those burning eyes. "You don't need to be here. Return to your slumber."

The beast blinked once, slowly, like it was trying to decide whether or not it wanted to obey. Then it turned and vanished through the palace gates. The barrier shimmered out of existence.

Her heart plummeted. She guessed Timothon had been right then, all along. Her father really was the bad guy.

Chapter Twenty-Six

Sighing, Redrinna's father turned back to her. Lady Cel Tradat's grip tightened on her hand. Redrinna's legs ached to keep running, but she wasn't sure if they wanted to run away or run to him. But that would've been stupid...right?

Xandrin landed close by, calling her from those thoughts. She looked at him, but he wasn't looking at her; he stared at her father, eyes wide.

"What?"

Distractedly, he glanced at her. "I-I know him. He's the man I met before, the other human."

What? The man who'd lost his family and blamed himself for it had been her father? She turned to him, but his gaze was fixed on the ground.

After a moment, he glanced in the dragon's direction. "Hello again, Xandrin. It's been a long time, huh?"

Xandrin just stared.

"What did you come here for?" Lady Cel Tradat abruptly snarled, earning a steely glare from her father. "You honestly think I'm going to let you get a second chance to kill your only daughter?"

Redrinna couldn't deny the rush of appreciation she felt with the woman was here. If she'd been alone, she didn't know what she'd do. All at once, something struck her. If her father and Lady Cel Tradat were here, then... "Lady Cel Tradat, where's my mother?"

The woman glanced at her with those dark eyes but didn't answer her question. Instead, she turned to her father. "I'm warning you, you stay away from her, Renoan. I won't let you mess with her again."

"Oh drop the act already. The only person who's been messing with her is you."

Hesitantly, Redrinna glanced back and forth between the two of them. They weren't best friends or anything, but they'd never spoken to each other like this. Lady Cel Tradat's grip on her wrist suddenly tightened. It almost hurt.

"That's rich coming from you," the woman snapped back. "She doesn't even know what you are."

"You think so? What about you? She doesn't even know your real name. Do you, Redrinna?"

What? When she glanced at the woman, she was startled to find Lady Cel Tradat staring at her, a hard gleam in her eyes. Almost like she was studying her. Something about it made Redrinna tense like she was pressing a blade against her own skin. The woman was closer than she'd been in months, but something was different now... Something was wrong.

"I wouldn't listen to him," Lady Cel Tradat said, the gleam in her eyes not vanishing. "Though I confess he's right about one thing: I did tell you one, teeny, tiny lie. My name isn't Cel Tradat. It's Reyna. But beyond that, I've always been exactly what I appeared to be. Unlike him."

Reyna. She knew that name. "Like Queen Reyna in the legends?" Redrinna began softly, her throat a bit tight.

The woman nodded.

"And like the Reyna who sided with Osiris?"

The woman's eyebrows lifted a fraction for a split second, so fast, she almost missed it. "How do you know about him?" she whispered, an edge in her voice.

Throat cinching a bit tighter, Redrinna said nothing. The better question was how did she? In all the legends Lady—Reyna had told her about the Dragon Kin, she'd never once mentioned Osiris. Redrinna hadn't heard about him until Timothon—who'd fought the guy in the flesh—had told her about him. So how did she know about him? Better yet, why was she here, unscathed from whatever had happened to the city? Redrinna could guess at her father, but why Reyna too?

Something flickered across the woman's face for a second—just a split second—something that looked a lot like annoyance. Redrinna might not have had many skills, but after spending her entire life on the lookout for who was going to smile at her before talking about her behind her back next, she knew when someone was wearing a mask.

So, for the first time since she'd met the woman as a child, she took a step back. Or tried to. The woman's grip on her wrist tightened, passing the point of uncomfortable and reaching the point of painful.

She squirmed, but the woman didn't let go. "You're hurting me."

"I asked you a question," Reyna said, a smile gracing her features. Her smile seemed different than usual, like it was being held in place by wooden stakes. "I'm still waiting for an answer."

Redrinna responded by fighting harder to get away. The woman let her go, and she stumbled back two steps. She had a feeling—a very nasty feeling—that there was only one way La—Reyna could know about Osiris.

She found herself sifting through her memories, searching for answers there. Now that she was looking for it, the woman was the same. Always, no matter the memory. Despite the fact that when they'd first met, the woman had been a war veteran, a full-grown adult, she sported no gray hairs now. No signs of the hours every day she spent out in the sun and elements. As far as she could remember, the woman seemed as much the same today as she had at their first meeting. Just like her father.

"You're that Reyna, aren't you?" Redrinna asked, her voice almost a whisper. The one the legends said could take on entire armies by herself. The one Timothon had fought against. The one who'd killed his dragon. "You're her."

The woman didn't say a word. She didn't confirm it. But she didn't deny it either.

All this time, Redrinna had been with the enemy. She'd been so desperate for friends, she'd made friends with a dragon murderer. But why had the woman wanted to be her friend if she'd known Redrinna might join the Dragon Kin, the one force that would stand in her way?

Without warning, Redrinna's father blasted Reyna in the side with shadowy magic. It looked like it was made from the same substance as the beast he'd just subdued. The woman flew sideways, hitting the ground. She lay still.

Then, he was there, in front of Redrinna, hand on her wrist, dragging her towards Xandrin.

She yanked herself out of his grasp, dodging out of reach. "Don't think I'm going anywhere with you after what you did." It hurt to say it—a little—but she meant it.

Holding up his hands, he took a step back. "I know, I know."

She didn't know what to say. She wanted to shout at him but also wanted him to hold her close and tell her it'd all been a bad dream.

"Oh my Little Princess," he began in a whisper, using her nickname from when she'd been five, his brow furrowing as he stared at her. "You shouldn't have come back here. Yet, I'm so happy to see you again. I feel like I'm in a dream that's going end any second. I bet that sounds crazy, right?"

"Dad," she breathed, stepping towards him before stopping herself. No. He couldn't be her dad anymore. He couldn't. It...it wasn't right.

"Are you sure you want someone like me as your dad?" he asked, dragging his gaze upwards until he met hers. "Even though I'm sure you know about my idiot mistakes?"

Redrinna didn't know what to think of what he'd done, even now. That was the truth. A part of her didn't want him to be her dad, but the rest of her refused to believe anything but.

"I wasn't lying, you know. About what I said when I pushed you."

"About how you love me?"

He nodded, a flash of determination lighting his eyes for a second. "I meant it then, and I still do. I know you don't get it—I don't expect you to—but there isn't time to explain anything. Not even this." He waved a hand at the city around them. "There's so much I need to say, but there isn't time."

"Why don't we have time?" It didn't seem like they were on a deadline here. Not anymore. "And where's Mom?"

He didn't answer that. Instead, a tiny smile touched his mouth. "You threw away your necklace, didn't you? The one I always told you to keep?"

A little self-consciously, Redrinna touched her collarbone. That had been so long ago. "You said it would prove who I was, and I thought you didn't want me so...of course I threw it away."

Her father remained still for a minute before his gaze flicked behind her and he suddenly pulled her into a tight hug. Automatically, she grabbed her knife, but she couldn't bring herself to draw it. Again. Why couldn't she keep her emotions straight?

"That necklace was all I could do to protect you from *him*," he hissed, making her heart shudder. She wasn't sure how, but she knew who he meant. "So without it, he already knows you're here, and that's why we don't have any more time. And because you have that gem, you're going to need this." Letting her go, he reached into his shirt and pulled out a slim sheaf of papers, placing it in her hands. "Don't read it now. Just take it and go. Hurry."

"But Mom—"

"There isn't time! You have to go." He pushed her towards Xandrin.

Before Redrinna could, there was something she had to know. "Why are you doing this after you tried to kill me?"

Her father blinked once before sighing. "I wasn't trying to kill you. I could never do that, but I wanted you to think that so you'd stay away from this place. Your mother and I had to keep you out of his hands."

"I could've died though," she said. A tiny flicker of anger sparked through her chest, but it didn't find anything to catch on.

"You weren't going to die. Because of your blood, it's impossible for something like that to kill you."

"What?" Blood again? Though, this was the first time she'd been told her blood would protect her in some way.

"Our blood, it's—"

"Oh, Father was right," Reyna said from behind them. "Renoan, you've gone soft after all."

The next second, shadowy magic caught her father in the chest, blasting him back. It pinned him to the ground like a massive spider hunkered over him. Spinning on her heel, Redrinna found Reyna stalking closer. Fear rooted her in place.

"Redrinna, go! Hide those papers!" her father shouted.

She didn't have anywhere to hide them, so for lack of a better place, she shoved them down her shirt.

Xandrin growled. As the woman's gaze flicked his way, panic like Redrinna had never felt exploded in her chest. Reyna had killed Timothon's dragon. That meant she could—

"Xandrin, don't!" she cried.

He took a step back, shooting her a concerned, confused look.

"Just...stay where you are, okay?"

"Clever girl," Reyna cooed, a grin lighting up her face as the sun caught her braided black hair, making it gleam. "Now give me those papers your father gave you, and I'll let you go."

"What do you want with them?" Redrinna said, taking a step back for every step the woman took forward.

"Save the dragons." The woman smiled. "Same as you and your Dragon Kin."

Redrinna didn't believe that. She wanted to, but she didn't. Not once had she, Xandrin, or her father mentioned anything about the Dragon Kin. Which meant she had to be that Reyna, didn't it?

It felt like she'd been carrying an open puzzle box and tripped, scattering the pieces all over, leaving her too startled to figure out what was what.

Slowly, Redrinna shook her head from side to side, heart hammering so hard in her throat it hurt. "I won't."

The grin vanished. "Excuse me?"

Redrinna's heart squeezed her windpipe, making it difficult to breathe. "I...I won't give these to you. They're for me to protect. Not you. Sorry. I-I have to go."

As quickly as possible, she turned towards Xandrin, but all at once, what felt like a large hand seized her wrist. Her gaze shot down. Her heart skipped a beat. A dark, shadowy hand coiled around her wrist, steadily morphing into something that looked more like a manacle. A long, taut, shadowy chain extended from it to Reyna's hand. She slowly met Reyna's cold glare, a chill shooting down her spine.

"I said," the woman began again, speaking in a harsher tone than she had before. "Give me those papers." The woman jerked the chain, yanking her off balance.

Xandrin leapt forward, claws raised to strike the woman. Reyna's icy glare flicked to him, and he went rigid, unmoving.

Redrinna's heart leapt into her throat again, threatening to choke her. "Don't hurt him!"

Reyna shot her a cold smile. "My business is with you, and you alone. Not this overgrown lizard, and definitely not with that half-wit father of yours. If they stay out of my way, they'll be fine. Give me those papers now, or I'll take them from your broken fingers."

Redrinna tried to step back, but the chain held her fast. Frantically, she glanced back, searching for her father. He was behind her, clawing at the shadow pinning him to the ground.

There wasn't anyone to protect her. Even if she'd been strong enough or skilled enough, she didn't think she'd be able to raise a sword against Reyna. Until today, the woman had been her friend.

"Stop fighting me," the woman demanded, yanking her a bit closer.

Redrinna fought to free her arm, her heartbeat roaring in her ears.

"You've never wanted to be an Empress or put yourself at odds with anyone. You've always wanted to be somebody else, always wanted to live a different life. How is this accomplishing that? If that's really what you want, then why are you fighting me?"

Redrinna didn't know that answer. But she didn't know what to do either. Her father kept urging her to run. Timothon probably would've told her to fight back. But a part of her couldn't bring herself to do it, like it believed if she stayed, Reyna would change, would go back to being the person she knew.

If she surrendered the papers, the nightmare that'd been the

Dragon Kin, the gem, the non-stop failing—all of it would leave her be. It wouldn't be her job anymore.

"Redrinna!" Xandrin said, turning his head towards her, but it looked like it was taking all his strength.

Reyna's attention didn't leave her as Redrinna stared at the dragon, tears burning against the back of her throat. If she listened to Reyna, she wouldn't have to keep trying to force herself into a life that was never going to fit. She could pretend this wasn't real.

That she hadn't met Xandrin.

She shook her head. She couldn't do that. She'd never forget Xandrin, despite the fact she wouldn't be able to join the Dragon Kin with him and ended up having to watch from the sidelines.

At the very least, even if she couldn't have anything else, she wanted to stay with him. No amount of books would replace him.

No amount of books would erase the destruction of this city from her memory either. Never, ever, would she be able to forget what had happened here and go back to a life of ignorant bliss.

"I don't want to fight you," Redrinna hissed, fighting desperately against the pull of the chain. "But I will."

That seemed to catch Reyna by surprise. "Redrinna, use your head. When have you ever done something right during all these years of trying to force yourself into something you're not?"

That stung worse than any insult anyone had ever said about her, whether or not they'd known she'd been listening. Her vision misted over as she glared at Reyna. She wanted to shout, to tell the woman she didn't know who she was. But that would imply Redrinna knew that answer, and she did not.

"Redrinna, she's lying to you," her father shouted. "You are not a failure!"

The woman's gaze suddenly flicked to the side, hovering there for a minute before she grinned. "If I can't convince you to play nicely, Redrinna, then allow me to introduce you to someone who can," she said with a wide grin. "He's been dying to meet you." The woman flicked her wrist, snapping the chain, the shadows melting away like snow. Redrinna staggered back. The woman flicked two fingers at her.

There was a moment of nothing. Then everything went pitch black. What felt like tiny hands scratched and clawed at her, dragging her somewhere she didn't want to go. After a long, silent, panic-filled minute, it all stopped.

Hesitantly, Redrinna opened her eyes, surprised she knew where she was. She stood in the great hall, the long room barren, the tables and benches smashed against the walls, most of the tapestries on the ground like trash. Timothon's still hung from the wall, dangling in tattered shreds. The fireplace in the center of the room lay black and empty. The only light came from the high windows along the far wall, muted light from the cloudy sky streaming through them. Dust filtered through the weak streams of light, twirling like they were floating through water instead of air.

Where was Xandrin? And her father? Reyna wasn't here either.

All at once, Redrinna's gaze flicked to the dais, where the weak sunlight illuminated the gentle curves of her mother's throne. A chill raced down her spine at the broken back, the wood in splinters on the ground. But what made all the blood in her body freeze was the man lounging on the second throne—her father's throne—like he owned it.

Smirking, he said, "So, you have arrived at last."

Chapter Twenty-Seven

The man's voice alone almost made Redrinna's heart leap out of her chest, something about the way it seemed to slither into her ears leaving her more than a little unsettled.

The man watched her with serene, unearthly blue eyes, a hint of a smile softening his expression. In the light of the windows, the whiteness of his skin and hair seemed to make him glow a little, accentuated by the fact he sat in a dark room. He rested his chin in his hand, his elbow on the arm of the throne.

Despite his smile, something about him made Redrinna feel sick like she'd eaten bugs and they were crawling around inside her. Why was he on her father's throne? Why was she here? How was she here?

The man watched her intently, something about his gaze reminding her a lot of a spider waiting for its prey. He didn't say anything for several minutes, each second that dragged by longer than the one before it.

"I have waited such a long time to meet you, Redrinna, and believe you me, it is such a pleasure. I apologize for not standing and greeting you properly. Even after all this time, I lack my full strength."

She tried to swallow, but her throat was drier than an empty well in summer. How did he know her name?

"A bit disoriented, are you? I suppose it is natural given the circumstances, and the kind of magic that brought you here always takes a bit to get used to anyway. Very well, allow me to introduce myself. My name," he paused, grinning like a cat with a mouse in its claws, "is Osiris."

Redrinna stiffened. Was this what an ant felt like moments before someone stepped on it, when the shadow of a shoe stole the light? Osiris was the guy...he was the one who'd murdered Timothon. The dragons. The one whose magic threw the world out of balance.

"However, something much more interesting to me, at the current moment, is you, and that blood you hate so much curling through those thin little veins of yours. It has always been your burden, has it not? The part of you that you could never wholly leech out."

She wanted to run, but her legs shook so badly, she was afraid she'd fall. This was bad. Really bad. Of all her screw-ups, this one outstripped everything else she'd ever done.

"Funny, is it not? How we humans always find something to hate about ourselves, whether it be our faces, our bodies, or our history. All things not easily changed and even harder forgotten. Even you, a girl born to the highest privilege, finds faults in herself, do you not?"

Redrinna's breath caught in her throat. If she survived this, Timothon might just kill her himself.

Chuckling, Osiris leaned forward a fraction of an inch. "You are a funny creature, that I cannot deny. Regardless, I have a proposition for you. It is the reason I have wanted to meet you since the day you were born, in fact." A wicked light appeared in his eyes, making Redrinna's heart shudder as far back in her chest as it could go. "Join me."

"J-join you?" she said, her stomach clenching with pain at the thought. The man who'd destroyed the Dragon Kin and nations alike wanted her? The man who'd taken her father from his family, and destroyed that family? There was no way, but she was too terrified to tell him no. She tried to step back, but her knees had rusted solid.

"That is what I said." He nodded once, leaning back in the throne. "Tempting, is it not?"

"You," she began, heart racing a thousand miles an hour, "you're the one who...you killed the dragons."

"I am." Osiris nodded once again.

"And you're the one...who hurt my father."

"I hurt your father?" He straightened, one pale eyebrow lifting before his smile widened. "Dear child, your father came with me of his own free will. Any pain he feels is human error."

She shook her head. That wasn't right. It couldn't be.

"No? Is it hard to think of your poor father that way? I suppose it must be hard to imagine him doing something like that when he appears so...human, is it not? After all, it is human folly to refuse to believe another human being, especially one with a special place in your heart, could ever be such a monster."

This was insane. She needed to get out of here as soon as possible. Working up as much courage as she could, Redrinna convinced herself to take a step back. She thought her knees might snap from the effort. Osiris's grin widened even further like he'd said a hilarious joke. Without warning, a sharp pain dug into her spine, rooting her to the spot. Hadn't it been just the two of them in here? Had Reyna come in while Redrinna had been distracted? Risking a glance back, her heart stuttered at the sight of empty darkness behind her despite the pain piercing her back.

"Appearances can be so deceiving," Osiris was saying, forcing her attention back to him. His grin was so wide, she was ready for his face to split from ear to ear, an idea that made her heart thrum in her throat. "That is a phrase known by many but understood by few. Perhaps you have joined the ranks of the learned now.

"Regardless, that," he sighed, grin dimming, resting his chin in his hand again, "is superfluous to the topic at hand. Alas, it is obvious the choice is unsavory to you. How disappointing. Truly. I even sent one of my best to fetch you, but you would have none of it."

His best? Did he mean the giant that had kept coming after her? Now that she thought about it, her father had said her pendant was the only thing protecting her from him, and the minute she'd thrown it away, the giant had come after her. Which meant Osiris had been the one trying to drag her off from the beginning?!

"So let us do this," he continued, pulling her unwilling attention back to him. "Would you like me to explain what, precisely, I am offering you? That would be more to your liking, would it not?"

The sharp pressure needling into her back made her too afraid to nod or shake her head, too afraid to even twitch.

"Not only could I give you power beyond your imagination, but I would also take the responsibility of this Empire from your shoulders." He paused, watching her with those unnerving, blue eyes of his. "Is that not what you have always wanted? A life without the burden of an empire, without a constant threat looming over you, forcing you to keep staring over your shoulder? Freedom? I can grant it if you wish it, Redrinna. All you have to do is ask."

Sweat trickled down the back of her neck, the pain in her back constant, making it hard to focus. She knew she shouldn't want to accept Osiris's offer, but she also really wanted to. Dangling in front of her nose, so close Redrinna could almost taste it, was the one thing she'd always wanted: her freedom. A life of her own choosing instead of the one where she was drowning under the weight of so much responsibility and guilt all the time.

A life where no one expected anything of her.

A life where she couldn't let anybody down.

Yet, at the same time, the things this man had done were terrible; she'd seen the evidence with her own eyes. Osiris hadn't even bothered to hide what he'd done. On the contrary, he seemed pleased about it. A shudder seized her, which made the pain in her back spike.

"It must be a difficult decision for you, though I imagine it would be for most anyone." Osiris lazily waved a hand. "So take a moment and think on it, long and hard. However, bear in mind, Princess: every choice comes with a consequence. Make sure it is one you can pay."

Redrinna didn't need a moment. Or, at least, she shouldn't have. His offer was tempting, but she wasn't so desperate to escape her blood that she'd side with a psychotic, mass murderer.

The pain digging into her spine vanished, allowing her the freedom to move without fear again. Slowly, she touched a hand to her shirt, the papers she was in charge of crinkling faintly.

Even if this man was offering what she'd always wanted, it didn't mean he'd give it to her. He'd been the one using her father, the one who'd caused the demise of the Dragon Kin a hundred years ago, and the one who'd been responsible for waging war after war on this continent. Who knew how much more pain and destruction he'd caused that she didn't know about? How much he would continue to cause?

And yet...she'd told herself if this trip wouldn't convince the gem to wake up, she'd admit defeat and return it to the ocean it came from. She couldn't bring herself to stay in the Mount or with the others. Maybe not even Xandrin, though she wanted to. Perhaps staying here and doing what Osiris wanted was what was best?

Her chest deflated like her lungs had been punctured. Was there much of an option for her? She wanted to believe there was, but...

Her hand reached for the knife at her belt, the one she hadn't turned to for guidance in a while. *Forge your own path,* Reyna had said. Had the woman actually wanted Redrinna to forge her own path, or merely walk the one Osiris had already planned out?

Lifting her head, Redrinna stared at the man. "Why do you want me?"

"I will not bog you down with the details, but you are different from anyone else who walks this earth. Because of your father's...let us say power, you hold in your very flesh something vital to my plans to rebuild this continent," Osiris said, his smile still intact. "That is why I need you and hope you will come of your own free will. It would be a shame for you to suffer like your mother."

Her heart stilled. "My mother? Where is she? Is she—"

"Hush for a moment," the man said, sitting up straight. "What I am saying is your mother lost so many children, which caused her much despair." He paused, his tongue running along the bottom of his top teeth as a twisted grin swept across his face."It was the only way to keep her in her place. Too much spirit, that one. Though that was not enough, I suppose. It was her idea to ferret you out of the palace and out of my grasp, you know."

The world stopped. Keep her in her place? That had to mean— Fear squeezed its fingers into her chest, making her muscles lock up.

"You...you're the one who murdered my siblings, aren't you? You killed them all."

Her parents had tried to keep most of the details from her, but Redrinna knew each and every one of her brothers and sisters had died with seemingly no explanation. It was eerily similar to the people in the city. Other than an excess of blood, she had no idea how they'd died. No cuts, no bruises.

"I am sure you will not understand my way of thinking, but I only need you." Osiris said that like he was discussing the weather. "An excess of children would simply serve as a distraction."

Redrinna froze, every muscle locking harder, so hard she was shaking from head to toe, her blood crackling with hundreds of ice crystals ready to rip her to shreds. Her mother had suffered so much trying to ensure the survival of every one of those babies and had suffered even more when she'd failed to protect them.

And she, Redrinna, had wanted so badly to be a big sister. Yet she hadn't even been able to do that right.

However, that was also because of this man. A century ago, he'd ripped her father out of his family. Now, he was trying to rip her out of her own, away from Xandrin, for something she could only imagine as horrible after what little of his methods she'd seen.

Forcing her body to work, she took a step back, keeping her hand on her knife. The idea of bowing her head to the man who had caused her parents so much heartache was revolting, more revolting than taking the throne or leaving Xandrin forever. She may not have had much choice, but she didn't have to choose that.

"I would prefer if you used words to share your thoughts," Osiris said, his grin shrinking by a hair. "I would rather not have to tear them out of you."

She had zero clue if he was serious or not, but the way he said it made her think he might be. Her throat was so dry she doubted she'd be able to make a sound even if she tried. However, she knew a way to make her intentions perfectly clear.

Her heart shivered at the hiss of her knife as she drew it out of its sheath. Holding her hand as steady as possible, Redrinna pointed the blade right at the man's chest, the metal gleaming in the light from the window.

That was her answer.

Osiris' smile vanished. "Are you sure that is what you want? You truly wish to point your blade at me?"

She didn't let her knife lower an inch.

Shadows curled over one of his hands, thrashing and flailing like a mass of writhing tongues. "Where will you go? You and I both know that Dragon Gem around your neck has remained silent as a grave for you. It wants to be with someone else. You don't belong with them."

Even if she didn't, there was still something important she had to do.

Still pointing her knife at him, she forced herself to take another step back, trying to ignore his words even though they hurt. If she could make it to the doors she knew were behind her somewhere, she could get out of here and back to Xandrin. Where she went didn't matter, so long as it was somewhere he wasn't.

"Leaving so soon, are you?" the man continued, using his free, non-shadow swarmed hand to pull something from within his robes. "First, before you go. Something...I think you will be delighted to hear."

He grinned again. Whatever he was holding lifted into the air before rushing towards her. She caught it—more from an instinct to protect her face than anything else—before looking at it.

It was a necklace, one Redrinna knew instantly, even before the tiny little gems caught the light from the window. It was her mother's favorite necklace, the one with the two intertwining hearts.

The chain was smeared with dried blood.

Chapter Twenty-Eight

The world dropped out from beneath Redrinna. The air rushed out of her lungs like she'd been punched in the gut. Her mother's necklace coated in blood. That didn't mean—it couldn't—

"What did you do to her?"

"It was unfortunate," Osiris said, watching her like he was studying the clouds in the sky. "On the bright side, she resides with all those little babies now."

Hot tears pricked her eyes as Redrinna glared at him. Unfortunate? Her mother's death—presumably at his hands since he'd held on to her necklace like it was a trophy—was *unfortunate*?

"All right, let us play a little game, shall we?" Osiris said, leering at her. "Since you are so insistent on running, I will let you have a chance. If you can get away, I will let you go about your business—for the time being. But if you fail and I catch you," he grinned, "you are mine."

Behind her, the massive doors grated open.

"I would start running if I were you."

Slamming her knife into its sheath, Redrinna turned on her heel and ran, faster than she ever had before. She didn't know why he was letting her escape, but she wasn't going to question it. Her first priority had to be getting out of here.

People were scattered along the path between her and the front doors, all of them as lifeless as the people outside. Some she recognized, some she didn't. She was too afraid to look closely, just in case Captain Brion had been caught up in this madness. Her heart wouldn't be able to take it if she found him here too.

Minutes later, she burst through the front doors, the dim sunlight blinding her for a second. Once she could see, she ran for Xandrin the second she spotted him. He let out a funny, squeaky roar when he saw her, the rain he had predicted starting to fall.

Just as she cleared the first gate and entered the city, Reyna seized her arm, jerking her to stop. Pain lanced up her arm.

The woman's brow was furrowed, twisted into an expression she'd never seen there before. "You think you can just go? After everything we—that I—?" A pained, confused expression flashed across the woman's features. "Redrinna, is this really what you want? I thought you were my friend. Does friendship mean so little to you?"

Redrinna blinked, her fist tightening on the chain of the necklace in her hand, metal biting her fingers. She was highly aware of the weight of her knife. When the woman had given it to her, she guessed neither one of them would have ever imagined their paths would be sliced apart like this. Or that she'd be the one cutting them apart.

"You were the only friend I ever knew in the palace," she said, trying to yank her arm free from the woman's steel-like grasp. "But you were manipulating me, weren't you?"

When the woman wouldn't let go, Redrinna drew her dagger, refusing to hesitate before slicing a deep gouge in the woman's arm and stepping back.

Reyna pressed a hand to the wound, blood dripping from her fingers as a heartbroken look swept across her features.

A terrible pain ripped through Redrinna's chest, but she kept her knife pointed at the woman. "You threw your lot in with him," she said, stepping back as Xandrin stepped up beside her, crouching low. "Even though you know what he's done. If that's your choice, I cannot—no, I will not be your friend. It's over."

Reyna's heartbroken gaze shattered, giving way to stone-cold fury. "So be it. If you're not with me, then I'm no longer with you, and that makes you my enemy. I destroy my enemies."

Redrinna didn't look back as she vaulted onto Xandrin's neck. Her gaze shot to the right, where her father stood, silent, his face drawn and ghostly white like he'd been given a death sentence. Their gazes met for one, nowhere near long enough second. He mouthed 'I'm sorry,' before Xandrin launched into the sky.

As they did, Reyna shouted after her, "You'd better get a good head start, you rat! When I catch up to you, you'll learn what it means to be hunted!"

The Imperial City shrank below them, the rain steadily falling harder, making the city seem more gray and desolate than before. Redrinna didn't want to think about it. She didn't want to think about anything. Swallowing, she hunched her shoulders and turned away.

Long before the city was out of sight, the storm's fury let loose, dumping the ocean on them. Lightning ripped the sky like it was made of paper. The gallons of rain spearheading towards the earth sizzled like fire with each lightning bolt that tore through it. Thunder burst so close, it hurt Redrinna's head and rattled her entire skeleton.

After another minute, Xandrin shot for the ground, diving under the cover of a thin cluster of trees. "Sorry," he said, glancing at her. "But I think we're going to get struck if we stay up there."

She nodded, her tongue and throat feeling swollen as she tightened her grip on her mother's necklace before tucking it away. Her mother...couldn't be gone, could she? No. She shook her head. There wasn't time to think about that.

Xandrin seemed about to say something before a war cry rent the air. It sounded close.

"What was that?"

Glancing back, it was too difficult for Redrinna to make out anything through the sheets of rain. Lightning flashed overhead, illuminating nothing but empty hills. What on earth had made that noise?

Without warning, the ground beneath them exploded.

Xandrin catapulted upwards, scrambling to escape the debris. Redrinna's heart stopped.

The giant ripped himself out of the ground, letting loose another one of those war cries. Her blood froze.

The second Xandrin's feet were back on the ground, he bolted. Redrinna clung tight to his wet scales, hoping the papers beneath her shirts would be okay. The giant raced after them, faster than she'd thought it could go, like they were the rabbit and he was the fox.

Apparently, Osiris had been serious about playing that 'game.' If she wasn't going to stay of her own free will, then he was going to drag her back to his side like a pet. She shuddered as panic ricocheted in her chest.

If they couldn't escape, she'd be trapped by the man who'd destroyed her family.

Xandrin raced on, his clawed feet thudding against the ground. No matter how fast he ran, the giant stayed hot on their trail.

Redrinna lost track of how long they ran, but soon Xandrin was panting so hard, it was almost louder than the rain cascading around them. They just broke the tree cover of the last of the forests that cloaked the foothills of the mountains when the giant lunged for them.

His enormous fist caught hold of one of the spiny parts of Xandrin's wing and yanked. There was a nasty snap as the force jerked them in a half-circle, Xandrin's claws ripping up chunks of earth as they spun. With a loud hiss, he clawed at the giant, slashing him across the face. Without waiting to see how much damage that had caused, Xandrin turned and ran.

Redrinna's heart pounded so loud in her ears, she almost couldn't hear anything else. The wing the giant had snagged hung limp by Xandrin's side, smacking the trees as they passed. Even though he didn't slow, she knew from the tension in his neck he was in pain.

Redrinna glanced back, waiting for a flash of lightning so she could spot the giant. A minute or so later, the lightning flashed. Her heart leapt into her throat. He was right on their tail. He leapt for them, making her cry out a warning.

As Xandrin glanced back, the giant latched onto his tail, yanking them backwards. She almost front flipped over the dragon's horns, just catching herself in time. Xandrin scrambled for a minute before kicking the giant so hard, it flew through the nearest tree.

His one good wing unfurled, and they half-flew half-jumped above the trees. He latched onto a ledge of the mountain, swinging wildly for a couple seconds before he scrambled onto the rocky cliff face. Redrinna struggled to keep her grip. This was her fault. It was all her fault. Why was she always so stupid?!

The dragon growled as he vaulted forward, and she glanced back to see blood streaming from his tail where the giant had dug its claws into his flesh. After a long moment, Xandrin paused and stared at her hard, a look she couldn't interpret etched into his features. It wasn't quite worry and it wasn't quite fear, but something in between. Something that scared her more than the giant scaling the mountain after them.

He took off again, faster than he'd been running before. There were no trees to hide them here, nothing but bare stone climbing high above them to one side and a steep drop off on the other. After several minutes, he skidded to a stop and rose onto his hind legs. Without making a sound, he reached up and pulled her off. Redrinna stared up at him, her heart threatening to dive headfirst from her chest.

"Xandrin?" she managed as he tucked her within a thin, scraggly outcropping of trees and bushes, barely enough to hide herself in. He arranged them over her to cover her better. Desperately, she wanted to ask him what he was planning on doing, but she was too scared of what his answer would be.

The war cry rang out, causing him to glance over his shoulder before looking back at her. "Stay here. Don't move until I come back for you, okay?"

Before she could argue, he turned and leapt a short ways ahead, to a spot where the cliff face was quite wide. Wide enough to fight, she realized. He stood there, waiting, blood-stained tail swishing from side to side, his gaze focused on the giant charging towards him. As thunder crashed through the sky, they leapt for each other. She dipped her head, rain racing over her cheeks as she tried to block out the crash of them fighting.

Struggling to keep her breathing even, Redrinna frantically pushed at all the thoughts crowding into her brain like insects, trying to keep them at bay. They scuttled in anyway.

Her gaze fell, finding her hands, the rain mingling with the mud and blood there. The blood must've been Xandrin's. Maybe she'd gotten some from running through the city. Honestly, she didn't know how her hands had gotten so dirty, but the rain pooling in them mixed all the filth together. Slowly, with her stained hands, she grabbed the gem dangling from her neck, still cold and lifeless as ever.

How had things ended up this way? All she'd ever wanted was to prove she was strong, but all she'd ever done was leave disaster after disaster in her wake like she was a hurricane, a menace. The people in the Imperial City, the people in the palace, all of them, were gone. Snuffed out with all the ease and indifference of putting out a candle.

That was Osiris' power. That was what Timothon and the Dragon Kin had fought against. That was what they'd died against. Redrinna shuddered. For the last one hundred years, people had been dying with no one to save them. And she, the one Timothon had believed would create some kind of miracle, had met him and ran like a dog with its tail between her legs.

Even then, he was still after her, and what was she doing?

Thunder and Xandrin's roar rent the air as though they were the answer her gem refused to give. She hunkered further in the bushes, holding the gem tight to her chest like that would give it life, some of the rain running down her cheeks suddenly becoming hot and salty.

"It's all my fault," she whispered. Like the coward she'd always been, she'd hid and thousands of people had been slaughtered like cattle. Her siblings had died because Osiris had decided she was perfect, the chosen one for his plan, whatever that meant. Her mother had been murdered because she'd raised her hand against the man to protect her.

Her breath caught in her throat and she had to fight the urge to start bawling as she stared at the gem she'd thought would fix everything.

"You were never going to wake up for me, were you?"

The ruby remained silent still.

Redrinna understood. If life was a tapestry with every soul woven into it, her strand wouldn't have been an important one. It would've been a frayed end destined to fall off sooner or later. If she'd been in the gem's place, she wouldn't have chosen her either. Why?

Because her people, her innocent brothers and sisters, and her mother most of all, had been beyond her power to save. Her cowardice had seen to that. There never would have come a day where she would've been good enough to save any of them.

Closing her eyes, she dropped the gem, making it thunk against her chest. Lifeless, as always. She'd tried—harder than she ever had before—and she had nothing to show for it.

When she opened her eyes, her stained hands caught her attention again, the hands that had failed over and over to break free from the blood pounding through her veins with every beat of her heart. The hands that had never been able to prove she could do anything more than fail.

Thunder rolled across the sky again. Burying her face in her hands, she let the urge to cry go, let her body shake, racked with quiet sobs that wouldn't stop, sobs that made the ache in her bones worse not better.

Why couldn't this have been the one time she'd been good enough?

All at once, a devastatingly familiar voice carried up to her from the cliff below, right below where she was. "Aw, you're looking a little rusty, Dragon Slayer! A century without dragons made you weak, huh? Normally, you'd already have him finished."

Lady Cel—no, Reyna. Redrinna's breath went still in her chest. She was too scared to even twitch.

There came a strange hissing from below. She braved a look. Her eyes went wide. Five shadow beasts, looking a lot like the one in the city but smaller, closer to the size of large dogs, slinked around Reyna, shadows curling off them as they prowled across the wet rocks.

"Yes, I know you're hungry," Reyna said, beaming at them. "You can join the feast in a minute. That beast has hidden the girl. If you find her, bring her to me unscathed."

The beasts snarled and one even howled, burning yellow eyes glaring at the dark sky.

"Yes, but your first order: Protect the Dragon Slayer. And as for the dragon?" Reyna laughed, sending chills down Redrinna's spine. "Kill it."

The beasts raced off, straight for Xandrin. A second later, the dragon roared, a high sound that reminded her of the first time the giant had come for them, back in the cave, a sound that made her blood run cold. He'd roared like that before, on that night. When he'd been in pain.

Parting the bushes a little more, Redrinna almost cried out at the sight of Xandrin being swarmed by those beasts while the giant—the Dragon Slayer—loomed over him. His sides heaved like the ocean in a storm, bright red blood streaming down his scales and his broken wing. As she watched, he staggered, back legs giving out beneath him.

She didn't know how she knew, but it hit her like a stone wall: Xandrin was going to die.

Chapter Twenty-Nine

Redrinna's heart went still, like a rabbit in the brush that knew the fox prowled inches away. Xandrin was exhausted from running with her for so long. Fighting with all his strength was wearing him out more. If he didn't stop, he would die.

As long as she stayed in the bushes, he wouldn't stop. He'd sworn he'd protect her, no matter the cost, but this wasn't a price she was willing to pay. If she lost him as well, she'd—

Panic flared in her chest, sparking in hot reds and oranges. Her heart shivered like the brush as a wolf parts it. Her breath came in short, hard gasps.

Maybe Redrinna had failed the people of the Imperial City and her family, but she would not let Xandrin die. If it hadn't been for him, she would've died several times over. Even if she could have, she never would have considered joining the Dragon Kin without him.

She leaned forward, resting her weight on one hand before freezing.

Xandrin had told her to stay here. He was a powerful dragon—a beast of legend—and she refused to believe he would've gone out alone unless he was sure he could win against those beasts. Right?

If she left the bushes now, would she make it past Reyna without getting caught? If she couldn't, would she be able to fight her friend— kill her if she had to? Better still, what if her going out there made things worse? She'd failed at so many things before, what if—

No.

Violently, Redrinna shook those thoughts out of her head. She didn't know what she could do, but she was going to do something. If she was just going to hide and let Xandrin fight her battles, then she should've stayed at Osiris's beck and call!

The bushes raked her skin as she burst out of them. Ignoring the sting, she ripped free of their clutches and fell the short distance to the shelf below. She landed somewhere in front of Reyna, but she didn't look back.

Just as she was about to race forward, shadows clasped her wrist, yanking her back and off balance. She glanced back, finding herself inches from Reyna's face.

The woman smirked. "I win."

Redrinna's heart thrashed in her chest. "Let go of me," she hissed, not wanting to fight, but desperate enough she would.

"Not a chance. The game's over, and you've lost. Now we wait for your dragon to die."

"No," she snarled back. "I don't care what happens to me, but let him go. He's got nothing to do with this."

"All dragons are a threat," Reyna said, still smiling. "And I eliminate threats. No exceptions."

Redrinna wanted to scream, but that wouldn't help Xandrin. She had to fight, no matter how much she hated it. And her opponent was Reyna, a peerless fighter who'd felled countless people.

Redrinna was only a scared, inexperienced seventeen-year-old who hardly knew how to use a weapon. But unless she wanted to watch Xandrin die, she was going to have to win somehow.

Taking a deep breath, Redrinna did her best to shove every other thought away, focusing solely on this fight. Reyna was amazing with those swords at her waist; Redrinna had seen it with her own eyes. So, she needed to make sure Reyna didn't get close enough to use them.

Focusing on the power coursing through the earth under her, she paused long enough to drink it in. She curled her free fist. Then punched. Flames ripped through the air, spinning off her fist, catching

Reyna in the stomach.

With a startled face, the woman staggered back. The shadows holding Redrinna disappeared. Turning, she bolted, racing for Xandrin.

The shadows clamped on her wrist again, jerking her to a hard stop. Her shoulder screamed in protest. Her feet scrambled for purchase on the wet rock, and she almost fell. Glancing back, her heart stuttered as Reyna charged at her, one sword in hand.

Quickly, Redrinna focused on the power flowing between her and Reyna. Several enormous plumes of fire shot up, their booms ringing off the mountainside. Reyna cried out, and the shadows on Redrinna's wrist vanished again. Without waiting to see what had happened, she ran.

Xandrin only had three of the shadow beasts and the giant on him now, but he could barely stand, hunkering so low he almost looked like part of the mountainside. There wasn't much time left. She had to get there now—

Something grabbed her ankle, yanking it out from under her. She hit the ground face first, eyes watering as the stench of iron filled her nostrils. Scrambling to her feet, she ignored the blood streaming from her nose.

Reyna was close, sprinting forward, her sword glinting in the rain.

Redrinna threw a wave of fire, knocking the woman off course and to a stop. Then another, making the woman retreat a step. They were getting awfully close to the cliff's edge. Redrinna tried not to think about it.

All at once, she had an idea. The woman wasn't going to stop chasing her, so she had to do something else.

As the woman recovered, Redrinna stepped closer, closing the distance. Her heart pounded so hard she thought it was going to explode. She stopped when she was close enough to be uncomfortable. Reyna readied her sword. Redrinna took the steadiest breath she could.

Then she fired her magic, as much as she could, as hard as she could. Reyna backed up a step, putting her dangerously close to the edge. As the last of the flames vanished, Redrinna leapt forward. And shoved as hard as she could.

One second, the woman stared at her with wide eyes. The next she vanished into the trees far below. And was gone. Thunder rumbled above as she stared into the canyon.

Redrinna...had just killed someone. It'd been quiet, much quieter than she'd imagined. She'd just—

Xandrin roared again, but this one was weaker than the others.

Spinning on her heel, Redrinna turned in time to see the remaining shadow beasts vanish like mist before the sun, but the giant remained. Steeling herself, she ran for Xandrin so fast, she could hardly feel her feet striking the ground.

It was almost like she flew.

Focusing, she seized the power flowing through the earth, the spirit pounding beneath her feet. Fire crackled at the tips of her fingers, and she shot it at the giant, consuming it in fire. It howled, clawing at the flames as she pushed them to burn hotter and faster.

After a minute, it fell, flames puttering against the torrent of rain. For now, it was dead. But that wouldn't last for long.

Skidding to a stop, gasping for breath, Redrinna glared up at Xandrin.

He stared down at her, and she focused on his face so she wouldn't see how badly his legs shook as his precious blood fell to the ground like rain. "What are you doing?"

"Go, Xandrin. Get out of here. I bought you a few minutes. They're doing this to get me. You can't get me out of here in your condition, so you need to save yourself. You can rescue me if I'm captured, but I can't save you if you're dead!"

Before he could speak, his legs buckled beneath him, sending him crashing to the ground. She cried out, but he shook his head, forcing himself back on his feet.

"I made a promise to protect you and keep you safe, Redrinna," he snarled, his voice so weak it almost broke her heart. "I intend to keep it, no matter what."

Anger sparked in her chest. It dissipated as a rattling cough shook his body.

Now what was she supposed to do? How was she supposed to save him if he wouldn't go?

While Redrinna stared at him, thoughts pounding her mind like raging river water against rocks, her heart fractured like it was made of glass. A crackling echoed from behind her. She glanced back as the giant began to rebuild, the burnt flesh melting away. They were almost out of time. Xandrin refused to leave, and she didn't know if he'd make it to the Mount in his condition. What was she—

Her breath halted in her throat.

All this time, Redrinna had been preparing to battle the Dragon Slayer. If Xandrin wasn't going to leave, then she needed to fight.

She didn't have a sword or any of the weapons she'd been training with, but it didn't matter. She'd been training with her magic too.

It blinked those snake-like eyes at her, but she stared at its chin instead. "Don't want you," it said in its slow, deep voice.

"Too bad." She channeled her energy. A second later, the giant erupted into flames, just like the night she'd first used her powers.

As she waited for it to die and most likely come back, she became aware of the fact she was panting so hard, it almost felt like she wasn't getting any air at all. Her back and shoulders burned. She'd never pushed herself this hard before. She'd never used so much magic all in one go.

The moment the giant recovered, Redrinna readied herself. It charged before she could pull on her magic. Xandrin snatched her to the side, barely getting them out of the giant's way.

Awful dizziness hit her. Of course. She'd used so much magic, more than she ever had before. If it was like any other muscle in her body, then it was at its limit. It couldn't go much further. And it was at such a bad time!

The giant prepared to charge at them again. There wasn't anywhere for them to go this time. If it came, Xandrin would undoubtedly shield her. There was a good chance he wouldn't survive that.

Before Redrinna knew it, she was moving. Forward, not backward. She didn't even know if she was breathing. Her heart fought to break free of her chest, but she snatched it, ramming it back in its place.

She was scared, yes. The last thing she wanted to do was die or surrender herself to Osiris. But she wasn't so weak she needed to sacrifice her friend's life to protect her own. Xandrin wasn't going to pay the price for her shortcomings!

"Don't." The command came out of her throat in a strangled snarl as she stopped between Xandrin and the giant. Her heart quivered in her chest as she stared up at the enormous creature, but it remained where it was for once. "You will not touch my dragon!"

The giant snarled in response and charged, hands stretched towards her.

She was too tired to move. Her hands ached from how much fire she'd used. So she held her ground, not even breathing as the giant raced straight for her. She hoped it wouldn't hurt when it hit.

All at once, a flash of light rushed outwards.

Dazzling.

Blinding.

Heat raced through her chest like it was a forest on fire.

All she could see was white light.

After a long moment, it faded, the rainy gray over everything seeming darker than it had a minute ago. Blinking, Redrinna stared at the giant who stood frozen mid-charge, still as stone. It was right in front of her, close enough she could touch it if she tried.

Had she done something?

Without warning, the Dragon Slayer shuddered before collapsing. Redrinna just managed to get out of the way. Was it dead? It didn't seem dead. It looked stunned, but she wasn't sure. Curling, dark mist coiled out from beneath it, looking a lot like the power Reyna and Osiris had been using, wrapping around the giant like a cocoon before it vanished.

Then there was nothing but the splattering of the rain and the occasional rumble of thunder. Her gaze drifted over the cliff face, waiting for something else to jump out at them. Everything was still.

What...had just happened? Her chest still burned like it was on fire, making her glance down. The gem hanging from her neck pulsed with a soft light, glowing fiercely in the rain.

That...that had to mean...

"D-did you just—?"

A heavy thud from behind her reverberated through her bones, threatening to rattle her heart apart. Redrinna knew what that was, but didn't want to believe it. Turning, her heart shattered like a window, bursting into thousands of glittery pieces.

Xandrin had collapsed.

"No, no, no, no," she whispered, racing to him, pressing her hands to his cheeks, trying to lift his head. "Xandrin, you have to get up! Please!"

He fought to open his eyes, those warm, dark pools trying to look at her, struggling to find her face. He took a shaky breath, eyelids fluttering, hauntingly reminding her of the rabbits in the wood seconds after she'd plunged her knife into their little chests.

"No, I won't let you die like this," she said, desperate to think of something, anything she could do. She couldn't lose him. It was more than she could take. "I need you."

He tried to look at her again, but his eyes slid shut. His head dropped awkwardly into the mud, completely still.

Her chest constricted. He...couldn't be dead.

Was he still breathing?

Redrinna couldn't tell.

What was left of her heart shriveled into a tiny ball. Her vision clouded over as she tried to take a breath. It felt like she'd been punched in the stomach and couldn't get any air in her lungs.

Xandrin couldn't be dead. He couldn't. Not him. Not like this.

"I'm sorry, Xandrin. I'm so sorry." Closing her eyes, she rested her forehead on his snout. "Please, get up."

She had to do something, but what? She didn't know how to help him. She couldn't just run and get Timothon. There wasn't anything she could do. Nothing she knew would save him. She'd failed again.

Redrinna.

She jumped at the quiet voice that whispered in her ear.

Don't give up just yet.

Confused, she glanced at the gem, which pulsed brighter than it had before. Did the voice belong to it?

There's still something you can do.

She repeated those words in a whisper, each one striking her heart like heavy raindrops against her skin. What was there for her to do?

Thunder rumbled across the sky as Redrinna ran a hand over Xandrin's forehead, her thoughts rushing to find something. What could she do?

Her thoughts stopped. There wasn't anything *she* could do anymore. She knew that. However, there was somebody else, someone she knew, who might be able to do something.

What will you do now? the gem asked, its light pulsing brightly with every word it spoke.

"I have to go back to Timothion," she said, grasping the gem in a white knuckle grip. "He saved me once. If I make it in time, I'm sure he can help me save Xandrin too. Can you help me do that?"

The gem didn't speak, but a red diamond of light appeared a hair's breadth from the ground a short distance away, hovering for a second like a lone star in the night sky before racing in a circle around both her and Xandrin. What it drew reminded her of the blood circle she'd seen in the Imperial City, but this was different somehow.

Heat flooded her again, and she closed her eyes, letting it flicker and churn inside her chest.

She would not lose him. Not this time. She would not lose Xandrin.

Chapter Thirty

When the heat and light faded, Redrinna opened her eyes to find herself and Xandrin back at the Mount. She blinked a couple times, trying to wrap her head around that. She'd had no idea the gems housed a power like that. What she'd been thinking would happen is it would... Actually, she didn't know what she'd expected to happen.

"Redrinna!" Timothon shouted so suddenly she jumped, jabbing the spikes on Xandrin's chin into her leg. The man skidded beside her, somehow ending up on his knees before grabbing her shoulders in a vice-like grip. "What happened to you?! Where have you even been? I don't like worrying about you, you know!"

Prying her shoulders out of his grip, Redrinna shook her head, wet hair whacking her cheeks. "It doesn't matter. What does matter is Xandrin's hurt bad, and if we don't do something he'll die."

His gaze jerked to the dragon, his cheeks going pale. "I don't know what happened, but whatever. Run to the kitchen, grab pans, and fill them with water from the spring in your room. If you find Tak, have him help you. Also grab towels. Those should be in the kitchen too—Hurry!"

Redrinna didn't need any further invitation. She raced down the hall, jumping out of Tak's way as he emerged from the library. Several emotions flicked across his face, from surprise to excitement to concern to bewilderment. She wanted to laugh, but saving Xandrin was what mattered. Dragging the young man with her, they grabbed as many pans as they could carry—and an armload of towels—and filled them in the spring in Redrinna's room.

Working swiftly, they mopped up Xandrin's blood. He had deep cuts everywhere, bruises already discoloring his scales, and his broken wing hung limp like a snapped twig.

Thunder rolled outside the Mount, muted but still sending chills zipping up Redrinna's spine. She focused her attention on the dragon's ribs, wiping away the blood and putting the strange mixture Timothon had whipped up on every cut she found. Timothon himself concentrated on Xandrin's wing, setting it and binding it to the dragon's side once he could. It was hard to stay focused when she felt the need to constantly check and make sure the dragon's chest still rose and fell.

Redrinna didn't know how much time passed while they worked, but she was worn out by the time Timothon released a sigh and stepped back. That sigh had sounded a bit ominous. Glancing at her hands, she bit her lip at all the blood smeared there. How much blood had Xandrin lost? She'd acted fast enough this time, hadn't she?

"He's going to be okay, right?" she asked, turning to the man, her breath catching in her throat.

Timothon looked her way, staring at her with his intense red eyes for a long second before nodding. "He should be fine. Eventually. We'll just have to wait and see."

All the air rushed out of her lungs and she lost feeling in her legs. She was pretty sure they wouldn't support her weight if she tried to stand. Her eyes closed almost of their own accord.

She hadn't failed him. At the very least, after all her mistakes, she hadn't let him down.

All at once, she was exhausted, her energy vanishing like thin, wispy clouds in front of the sun. Timothon's voice echoed around in her brain, but she had no idea what he was saying for a long time. Dragging herself back to the surface, she glanced at him.

"Are you going to tell me what happened?" the man asked, his face set in a scowl.

There was so much to tell, Redrinna had no idea where to start.

Her memories swirled together, linking in patterns she couldn't puzzle out. And there were some things...she didn't want to puzzle out yet. However, there was one thing she could tell him.

She lifted the gem so he could see it. For a long moment, he simply stared at it like she was showing him an ordinary rock, not one that burned with a soft, red light.

His eyes went wide as saucers.

"It woke up," he breathed, kneeling in front of her. "You did it. How?"

The only answer she could give him was a shake of her head. Right now, she just wanted to sleep. She could think about those things later.

"Oh," Timothon said before he leaned back a bit. "I suppose you should get some rest. You'll have to try to stay awake long enough to clean up, which I'm already guessing is going to be difficult. After that you can explain everything that happened after you left."

"But Xandrin—"

"I'll keep an eye on him. I promise."

Redrinna dipped her head, unable to express the relief in her chest. However, her legs still lacked any feeling. They sat there for a long time, Timothon's eyebrows rising higher and higher. There still wasn't any feeling in her legs, but she figured it would come back soon.

"Do you like it there or something?" he asked, his head tilting to the side.

"Oh no, it's not that," she said. "I was just so relieved when you told me Xandrin would be okay, I kind of lost the feeling in my legs."

A short laugh escaped him before he rose and picked her up. "How about I take you to your room? Maybe your legs will be able to get themselves back together by then."

She felt a bit conspicuous being carried like that, but after a minute, she remembered her father used to carry her like this when she'd been little and had fallen asleep in her parent's bed or the library. She'd always woken up but had pretended to be asleep so he wouldn't make her walk. Thinking about how tenderly he'd tucked her under her sheets—which had been warmed before they'd arrived—left her empty and miserable, something she didn't want to be yet.

Timothon set her down once they'd reached her doorway, bringing her back to the present. "Are those legs of yours working now?"

"I'm fine," she said with a small nod.

With a nod of his own, he left. As she watched him go, it finally dawned on her why she'd trusted him from the second they'd met: his walk, his smile, and even the way he stood, all of it was exactly like her father.

Frowning at the thought, she turned away and entered her room.

ঙ৹৩ ৩৹ঙ৹

Redrinna only slept for as long as she needed to before she was awake and as alert as a rabbit with a fox on its tail. The thought of trying to go back to sleep crossed her mind before she shook it away and left the confines of her bed. She quickly went back in the main hall, curling up beside Xandrin's head, listening to his slow but steady breathing for a moment she wanted to hold on to for as long as she could.

It'd occurred to her many times that if she had given up and done her usual, the dragon wouldn't be here with her. It scared her a bit, but also...it felt good. Refreshing, like water on a hot day, sweet fruit on a warm spring evening, or a crackling fire during a quiet snowstorm.

Timothon had been here a minute ago, but he'd left with a nod when she'd arrived. She caught a glimpse of his retreating form and couldn't help wondering whether or not he'd keep his word and scold her for what she'd done. The idea didn't stop her stomach from yanking itself into hard knots, but she hoped he'd spare Xandrin. The dragon had just gone along with her idea.

Plus, the Dragon Gem had woken up. Her heart leapt in her chest at the thought. She'd done it! She'd proven her strength and herself, even though she'd been ready to throw in the towel.

Yet, the dancing in her chest faltered when she remembered what that meant. The idea of confronting Osiris and his unnervingly blue eyes made her tremble from head to toe, but if it would keep Xandrin safe, then she'd do it without hesitation.

She'd protected Xandrin and successfully evaded Osiris for the time being, two things she hadn't known or believed she could do. Yet now that she had done them, she wondered what else she was capable of.

Footsteps pulled Redrinna from her thoughts. Looking up, she was a bit startled to find Timothon coming back towards her.

"Do you ever sleep?" she asked, scooting a little closer to Xandrin.

"Well, I am a spirit, so I don't need to sleep," he said, shifting something he was holding behind his back. "But, since you're awake, I figured this would be the perfect time for you to explain where you and Xandrin disappeared to for an entire day." He sat beside her, a stern glare on his face.

Redrinna ran her hand over Xandrin's snout a couple times before she started. She left out a lot of the parts with her dad, unsure how to process any of them, but she kept in just enough for him to get the idea. When she mentioned Lady Cel—Reyna, Osiris, and the Dragon Slayer, he sucked in a breath so fast, she worried he might choke.

"I should've guessed those three would still be going strong if your dad was. And it freaks me out that the Dragon Slayer himself was on your heels this whole time. But you actually saw Osiris? Like, in flesh and blood?" His eyes were wide and his face ashen.

She nodded. "As far as I could tell. I didn't try to get close enough to find out. However, he did say he was still really weak."

He sighed, rubbing the side of his head. "I wish I knew what he was after, but it's not like he carried around a giant banner saying 'This is My Evil Plan' when I fought him."

After a long minute of silence hung over them, she continued explaining, pausing when she got to the part with her mother's necklace. Her hands went to her pockets. Not there. Had she dropped it somewhere? Had she lost the last thing of her mother's she had to hold on to?

"Tak might have it," Timothon interjected, putting a damper on the panic flaring in her chest. "I saw something on the ground in here, but Tak picked it up. However, you're not allowed to bug him until he wakes up. He has enough trouble sleeping as it is."

"He does?"

"Sure, but you're not one to talk either considering how early in the morning it is right now."

Redrinna frowned, waiting until he motioned for her to continue before speaking again. He stayed quieter than the snow on a winter's night until she finished telling him what'd happened. He remained silent for a while after too.

"So that's what finally did it, huh?" His gaze flicked towards the gem hanging from her neck. "You know, I had something I wanted to give you. I thought it might help you figure this whole thing out, but it seems I was a bit slow. Do you want it anyway?"

Curiosity bit at her heels, making her say yes almost instantly. A smile tugged on his mouth as he turned and grabbed something wrapped in a soft cloth. A towel, she realized, which made her hide a smile. Timothon was a bit strange, but he meant well.

Pulling the towel back, Redrinna gasped, tempted to rub her eyes to make sure what she was seeing was real. A shirt lay in the folds of the cloth, but what caught her attention and held it was the fact it was made of scales. Glittering scales the same red and smoky black shades as Xandrin's.

Holding it up, she turned it so that the scales on the long sleeves caught the light, shining like little jewels.

"This is amazing," she breathed, running her hands down the sleeves.

"It was something my dragon did for me, so I figured maybe if Xandrin made you one, it might give you the push you needed. There's nothing quite as special as having a dragon care about you so much they make you armor out of their own scales."

"Armor?" She cocked her head at the shirt. It was light and moved like an actual shirt. It was nothing like the heavy, clanking armor the knights were required to wear.

"Dragons are born with magic in their scales that protect them from all kinds of weapons and things, so they'd sometimes make shirts like these for the humans they care about as a way to show their friendship. It was considered a high honor to receive one in my time."

"Xandrin made this for me?" Her heart quivered a little at the thought. Was this what he'd been up to while she'd been trying to wake the gem?

Timothon nodded, a faint smile touching his mouth. "Yep. While you were focused on your training, he was very determined to make this shirt for you. In the end, I think I ended up doing most of the work, but he was very enthusiastic. He told me if he made you a shirt, then he'd be able to protect you all the time, even when he couldn't be with you."

She couldn't help the smile that touched her mouth as her heart melted. Typical Xandrin. Once again, she reached out and traced her fingers across his scaly forehead.

A few months ago, Redrinna wouldn't have believed that she'd find such a devout friend in a dragon, especially in such a short amount of time. Now though, she couldn't imagine being without him. Funny how that had all worked out.

"And...I think I owe you an apology," Timothon continued, shifting slightly.

"You owe me? I thought I owed you."

"Okay, but I get to apologize first," he said, shooting her a grin—another one of those smiles that didn't seem able to reach his eyes—before he looked away. "I need to apologize for pushing you so hard. For me, I had this constant, incessant dream until I went and got the gem, so it didn't even cross my mind that the gem wouldn't accept you once you found it. Then I kept pushing you and pushing you because I was afraid if I was more sympathetic, you'd stop trying so hard. But because of that you and Xandrin almost got killed. I guess I was so determined to find a way to make up for my own failures and ease my guilt that I tried to force my burden on you. That's why I'm apologizing."

She didn't know how to respond to that, so she didn't. "I'm sorry too," she said, fingering the sleeve of the dragon scale shirt. "For not realizing my limits, I mean. And for being so reckless, I almost got Xandrin killed and myself captured."

He shrugged, glancing her way out of the corner of his eye. "We both still have a lot to learn, eh?"

A tiny laugh escaped her. "It seems so."

She rose to her feet, wanting to put on the shirt as soon as possible. Timothon smiled, a real smile. Unable to resist matching his smile with one of her own, she headed to her room.

Chapter Thirty-One

Later that morning, Redrinna stood on the ledge of the Mount, watching the early morning sunbeams poke their heads out from behind the mountains in the distance, the light making the scales on her shirt glisten. The shirt was a bit big, but it was easy to move in and surprisingly comfortable. Seeing it made her grin. She could imagine Xandrin laboriously arranging all the scales so they'd overlap like the ones on him did, an image that made her chest all bubbly. If that was how much the dragon cared about her, then she'd have to try even harder to be worth him almost getting killed.

Shouldn't you be getting some rest? The gem around her neck said, making her jump.

It seemed weird to answer the gem out loud, but it was comforting that it didn't seem able to read her thoughts. "I tried, but I'm too worried about Xandrin to sleep. Besides, isn't this shirt he made me beautiful?" Should she try being friends with the gem? Would it care? What would it do if she made it mad or something? Did it even experience emotions?

It truly is. I'm sure it's a great honor for you.

She nodded, trying to think of something to say but only managing to make herself acutely uncomfortable. Maybe it was a good time to ask it some of the questions she'd had for a while?

"Can I ask you something?"

Besides that, you mean?

"Oh...I guess so."

Go ahead.

"Why did you choose me?"

That? It remained silent for a moment, the wind tugging on Redrinna's hair. *There was something you did when you were small that stuck out to me. It was a long time ago. Do you remember?*

She did, or at least, she thought she did. "Wasn't it the day that little boy and I almost got kidnapped?"

That was the day, yes. You showed such outstanding courage I couldn't resist marking you. Though I suppose I should apologize for that. Because I marked you then, I'm the reason you're trapped in this now.

"I chose this path too," she said, half-closing her eyes.

There was more to that memory, to that day. Before, she hadn't wanted to think about it. But, for just a moment, she let it play out in her mind.

⁂

After they'd been rescued, Redrinna and the little boy were kept in the same room as their fathers while the two men did business. A maid gave the two of them a plate of kürtőskalács, which Redrinna was quite pleased with, but for some reason, the little boy split all of his crispy treats in half, eating one half before pushing the other halves to her.

"Eat your food," she hissed, trying to stay quiet since they were hiding beneath the table their dads were using for their meeting.

"They're to thank you, so you have to eat them all," the boy hissed back.

"I can't eat all of them, and what're you trying to thank me for?"

"You protected me from those guys, and I'm not staying in your debt, so you have to eat half of all mine."

"I don't want yours, and I don't want you in my debt, so you're not, okay?"

He scowled. "That's not how it works. In the legend of the priestess, when she saved the farm boy's life, he owed her a life debt."

"That's for grown-ups," she hissed, pushing the tray towards him.

He shoved it back, locking it between them. It inched towards her, much to her frustration. Despite how tiny he was, he was stronger than she'd expected.

"You have to eat them," he insisted. "Or I'll make you!"

Redrinna's father tapped on the table, making them both jump. "Redrinna, wish your friend farewell. He and his father are going to retire for the evening."

"Take your kürtőskalács," she snapped.

"Eat them!" The boy shot out from under the table, leaving her with the tray of half-eaten sweets. "Bye, Princess!"

Scowling, she pushed the tray back and forth with one finger, making the crisp desserts rock back and forth.

Now that their guests were gone, her father might give Redrinna a scolding. She was forbidden to leave the palace without her parents, but she'd broken that rule today. Maybe he'd take pity on her because they'd almost gotten hurt?

"Redrinna," her father said, the tone of his voice making her flinch. She swallowed, pushing her tray back and forth a little faster. There was an excruciating minute of silence before he quipped her name again.

With a resigned sigh, she crawled out from under the table, pushing the tray out first. She slid it onto the table before approaching the chair where he sat, head bowed.

"What do you call your behavior today?"

She didn't know what to call it, so she didn't call it anything.

"You and that boy could've been hurt, kidnapped, or worse, killed. You know the rules of the palace, and you disobeyed them. You disobeyed your mother and me. You caused her a great deal of worry today. I told you she needs time to heal after losing your little sister. How do you think she'd be feeling right now if she'd lost you too?"

Redrinna's lip quivered and her vision went all blurry and then she was crying. "I'm sorry, Daddy. But he wanted to go and you said I had to watch out for him. I didn't mean to make Mommy upset."

He thumbed the tears off her cheeks before lifting her chin. "I know, and you were very brave. However today only happened because you were reckless. If you truly want to protect someone, you need to think things through. Carefully."

Her lip still quivered as he lifted her into his lap. Sniffling, she fingered the hem of his sleeve, remembering the way he'd burst through their attackers to get to her.

"I want to be like you someday," she whispered. "You're not afraid of anything."

"You think so?"

She nodded.

"I was scared today though."

"What? How?"

"I thought I might not find you and you'd be gone forever." He rose, carrying her with him. "But I wasn't going to stop searching until I did find you. And you don't have to wait for someday; you showed today that you are just as brave as me. Maybe even braver."

She sniffed and smiled at him. "I don't think you were scared. You're just trying to make me feel better."

"Oh yeah?" A grin split his features too. He tossed her into the air and caught her, spinning her round and round until they were both dizzy and laughing so hard they couldn't see through the tears. They collapsed on the ground, lying side by side for a long while, watching the sun slant further into the room, chatting about things she didn't remember anymore.

When Redrinna could see straight again, she fetched the kürtőskalács from the table, offering the remaining halves to her father. He took one and so did she. She was pretty sure she loved the sweets so much because he did.

"Daddy?"

"Hmm?" her father said through a mouthful of crisp pastry and caramelized sugar.

"If I keep trying, I'll be brave like you someday, won't I?"

"I have no doubt."

"And you and me are always going to be friends, right?"

"That's right."

"And we'll always be together?"

"That's my only dream."

She'd smiled so much her cheeks had hurt the next day.

⚬⚬ ☙ ❧ ⚬⚬

Redrinna closed her eyes, wind rushing over the ledge of the Mount. It'd been a long time since she'd thought about that memory whose taste was both bitter and sweet. There was a good chance she and her father would never spend time together like that again, and truthfully, she didn't know if she even wanted to.

He'd done a lot of wrong things and so many people had been hurt because of it. People were still getting hurt because of it.

However, maybe she was crazy, it seemed like he was trying to stop it. He'd started her on the journey to join the Dragon Kin, the force necessary to stop Osiris. He'd given her the information she'd needed. The papers he'd given her? A list of every dragon he'd hidden and where to find them. That didn't excuse anything he'd done, but she couldn't hate him.

All these feelings were so complicated, they were giving Redrinna a serious headache.

What's on your mind?

"I was thinking about my father," she said, stopping there because she couldn't explain these feelings.

I remember him. He's different now than he was before.

"How so?"

Before, he was practically a puppet. Now, he seems human. He can think for himself, it seems. It makes me wonder where his heart truly lies.

"It does," she breathed, fingering the gem's smooth surface. "I wonder if he's going to help us or hinder us."

Redrinna didn't say the rest of what came to her mind. Her mother had been killed protecting her. How much about this had she known? She must've known something, at least, to hatch a plan to give her to Xandrin, but how much had she really known?

And Captain Brion. Now that she knew Reyna had been lying, guilt filled her for thinking he'd betrayed her. If anyone had truly been her friend before, it'd been him. He'd sworn his life to her and kept that oath, but the kindness he'd shown her had gone above and beyond a mere promise.

She had no way of knowing if he was alive or if he'd been killed alongside everyone else.

Lastly, there was Reyna. Redrinna still shuddered when she thought of how she'd killed her. She'd been so desperate, she hadn't even hesitated. That terrified her. Never, ever, did she want to do that again, but she might not get a choice in the future. If her friends were danger again, would she make the same choice?

I suppose only time can tell. Silence stretched between them, measured by the shortening of the morning sunbeams in the sky and the growing swells of birdsongs. *Can I apologize for one more thing?*

"What could you have to apologize for?"

Not waking up, and causing you to feel like such a failure. Of all the people I've marked, you were the one I wanted, but you just seemed so…unready. Not fully prepared to pay the price that war costs. So I didn't wake up.

Redrinna dipped her head. So that was why.

Timothon died because I chose him, and the last thing I wanted—and still want now—was to choose someone who wasn't ready and trap them in war. Even now, even if I did what I did to save you, I still ended up trapping you in this, whether or not you're ready.

Redrinna had to swallow a couple of times to get the lump out of her throat. The gem was right. She hadn't been ready. In many ways, she still wasn't, but—

The Mount doors abruptly opened, causing her to turn. Tak was there, eyes wide.

"What?" she asked, startled by his appearance.

"Xandrin's awake."

⁕ ⁕

Kneeling by Xandrin's head, Redrinna could barely breathe as the dragon's eyelids fluttered, his head lifting slightly from the ground. Seconds later, his dark eyes opened, reflecting the mountain's soft light.

For a long moment, he mutely stared at her before managing a small, toothy grin. "You're okay," he said, his voice a bit raspy and quiet.

"So are you," she said, a part of her wanting to scold him for pushing himself to the brink of death to save her while the rest of her didn't care, happy he would be okay.

His gaze flicked to the side, to Timothon and Tak, both of whom stood right behind her. His spiked eyebrows furrowed a bit. "How did we make it back to the Mount?"

Lifting her softly glowing gem, Redrinna couldn't help smiling as his eyes went wide and his smile broadened.

"It woke up!"

"It did. It helped us come back here."

"That's so cool," he said, making her laugh a little. Such a Xandrin thing to say.

"H-hey, Redrinna?" Tak whispered from beside her.

She turned, a bit surprised. He held his hand out to her. Her heart skipped a beat. Resting in his palm was her mother's necklace. The chain was no longer stained with blood. Had he cleaned it for her?

"I-is this yours?"

"It is," she whispered, taking it from him.

"What's that?" Xandrin asked, shifting slightly before putting his head on the floor like moving had worn him out.

"It's my...it was my mother's favorite necklace. She used to wear it all the time. But...Osiris killed her." Her throat tightened, but she pushed the feeling away. She didn't want to let that emotion in at that moment.

"Oh." Xandrin touched her knee with his snout. "I'm sorry."

Smiling a little, she rubbed his snout. "Thank you."

After staring at the necklace for a moment longer, Redrinna fastened it around her neck. For a minute, she held a hand over the charm, staying quiet. The others remained quiet too, just until she lowered her hand.

"Xandrin, do you notice something else a bit different about Redrinna?" Timothon asked, smirking a little. She smiled too.

The dragon stared at her, brow furrowing. The longer he stared, the wider her smile became.

All at once, his ear frills shot up, his eyes wide. "You're wearing my scales!"

She laughed. "That's right. What do you think?"

He grinned, then yawned before grinning again. "They suit you."

"Thank you," she whispered.

He smiled at her before his eyes closed again. Before he drifted back to sleep, he shifted so his head settled in her lap. She didn't object, rubbing a hand across his cheek. All at once, she felt it: thrumming against her foot was his heartbeat. That was all she could think about. Because of her, it was still beating, still pounding with life; his great, big, dragon heart.

ఎలి ఎ౬

A few days later, once again, Redrinna stood on the ledge of the Mount, gazing out at the landscape before her, all the mountains carpeted in green and the sky an almost inky blue in its final moments of twilight. She took a deep breath, drinking in as much of the cool, night air as her lungs could hold.

It was kind of odd to see the world going on like normal after seeing the destruction of the Imperial City. That in and of itself was cathartic, something that made it a bit easier for her to sleep at night. Her heart ached at the thought that her mother no longer walked the earth, but the fact that the world hadn't stopped yet helped her think she didn't have to stop either. Even though, just that morning, she'd woken and cried until the pain in her chest eased a bit, the pain had eased.

Running her fingers over her newest necklace, Redrinna let out a tiny sigh.

Above her, the stars were beginning to show their faces, sometimes winking at her. As she stared at them, she reflected on the events that had led her to be standing on the ledge of the Mount. Her mind wandered back to her days in the palace, then to Xandrin's cave, next to the forest, and finally to the Mount.

To home.

She smiled a little. In retrospect, it was kind of funny how all of this had happened. Well, some parts of it were.

Warmth filled her chest, causing her to look down. Her gem glowed softly, like the last sliver of red-orange sun before it vanished beneath the horizon. Even though it didn't always speak to her, she was growing attached to its company.

However, now that it had officially chosen her, the weight of the war settled on her back like she carried a mountain. The weight further intensified when she thought of how many people she'd already failed, but at the same time, she'd been able to save two people: Tak and Xandrin (well, one wasn't quite human, technically). There had to be more people out there like them, people or dragons she could do something for, especially since her father had given her those papers with the location of all the dragons on them. Fortunately, they hadn't been badly damaged in the rain.

At the very least, as long as Redrinna tried her hardest, she hoped that wherever her mother was now, she'd be proud. She tried to ignore how much she missed her mother, how much she wished they could still be together, but she knew they couldn't.

Closing her eyes, she listened to the sounds of the night, the quiet seeming different now that it was dark. Her thoughts turned back again, a part of her missing the life of the forest. She missed the peacefulness of Xandrin's cave. And her mother's smile. And Lady...Reyna sneaking into her room a lot. And Captain Brion following her all over creation.

That last thought made her stop. Was there a chance the Captain had survived what had happened? She'd seen nothing to suggest he hadn't, but she also hadn't seen anything to suggest that he had... She would simply have to hold on to the hope he was safe, and they'd meet again someday. That, she could do.

Sometime later, Redrinna heard steps behind her, shaking her from her thoughts. To her surprise, it was Tak.

"H-hello," he said, stopping a short distance away.

Turning her attention back to the land spread out before her like an ocean, she asked, "What brings you out here?"

The young man stayed quiet for a minute, his gaze on the landscape as well. Turning to face her—though he didn't meet her gaze—

he said, "C-can I ask you a question?"

"Yes?"

"Are you really the Imperial Princess of Eridia?"

She raised an eyebrow. "What makes you say that?"

"N-nothing!" His cheeks reddened. "Well, it's just—you're smart, you know how to read and—" Abruptly, he shut his mouth. His cheeks flamed a vivid red.

"And?"

"A-and you're nice. Nicer than most people, actually." He shrugged, hunching his shoulders like a turtle, reminding her of when they'd first met. "A lot of people in my village said you stayed in your palace because you were weak or you didn't care about us, but...you...you're actually really brave."

He was unquestionably avoiding her gaze on purpose.

For a minute, Redrinna stared, studying him. To be honest, when she'd first found him, she hadn't been sure what to expect from him. Her expectations had been kind of low, which made a guilty feeling settle in her chest.

"Well, as surprising as I may be, I really am—well was, the Imperial Princess of Eridia. And if I'm the nicest person you've ever met, you can't have met too many decent people."

He almost smiled, but for some reason, he couldn't quite seem able to. He peered at her like he wanted to say something else, but didn't. As neither of them said anything for a while, she became aware of how quiet the night had become.

"So," Redrinna said, breaking the silence that had fallen between them. "Do you like it here in the Mount? You're not mad at me for taking you from your home, are you?" She noticed his cheeks weren't nearly as hollow as they'd been when she'd first met him. Maybe coming here had been a good thing after all.

"Oh no, I'm not mad," Tak said hurriedly. "I like it here. It's...nice. Better than what I'm used to."

That caught her off-guard. "You must not be used to much," she said carefully.

He didn't reply, looking away instead.

Not for the first time, she wondered what his life had been like before they'd met. She was starting to gather it hadn't been great or even good, but the important thing was that he was doing all right now. She was satisfied with that.

"You know," she began, getting him to look at her. "I overheard Timothon saying you could go claim one of the gems if you wanted to the other day." It was kind of hard to believe that had only been a few days ago.

"You heard?" The young man winced. "I'm sorry."

She shook her head. "Why should you be sorry? If a gem has decided you're the one it needs, then you should be happy. Unless you didn't want to be chosen, of course. However, there's no point in worrying about it yet since Xandrin's in no condition to fly anywhere. Unless you wanted to walk there?"

He made a face that made her laugh.

"I wouldn't want to either," she admitted. Maybe it would be nice to have some time to relax and unwind.

At that, the young man smiled—one of the first of his she remembered seeing.

Maybe this whole Dragon Kin thing wouldn't be so bad, Redrinna found herself thinking. She had friends like Xandrin, Tak, and the gem. More importantly, though, she was more ready than before. More prepared. Maybe she could do this after all.

Epilogue

That had been unexpected. Reyna winced as she entered the great hall, still rolling her neck from side to side even though it didn't hurt anymore.

"So, the little princess won the game," Osiris said from where he lounged on his throne, his bottom lip sticking out in a pout. "Not what I was hoping for. Nevertheless it works in our favor."

"It would've been a bit easier if you would've let me to rough her up a bit," Reyna said, crossing her arms. "Holding back against a magic user is the worst."

"Yes, you were a bit caught off guard by that trick of hers, were you not? It seems the Dragon Slayer is not the only one who is a bit rusty."

"Yeah, yeah whatever. It won't happen again. So what do we do next?" she asked, noting Renoan wasn't here. What was the fool up to now? Why did Osiris keep letting him roam free?

"She did escape, but the gem awoke. Her next course of action will be gathering the rest of the Dragon Kin. If that is the case, letting her roam free will help our plan along, since it does require the power of all the awakened gems to complete. It also means we can redirect more of our focus onto other projects."

Reyna smiled a little. Father always had a plan.

He smiled, resting his chin in his hand. "Yes, this will work out nicely. We shall simply have to help her along here and there."

"Are you sure? She could find a way to thwart us regardless of how closely we watch her. After all, the previous Dragon Kin did put you in your current state, and she managed to escape today."

"Half the fun depends on how much risk is involved, is that not so?" He glanced her way, a gleam in his eye. "Do not worry. I do not intend to make things easy for her. After all, she did point a knife at me. That was quite rude."

Reyna couldn't help the smile spreading over her cheeks. Making things difficult for Redrinna was something she would gladly do after the girl had turned her back on her.

As that thought crossed her mind, there was a small zing in her chest, a tiny painful shock. Was that remorse? Pathetic. She didn't have time for stupid emotions like that. There were more important things she needed to do. Something as petty as a spoiled friendship wasn't going to stop her from winning. Absolutely nothing.

Don't miss the next book...

SHATTER

Book Two in the Rise of the Empress Series

Coming Soon

Thanks for Reading!

No, seriously. I mean that!

If you enjoyed this book, then I have a tiny request for you (I promise it's small. It'll take maybe five minutes of your time). You may not be able to tell, but I am an indie author (indie stands for independent). That means I published this book alone, without the help of a publishing house and the team that would go with that. I spent the money from my own pocket in order to put this book in your hands.

Since I chose not to enlist the services of a publishing house (there are several reasons why), then I need your help in order to keep making books like this one. How? Please, if you liked this book, leave a review! That's it. You don't even have to be on social media or anything like that. The best place to leave it is on Amazon, but you can do it on places like Goodreads too, if you're familiar with that. And if you liked it, just tell people about it. That helps me so much.

And, of course, if you liked it enough, buying the next book helps too.

Once again, thank you! Enjoy some artwork as a treat.

Acknowledgements

I've been dreaming of the day when I finally got to sit down and write this, and it's weird that it has finally come. In a good way, of course. This book has grown up with me, and it and I are both completely different from where we started.

So first, a big thanks to the many family members without whom I would not have made it this far (you guys know who you are). The rest of you, I appreciate you simply giving me space to work and figure out this career I've chosen. The next big thanks goes out to my lovely English teachers—several of them—without whose encouragement I wouldn't of even realized this career existed or was an option to consider. But thank you for helping me see that and pushing me down it (because it took many of you and many, many years of persuasion...).

The next enormous thank you goes to Erin Young, my fabulous editor. I must admit, until you got your hands on this book, I was ready to give up on it. Thank you for seeing its potential and helping me turn it into the lovely beast it is. Thanks also belongs to Lauren Thompson for her beautiful (and free) font I used for the ornamental breaks! They literally made my heart flutter (check out her blog here: http://nymphont.blogspot.com). And a special thanks goes to Lexi for the beautiful cover she bestowed on this book.

Thanks also goes to my younger self, for not only starting this book, but sticking with it throughout the years. I know you never did get to read a book quite like this one, but because of you, there may be someone like you who does.

I would also be remiss if I failed to express my gratitude to God for helping me on this journey and with this book specifically. My own hands and mind would not have been capable without Him and His help and encouragement. I'm also endlessly grateful for the gift of stories that has been given to me and for the opportunities I have to share them with others.

Last, but not least, thanks to you, reader, for picking up this book. I hope you'll stick around for all of Redrinna's adventures and all the friends along the way. Maybe even beyond (if you like, of course).

About the Author

C. S. Doraga is the author of the *Rise of the Empress* series, and *Defy* is her debut novel. She grew up in the shadows of the Rocky Mountains with her nose stuck in any book within reach and imagination constantly running wild (to her parents' chagrin, at times). Her favorite author is the amazing Mangaka, Hiromu Arakawa, the author of *Fullmetal Alchemist* and *Silver Spoon*. What little free time she has, she spends playing the *Fire Emblem* video game series and a few, choice others. She has a deep love for the fantastic but also loves mystery and those characters that sit with you long after the story is over.

She has a Bachelor's Degree in Creative Writing from Weber State University and lives in beautiful Northern Utah with her family, one hungry dog, and two, crazy cats.

Follow me on Instagram to get all the latest news and other fun things!

https://www.instagram.com/bookdragons.nest/